5/66

P9-ELW-319

WITHDRAWN

Dreamhunter

Dreamhunter

BOOK ONE OF THE DREAMHUNTER DUET

ELIZABETH KNOX

Frances Foster Books
Farrar, Straus and Giroux / New York

Copyright © 2005 by Elizabeth Knox
Maps copyright © 2005 by Philip Hood
All rights reserved
Printed in the United States of America
First published in the United Kingdom by Faber & Faber, 2005
Designed by Robbin Gourley and Vera Soki
First American edition, 2006
1   3   5   7   9   10   8   6   4   2

www.fsgkidsbooks.com

Library of Congress Cataloging-in-Publication Data
Knox, Elizabeth.
    Dreamhunter: book one of the dreamhunter duet / Elizabeth Knox.—
1st ed.
        p.   cm.
    Summary: In a world where select people can enter the Place and
find dreams of every kind to share with others for a fee, a fifteen-year-old
girl is training to be a dreamhunter when her father disappears, leaving
her to carry on his mysterious mission.
    ISBN-13: 978-0-374-31853-6
    ISBN-10: 0-374-31853-0
    [1. Dreams—Fiction.   2. Family life—Fiction.   3. Fantasy.]   I. Title.

PZ7.K7707 Dr 2006
[Fic]—dc22

                                                        2005046366

To my son, Jack Barrowman

✤ ✤ ✤

Contents

RIFLEMAN RANGE

WHYNEW
FALLS

WHYNEW STREAM

SISTERS
BEACH

TRICKSIE
BEND

MORASS RIVER

RIFLEMAN PASS

RIFLEMAN RIVER

DOORHANDLE

HELIOGRAPH RANGE

WRY
VALLEY

WESTPORT

SVA RIVER

FOUNDERSTON

LIGHTHOUSE

SO LONG SPIT

Bay

Road

Railway
++++++++++

Border of Place
- - - - - - -

Rivers and
Streams

AWA INLET   MT
KAHAUGH

Prologue

(1905)

✢ ✢ ✢

ON A LATE WINTER NIGHT, THE ISLE OF THE TEMPLE LAY QUIET, STREETS EMPTY AND SHIMMERING. THE MOON WAS AT the top of the sky, and the dew had set as frost on copper roofs, iron railings, and window glass. But the roof of the Rainbow Opera was clear of frost and lit from without by tall gas beacons that rose, a crown of flame, from the coping around its dome.

Inside the dream palace all was silent. Its central pit was illuminated by low night-lights, and by a mix of moonlight and the unsteady gas jets shining through stained glass. The Rainbow Opera seemed deserted. But behind the doors that lined the four tiers of its balconies were bedchambers, all occupied and all with their padded doors shut fast. Each chamber was at an equal distance from a dais that rose in the center of the pit, a platform upholstered in white silk.

The dreamer's bed.

It had been a hard winter, the kind that kills the old, the ill, and unlucky infants, and at the Opera that night, the great dreamhunter Tziga Hame was performing his most famous dream—Convalescent One.

Tziga Hame lay on his back in the dreamer's bed, his sleeping face serene, paralyzed by his dream and holding all the Opera's patrons still in its priceless healing spell.

Dreamhunter

. . . The invalid had been gravely ill but was better and was to be allowed out. He was to take the air. But he wasn't just lifted into a wheelchair and wheeled into a garden. Instead, he was bundled up and taken by carriage to a small country station. There he was transferred to a white canvas pavilion that had been built on the roof of a rail carriage. His attendants joined him, and picnic baskets were passed up to them. The train pulled slowly away from the station. It went on quietly, its motion only fast enough to raise a pleasant breeze. It was a late afternoon in summer, the air balmy, the light gold.

The train took them through tunnels of elms and black beech trees, a cool green and red gloom. It ran along cuttings with its roof at the level of meadows. Young horses galloped beside the train, sometimes plunging through the trailing banner of the engine's white steam. The train passed over a viaduct, high above the meadows, then ran alongside a canal, passing barges with bright paintwork. It picked up its pace a little on a winding, graded stretch of line that took it through pastures where rabbits grazed and crouched, washing their black noses and ears in the evening light. The train ran along beside low sand dunes and showed the invalid the sea, the sun setting over its quiet surface.

The scalloped edge of the white cotton awning fluttered in the breeze. The invalid's attendants handed him strawberries, each the size of a child's fist, firm fruits with foamy white cores. They gave him milk sweetened with honey.

The train ran onto a causeway, a narrow strip of land, wide enough to carry only one set of rails. The causeway went out across the water. The train seemed to glide over the sea itself. Everything was peaceful, the air cool and caressing. The invalid lay in the safe embrace of his bed, yet there was space all around him, open air and flaming light . . .

Almost as one the Rainbow Opera's patrons breathed in deeply, and out slowly, and seemed to melt into their beds, let gently down into a deep, restoring sleep.

But Tziga Hame opened his eyes. He looked up at the fluttering light filling the air. He listened to the auditorium's dedicated hush. Nothing had disturbed him. He had roused himself.

Like other dreamhunters, Tziga Hame could edit any

dream that needed editing *as he caught it.* He'd wake himself up before the dream managed to load him with any distressing dark turn. But he had never learned how to edit Convalescent One in the catching. And so, when the dream reached the point where the train moved out onto the causeway, Hame had taught himself to wake up. To ease out of sleep without hauling his audience with him. Their dreams would trail off with the train into the beautiful sunset. There would be no dark turn.

For the dream went on. The train slowed because there was work being done on the line. Men stood on the stony railbed, their hands hanging idle, while the train glided by. The invalid looked down on their upturned, grimy faces. He saw that the legs of their pants were gathered at the ankles, as if tied there. The invalid was innocent and curious. He didn't know why he felt frightened by the exhausted men, and unhappy for them.

But the dreamhunter Hame had caught and performed Convalescent One many times and had understood long ago that the invalid felt frightened because the men looked up at him with eyes full of menace and a kind of hungry expectation. And that their pants were gathered at the ankles because their legs were in chains.

Hame had begun to suspect who the men might be, and that their presence in the otherwise beneficial dream was not a mistake but a *message.*

That night at the Opera, Hame lay gazing at the dome high above him as a drowning man looks back at the surface, the underside of the world of air. He lay under silence like the weight of water and thought: "What do they want *me* to do? Tell their story? Or break their chains?"

I
A Talented Family

(1906)

1

✢ ✢ ✢

*O*N A HOT DAY NEAR THE END OF SUM-
MER, LAURA HAME SAT WITH HER FA-
THER; HER COUSIN, ROSE; AND HER AUNT
Grace against the fern-fringed bank on a forest track. She
watched as her uncle Chorley and the rest of the picnic party
passed out of sight around the next bend.

Chorley turned and waved before he disappeared. Laura
stared at the empty, sun-splashed path. She saw black bush
bees zipping back and forth through the air above the nettles
and heard the muffled roar of Whynew Falls, where the rest of
the party were headed.

Laura and Rose; Laura's father, Tziga; and her aunt Grace
were sitting under a sign. The sign read, *CAUTION:* YOU ARE
NOW ONLY 100 YARDS FROM THE BORDER TO THE PLACE.

"The falls are loud today," Tziga said. "It must have poured
up in the hills."

They listened to the cascade pound and thump. Laura, who
had never been allowed near the falls, tried to imagine how
they would sound up close.

Her father said, "Think how startled Chorley would be if
one of these girls suddenly skipped up behind him."

Aunt Grace squinted at Laura's father. "What do you
mean?"

"Come on, Grace. Why don't we just get up and wander along that way?"

"Tziga!" Grace was shocked. Laura and Rose were too. The family had owned a summer house at nearby Sisters Beach for ten years, and at least once a year they would go with friends for a picnic up in the old beech forest. Every summer those who *could* would continue along the track to see the falls. And every summer the girls were forced to wait at the sign with their dreamhunter parents. Tziga Hame and Grace Tiebold couldn't go and view Whynew Falls themselves because, one hundred yards from the honest and accurate warning sign, they would cross an invisible border. They would walk out of the world of longitude and latitude, and into a place called simply the Place. Tziga and Grace could no more continue on to Whynew Falls than Laura's uncle Chorley could walk into the Place. Uncle Chorley, like almost everyone else, couldn't go there. Tziga and Grace were part of a tiny minority for whom the rules of the world were somewhat different.

"Come on, Grace," said Tziga. "Why should we make the girls go through all the ceremony of a Try? It's only for the benefit of the Regulatory Body, so they can see their rules enforced. Why can't we just find out *now*, in a minute, in private?"

Rose wailed, "It's against the law!"

Tziga glanced at Rose, then looked back at Grace. He was a quiet man, self-contained, secretive even—but his manner had changed. His *face* had. Laura thought that looking at him now was like peering into a furnace—its iron doors sprung open on fire. Her father was a small man. He was a mess, as usual, his shirt rumpled and grass-stained, his cream linen jacket knotted around his waist, his hat pushed back on his dark, springy hair. Laura's aunt Grace wasn't any better turned out. Both dreamhunters were thin, tanned, and dry-skinned, as all dreamhunters became over time. Rose was already taller than her spare and weathered mother. She was white and gold and vivid, like her father, Chorley, and like Chorley's sister, Laura's dead mother. Laura had, unfortunately, not inherited her mother's stature or coloring. She was little and dark, like her father. But—Laura thought—her father, though small and shabby, still had the aura belonging to all great dreamhunters. She liked to imagine that the aura was a residue of the dreams they'd carried. For when Tziga Hame and Grace Tiebold ventured into the Place, dreams were what they brought back with them. Dreams that were more forceful, coherent, and vivid than those supplied to all people by their sleeping brains. Dreams they could share with others. Dreams they could perform, could *sell*.

Laura's father was saying, "We were pioneers, Grace. You didn't 'Try,' you crept past the cairn beyond Doorhandle early one morning when there wasn't a soul on the road. Do you remember? That moment was all your own. There wasn't anyone standing by with a clipboard and contracts."

Laura saw that her aunt had gone pale. Grace stood up. Laura thought Grace meant to walk away, back toward the road, to go off in a huff and put an end to Laura's father's crazy talk. But then she saw Grace turn to look up the track toward the border.

Laura's heart gave a thump.

Her father got to his feet too.

Rose didn't move. She said, "Wait! What about our Try? You've even bought us outfits—our hats with veils."

"Rose thinks she's a debutante," Laura's father said.

"I do not!" Rose jumped up. "All right, I'll go! I'll go now! I'm not scared. I was only trying to follow the law. But if you don't care about it, why should I?"

"Good," said Laura's father. He offered his hand to Laura. She looked at it, then took it and let him help her up. She busied herself brushing dry moss from her skirt. The others began to amble slowly along the path. Laura caught up with them and gave her hand to Rose, who took it and squeezed it tight. Rose's hand was cold, much cooler than the air, which, even in the shade of the forest, was as marinated in heat as the open paddocks, the dusty roads, and the beaches of Coal Bay. Rose's hand was chilly, her palm coated with sweat.

Around the first bend was another, very similar. The track was flanked by black beech trunks. The sun angled in and lit up bright green nettles and bronze shoots of supplejack.

"I guess we won't see the Place until we're there," said Rose.

"That is right," Grace said. "There's nothing to see. No line on the ground."

Tziga said, "The border is around the next corner."

They didn't slow, or hurry. Laura felt that their progress was almost stately. She felt as though she were being escorted up the aisle, or perhaps onto a scaffold.

She didn't want to know yet. *It was too soon.*

In two weeks Laura and Rose were due to Try. Any person who wanted to enter the Place for the first time had to do so under the eye of an organization called the Dream Regulatory Body. The Body had been set up ten years before. It employed rangers—those who could go into the Place but couldn't carry dreams out of it—to patrol the uncanny territory and its borders. The dream parlors, salons, and palaces in which working dreamhunters performed had to obey laws enforced by the Regulatory Body and its powerful head, the Secretary of the Interior, Cas Doran. The parlors, salons, and palaces were businesses and had to have licenses. Dreamhunters, too, had to have licenses. A Try was the first step on the road to a license, and a livelihood.

The Body held two official Tries a year—one in early spring and one in late summer. Each Try found hundreds of teenagers lined up at the border. It wasn't compulsory to Try, but many did as soon as they were allowed, because dreams represented a guarantee of work and the possibility of wealth and fame. Any children who showed an inclination—vivid dreaming, night terrors, a tendency to sleepwalk—were thought, by hopeful families, to have a chance at the life. A dreamhunter or ranger in the family was another indicator of potential talent. More boys than girls Tried, since parents were more permissive with boys, and the candidates were, by and large, in their midteens. The earliest age of a Try was legally set at fifteen.

Rose and Laura had celebrated their fifteenth birthdays that summer.

Walking along the Whynew Falls track hand in hand with her cousin, Laura felt desperately unprepared for an impromptu Try. Every night that summer as she'd put her head down on her pillow, she had mentally ticked off another day—the time narrowing between her and her life's big deciding moment. She had felt as though she were hurtling down a slope that got steeper and steeper the farther she fell. For Laura knew that, after her Try, she would either be in her father's world or remain at her school—Founderston Girls' Academy. She would have a calling or be free to continue her education, to travel, to "come out" when she was sixteen and appear at every ball that season. If she was free, Laura knew she'd inherit the Hame wealth—but not the Hame glamour. And, free, she would lose Rose, because *Rose* fully expected to walk into the Place, fall asleep there, dream, and carry back her dreams intact, vivid, and marvelous. For Rose had already been into the Place, had been a number of times, because Grace Tiebold had gone on catching dreams when she was pregnant with Rose. (When her sister-in-law Verity said to her, "Did you ever think that you would go there and leave the baby behind?" Grace had put a hand on her stomach and laughed at Verity—also pregnant—saying, "Oh! Darling! What a bloody thought.")

As Laura approached the bend around which her father had said the border would be, she began to drag her feet. Rose gave her hand a sharp tug. "Come on," she whispered. "Stick with me."

"Tziga," said Grace. "Just tell me this—why now? We could have tried last year, or the year before, or when they were only ten. We could have whipped them across quickly when they were really tiny, and they wouldn't even have known where they were. We would have learned whether they could cross or not, and just waited to make it official."

Laura saw her father shake his head at Grace, but he didn't answer her.

"Why do you need to know *now*?" Grace asked again.

Laura gave a little sob of tension. Then she crashed into her aunt, who had suddenly stopped in her tracks. "Jesus!" Grace said. They all stepped on one another. When Laura righted herself, she saw a ranger approaching along the path.

The man came up to them. He looked, in quick succession, surprised, suspicious, and polite. "Mr. Hame, Mrs. Tiebold," he said respectfully. "Good day to you. Are you going In?" Then he looked beyond the adults at the two girls. He stared pointedly.

"No, of course not," said Grace. "We are just waiting for my husband and our friends. They went along to the falls."

"I see," said the ranger. He stood blocking their path. He cleared his throat. "Perhaps it would be wiser to take these young ladies back to the sign."

"We do know exactly where the border is," Grace said, frosty. "It isn't as if it moves."

"It *is* very well marked," Tziga said, neutral. "We're not likely to make any mistakes."

"But you can't always keep your hand on your children near the border—best not to go too near." The ranger was quoting a bit of the Regulatory Body's official advice, saying something he no doubt had to say to many people on his patrols. But because he was addressing the undisputed greatest dreamhunters—one of them the very first—he at least had the decency to blush. "I'm very sorry," he said.

"We're not dopes, you know," Rose said, indignant. "Laura and I are Trying in two weeks, for heaven's sake. Why would we spoil that by sneaking across now?"

"It is better to be careful," the ranger said. He focused on a point above Rose's bleached straw sun hat and composed himself into a stiff state of official dignity. He looked blockheaded.

"Come on, girls," Grace said. She turned Rose and Laura around and propelled them back along the track.

Laura swallowed hard to suppress her sigh of relief.

The ranger hovered for a moment. He seemed to realize that Tziga Hame meant to stay put, so he followed Grace and the girls.

✧ ✧ ✧

At Whynew Falls, Laura's uncle Chorley Tiebold filmed the other picnickers as they requested. He shot them pointing up at the waterfall, wet from spray. He filmed them jostling and giggling at the pool's edge.

When he was finished, Chorley packed up his movie camera, hoisted it onto his shoulder, and followed his neighbors back along the track. He was itching to return to his workshop in Summerfort, the family's house at Sisters Beach. He wanted to see whether he'd managed to capture on film the scales of shadow pushing down the white face of the cascade. Chorley picked up his pace to catch up with the others. He passed the orange-painted circle of tin tacked to a tree trunk—the border marker. He went on a few steps, then for some reason glanced back. He saw the track, tree ferns, gray, knotted sinews of a redbush vine. Then he saw a flicker of color and shadow in the air, and his brother-in-law, Tziga, materialized on the track behind him.

Chorley flinched. He had filmed this phenomenon—people passing into and out of the Place on its busiest border post, the cairn beyond Doorhandle. It was Chorley's best-known film; he'd sold copies to all corners of the world. Everyone wanted to know just what it looked like—and that it didn't look like trick photography. It didn't. It was a quiet, unfussy, terrifying sight. The only time Chorley had seen it and hadn't felt frightened was when, shortly before they married, he and Grace had played a stalking game in the long grass on the bluff above the river at Tricksie Bend. Grace, inside the Place, hadn't known where Chorley would be outside of it, and he hadn't known where she would emerge. She jumped back and forth, sometimes startled to find he was close by and could grab her. It had made Chorley anxious, made his heart ache to see Grace come and go like that—go where *he couldn't follow*. But it was magical too.

"There you are," said Tziga. "You always come last when you're carrying your camera." He stepped around Chorley and walked ahead of him, turning back now and then to speak. Looking up, for Chorley was quite a bit taller. "You know—there's far too much interest in Laura's and Rose's Try," he said.

Chorley couldn't remember anyone mentioning the girls' Try at the picnic. Not even Rose, who grew more excited the nearer the event came. He said, "I may be following you, Tziga"—he poked his brother-in-law with the legs of his camera—"but I don't follow you."

"There's too much interest in the *outcome* of their Try. That's all I'm saying. I don't want them besieged with publicity, or contracts."

"That's why we've bought them hats with veils, to keep their faces out of the newspapers," Chorley said. "To keep it all as private as possible. We could, at least, all agree to do that much. You *do* realize that I've been trying to talk to you—and Grace—about this for months now?"

"I know. But there was never any question that they'd Try as soon as the law allowed."

Chorley took one hand off his precious camera to grab Tziga's arm. "*I* questioned it," he said. "The law can say what it likes, but I think they're still too young."

"They *want* to Try," Tziga said. He looked very unhappy.

Chorley said, "Rose wants to—Laura just doesn't want to be left out." He watched Tziga's face go remote. Even Chorley, who knew his brother-in-law better than anyone, couldn't tell whether Tziga was offended, angry to be told something about his own daughter that he should know himself, or whether he had just dropped down into a colder and deeper reach of his usual sadness. "Tziga," Chorley said, and gave the arm he held a little shake. He was annoyed with himself for poking the chisel of his complaints into this crack in his brother-in-law's certainty. "Look," he said, "it'll soon be over. It'll be decided one way or the other."

"Yes."

Chorley told Tziga to get a move on. The others would wonder where they were. "You do know it will be all right whatever happens," he said as they went along. "I'm not a dreamhunter, and I'm all right. Grace and you are dreamhunters, and you are too—all right, I mean. Aren't you?" He gave Tziga yet another chance to confide in him, to tell him why, lately, he'd seemed so *hunted*.

Tziga just made a faint affirmative noise, then asked Chorley if this was the camera Chorley wanted him to take into the Place.

Chorley immediately forgot his worries. "Yes," he said. "Are you saying you will? Finally?"

Tziga said yes, he'd take Chorley's camera In tomorrow.

Chorley was rapt, and for the next hour, long after they'd caught up with the others, he talked. He gave instructions, advice, almost gave a shooting script for the film he most wanted to make but couldn't make himself.

Tziga interrupted only once, when they reached the cars, which were parked at the gate of the farm beside Whynew Falls Reserve. He said to Grace, "There he is," and tilted his head in the direction of a man in a duster coat, a shadow against the tangled trunks of the whiteywood forest.

"He's seeing us off," Grace growled.

"Who is it?" Chorley asked.

"A ranger," said Rose.

Chorley saw Grace give Rose and Laura a sharp look. The girls got into the car. Chorley said to the dreamhunters, "Do you think that ranger is watching you?"

"Of course not," said Grace.

"Yes," said Tziga. "I'm being watched. The Regulatory Body has a big investment in me. Contracts. That sort of thing." He made one of the gestures peculiar to him—seeming to crumble something in his right hand and cast it away into the air. Then he went around the front of the car to crank it for Chorley.

2

✣ ✣ ✣

THE RANGER CAME IN AT THE END OF THE DAY AND SHUT HIMSELF IN HIS HOTEL ROOM. IT DIDN'T HAVE A SEA VIEW, but it looked along the Strand toward the hill at the western end of Sisters Beach and the gates of Summerfort, the Hame and Tiebold beach house. The ranger opened his windows, dragged an armchair across the room, and sat facing the view. He pulled a crumpled paper from his coat pocket. It was a letter containing his instructions. He looked again at the figures penciled on its back. He had been doing sums, figuring how best to spend his extra cash.

The letter told the ranger to tail Tziga Hame.

. . . the dreamhunter has failed to register the location of a dream about which I have grave concerns. Keep close to Hame at all times. As he is concealing a site, it is reasonable to suppose that he will attempt to enter the Place on a quiet section of the border, and without registering his intentions at a rangers' station. Follow him and find out where he goes.

And—this cannot be stressed enough—do not sleep when, or where, Hame sleeps.

The ranger had spent that day lurking in the beech forest near Hame's picnic party. The picnickers fortunately hadn't had any dogs, and the ranger had been able to position himself between the group who went up the track to admire Whynew Falls and two dreamhunters and their unTried daughters. He hadn't expected to run into the four right by the border. He'd been just as surprised as they were. It was an awkward moment.

As he sat at the hotel window, the ranger decided that he would not report today's incident. He was afraid he'd be taken off his lucrative job, a job he was no longer the best man for now that he had been seen by his quarry. If Hame spotted him again, the dreamhunter would know for sure that the ranger hadn't just stumbled upon him. He would know he was being followed. The encounter near the Falls had been unfortunate, but the ranger decided that he would not let it ruin his opportunity to earn some good money.

He produced matches from his coat pocket and tore the letter in half, kept the portion with his calculations, and set a burning match to the other half. He held it while it flared up, then released the flaming fragment onto the evening breeze and watched it blow away, shedding threads of floating embers.

3

✣ ✣ ✣

*L*AURA DRAGGED HERSELF OUT OF BED EARLY AND WENT DOWNSTAIRS TO SEE HER FATHER OFF ON HIS LATEST FORAY into the Place.

As she pushed through the padded doors to the kitchen, she heard singing. The song was strange, and the sound of it made her scalp prickle. She reacted to the music before she recognized the singer's voice. It was her father—singing something disturbing and incomprehensible.

When Laura appeared, her father stopped in the middle of a phrase. The air in the room smelled of oatmeal, and brown sugar, and something else—moisture and electricity. It was as if her father had been joined for breakfast by a thunderstorm.

Laura pushed a chair up next to his, sat down, and leaned against him. She said, groggy, "Has someone left a door open? Is it going to rain?"

He put his arm around her. There were two places set at the table, two empty teacups, and one empty oatmeal plate. Tziga's plate was still full. He had gathered the glutinous oatmeal into a mound and shaped the mound into a rough, mealy sculpture, *a face.*

Laura picked up a napkin and wiped her father's fingers clean. "Who is that supposed to be?" she said.

Tziga smiled. "Someone bran-knew," he said.

Laura giggled. "Bran new and feeling his oats," she said. Then, "What were you singing, Da?"

Laura's father rested his cheek against her hair. " 'The Measures,' " he said. "A song my great-grandfather taught me. Or rather, *tried* to teach me. He was always trying to teach me and your aunt Marta the old folk songs he knew. I was too young and callow then to understand that the songs were our family inheritance. The songs, and stories, and—*other* things. I used to say to the old man that I didn't have time for that ancient stuff, that I was expected to earn a living, and that nobody in the fashionable places wanted to hear 'Of His Name' or 'A Stitch in Time.' " Laura's father sighed. "So I never did master 'The Measures.' I've been trying to remember how it goes."

"I didn't understand a word of it."

"You wouldn't. It's Koine, demotic Greek, the common tongue of the Roman Empire. Or—rather—half the song is in Koine; the rest of it is just sounds, what doctors in insane asylums would call glossolalia—articulate, nonsensical noises, noises like words. A priest would call it 'talking in tongues.' So—'The Measures' might be described as a mixture of Koine and tongues."

Laura leaned away from her father to take a good look at his face. She asked him whether his great-grandfather ever told him where *he* had heard the song.

"Do you know the story about how the survivors from the island of Elprus first came to settle in Founderston?"

This was something Laura had had in her history classes. She knew that Elprus was an island depopulated some two hundred years before by a catastrophic volcanic eruption. Most of the island's population were poisoned and buried when the volcano in its center vented corrosive gas and a burning cloud of ash that filled the air for fifty miles and fifteen days. The survivors were either from the island's fishing fleet, who were at sea when the volcano blew, or from a convent school on a peninsula, the only place upwind of the volcano. They were gathered together by Laura's ancestor, one John Hame. The history books said that this John Hame took the Elpra far across the seas to Southland, finally to settle in Founderston, then a small pioneer settlement around a fort and river port. But before they left their island, the survivors excavated their main holy site, the tomb of St. Lazarus. (Lazarus of the Gospels, whom Jesus raised from the dead, had apparently spent most of his long, miraculously restored life on Elprus. There he had married, fathered children, worked his own miracles, written his own gospel, grown old, and died—*again*.) John Hame and the other Elpra dug down through the ash to the saint's tomb, removed his bones, and carried them away.

Laura said to her father, "I know the story. Our ancestor brought the relics that are now in the Temple."

"Yes. 'The Measures' was passed down through our family. It's the oldest of all the Hame songs. Legend has it that John Hame was a descendant of St. Lazarus. That's why Lazarus is a family name."

"Is that true?"

"Well—it's a story I inherited, not one I made up."

Laura pulled a face and said, "But it can't be proven, right? It's what Uncle Chorley would call unscientific."

"History, unlike science, doesn't need *repeatable* proofs. A story can be true if its sources are sound. The Gospels are a good source of things Chorley would call unscientific. St. Lazarus's Gospel mentions a song he heard in the tomb. But the Gospel According to Lazarus is the only *documentary* source. All the rest of it is lore—family lore."

Laura gave her father a worried look. "I would have thought that all St. Lazarus heard in the tomb was Jesus telling him to come forth."

"Yes—to return to the land of the living. But perhaps Jesus was singing." Laura's father blushed and pressed his lips together. He'd said something blasphemous and was embarrassed by it.

"Da, you'd better stop before Uncle Chorley comes back. You wouldn't want to offend his *irreligious* feelings."

Tziga laughed. "Chorley's getting the car out and putting his camera in it. And, probably, fifty pages of instructions. Perhaps when I come back I should pretend I forgot to remove the cap on the lens. See what he does."

Chorley Tiebold was hard to tease, even-tempered, and too quick to fool easily. But the fact that he was so hard to tease meant that it was a challenge—a challenge his wife, daughter, and brother-in-law frequently took on.

"No one thinks you're *that* vague, Da. And you shouldn't start acting vague in case you do forget something important, like coming back in time for my Try!" Laura let go of her father and drew back so that she could hold his gaze. "You *will* make sure to be back in time, won't you?"

Tziga nodded.

"You can just go In and get something therapeutic for the old ladies who go to matinees at the Beholder. A nice dream for the afternoon naps of vacationing biddies. *Promise*," said Laura.

"Sweetheart . . ."

"Just promise."

Tziga put his hands, still slightly tacky with oatmeal, on either side of his daughter's face. He said to her, "Darling—do you want to be a dreamhunter?"

"Yes!" She was surprised but answered instantly. "And before you ask me— No, I *don't* mind being tired all the time, being in and out of different worlds, being weirdly imperiled. I've heard you say that to Aunt Grace: 'Weirdly imperiled.' And she always says: 'Some things are worth the risk.' I am very nervous about my Try, but dreamhunting *is* worth the risk—isn't it?"

Laura's father sighed. He looked sad. "Yes," he said. "It is. But not to supply tonics for old ladies at matinees."

"But, Da. That's just *this* week. So you'll be back in time for my Try." Laura kissed her father on his cheek.

Chorley came into the room, grinned, said, "Good girl. I'm glad you got up," and ruffled her hair. Then he began to hustle Tziga out of the house. Laura went with them. She carried her father's bedroll. Chorley carried Tziga's pack and water bottles. They put everything in the car, and Laura stood, dew soaking the hem of her nightgown, waving until the car disappeared down the drive.

4

✧ ✧ ✧

A WEEK AFTER LAURA'S FATHER HAD LEFT ON HIS LATEST EXPEDITION, SHE AND ROSE LAY BUNDLED UP BESIDE A fire on the beach beneath Summerfort. They had a pile of firewood near at hand and were nursing the flames stick by stick so that the blaze would provide a pleasant heat.

All the other beach fires had been put out. The stars were coming clearer as the land cooled and the forest on the high headland to the east finished breathing out a day of sun in the form of heat distortion. Those stars at the zenith were steady, cold, and piercing.

The sea was calm. The tide had turned only an hour before. The girls could hear an occasional flipping splash as a small fish feeding on insects was startled up into the air by a larger fish hoping to feed on it. Laura, who lay facing the curve of the Bay, could feel heat on the back of her neck radiating from the rocks at the skirt of Summerfort's headland. There was flax growing on the rocks, and she could smell its baked black flowers and the perfume of the tea-tree scrub.

Earlier in the evening they had made the rounds of other fires, chatting with this and that friend—people they saw only in summer. They cooked potatoes in the embers of their own fire—then peeled them in the shallows and let seawater cool and salt them. They baked clams open on a sheet of tin, then balanced a pot on the embers to brew black tea. They toasted marshmallows and scalded their lips with molten sugar. They sang songs and cooled their overheated feet in the sea. Now they were tired, and taking slow turns to speak about what they had ahead of them.

The trip back to the capital, Founderston, was quite a journey, ten hours by rail, for the rail line, completed fifteen years before, took a long way around in order to avoid the border of the Place. The family traveled back on an overnight train, and their arrival in Founderston always seemed an abrupt end to the summer. Founderston was inland, and colder. The Tiebold town house was grand but old, built of stone, not timber like Summerfort. It faced the river, the bright Sva, but its windows were small, leaded, and composed of tiny panes of greenish, uneven glass. The house had electricity, and a fireplace in every room, but it seemed close and gloomy. Its walls and doors were thick, and anyone closed in a room alone *felt* alone.

For seven years the end of summer had meant for Laura and Rose a return to the old house and to school—Founderston Girls' Academy, where they began at eight years of age after two years of patchy learning with day tutors. These tutors were always being encouraged to go home early by either Laura's father or Rose's mother. The dreamhunters might arrive back home at any hour, leather coats covered with the white dust of the Place. Overexcited by the dreams they had caught, Tziga and Grace would want company, and cuddles from their daughters, before they had to go out and sleep, in Tziga's case at a hospital and in Grace's at the Rainbow Opera.

At the end of every summer the girls found themselves anxious about going back to school, because every summer they had been drawn into the family culture of late nights, broken sleep, and napping during the day. They often arrived at school as dazed and feverish as their dreamhunter parents, and full of irregular habits they had quickly to give up. This year Rose and Laura were more nervous than ever because *this year* it was possible that they would not be returning to the Academy at all.

✧ ✧ ✧

On the last day of the term before the summer holidays, Laura and Rose's classmates had tried to talk to them about what would happen. The other girls needed to talk—Rose was very popular and would be missed, and her friends were aware they might have to do their mourning before her departure.

After the final assembly, the girls' class gathered in their favorite meeting place, the peach tree in one corner of the quad. Everyone swapped gifts. Laura and Rose passed out their presents—carefully chosen gifts, beautifully wrapped, for the girls they really liked, and pricey soaps, perfumes, and manicure sets for those they liked only diplomatically. Mamie Doran was one of these, and as Rose handed her a ribbon-festooned tray of soaps, Mamie said, "How will we manage without you, Rose? In the choir, and as goalie in hockey. And who will counsel Jane when Miss Melon is stern with her, or console Patty when she breaks out in blisters again?"

"You could take up the slack, Mamie," Rose said. "And it's not as if we're going to the other side of the world!"

"But it's such a different life. A life apart," said Mamie, falsely sentimental, and as though to suggest that this was what Rose and Laura in fact thought. As if Rose and Laura were disdainfully shaking the dust of some provincial place off their feet.

Rose, being Rose, moved into Mamie's attack rather than away from it. "Mamie," she said, "I promise to blow you kisses when you're eating ice cream on the balcony of your father's suite at the Opera."

Mamie Doran's father was the Secretary of the Interior, a man whose power and influence were, according to some, now greater than the President's own. Mamie wasn't popular, like Rose, but she had her followers and, when she could be bothered, she was very good at managing the opinions of others. Now Mamie seemed to be determined that everyone discuss the possibility that Rose and Laura wouldn't be coming back to school. Like the cousins, almost every girl in their group had attended the Academy for seven years. Founderston Girls' Academy was their universe, a universe in which, year by year, they all rose nearer to the exalted status of seniors. Some were already the womanly heroes of the cricket and hockey fields. And soon they would play the leads in end-of-year productions, edit the yearbook, chair the school council.

One girl, too dependent on Rose's morale-building presence and made bold by Mamie's chiseling, said, "How can you think of leaving?"

"Aren't you scared?" said another girl.

Mamie looked keenly at this girl, then smirked at Rose and Laura.

Mamie Doran, unlike the other girls, was prepared to talk about where the cousins were—*or might be*—going. She knew something about dreamhunters. Ten years before—when they were all little—Cas Doran had headed the government commission that produced the legislation controlling what dreamhunters did. The Dream Regulatory Body reported to Mamie's father. So Mamie could talk about "the industry."

"Well," she said. "Dreamhunters are an independent and unmanageable group of people—I can see the charm for Rose."

Rose said, "Money's the charm."

Mamie turned pink. For a moment she held her breath; then she said, "I'm surprised to hear you say that, Rose. Dreamhunters must also have professional ethics. And they have to think about public safety."

"Oh, I can do all that and think about money too," Rose said. "And fame. And what outfit to buy for my debut at the Rainbow Opera."

"All right, be facetious," Mamie said. "But at least I'm actually talking about dreamhunting, not just going 'Aren't you scared?' like Patty."

Laura turned to Patty and touched her arm. "We don't know what will happen. I can't think yet about missing school. I can't think what I'll wear at my debut at the Rainbow Opera either. It's all too far away, and uncertain."

"Well, at least Laura is taking it all seriously," Mamie said, and managed to sound as though she was criticizing Laura as well as Rose.

"Laura's seriousness sounds like seriousness," Rose said, "and mine does not."

Rose and Mamie might have gone on fencing, but Laura discovered one unclaimed present in their basket, looked at the card, and realized that a classmate—a quiet, mousy girl—was missing, and they all had to go look for her and fuss over her.

✦ ✦ ✦

Lying on Sisters Beach after midnight, Laura was thinking about that last day of term. "Rose?" she said, then freed her arm from her bedroll to poke another stick into the flames. The driftwood caught, and for a moment its salt-saturated timber burned green. "Isn't it strange not to be thinking about school?"

"But you *are* thinking about it. You just mentioned it," said Rose.

"I just realized I hadn't thought about school all summer. I've only been thinking about our Try." Laura listened to her cousin's silence.

Finally Rose stirred, her blankets rasping softly in the hollow she'd worn herself in the sand. She said, "I'm trying not to be impatient for the time to pass. These last days at the beach are always so special."

Laura, frightened by the prospect of her Try and not wanting to be alone in her fear, asked her cousin, "Aren't you nervous? I'm miserable with nerves whenever I stop to think."

Rose was unperturbed. "But we're so lucky, Laura. We have Ma and Uncle Tziga as guides. We don't get pushed off into the Place in the company of rangers and a gaggle of poor piss-pants kids with fortune-hunter parents."

It seemed that Rose hadn't considered that she wouldn't go. That, like almost everyone, she wouldn't be able to enter the Place but would be left standing on the everyday road. "But—" Laura began. She was about to say, "What if you don't go there?" Then she stopped. She could feel Rose's confidence like the noonday sun, shrinking and blackening her own doubts. If she were to say, "What if it doesn't happen?" she would sound mean. She felt the difference in their expectations like a poison between them, a contamination that only she was aware of. She decided not to say anything. She felt that her cousin's confidence would contaminate her own luck—but only if she spoke and spoiled it for Rose.

"It'll be an adventure," Rose said, as though she were reading Laura's mind.

"An ordeal," Laura thought. But her father would be there. Her father, at least, would understand her disappointment if she didn't succeed. Laura was quiet for a time. A breeze had come up. They were sheltered from it by the rocks, but Laura could hear the flax bushes clapping. That, and the clucks and groans of roosting gulls.

"Wasn't Mamie a pain, though?" Rose said sleepily. "All her false sentiment about how the school will do without us."

"Without *you*," Laura said.

"Oh yes. Perhaps she thinks I'm flattered. But the way she talked about our Trying, as if it's never bravery we're showing—it's only pride. Implying that we are horribly confident. We're forward, so if we fall on our faces, then it serves us right. And the other girls saying, 'I don't know how you do it' and 'I'd never have the nerve.' " Rose hissed with contempt. "It isn't admiration—it's an effort to control us. To make us see sense, or show fear—or something!"

Laura could see Rose's profile, her cocked elbows. Her cousin was gazing up into the stars, and Laura knew her eyes would be wide—she'd be wearing her fighting look.

"They're so transparent," Rose said. "Honestly."

Laura realized that Rose, in taking her friends' concern as their attempt to make her feel fear, must be resisting fear. At some level Rose was nervous too. As soon as she'd thought this, Laura felt the late hour, the long day. She felt herself slipping, falling down into the soft dark below the clear black of the open air. "They're your friends, Rose," she said sleepily. "They care about you."

"I know. But they want me to stay with them, at school. They want me to fail."

"Not you," Laura said, and fell asleep—and into dreams, her own dreams.

5

✧ ✧ ✧

HE RANGER LAY CONCEALED IN A
THICKET OF BROWN GORSE BY THE
DRY RIVERBED. HIS VIEW OF TZIGA HAME
was unimpeded by haze or shade. The scene was saturated
with light, as though the sun had dissolved, whitening the air.
It had taken the ranger hours to creep close to his quarry. The
Place was silent, there was no birdsong, sawing insect chorus,
or wind to mask his approach. For each movement he'd
made, the ranger had had to wait for Hame to make some
covering noise. He'd been patient and was now in a good position.

Tziga Hame knelt in a damp excavation in the dry riverbed.
He had unwound the bandages from his hands in order to use
them. His injuries were troubling him, and it was his pained
gasping that had masked much of the ranger's stealthy
rustling. His hands were now gloved with a mixture of blood,
blue clay from the riverbank, and silver river sand. He was
sculpting. A form was beginning to emerge from the long
mound of sand beside his excavation. He worked quickly, as if
against a clock or in a competition.

This impression jogged the ranger's memory. He remembered Hame's picture in the *Summertime Weekly*, the newspaper
of Sisters Beach. The ranger had seen the picture among
other photos taken at an annual sand-sculpting competition.

In it Hame, barefoot, his trouser legs rolled, stood behind his daughter and niece—girls really too old for buckets and spades—and their competition entry, the recumbent form of a man.

It occurred to the ranger that this was what Hame was busy sculpting now—a recumbent human figure. Hame's work was quick, but not crude. It seemed he had practiced.

The ranger was puzzled and attempted to make mental notes for the report he would have to give. A verbal report, since the man for whom he was tailing Hame wouldn't want anything committed to paper.

For the last seventy-two hours the ranger had been chewing a grainy paste of Wakeful, a stimulant that dreamhunters and rangers used to stave off sleep. The ranger knew he was no longer at his best and hoped his watch would end soon. It would have to—for Tziga Hame had put his first wad of the drug into his own mouth forty-eight hours before. Hame would need to sleep soon. He didn't have any time to muck around, yet here he was, digging, patting, shaping sand like a child at play—except that he moaned as he worked. For as he worked, Hame was driving dirt into the wounds on his hands.

The ranger had picked up Hame's trail the day after the picnic. He followed Hame into the Place. The dreamhunter had led him farther into that silent wilderness than he'd ever been on his normal patrols. Hame was hard to follow—he'd been followed before, by claim-jumping dreamhunters back in the days before the Place was patrolled. The dreamhunter was wary and slow, and the ranger had kept nearly overtaking him. Hame was burdened with the usual provisions, food and water and a bedroll, but he also carried a camera, a big instrument with a collapsible crank and telescopic brass legs. Chorley Tiebold's movie camera.

Hame had led the ranger deep into the pressing silence of

the Place. And as he walked, the ranger worked on his verbal report. He composed it in his head and rehearsed it. It was terse. "I followed Mr. Hame fifty-two hours in. He made camp at a place with a ruin, a burned timber-frame building of some considerable size, standing at the edge of what appeared to be an expanse of dry seabed. Mr. Hame set up his camera, pointed its lens at the building, and cranked its handle for two minutes by my watch. After that Mr. Hame ate, then settled himself to sleep. He caught a dream."

"A bad dream"—the ranger could have added, were he able to find some way of describing what he had seen.

The ranger had watched Hame struggle in his sleep, moving violently but as though constrained, as though he were beating his forehead, elbows, and knees against invisible walls. The ranger's report would have to include an explanation of the wounds on Hame's hands. But how to put it? Perhaps like this: "Mr. Hame appeared to be distressed by his dream. He tore at his own hands with his teeth. I could not say for certain if he was asleep or awake when he inflicted these injuries on himself."

A report was required to give directions, to record actions, to measure the duration of events. The ranger had stayed under cover and watched Hame suffer some horrible, mysterious ordeal. He had trembled with the effort of remaining hidden, of not rushing to the dreamhunter's aid. He had never felt more alone—alone with his task and its limitations. Still he composed his notes. "At fifty-seven hours Mr. Hame broke camp and carried the camera back to map reference Y-17."

Back onto the known map. But how should the ranger describe what he was watching now, at map reference Y-17? When Tziga Hame began to dig in the riverbed, the concealed watcher had thought that perhaps Hame meant to bury the camera, or the cartridge of film. He saw Hame's hands bleed and listened to his hoarse breathing. He saw mad purpose in the man's actions.

"At map reference Y-17, Mr. Hame dug a trench," thought the ranger, attempting to shape his report as Hame's hands were shaping the long mound of sand. Hame was using clay as well, to fashion forms too delicate for sand to hold. He made hands from the clay and laid them at the ends of the arms. The shape he'd sculpted on the riverbed was that of a man with a broad torso and powerful limbs, a man half again Hame's height.

The ranger cowered in the tunnel of dry gorse, his shirt collar clutched over his mouth, although the vegetable dust he'd stirred up had long since settled. He watched Hame scrape the blood and soil from his hands and use this paste to form a face for his sandman. Hame took his time, and took care. But *why*? This waterless crease of unpopulated land, this most remote of remotenesses, was no place to pursue a hobby or perfect an art.

Hame sat back on his heels and surveyed his work. He nodded slowly to himself. He took out his water bottle and splashed the last of his water over his hands to wash them. His injuries oozed blood through scabs of sand. Hame raised his hands over his head, to ease the flow of blood, the ranger supposed, though the dreamhunter seemed to be praying. Indeed, the ranger imagined he heard Hame *singing* softly.

For long moments the dreamhunter remained in this incantatory position, and the ranger, tormented by puzzlement and gorse prickles, was able to get only a little relief by formulating a final sentence, at last allowing himself to express an opinion: "Mr. Hame's behavior was highly irrational, and I believe he requires further close observation.

"I've warned them," thought the ranger, though he hadn't.

He was miles and hours away from the end of his task—the delivery of his report—and alone with crazy Tziga Hame.

Hame finished his appeal to the gods. He put his hands down and stooped over his figure once more. He hesitated, one finger pointed at the figure's face. Then he leaned closer and wrote with a fingertip on its sandy forehead.

The ranger could have sworn that the air became suddenly humid as, on certain sorts of summer days, the sun uncovers itself and creates a heat sink from the water vapor in the air. But it wasn't waterborne heat that thickened the parched air. It was something else. Something as stifling and invisible as humidity but not made of water.

The figure, the man made of sand, got up out of the excavation. It stood up before Hame—stood up to face its maker. It shimmered, its surface blurring, the sand there in motion like smoke rising.

The ranger gasped and flung himself back through the tunnel in the gorse. He rolled free from the thicket, out into the open, and ran. He heard Hame call out—an angry summons or perhaps an order.

The ranger was fit and fast, and there were times, as he fled, when he imagined he'd finally been able to outstrip what followed him—till he caught again its soft approach, the hissing, sifting sound of its walk.

THE FIRST THING LAURA SAW WHEN SHE OPENED HER EYES WAS A SEABIRD, A SHAG STANDING IN THE SHEL-ter of a big log at the high-tide line. It stood with one wing tucked into its side and the other drooping, tip trailing in the sand. The bird was injured. Laura wriggled out of her bedroll and crawled toward it. She came closer, but it seemed not to see her, didn't even turn its head until she was right beside it and her human shadow was at its feet. Then it looked at her, dazed and exhausted, and shuffled a few feet away from her. It moved slowly, stumbling as it went.

Laura shook her cousin awake. For the next quarter of an hour they discussed the bird, what to do about it, what might have happened to it. There had been a big storm four nights earlier—perhaps the bird had been hurt then. They were planning to catch it in a blanket and carry it up to the house, when Rose's father appeared.

The girls had lain awake talking and thinking until dewfall, then until the cool perfume of dew gave way to the smell of bread from the two bakeries along the seafront of the resort. They'd had only a few hours' sleep, so it was easy for Rose's father to talk them out of their plans of rescue. He asked which of them knew how to set a broken wing. And if the wing was only wrenched, the bird might still gather its strength and fly away. He suggested that if they wanted to go to bed till lunchtime, he could check on the bird now and then.

Rose and Laura went up the beach yawning. Chorley bundled their bedrolls and picked up their picnic basket. He doused the gray but still smoking coals of their fire.

Once his daughter and niece were in bed, Chorley went back to the beach to find the shag lying facedown in the sand. Its head was turned, and its smooth feathers and round shoulders made it look like a sleeping baby. Chorley picked it up and carried it to the water. The tide was still going out, and if he threw the bird far enough, the tide would carry its body away. He would tell the girls that it had been gone when he'd checked. He wouldn't lie for Rose, who would think that the bird's death was a shame, and might wonder whether or not it might have been better off if she had taken it up to the house. She'd wonder, but she was tough-minded, and the bird's death wouldn't trouble her. Chorley disposed of the small corpse for Laura's sake. Laura had said, "How lonely it looks. How tired." Laura was sensitive, and her uncle had the habit of protecting her from upset whenever he could.

Laura was the only child of Chorley's dead sister—his only sibling. He loved his daughter, naturally, but Laura was all he had left of Verity.

Verity and Chorley Tiebold had been inseparable, and so after they married they combined their households. The brother and sister were support for each other in their mutual peculiar marriages to the great dreamhunters. Grace and Tziga were friends. Friends who went away for weeks at a time foraging for dreams. When the girls were born, their care naturally fell to Verity and Chorley. It had made sense for them all to live together. And to combine their finances.

But when Verity's marriage was only five years old, and her daughter only four, she fell ill, and it became apparent that she wouldn't recover.

The family, so dedicated to one another and to their un-conventional lives, had found themselves facing a creeping disaster. They were already financially overextended by Chor-ley's ambitions to restore the Tiebold Estates, refurbish the Tiebold town house, and build a beautiful summerhouse at Sisters Beach. They had to struggle to keep up payments.

Yet while Grace scaled up her dreamhunting to meet the family's commitments, there came a time when Tziga would leave his wife only to catch the kinds of dreams that might help restore her health. Later he caught the kinds of dreams that might prolong her life. And at the last, he sought and pursued the kinds of dreams that might help ease her dying. Tziga caught and performed for nobody but his wife. Every night, for Verity alone. She and he would disappear together into her darkened sickroom and into his dreams. Apart from his hurried forays into the Place, Tziga was always with Verity. His savings ran out. Chorley and Grace supported him, and his neglected daughter. To Chorley it seemed that his sister, in dying, was taking her husband with her. He imagined that Verity would die in her sleep—in Tziga's sleep—and that nei-ther would wake.

In the end Chorley begged his sister to stop Tziga. He was in anguish, but he said to her, "Please, dear, you must refuse his help now. You must ask him not to go to the Place again. Can you *please* try to go from us awake? Forgive me. But please, Verity, don't let Tziga go with you in his sleep."

Verity promised to do what her brother asked. "But only when my time has come," she said. She postponed her sacri-fice, while Tziga worked to banish her pain and stave off her death. Little Laura asked her uncle Chorley, "Is Daddy sick too?" Even the child could see how it was—that her father was desperately active but fading.

Tziga went away to get another dream. "It's only overnight," he promised his wife. "Be brave." When he'd gone, Chorley told his sister what her daughter had said. Verity asked to see Laura. They had a little talk. Then Verity kissed her daughter and sent her off to play. She summoned Chorley and Grace. She said she wanted to get up. She put on a robe, and they helped her out onto the terrace. She sat watching the river traffic go by in the afternoon sunlight. An hour later Chorley and Grace carried her inside, unconscious. They called the doctor and watched by her bed, and in the small hours, Verity Hame died without ever coming around again.

Tziga carried his dream home and found a hearse parked at his gate.

Verity's funeral was held three days later. Tziga stood at his wife's graveside, his eyes sunk in circles of bruises. He refused to sleep or eat, took nothing at the funeral breakfast, and sat in the chief mourner's chair oblivious to the approaches of friends and relations who steeled themselves to offer their sympathy; oblivious to his daughter, who was ruining her black velvet dress by lying on the floor under his chair.

When the guests had gone and the girls had been carried off to bed, Tziga prowled around the house. Chorley got out of bed at dawn to find his brother-in-law in the kitchen yard, his head held under the stream from the pump. "You can't stay awake forever," Chorley told him—though he could smell the spice of Wakeful in Tziga's sweat and see that his lips were stained mauve from the drug.

"This dream isn't anyone else's," Tziga said. "It was for her. The best yet. The best I've ever caught." He raised his wet, white face and glared at his brother-in-law. "You can bury me with it," he said.

By the next morning he was swaying and stumbling. He tripped on the stairs and sat on the landing with his head

hanging. Chorley followed him around. Tziga called him a
vulture and threw things at him. Grace sent the servants away
and sat with the girls in the nursery. She read to them, sang
lullabies, and put them in their beds. She listened to the
house. Rose's bright, sleepless eyes regarded her mother
through the white mosquito net around her bed. Laura poked
her head out of her netting—sat veiled in it, like a little com-
municant. At sunset Chorley found Tziga holding himself up
against a doorframe on which he was rhythmically beating his
head. Chorley inserted his hand between the bloodied mold-
ing and Tziga's oozing forehead. Then Tziga collapsed, and
Chorley picked him up. Tziga was light, worn thin by walking
Inland after the consoling beauties of the Place, by watching,
by keeping himself awake. Chorley carried Tziga to his and
Grace's bed.

Tziga woke in the morning—at the same time that a whole
city block woke weeping with joy at a dream so powerful and
beautiful that it altered each of its dreamers forever, a dream
caught to carry a beloved, pain-racked woman into paradise.
Tziga woke, weeping himself, and saw that Grace was beside
him and Chorley beside her, looking over her shoulder with
pouring eyes, and between them were the little girls, Rose
laughing at her dream with nervous, puzzled delight and
Laura calling alternately, "Mummy!" and "Rosie!"—as though
she wanted to share some wonderful news but didn't know
who to tell first. Tziga could feel his dream echoing in the city
like a thunderclap. He lay floating in breathing light. Grace
cupped his wet face in both her hands, and Chorley's hands
covered hers.

Tziga wasn't good for much after that. He rested, and the
bills mounted up. Grace, meanwhile, foraged deep into the
Place, looking for wonders and novelties, overwriting one
dream with another till she got something she knew she could

sell at a very high price. Sometimes she would encounter dreamhunters who had abandoned their own plans in order to wait for her, dreamhunters who would offer to empty their heads for her. She was exhausted—so they might offer also to carry her out. They'd carry her out and delete their own dreams, replacing them with what she had—not so that they could part from her and peddle their poor copies of her dreams but so that they could act as amplifiers, dream in unison with her, share the dreamer's bed and a small part of her fee. For remembering with what force her presence in Tziga's sleep had amplified his last dream, Grace was ready to accept these offers.

Chorley was busy. He reorganized the family's finances— budgeting and juggling due dates on payments. He kept his brother-in-law company—Grace had been very clear to him about this. "Tziga has to get well," she'd said. "He's worth more than we are. He is the beauty of dreamhunting. He is the good of it."

Chorley also had the girls to care for. Grace was clear on that score too. "Watch poor Laura. And—you know, love—I can work, and work, and work, so long as Rose is happy."

Chorley did all that he had to—and he failed to notice things. He didn't see the dubious looks people had begun to give him in the street. He didn't hear the odd stifled snigger in acquaintances, or see how embarrassed, fastidious looks would appear on the faces of certain friends whenever he spoke about his wife.

One evening Chorley took Tziga drinking to shake him out of his misery. At six in the morning he and Tziga decided to go quietly—or as quietly as a couple of scuffling, giggling drunks can—in the stage door of the Rainbow Opera. They had decided to wait for Grace in one of the galleries (this was before they owned private suites). They'd carry her off to a café and eat a pile of potato cakes and sour cream, just like they used to. "She must want a change of scene," Chorley said. "She spends half her life in this place—or the Other."

Chorley and Tziga stumbled up the back stairs to the first-floor gallery. The Opera was silent. The men of the fire watch, who were sitting one level above and opposite, leaned out to gesture, fingers across their lips. Chorley mirrored the gesture. He put a finger to his lips and shushed Tziga. Then he tiptoed to the balustrade and looked over.

Chorley Tiebold saw that his wife was asleep in the Opera's dais bed and that there were two men lying on either side of her.

✣ ✣ ✣

The Dream Regulatory Body was set up under a piece of legislation known as the Intangible Resources Act. The Body came into existence six weeks after Chorley Tiebold's discovery and, in a way, owed its existence to him. For Chorley had caused a scene, he and the fire watch had come to blows, and some furniture had been broken. Grace, hearing her husband's drunken bluster, flung herself and everyone else out of sleep. Several hundred people woke up abruptly, before the happy conclusion of their dream. It was—one man later told his cronies—like being thrown into an icy pond while in the act of love. Behind the Rainbow Opera's padded doors, people surfaced shouting, gasping, and gagging.

There were complaints to the Rainbow Opera, of course. Some patrons demanded the return of their ticket price. Others canceled their season tickets. The police considered charging Grace Tiebold with criminal negligence. But no current law quite covered what went on in dream palaces.

The newspapers reported the incident, then refused to let

the matter drop. For ten years fastidious fear, suspicion, and disapproval had been brewing about dreamhunters and their performances. Even when dreams were only a therapy, even when Tziga Hame was the only one able to broadcast a dream wider than a room, there were people who said that dreams were wicked seductions, that dreamhunters interfered with people's souls, and that the Place was alien and unhallowed. The public was ready for a moral panic, and the newspapers whipped up their fears.

The President called a special meeting of Congress. This was the meeting at which the young Deputy Secretary of the Interior, after making a number of alert and thoughtful remarks, was appointed head of a commission of inquiry.

Over several months the commission called its witnesses, asked its questions, and discussed the testimonies. The commission gave its report, and its head, Cas Doran, wrote a draft bill based on its findings. Doran's Intangible Resources Bill proposed that a body be set up: to regulate traffic in and out of the Place, to police the Place and its bordering countryside, and to act as a licensing body for dream parlors and palaces—deciding where they could be set up and how they would be run. "The Place is not a mirage that will disappear," Doran wrote in the commission's report. "It is a valuable resource belonging to our nation, and, as such, it cannot be an ungoverned frontier."

When the act was passed, and the Dream Regulatory Body set up and its regulations written, almost everyone was satisfied.

Chorley Tiebold was not. He complained to his wife that nowhere in the regulations did it say that a dreamhunter wasn't allowed to sleep in the same bed as any amplifiers she used. The legislation got its start in public concern about public morals. Where was that reflected? All the government seemed to care about was that they got *control*.

Dreamhunter

Chorley Tiebold stood on the beach, watching the dead shag floating a foot under the calm surface of the morning sea, slowly drawing away in the ebb tide. He was thinking about the life of a dreamhunter. Not "the beauty of it," as his wife had said to him about Tziga all those years before, but its dangers. His daughter and niece might congratulate themselves on having lived in a liberal, adventurous household, but really they'd led sheltered lives. Chorley had led a sheltered life too—and was very grateful for it. He wanted to see the girls grow up surrounded by pleasant, civilized people. Grace, in her fantasies about Rose's future, couldn't seem to see past that magical moment on the border, at a Try, when one child in a hundred walks out of the world everyone can see. Dreamhunting had brought Grace everything—fame, wealth, pride in her work. But the girls already had everything they could ever need. They were well-off, and well-informed and confident. They didn't need a job that would see them limping home haunted and hollow-eyed, as Tziga often did. Increasingly often. If the girls went into the Place, they would be going where Chorley couldn't walk after them, couldn't look for them if they got lost. And he was the parent who'd *done* those things, who'd rounded them up at dusk from the safe little park a few streets from their house in Founderston, who'd called them in from the beach below Summerfort. He was the one who was always there at bedtime. Chorley didn't want his daughter and niece to Try—especially not Laura, who was small for her age and always had at least one serious cough every winter.

He didn't want it, he'd argued against it, but he hadn't stood a chance against everyone else's wishes. For a while it had seemed as though Tziga was of two minds about his daughter's Try, but now he was in just as much of a hurry as everyone else.

Chorley lost sight of the dead bird. The sea dazzled him. He trudged back up the beach to Summerfort, where he stood listening in the lower hall. There was no noise from upstairs; the girls had fallen asleep.

7

✤ ✤ ✤

THE RANGER THOUGHT HE WAS FINALLY SAFE, WITH THE BALDING EARTH AND PALE, TRAMPLED VEGETATION OF THE BORDER before him. But still he jogged on, his feet dragging and sweat dripping past his belt. He was gasping for breath and making a lot of noise, but when *it* came, he still heard it. He heard the whisper of his mineral pursuer.

The ranger put on a burst of speed. The nightmare that was chasing him must belong to the Place, he reasoned. Once he was across the border, the monster would vanish.

He felt the creature's heavy, semisolid hand drop upon his shoulder. He let out a raw scream.

The hand solidified enough to grip and jerk the ranger around. He faced the creature, its dry, lumpish face and the horrible, swarming attention in its holes-for-eyes. The ranger felt the creature fumbling at him and imagined that it was searching him. As he tried to tear the creature's hands from him, the ranger's own hand found the remnant of his letter of instruction. He took the paper and stuffed it in his mouth and began to chew. At the same time he threw his weight backward and hauled himself away toward the border.

The sandman's muddy, fused-together fingers separated. He poked two into the ranger's mouth.

The ranger tried to swallow the letter and began to choke.

He and the sandman rocked back and forth, fighting but moving ever nearer to the border.

The ranger bit down on the fingers. His mouth filled with loose sand. Sand packed down the partly chewed letter.

The sandman released the ranger, who saw the monster's bitten fingers re-form, grow from a trickle of sand running like veins down the surface of its arm. He saw the fingers lengthen till the hand was whole.

The creature was holding a fragment of the letter.

The ranger saw all this before he staggered, gagging, through the border, into the heat and color and noise of the world.

The noise was that of running horses and iron-rimmed wheels rolling on sunbaked earth.

The ranger turned toward the sound and threw up his arms to ward off what instantly overwhelmed him—the Sisters Beach stagecoach, which had come, at full tilt, around a bend in the road above the village of Tricksie Bend.

8

✢ ✢ ✢

THE DAY AFTER THEIR CAMPOUT, AT AROUND FOUR IN THE AFTERNOON, LAURA AND ROSE WERE ON THE INFANTS' beach. For the last few weeks of that summer, the cousins had made a daily visit to this sheltered spot. There was a lifeguard they liked to look at. The girls tried not to be conspicuous in their admiration, so they would park themselves at the edge of the ranks of for-hire lounge chairs. The chairs were usually empty at that hour—the infants and their minders having packed up and gone home. The sun was well past its zenith, and the sun umbrellas cast their streaks of shade along the sand behind each slatted chair.

That day the handsome lifeguard wasn't at his station but was prowling up and down before the shallows in the shelter of the breakwater. Rose and Laura ambled as near to him as they dared, finally settling down partly concealed behind a lounge chair.

The chair they chose was occupied, but Rose and Laura were looking elsewhere and scarcely noticed its occupant. He was quiet, reading. But as the sun settled toward the horizon and the shade of his umbrella thinned and swooped eastward, the girls moved to stay in its shadow. Eventually, they were lounging on the sand to one side of the chair.

Rose craned and squinted. She shuffled a little closer to the

lounge chair. Then she said, "We have that book in school."
She turned to Laura. "Well, next year we do. It's Dr. King's *A History of Southland*."

Laura peered at the book. People usually read magazines on the beach, or didn't read but draped their faces with them.

Rose said, "He's up to chapter sixteen, 'Tziga's Fall.' "

The occupant of the lounge chair grunted. He sat up, swung his feet onto the sand, and looked at Rose. He appeared to be a few years older than the cousins. He was already sporting a small, experimental mustache and a thin strip of brassy whiskers, a shade darker than his hair. He was fair-skinned and freckled—and very pink.

Laura said to him, "You're getting a sunburn."

"I'd say, judging by your color, that you are a little more practiced at beach holidays than I am. This is my *first*, and I'm making the most of it. I rented this lounge chair for the afternoon, and I'll not leave it till the afternoon is over."

"I can never read on the beach," Laura said.

"I'm not at leisure to choose when I do my reading," said the boy.

"Won't you at least take my towel?" Laura said. She rolled off it and held it out to him.

"That's hardly necessary," he said.

Rose said, "You could get off your lounge chair and drag it into your shade. Your shade is oozing away from you—it doesn't seem to understand that it's been hired for the whole afternoon." She asked him where he was staying.

"My uncle has an apartment in Bayview."

"Oh!" Rose said. "Someone was killed there last year! A potted plant fell from the terrace on the sixth floor and killed a man on a first-floor balcony. It was dreadful!" Rose mused for a bit. "But they did manage to repot the geranium," she said.

The boy stared at her, baffled and skeptical at once. "What are you girls doing on the infants' beach?"

Rose tossed her head. "I am the mother of one of those infants, naturally," she said.

"Only *one*?"

Laura asked, "What are *you* doing on the infants' beach? Can't you swim?"

"I thought I'd get some peace and quiet—get away from youths stuffing sand down one another's fronts. All those splashing, dunking, shrieking, sidling, flirting nuisances."

"Laura and I are only interested in what you're reading," said Rose.

"Really?"

Laura said to her cousin, "He's here to Try. He's doing research." Then she asked the boy, "Are you Trying at Tricksie Bend?"

The official Tries took place at two locations. One was at Doorhandle, an hour and a half by coach from Founderston. That Try took place on a strip of land cleared from the forest a mile out of the village. The clearing followed the border for a short way before letting it go in the thick woods that—with patrolling rangers—helped to guard it. The second location was some fifteen miles away, across Rifleman Pass, on the Place's seaward border. There the candidates Tried in a meadow that sloped up to a bluff above the river at Tricksie Bend.

"No," said the boy. "I'm going back to Founderston tonight, and I'm Trying at Doorhandle."

"Uh-huh," said Laura. Then she asked him, "Do you have that book in your school?"

"We *had* this book at my school."

Laura and Rose exchanged a look—he was perhaps more a young man than an oversized boy. "What school?" Rose asked. Founderston Girls' Academy's annual ball was attended by the seniors of several boys' schools and military academies. Rose was trying to place him on her social map.

"A school in a town south of the Corridor."

The Corridor was a wide valley that cut through the mountains which divided their country. The south was all plains and grain, vineyards, small towns, pasture and cattle. The north had the capital, Founderston; the nation's next largest city, Westport; its mines and industries, forested mountains, and beautiful Coal Bay. The north also had the Place.

Rose said, "What does Dr. King have to say about Tziga's fall?"

The boy leaned his forearms on his knees and opened the book. "He seems to be saying that it was no accident. And I keep feeling sorry for Hame's sister, Marta. She's 'just folks' in this story. Everyone else is special and involved."

"Yes, poor her," Laura said of her aunt Marta. She was fond of Marta, whom she never saw often enough. It was Laura's impression that her father didn't invite his sister over because she and Chorley didn't see eye to eye. Marta was very religious, and Chorley, a firm atheist, was rude about her beliefs. He wasn't rude to her face, but Aunt Marta seemed to be able to tell that Chorley said things behind her back.

Rose wriggled a little closer to the boy, put her finger on the corner of the book, and pushed it down so she could see it. Laura hoped Rose wasn't going to do her showy upside-down reading. Rose could read upside-down in mirrors too. "So," said Rose. "You live in the south, but I suppose you've shared dreams."

"One or two. My uncle is a dreamhunter."

"Which one? Is he famous?"

"George Mason. He usually works only in hospitals. Pike Street, and St. Thomas's Lung Hospital."

"Well—that's good," said Rose, in the tone of someone thinking of something nice to say.

"I think we might have King's history at home, in the library," Laura said.

"You have a library so large that you're not sure what's in it?" For some reason the boy seemed to find the idea of a large library offensive. Or perhaps it was only the idea of a large library largely unread by girls who had access to it.

Laura could see that Rose would strike back at the boy's remark; she had sparks of white in her blue eyes. "Actually, we have *two* libraries too large to know what's in them. One here, and one in Founderston."

Laura said, "*Rose.*"

"Rose," said the boy. He said it as if he had a pen and was writing it down.

"My cousin has had too much *afternoon* this afternoon," Laura said.

Rose said, "We can look for the King if you'd like, Laura—and check his history against the facts. You know, I don't think I've ever *read* about dreamhunting."

When Laura and Rose were four, they had been told what Laura's father and Rose's mother did for a living. That simple explanation went something like this: "Laura, your father and, Rosie, your mother go to the Place to catch dreams. Other people pay to go to sleep with them and share their dreams in hospitals and dream palaces." The little girls had accepted this explanation because they were very happy with the arrangement. Laura's da and Rosie's ma were only sometimes at home in the evening, and so Laura could climb into bed with her ma, and Rosie with her da. There was room in each adult bed for *two* girls if that was what they felt like. But for Laura, who had this lovely privilege explained to her only a few months before her mother fell ill with the cancer that killed her, her knowledge about what her father and aunt did for a living became connected with the terrible changes that came later. She had questioned how things worked in her world, and then things had changed for the worse. Laura was careful about asking questions after that. She kept looking at her life, her family—her *happiness*—only out of the corner of one eye.

The boy's jaw had dropped. He was staring at the cousins as though they'd grown horns. After a moment he collected himself and glared. "You're a Tiebold," he said to Rose. "You're Grace Tiebold's daughter, aren't you?" Then he turned, with a different expression, to Laura. "So you must be—"

"Gosh it's nice to be famous," said Rose.

"Honestly, you girls are just playing with me, aren't you?" said the boy. "Saying 'What does the book say?' as though you really are infants. Big joke on the country boy, right?"

Rose tilted her nose in the air. "No," she said. "My motives are completely pure. I only wanted to pilfer your bought-and-paid-for shade."

The boy stood, shut the book with a snap, and picked up his towel from the lounge chair. He stepped between the cousins and began to walk away.

"Hey!" Laura called. "Good luck!"

He spun back. "I suppose you expect me to wish you good luck too? But *you* don't need luck. After all, I'm sure it's not what you know but *who* you know."

"No. It's who you *are*," Laura said plainly.

He turned and stalked off.

"That was interesting," said Rose, looking after him. "If we say who we are we're boasting, and if we don't we're sneaky." Then she said brightly, "Let's go for another swim."

✢ ✢ ✢

Half an hour later a wind picked up on the beach. It bowled sun umbrellas, flipped picnic blankets, and made the wide brims of fashionable sun hats take on unfashionable shapes. Everyone began to abandon the shoreline.

The cousins were very quick to pick themselves up off the prints their wet bodies had made on their rented towels and sprint up the steps to the Strand. Because Laura and Rose spent three months of every year at the beach, they knew that when a westerly set in around five, it was bound to blow until the early hours of the following morning.

The girls hurried across the Strand to the corner of Main Street. They tumbled through the glass-and-brass doors of Farry's, the confectioner, and stood shaking sand from their knitted swimsuits and printed cotton kimonos. Rose, seeing her favorite table emptying, made a dash for it. She came around from one side as the previous occupant was leaving by the other. Rose slid into the warmed iron chair, and the woman who had just left it looked back at her, rather startled. Rose didn't notice. She was issuing orders to the countermen: "I want my usual, chocolate-and-ginger ice cream with candied apple and cream." She repeated her order to the waiter who'd come over to clear the table. Then, as he made space, transferring plates from the marble tabletop onto his tray, she stretched her tan, salt-silvered arms out of the sleeves of her kimono and laid them on the table. She said, "Do you think my skin looks dry?" She pinched the taut flesh on her sharp elbow joint.

"If you like, Miss Tiebold, I can give you a bit of butter to rub on your elbows."

"I asked for your opinion, not for assistance," said Rose.

The waiter said, "Ah." Then, "I'm sorry to have to admit that my experience of female elbows is rather limited."

Rose dismissed him with a wave of her hand.

Laura was up at the counter, choosing a cake.

Farry's had two curved counters at the back of its round room. Behind the glass front of one, sweets were displayed—

marzipan in the shape and flavor of every fruit, and filled chocolates, bitter dark chocolate, milk chocolate, and white. There were glistening fruit jellies and thick slabs of marshmallow dusted with sugar. There were caramels and fudges, peanut brittle, sugared almonds, sherbet in paper envelopes with licorice straws, and hokey-pokey stacked high like gold bars in a treasury. The shop smelled of sugar and fresh cream. Behind the glass of the other counter, glittering beneath the light of electric bulbs, were huge slabs of ice and—nestled between them—steel tubs of Farry's famous ice cream.

Laura saw that a counterman was waiting for her order. She was having trouble making up her mind. She felt vague, stupefied by sun, weak and watery from swimming. She told the man she'd have the same as her cousin.

"Again," he said.

This was a little rude, but the girls had practically lived at Farry's every summer of their lives, and, Laura supposed, the staff was entitled to remark on their habits. "Again" was true. Laura was in the habit of following Rose, of letting Rose make arrangements, shape their days, choose their food. The man was telling Laura off. Teachers would do the same. They'd say, "Laura Hame, if you don't come up with your own topic, we're just going to have to separate the two of you." Or they'd say, "Miss Hame, could you please show a little more initiative?"

It was easy for Laura to follow Rose. Rose always made headway, whichever way the wind was blowing. And following Rose left Laura free to watch what was going on around her.

As Laura walked back to the best table in Farry's big bay window, she looked around, her mind floating, unburdened by decisions. She saw a woman come in the front door shepherding a wind-tossed flurry of girls—of three different sizes but in the same white flounced dresses, their straw hats clapped flat to their heads by their lace-gloved hands. Laura saw the woman assess Rose, slouching in her chair at the front table, point by point: Rose's damp kimono, her gold hair clumped in salt-dulled rattails. She clicked her tongue against her palate, went "tich" like an angry thrush. Then Laura looked past the woman and saw, across the road, the manager of the stagecoach posted out on the pavement, looking at his watch, then up Main Street toward the rise to Rifleman Pass.

Laura glanced over her shoulder at the clock above the door to Farry's kitchens. She saw that the coach was already more than half an hour late.

Half an hour, of a four-hour journey.

"Look," she said to Rose, pointing at the clock, then the anxious manager.

The waiter returned. He carried a tray with a plate of ice cream and pink curls of candied apple. He put the tray down on the table, shook napkins open, and dropped them onto the girls' laps. The cousins leaned back to let the linen settle.

Rose dug into her ice cream, then immediately began to talk around her spoon. "Perhaps it's broken an axle," she said.

"I don't think so."

"You're a ghoul, Laura."

"*I'm* the ghoul? It'd be pretty gruesome to break an axle above the bluffs in Rifleman Pass."

Rose shrugged. She said she was going to get a conversation cake too. "Do you want one?" She jumped up, dodged the matron's table and the waiter carrying the matron's tea, and ducked under the brass rail before the cake display case. She draped herself on its glass. She gave a moaning sigh and pressed one pink cheek against its condensation-covered surface.

"Miss Tiebold," said the counterman.

"Two conversation cakes. With cream and lemon curd."

"Certainly. Will that be all?"

"And a pitcher of mint tea."

Rose brushed the glass with her nose, leaving a smear. She came back to the table. She didn't say thank you.

The matron's daughters were all managing to sit straight in their chairs and eat with their cake forks. They were a contrast to the cousins who sat in Farry's prime spot, clearly visible from the street, dusted with crumbs of baked egg white, licking their fingers and staring fixedly, rudely, at the people waiting at the stagecoach stop.

Laura said, "It's nearly *an hour* late."

"Come to think of it," Rose said, "you haven't even *seen* the bluffs at Rifleman."

"Your da took us up to the surveyor's station near there. Remember? It was one of his educational outings. The station was right on the border to the Place."

"Did *your* da know about this?"

"Uncle Chorley lied about it. He said we'd stopped at Tricksie Bend."

"I remember *that*. We bought honeycomb."

The three girls at the next table had removed their gloves to eat. After each bite they dabbed at their lips with Farry's white linen napkins. They were so ladylike, so poised and mild that they raised their heads only when Laura and Rose suddenly dropped their teacups into their saucers and jumped up, shoving their chairs back so hard that one fell over with a clang.

The stagecoach had appeared behind other traffic on the long avenue of Main Street. Its driver was standing up in his seat, his whip flicking and biting above the backs of his horses. The coach sounded its horn, then kept sounding as it made its way through Sisters Beach's shallow settlement to the stage post. The coach pulled up—a noisy emergency.

The cousins rushed out of Farry's and across the road.

Rose's kimono billowed open in the wind—its co̶ ̶ ̶hed itself and, unnoticed by her, blew away leeward, traveling along the pavement like a thin sidewinding serpent.

The girls plunged into the little crowd and pushed to its front in time to see the stage doors open and passengers spill out.

A man and woman were clasping each other. She had a handkerchief stuffed into her mouth.

Rose leaned back on the jostling crowd. She called out, "Driver! Have you lost someone?"

The driver and passengers all looked at her.

It did happen that, every so often, an adult might vanish by the cairn that marked the border on the road beyond Doorhandle—might melt from the coach. It would turn out that this person hadn't, for whatever reason, chosen to Try at fifteen. Hadn't attempted before to pass across into the Place.

Rose called out her question, and the crowd hushed. People looked from the stage post manager to the driver to the girl in a kimono and bathing suit. "Because"—continued Rose, managing and informative—"you should go straight to the telegraph office at the station and send a wire to Doorhandle."

Most of those who fell were missed right away and, when they emerged, were recovered. Some wandered in the wrong direction, disoriented, deeper in. Rangers were dispatched to find them.

"Have someone send a ranger," Rose said. She gestured at them to hurry.

The driver lifted his hand, the hand with the horse whip gathered in it. He pointed with his whip, showing something to his employer, the bossy girl in beachwear, and the gathered crowd.

Laura saw what was fastened to the roof rack among the

luggage on the top of the coach. A long, limp, blanket-wrapped bundle.

She backed out of the crowd.

Uncle Chorley's cream-and-chrome motorcar had pulled up by Farry's. Laura's uncle was at the confectioner's door, his hands cupped by his eyes and his face pressed to the glass as he tried to see inside. He peered, then took a step back and opened the door for the matron and her daughters. They nodded their thanks, then clapped their hands onto their hats and turned into the wind coming up from the beach. The sand lying on the road rose to make a sparkling golden stream at knee height, in which the woman and girls seemed to be paddling.

Chorley caught sight of Laura and waved.

She ran across the road to him.

"I've been looking for you, Laura."

His niece interrupted him. "There's been an accident. Someone is dead." She pointed at the crowd around the coach. "Rose wanted to help," she said as her uncle opened the car door and helped her into its backseat. "She wanted to take charge," Laura added, currying favor—she knew that Rose's father was sometimes irritated by what he called "Rose's prefect manner."

Laura watched her uncle walk away from her across the road. She saw him stop at the edge of the crowd and crane over the people's heads.

The wind dropped and the sand settled. The girl heard Chorley asking questions. The crowd became quiet. The wind gusted again, and sand rose in one place, in a humped wave. Laura watched as her uncle, the driver, and the manager climbed on top of the coach to inspect what was tied there. They removed some of the wrappings. Chorley put his face down, close to the wrapped corpse. His hand went into the wrappings where Laura knew a head would be. He straightened, looked at something he held. He showed it to the manager, then they both climbed down. Several men from the crowd clambered up to help the driver unfasten the body and lower it to others on the ground, who carried it into the stage post.

Laura's uncle came back across the road leading her cousin. Rose got in beside Laura. Her expression was sober, and she didn't say anything. Chorley released the brake, and the car rolled away from the curb. He raised his voice above the engine noise. "Your father is back, Laura. But they've sent a special train for him." He sounded sympathetic.

Laura put a hand to her throat. She felt breathless, as if the air in her lungs had set hard.

A special train meant that her father had had one of his rare, priceless dreams—a dream that was contracted to the government and would be commandeered for the public good. He would be performing it for as long as it lasted—a week to ten days. The girls had once asked Rose's mother—who was always more open about her profession and its mysteries—where exactly Laura's father took these dreams.

"Insane asylums—and the like," Grace had said.

In the car, on their way to the train station, Laura said to her uncle, "But Da has to be *here* a week from today. He *promised*."

"The Body has him under contract—and that's a promise too," Chorley said, patiently explaining what Laura already understood. "Sorry, darling," he added.

"Why didn't he avoid getting a dream they'd want? He knows where his dreams are!"

"I don't know what he was thinking," Chorley said.

"He can't make it to my Try!" Laura wailed.

Laura's uncle didn't say anything, but she saw him clench his jaw.

Rose looked at Laura and blushed, then bit her lip. Laura turned away from her cousin. She didn't want to see Rose concerned for her, Rose excited by concern, alive with it.

The Strand was almost deserted. A few people walked, tilting forward or backward, against the wind. The waves were still small but tipped white. There were flags flying on the twin turrets of the resort's dream palace—the Beholder—long green pennants, Grace Tiebold's sign.

"Mother's back too!" Rose said. Her mother had gone In three days before.

"She's dreaming tonight," said Chorley.

Rose squeezed Laura's arm. "That's something to look forward to, at least."

9

✧ ✧ ✧

T HE STRETCH OF THE PLATFORM THAT
WAS UNDER COVER FROM THE SUN
WAS CROWDED WITH PASSENGERS, ALL KEEP-
ing an eye on the luggage trolley, smoking porters, and their
train, which sat in a siding five hundred yards up the line,
breathing wisps of steam. The Sisters Beach Express was waiting for the special train to leave so that it could pull into the
station.

The special train was at the far end of the platform. Only
one or two brazen travelers had wandered up to have a look at
it. The train had only two carriages—a luxury coach and a
guard's van. Its engine was new, bull-nosed, and black. The
train flew red flags, two on the engine and two on its back
deck—danger signals.

A group of officials waited by the train. They all wore
dark suits and city hats. Several were mountainous, broad-
shouldered bodyguards in the guise of civil servants. Also attending on the train was a famous flamboyant physician from
Sisters Beach. Dr. Wilmot was resplendent in gray pinstripes
and a gold cravat. He was playing with a monocle; it flashed as
he twirled it.

Grace and Tziga had come straight from the Place and were
dressed in linen shirts and trousers, leather jackets, and sup-
ple leather lace-up boots. Grace Tiebold wore a duster over

her clothes, and Tziga Hame had bandaged hands. He carried a handkerchief with which he sometimes dabbed at his mouth.

The special train had a full head of steam. Steam escaped from all its engine's valves, wrapping the black iron in a tissue of white vapor.

The passengers waiting for the delayed Sisters Beach Express saw Chorley Tiebold's car pull up, the two girls jump out of its backseat and sprint along the platform past them. Chorley hurried too but was less headlong.

Long-legged Rose was the first to reach Tziga. She clasped him around his chest and leaned close to issue a warning. "Laura's mad at you!" Then she let go, drew back, and noticed how he held his hands clear, so that his blood-spotted bandages wouldn't foul her clothes. She saw his hollow eyes and scabbed lips. Then Laura barged in, and Rose stumbled back, too surprised to stand her ground.

"Goodbye, Rose," Tziga said. "Good luck."

Laura had begun to talk, low and accusing. Her father didn't meet her eye but took her arm and walked her along the platform away from the others.

✧ ✧ ✧

Laura let her father lead her away. She knew that she would cry. She collected her thoughts and tried to tell him how she felt. She said, "You've always talked as though you'd be there for my Try. I expect you there. You should understand that, Da. Don't you know that all my life people have looked at me as if they imagine they can see something in the air around me? Dreams. It might be *you* they are thinking of, but it's *me* they're staring at. *Hame*, those looks say, like people sighing when they're in love. How do you think that's made me feel?"

Laura stopped walking: she dug her heels into the platform's rust-browned bitumen, and her arm slipped through her father's hand. He gave a sharp cry and snatched the bandaged mitt of his hand back against his chest. He hunched over, cradling it.

Laura wiped her eyes and looked at him. She saw his torn lips and the red seepage on the white linen. She forgot the rest of what she'd meant to say. She said, "What happened to your hands?"

"I bit them," he said. He straightened, gathered her in an arm, and hustled her along the platform again. This time Laura took in the movement he had suppressed, a glance back at the officials by the waiting train.

"I'm afraid," she said.

Her father didn't look at her, but he said, "What are you afraid of?" He was brusque.

"When you come back, it'll all be over. That's what I'm afraid of," she said. "It'll be decided." She shouldn't have to explain—he should know. "My whole life will be decided."

He had walked her to where the platform began to slope down to the railbed. He stopped, and Laura, looking for an expression of understanding and sympathy, saw instead a look of desperation cross his face. Beyond them the silver rail lines, siding, and waiting express all shimmered in the hazy middle distance.

Laura said to her father, "You should have told those people no!" She pointed back at the officials and the special train, keeping her eyes on her father's face. She was crying now. He should at least say he was sorry. At least dry her tears. "Rose will go there," Laura sobbed. At last she let it show—all those weeks and months of being slowly crushed by Rose's confidence. Rose was her mother, Grace, all over again—fearless and full of appetite. Rose had hung at the front of the crowd to look at the corpse, while Laura flinched and fell back.

Laura cried, "Rose will go and I won't!"

Her father sighed. "Don't be so softheaded," he said.

"It's how I feel!" Laura said. She heard herself, her aggrieved whining.

"As if confidence can affect the outcome," her father said—cold and impatient. Then: "Laura."

His voice had acquired some warmth and urgency, so she looked at him. He was frowning back along the platform. There was a figure apparently wading toward them through the heat haze, one of the black-clad officials, his hand on his hat, head bowed into the wind.

Laura's father grabbed her arms and leaned down to look into her face. Laura could feel the bandages, and his fingers beneath them, held stiff, so that his palms and not his injured digits took the pressure of his grip. He said, "Do you remember any of the songs I taught you?"

Laura was so surprised by this question that she didn't answer.

Her father gave her a little shake. "The old family songs. I sang them to you night after night when you were small."

"The bedtime songs?" Laura said. " 'The Hame inheritance'?" She was unimpressed.

"Do. You. Remember. Them?" Her father demanded, separating each word.

He was frightening her. Only the fact that she was frightened stopped her from breaking away and shouting at him "What is all this!" She did manage to mutter, sullen, "Why should I bother to remember any old songs when you aren't going to take the trouble to be there for my Try?"

Her father's eyes were wide, his face so pale that Laura could see, very clearly, that the wounds on his lip were crenulations, the marks of teeth, his own upper incisors having bruised and broken the skin on his lower lip. And she saw that his teeth were streaked with blood, as though he had further wounds inside his mouth.

He shook her again. "The songs," he said.

" 'Button Thread,' 'A Stitch in Time.' The *baby* songs. Yes!" Laura shouted at him. She'd heard her aunt calling, far away at the other end of the platform. Aunt Grace yelled, "Tziga! It's time to go!"

Laura's father's grip loosened. He whispered, "Of His Name." It was the title of a song.

"Yes." Laura sobbed. "That nonsense."

"*Noun* sense," said her father. Laura felt his wadded hands on her hair, the sticky edges of the bandages catch at her curls. Her father asked her if she could just say the words for him.

"The words of?"

" 'Of His Name.' " Tziga Hame glanced again at the hurrying figure of the official—the nearest one, and all the others coming hard on his heels, Uncle Chorley with them, his pale coat flying. "Quickly," he said. "Please, Laura."

She couldn't sing; her voice was too choked. She recited it, the nonsense nursery song.

> *The final measure is his Name.*
> *Four letters, and four laws.*
>
> *The first gives life, the last speech,*
> *though they are the same.*
> *Two letters remain within,*
> *death and freedom.*
> *Make his name his Own and he is.*
> *If your Will departs he will.*

Laura's father released her. She stood, her eyes squeezed shut, weeping. She could hear the hard shoes of the first official, and a scattering of footfalls following him. She didn't open her eyes. She didn't know if her father was still standing near her or not. But then he said, from a short way off, "Those are capitals. Name. Own. Will." Then, "Name," he said again. "Remember that."

"Mr. Hame," said the official. He sounded breathless.

Laura heard her father say, "I've been trying to explain how little time I have." He addressed this remark to the official but seemed still to be speaking only to her. Then Chorley arrived and wrapped his arms around her. Laura smelled the bergamot in his hair oil. It was a smell that always made her happy. She opened her eyes and looked over her uncle's shoulder at her father, who was standing beside the official, looking shabby, rumpled, and small.

"For heaven's sake, Tziga! Is it really necessary to browbeat the child?" Chorley said.

Laura's father said that Dr. Wilmot had given him a shot so he'd stay awake throughout the journey. "I'm overmedicated, I think," he said.

"He won't be here for my Try!" Laura said, aggrieved, to everyone but her father.

"I know, honey," Chorley said. "But your aunt Grace will take care of you."

"Mr. Hame," the official said again. He had a grip on Tziga's arm. Laura's father turned away with the official and started back down the platform. Chorley put his arm around Laura, and they followed, walked up to Laura's aunt Grace and Rose. They went along together, all of them touching Laura, while her father walked ahead. Laura noticed the moment the official collected himself enough to release her father's arm.

They reached the special train's private car. Inside it a maid was lowering the silk blinds against the glare of the low sun. Laura could see tables, white linen, silver, a steaming tea urn.

"Tziga," Chorley said. "Where's my camera?"

"I had to leave it," Tziga said.

Chorley flushed and compressed his lips.

"It won't be rained on, at least," Tziga said. Then he held up his wounded hands, reminding his brother-in-law.

Chorley blinked. He seemed distressed. He glanced around him at all the men from the Regulatory Body and swore.

"Look, Grace," Tziga said, "Chorley's camera is at the dry stream with the blue clay bed."

"I know the place," Grace said to her husband. "It's two days In. Don't worry—I'll drag some ranger along to carry it for me." None of that country's pioneering filmmakers had yet been able to build a camera light enough for a person Grace's size to carry with comfort.

It was Grace who first put a hand out to Tziga. She squeezed his arm. She said she'd mind Laura at the Try. Rose kissed his lapel—and shot him a stern, disappointed look on her cousin's behalf. "Bloody government contracts," she said, quite audible to the officials. "I won't be signing any."

"Our loss I'm sure, miss," one of the officials said.

Tziga Hame opened his arms for his daughter.

She made him wait, nestled against her uncle, the ever-present, constantly attentive and affectionate Chorley. Then she conceded and went to her father. He pressed her into his shirtfront and kissed her hair. Was he asking for forgiveness, or forgiving her? It was more than just a going-away embrace.

"So," Laura said. "When I see you next, it'll all be over." She rubbed it in.

Her father whispered, "I'm sorry." He said, "Goodbye, darling." And then he let go and climbed the folding steps into the train. Dr. Wilmot and two officials swung up behind him into the private coach. The rest went in the guard's van. The stationmaster blew his whistle and waved his flag, and the engine shot out a blast of steam; then it drew slowly out of the station.

✧ ✧ ✧

The delayed passengers saw, with relief, the special train pass the detained express, and that train begin to shunt out of the siding. The porters wheeled their luggage trolleys up to the red line where the baggage car always came to a stop. More attendants appeared with linen for the sleeping car and food-stuffs for the dining car.

It had all been very interesting—especially those final moments when the men from the Dream Regulatory Body ran to retrieve Tziga Hame from the end of the platform. It had been interesting, but it was late and the passengers had a ten-hour journey ahead of them. Some were thinking "hurry up"; others were content to go slowly, happy to see the smokestack of the special train recede up the line. "Let it get well ahead of us," they thought. "Let us not catch up with it in the two-mile tunnel. Not in the dark. Not with our heads down on starchy railway pillows. Not *asleep*."

Whether impatient or prudent, whether thinking "hurry up" or "let it get ahead," the passengers were all looking up the line, measuring the distance between one train and the other. They all saw the dark girl, the Hame daughter, shrug off the adults who were comforting her. She slipped back between them. She was looking at the tracks, or at something on the tracks. The girl jumped down onto the sleepers between the rails, then stooped and picked something up.

Her cousin shouted, "Laura!"

Her uncle rushed to the edge of the platform.

The dreamhunter Grace Tiebold ran the other way, yelling, "Stop the train!" and waving furiously at the engineer, in his cab, at the far end of the shunting express.

The engineer hadn't seen the girl jump, but he did see the woman waving. He put on his engine's brakes and sounded its whistle. The brakes caught and sparked as the engine slowed. The wheels locked, but the engine kept sliding, pulled on by the momentum of its freight.

Chorley Tiebold jumped down to the tracks, picked up his niece, and rolled her back onto the platform. He didn't have time to scramble up himself, so he threw himself across the rails and tumbled down the slope on the far side.

The train passed between him and his family, and finally came to a stop.

Chorley got up and tramped around the back of the halted train. The engineer climbed down from his cabin. The stationmaster dropped his flags and hurried up the platform. Some of the passengers followed.

Grace was shaking Laura, who knelt on the platform, hunched over something she had in her hands. "Put it down!" Grace was saying. "Are you mad?" She was furious.

Chorley clambered back onto the platform, restrained his wife, and got his niece to her feet. He moved her away from the converging driver and stationmaster, and flung out an arm to ward them off. Then he gathered Rose to him too and strode away toward his car.

Grace faced the stationmaster and, before he could speak, said, "Just name your amount, your fine for Laura's stunt. Go on, give me a figure." She gripped the stationmaster with one brown hand and put her other hand into her duster to produce a wallet.

The stationmaster blustered. "You think it's enough to offer me money? This is a serious incident. That child needs a good talking-to at the very least!"

Indeed, the child, the curious onlookers thought. What had she seen? Some dropped treasure, or injured animal?

They imagined the extravagant childishness of a spoiled rich girl. They peered at her as her uncle hustled her past, pale and tearstained. And some saw that what Laura Hame had in the fist curled to her chest was a large, rust-stained rock. A rock from the railbed.

10

✢ ✢ ✢

WHEN THE SPECIAL TRAIN PULLED AWAY FROM SISTERS BEACH STATION, SOMETHING STRANGE HAD HAPPENED to Laura.

She was walking along the platform with Rose, Grace, and Chorley. She was dragging her feet, feeling defeated. Her father had gone, and she felt abandoned, resentful, deeply anxious about her Try. And then—all at once—she felt all these things an emptiness, like extreme hunger. Hunger without exhaustion. It was as though a gap opened within her and yawned wide. For a moment Laura felt this open chasm; then something rushed to fill it. Something was suddenly *in* her—it felt like sorrow and need and power too.

Laura stumbled. Then she came to a stop, and her family went on for a few paces without her. She looked over her shoulder, back along the line through the haze, at what, she thought, was the end of the receding special train. Then her gaze drifted down, and she found herself staring at the rocks between the bright rails. She looked at one in particular. It occurred to Laura that if she picked up that rock, the thing that had rushed to fill the gap inside her—the weighty, cold, roaring thing—would jump out of her and into the rock. It was a mad thought, but it seemed true. True and urgent.

Laura jumped and grabbed the rock and turned, meaning

to fling it after the special train. She could see only the back of the train's caboose—like a black door in the heat-distorted air. But, of course, what she really saw was the express bearing down on her. The rock stayed in her hand. In fact, it seemed to stick to her hand.

Then Chorley jumped down beside her. He lifted her up onto the platform, and Aunt Grace took her by the wrist and shook her hand hard, twice, to make her drop the rock. Grace was shouting at her, but Laura kept her fist clenched.

Then Uncle Chorley intervened; he put an arm around her and urged her to go with him. He and Rose hurried her along the platform. They walked her out of her shoes, seeming not to notice that she'd lost them. The soles of her feet were scorched by the hot pavement. Then she was back in Chorley's car. She was crying. She sat beside Rose, who put an arm around her and kept quiet—which must have cost some effort.

Laura felt that her family was thinking she'd behaved badly but was sorry for her, and so wouldn't say anything about it, would let her forget it. Except Rose, of course. Rose, who held her with one firm, friendly arm but vibrated with suppressed excitement.

❖ ❖ ❖

Back at Summerfort, the nor'wester was combing all the grass clippings missed by the gardener's rake out of the new-mown lawns and was scattering them across the polished floors of downstairs rooms. Grace went around closing the doors. She sent Rose and Laura upstairs to bathe.

In the bathroom, Laura climbed into the tub and turned on the taps. Tepid water splashed her feet. She pulled the chain that diverted water to the showerhead and stood in the downpour. The water coaxed a saner self back into her body, so that when she got out and wrapped herself in a towel she began to wonder about the rock.

She went into her bedroom and found the rock where she'd put it, beside her jewelry box on the dresser. It was quarry stone, a lump of crushed granite. Its edges were still sharp, although its whole surface was softened by a velvet of accumulated dust, the iron rust that slowly salted from the rails, ground away by the wheels of trains. The rock had made a mark on Laura's dresser, as it had marked her palms. She stared at it—a dirty stone.

Rose came to the threshold of the room. She stroked the door with her knuckles. "May I come in?"

Laura put the rock in her jewelry box and closed its lid. She carried a string of amber beads to her bed and put it down on the outfit her aunt had laid out—some of the extravagant sleepwear fashionable people wore to dream palaces.

Rose came in, kicked off her beaded slippers, and sat on Laura's bed. "So," she said, "we're on our own." Rose said that the girls—Summerfort's two servants—had gone for the night. "Ma is doing something with chopped egg and chives and bread." (Dreamhunters ate sparingly before each performance of a dream, enough for comfort but no more.) "Da's threading the projector. He's screening his film of the sand-sculpting competition. He finished it this morning when we were asleep," she said, then asked, "Shall I brush your hair?"

Laura dropped her towel and got into her pajama pants and jacket. Her pajamas were pale yellow, her robe pale green with a broad band of dark pink around its hem and collar. Laura sat on the edge of the bed and let her cousin tame at least the surface of her bushy hair. Rose made noises of effort and once or twice clicked her tongue, as the matron at Farry's had done.

After a moment Rose said, "Have you still got that rock?"

"I put it in my jewelry box."

"Is it like—a memento?" Rose was cautious.

"No." Laura was happy for Rose to think that her feelings were Rose's business. She wanted to be checked on and worried about. But she didn't know how to explain herself.

"Maybe 'memento' is the wrong word, since a memento would be to remind you of a time you treasured," Rose said. "Just a reminder then. But, Laura, your da let you down. He did. I'm really mad at him. *I* won't need reminding."

"I was going to throw it at the train."

"I see. But if you'd thought to throw your *shoe* instead, you wouldn't have had to jump down in front of the express. I bet Ma and Da are worried that you meant to kill yourself." Rose hurried on. "*I* know you wouldn't do that—but I'm still pretty puzzled by what you *did* mean to do."

Laura turned around and stared at her cousin. "Why would anyone think I'd do something like that? Try to kill myself."

"You jumped down in front of a train."

"It was still a way off."

"Laura. It was close, and you were dithering on the tracks."

Laura began twisting her hair into a thick, crackling rope. "I had to pick up the rock, because something was in me and when I saw the rock, it occurred to me that if I picked it up, the thing that was in me would go out of me and into the rock."

"That's crazy," Rose said—though not as if she disbelieved Laura. "*What* was in you? And why *that* rock and not the one next to it?"

"I think it could just as well have been the one next to it," Laura said.

Rose asked whether she could see the rock, and Laura pointed at her jewelry box. Rose wriggled off the bed, took out the rock, and gave it a serious inspection. She said, "So what do you think you put into it?"

"I don't know. Bad feelings. Disappointment. And I meant to *throw* it. But I got mixed up about how many minutes had passed. I thought the express was the special train still pulling away." But—Laura thought—she hadn't thrown the rock. She couldn't release it. And, although she had been angry, what had seemed to pour from her into the rock was more longing than anger. Longing for what she believed she deserved from her father—his undivided loyalty, and love in any measure she asked or needed.

Rose caught her cousin's eye and gave the rock a little shake. "So you want to keep this?"

Laura nodded. Rose put it back in the box, then came back to sprawl on Laura's bed. "You know, you Hames have always been kind of peculiar about dirt and sand and stones. Uncle Tziga is always feeling the soil, as though he's a farmer planning to buy some land. You do that too. You love sand castles, and do you remember all your little earthworks in the kitchen garden at Founderston? 'Mucky Laura,' the cook used to say. There's a word for it—all that fiddling with dirt."

"There's a word for people who *eat* dirt," Laura volunteered.

The cousins gazed at each other, grimacing and trying to remember what they'd learned from a book they'd sneaked a look at. A girl had brought it to school. The girl's father was an asylum doctor, and the book about mental aberrations. Rose turned pink, then gave a shriek of laughter. "I can only think of the names of the sex disorders!"

They swapped a few words and definitions, and had a good giggle. Then Rose changed the subject. "Did you get a look at the body tied to the top of the stagecoach? Did you hear what the men said?"

"I didn't manage to keep my place in the front. I didn't push hard enough." Laura sounded prim, even to herself.

"Oh blah," Rose said, impatient. "Please show some interest, Laura."

"I'm listening," said Laura.

"Being sullen doesn't suit you," Rose said, annoyed.

"You sound like your mother," Laura said, "telling me to be 'ladylike.' No one ever says that to you! They think you won't need to be." She lay down and began to cry. "They think you'll succeed and I won't. I'll have to be 'careful of my station in life,' like the women in novels about women who make mistakes and end up miserable."

"Laura," Rose said. She stroked her cousin's back. "You've got it all wrong. They don't say those things to me because I bite their heads off. Instead they pretend to be brightly positive about me and all my habits. 'Rose is a big, robust, forthright girl,' they say, as if by their describing me I'll start feeling properly self-conscious and pull my head in. It doesn't have anything to do with our Try and what they think of our chances. Your da never tells you to be ladylike. Nor does mine. Your da is too artistic, and my da is a *real* gentleman and a lot less worried about being proper than poor nervous Ma and our teachers. Our teachers have had to think about being *respectable* to get ahead themselves. And Ma was *poor*. She's had to put up with all sorts of snubs since she got rich and married Da. Ma's worried about *both* of us, but only *you* ever listen to her when she goes on about how we should be 'ladylike.' "

Laura had stopped crying to listen to Rose. She kept still and let her cousin pet her. After a moment Rose said, "I'm bursting to tell this story."

Laura lay quiet. This was enough of an invitation to Rose. "The dead man tied to the top of the Sisters Beach stage was a ranger. The driver said he staggered out of the Place—not in the safe spot beside the old telegraph pole but in the middle of the road, right in front of his horses. The man was trampled and died on the spot. Or almost. When they picked him up he was still 'making mouths,' the driver said. And when the driver, stage post manager, and Da climbed up on top of the stage and unwrapped the ranger, Da discovered that the man's mouth was full of sand—fine, silvery sand. And in the sand was a shred of paper, with fragments of words written on it."

Laura rolled over, sat up, and swept her hair back from her face. "That's what your da was saying under his breath when he got in the car. 'Fragments of words.' "

Rose nodded. "I got a glimpse of the paper," she said. "The phrases were separated and stacked."

Laura scrambled off the bed and found a notebook and pencil. She gave them to her cousin.

Rose wrote. She said, "I'm pretty sure there was a gap between 'as' and 'D.' And I think the 'D' was a capital."

They put their heads together and looked at what they had:

ours

as D

ecre

"The 'as' is the end of one word, and the 'D' is the start of another," Rose said.

Laura said, "Should we check this with Uncle Chorley to make sure we have it right?"

Rose shook her head. "He was angry with me for being so nosy. Or bossy." She wriggled her shoulders, shrugging off her father's disapproval. Then she slid off the bed and bounced up. "That poor ranger," she said, bringing the talk back to the dead man briefly, only to dismiss him.

"The border can be dangerous. It's like diving into a river

when you can't see the bottom," Laura said. "He was only a few feet off the safe path, and unlucky in his timing."

"The sand is a puzzle though," Rose said. "How did it get in his mouth?" She rubbed her stomach. She was thinking about dinner. She gave her cousin a hand and hauled her up. "Eggs and toast," she said, and led Laura downstairs.

✧ ✧ ✧

Chorley's film was less than ten minutes long. He'd filmed a sand-sculpting contest held six weeks earlier on the beach. Grace had been asked to judge it, and there was a lot of footage of her with the mayor and several other dignitaries, going around among the entries and asking the competitors questions. Grace holding her sun hat and bent at the waist to speak to sand-caked children. Grace inspecting shell-studded ramparts. All in ghostly black and white—the small waves flickering in, soundless and a little too fast.

Grace told Chorley he should put this footage together with his balloon flight and his film of whales stranded on the western shore of So Long Spit. He should hold another screening.

Chorley had held a number of public screenings. His most recent hit was a film of a state funeral. People were grateful for the record—for film's power to capture a real event and repeat it infinitely.

"People like to see themselves," Grace said. "A newspaper can only report."

"Miss Laura Hame and Miss Rose Tiebold, the niece and daughter of the competition's judge, while not eligible to enter the competition, were still able to join in the fun," Rose said, imitating a newspaper's social events page.

On the screen, a sandy Rose and Laura were sculpting with butter knives. Laura's father stood between them, his feet bare and his pants legs rolled. He was giving the girls advice. "Miss Hame and Miss Tiebold's 'reclining man' was admired by all the other competitors," intoned Rose.

Chorley had caught the moment when Laura's knife slipped and the sandman's nose collapsed and crumbled down his cheek. The black-and-white Rose burst into silent giggles; Tziga Hame's hands flew up in mock horror. Black-and-white Laura paused, then smoothed the sandman's face with her knife, like someone spreading icing on a cake, till the mouth and eyes had gone too.

The film ran out, slipped off the end of the reel and spun flapping in the projector. The room filled with radiance from the screen.

Grace got up and opened the curtains on the dusk. She went out to make a pot of tea, and Chorley switched off the projector and packed his film away. He said it was a shame that he couldn't make a motor to crank the camera so that the speed of the film would always be even, and lifelike. Or—at least—he hadn't yet been able to make a motor light enough or with a portable source of power. He'd shown his balloon film to the Government Surveyor, who was interested, but not in motors to crank a camera or batteries smaller than hatboxes. "No," Chorley said, "this will continue to be a rich man's hobby until I travel to remote places and film horned whales and witch doctors' ceremonies. That should get more people interested."

Rose yawned to interrupt her father's complaining. "Mother can catch horned whales, a dream of horned whales. Dreams have sound and sensations, colors and tastes. Films don't."

"So you think films are only a novelty?" Chorley asked his daughter.

"No—but they're for recording *facts*. They can't do fiction, like dreams can."

"Has anyone been able to establish that dreams are fiction rather than fact? They may all be true. They might be like mirages—strange images of distant places. No one knows what they really are."

Grace came back in with the tea.

Laura said to her uncle, "Is that the sort of thing people discuss when they write about dreamhunting in books?"

"What kind of thing?" said Grace.

"What dreams really are," said her husband.

"Oh—that."

Rose said, "There was a boy on the infants' beach reading Dr. King's *A History of Southland*."

Chorley looked interested. "Some kind of prodigy?"

"No, a boy around our own age," said Rose. "He's Trying."

"If he was so trying, why did you talk to him?" Chorley asked.

"Da!"

"The boy said his uncle is a dreamhunter named George Mason," said Laura.

"Is this boy's uncle, this Mason, respectable?" Chorley said to Grace.

"You're such a *father*," Grace said. "It's very sweet. Mason's perfectly respectable. He's a Soporif—the surgeons at Pike Street Hospital use him to enhance their anesthetics. If you're in the same room with him when he drops off, he can knock you out."

Chorley was shaking his head. "You're all terrifying," he said. "You dreamhunters. You do know that, don't you?" And then, as if the action were somehow related to his remark, he took two extra sugar lumps for his tea.

✣ ✣ ✣

In the half hour between tea and her family's departure to the dream palace, Laura went into Summerfort's library. She found Dr. King's book on the shelves devoted to encyclopedias and Chorley's science journals. She took the book down and curled up in a chair with her feet tucked under her.

11

✧ ✧ ✧

Excerpt from *A History of Southland* by Dr. Michael King (1904)

*J*T IS DIFFICULT TO CONVEY TO ANY-
ONE BEYOND OUR SHORES THE EX-
TRAORDINARY INFLUENCE OF DREAMHUNTING
on the life and culture of Southland. Since the arrival of the
first settlers nearly two hundred years ago, much has been
made of the tyranny of distance, the fifteen hundred sea miles
between ourselves and our nearest neighbor, and five thousand between us and the Northern Hemisphere's great cen-
ters of civilization. Ours is a productive but isolated country.
Southland can export wool and leather but not meat or milk;
wine but not fruit; grain and linen, steel, tools, and machin-
ery—but not dreams. Dreams are a highly perishable commodity and are yet to be sent offshore.

Dreams are found in a territory in the northwest of our
country, a territory known simply as the Place. Certain facts
about the Place have been hard to establish—for example,
when did it first appear? Southland is a landmass without a
native people, and so there are no songs or legends for us to
consult. Has the Place always been there, its borders concealed in the rugged terrain of the forested Rifleman Mountains? Did it remain secluded because only a very few people
were able to go there? For dreamhunters and rangers, those

able to enter the Place, represent only a tiny proportion of the population—perhaps one in every five hundred people.

We do know that Wry Valley, the fertile land between the Heliograph and Rifleman mountain ranges, was first settled in 1750. Sparsely settled, but I imagine that, were the Place present, there would be some record of it, if only of the occasional "disappearance." Timber has been cut in the Rifleman Range since the first settlement. In the 1790s the bullock trails used by foresters to haul timber linked up with the road from Founderston to the Wry Valley. And yet I have found no reports from that time of the kinds of mysterious disappearances that would indicate that the Place was there.

By the middle of the nineteenth century, Sisters Beach in Coal Bay had become a summer retreat for the wealthy. The Bay's visitors arrived mostly by sea, but the road from Founderston was improved, and in 1860 the Sisters Beach stagecoach made its first run from the capital. And still there were no disappearances. It wasn't until 1886 that the Place first made its presence felt—for that was when Tziga Hame vanished from the Sisters Beach stagecoach.

✤ ✤ ✤

Tziga Hame, a seventeen-year-old violinist from Founderston, was making his first journey outside the capital. He and his elder sister, Marta, had been hired to play at the summer assemblies at Sisters Beach. The Coal Bay railroad was, at that time, still only a plan on paper—a plan that had to undergo a radical alteration after the discovery of the Place. The young Hames chose to travel overland, so they booked seats on the stagecoach.

It was early summer, November the fifteenth, and the weather in the mountains was wet. Tziga Hame gave up his seat inside the coach for his sister's cello, which was particularly vulnerable to damp. Hame rode up on top of the stage, on the box seat at the back.

Halfway through its journey, the stage made its usual stop in Wry Valley at the village of Doorhandle. Marta Hame got out to stretch her legs. When she climbed back into the coach moments before it departed from Doorhandle, Marta saw that her brother was in his place on the box. Yet when the coach arrived at Sisters Beach four hours later, Tziga Hame was missing. Marta Hame, desperate with worry and sure that her brother had fallen, tried to raise a search party at the stage post. She was still making her arrangements when a summons came from Doorhandle for a surgeon. A farmer from that village had discovered the young man lying on the road.

Marta Hame traveled back to Doorhandle with the doctor, a holidaying Founderston physician, Dr. Walter Chambers.

Tziga Hame had broken his left leg. It was a serious injury and a cause of grave concern to Dr. Chambers. The doctor knocked Hame out with ether and set the leg as well as he was able. And while Hame was unconscious, he had a dream. In fact, Tziga Hame repeated the dream he had first had when he fell from the back of the stage.

The road through Wry Valley had been wet and green, but the ground on which Hame landed when he fell wasn't even a proper road—he later said—only a track, a streak of bald earth showing through parched grass. Hame said that he fell because his seat suddenly "wasn't there." One moment he was on the box at the back of the coach, the next he was apparently sitting in the air, and the next he lay on the dry track with his thighbone shattered. "At first I didn't understand that I was injured. But when I sat up and looked, I saw a tear in the cloth of my trousers and the broken bone jutting blue against my skin," Hame recounted. He fainted at the sight, lost consciousness, and had a dream.

All famous dreams have names. The dream that came to be

known as Convalescent One can be found in a stable dream site directly across the border of the Place beyond the village of Doorhandle. For the first seven days of Tziga Hame's convalescence in Doorhandle, he repeated Convalescent One till, eventually, the whole village had managed to sleep when he was sleeping and share his dream. Its effects were noticed. A girl who had coughed all winter and spring finally had a good night's sleep and woke with color in her cheeks. A troubled man woke feeling the dark haze lift from his mind. The people of Doorhandle felt invigorated and at peace. Eventually, comparing their experiences, they realized that, over the course of the week, they had all had the same dream, and many had had it several times.

Hame's dream faded. He was on the mend. His sister, Marta, was paying their board by playing her cello in the Inn parlor. The Hames' father sent money for their passage back to Founderston; they were to make the journey once Tziga's leg had healed well enough to travel.

Tziga Hame was distressed by his father's orders, for he and Marta had failed in their plan to spend the summer earning their fees for a final year at Founderston's Music Conservatory. Without their fees, the brother and sister would be unable to attend.

Dr. Chambers passed through Doorhandle in late January on his way back to the capital. He removed the plaster from Hame's leg and told the young man he must exercise it to unthaw the stiff knee joint.

Tziga and Marta Hame returned to Founderston. Throughout late summer and autumn, Hame exercised his leg. He climbed up and down the six flights of stairs from the family's rooms in their tenement in the Old Town. He walked the streets. When a number of weeks had passed, he visited Chambers in the doctor's rooms at the front of his residence on the west bank of the Sva River. Hame showed Chambers how, when he planted his feet to play reels, his bad leg would tremble. Chambers told Hame that although he could still expect some improvement, his limp was with him for life.

Hame was cast down. After seeing the doctor he took to his bed for a time, using the winter's first cold snap as an excuse not to exercise. Hame lay in bed and did some thinking. He thought about the dream he had had, night after night, in the first week after his accident. He felt that the dream had helped him to heal. He reviewed what had happened to him. He'd had a fall and broken his leg, and while unconscious, he had caught a *dream* as one catches a cold. When he'd caught his dream, he'd seemed to be in *another* place—somewhere dry and silent, a place whose trees had bark that was peeling in sooty strips, somewhere unlike the road through the lush Wry Valley.

Hame later explained that he would never have known that he had gone into another place had the farmer who found him come from the Doorhandle direction. Fortunately, the farmer was coming from the coast with a cartload of seaweed for compost. Hame, crawling back the way he'd come, slithered from the dusty trail onto the muddy road and heard a cart coming up behind him. He looked over his shoulder and saw the farmer coming around the bend of a road *he hadn't crawled along*. The farmer stopped and looked Hame over, then picked him up and tried to carry him to his cart. But Hame simply dropped out of the farmer's arms and fell back through what he called "a fold in the map."

"I've always imagined the Place is a whole territory hidden in a fold in a map. Everything on the map apparently joins up—the roads, rivers, mountain range—but the map can open wider, and show a whole concealed country," Hame said.

The farmer, finding his arms empty, to his credit did not immediately decide that Hame was a ghost and flee. A calm and practical man, the farmer waited on the spot at which

Hame had disappeared until the young man managed to collect himself and crawl out again. The farmer saw Hame's arms break through the air. He said later that it was like watching a calf born from an invisible cow. When Hame appeared the second time, the farmer led his horse past the spot where Hame lay and *only then* picked the young man up and put him in the cart.

Hame, lying in his attic room in Founderston's Old Town, discouraged and in pain, thought about his fall and came to a conclusion. He concluded that he had caught his dream in *a place* he might be able to find again. A place on the road beyond Doorhandle. And so he pawned his violin and bought a seat on the Sisters Beach stage as far as Doorhandle. He found the farmer and asked the man to accompany him to the point on the road where they'd first met. The farmer was quite clear about the location where he'd found Hame—a section of road shadowed by a mature hawthorn tree.

It was late afternoon when they reached the spot. The road was narrowed by drifts of fallen leaves. There was a cloud of midges under the hawthorn—but it was otherwise an empty, everyday road. Hame and the farmer crept under the tree, their hands held out before them. Then Hame disappeared— and the farmer walked on a little alone. A moment later Hame reappeared out of the air and asked the farmer to build a cairn by the tree to mark the border. And then he went back In.

It is possible that, having injured himself on his first arrival in the Place, Hame had been pushed into a certain kind of adaptation to its weather. I will use that word—"weather." Sailors talk of winds, of trades and variables, doldrums and roaring forties. Just as different vessels are adapted to different weather conditions, each dreamhunter is adapted to sail down different winds of sleep. Directly over the Doorhandle border is a band of "dream weather" full of powerful beneficial dreams. Tziga Hame emerged from his second, purposeful excursion into the Place with the dream now known as Starry Beach. Starry Beach is a less effective dream than Convalescent One. It is soothing rather than healing. The dream did make Hame feel better, but it wasn't enough in itself. Hame decided to use it to bargain somehow for better medical treatment. He hoped to persuade Dr. Chambers to do something more for him.

Tziga Hame took the dream back to Founderston and to Chambers. He asked if he might spend the night in the doctor's house. Hame attempted to explain, but Chambers wasn't of a mind to listen. It was totally out of the question, Chambers said, *preposterous*, what was the young man thinking?

Hame left the doctor's residence but returned at nightfall and camped on the porch stairs. He went to sleep with his head resting on the back doorsill.

Walter Chambers later reported what happened that night. He said that he had a wonderful, refreshing sleep and a blissful dream. The following morning over breakfast his wife told him about *her* dream. The doctor recognized his wife's description of the warm sea, golden beach, the fish baking in crumbling white coals, the sunset, kind friends, campfire singing. Chambers recognized the dream's air of languid wonder, and its mysteries, like the line of lights moving through the forest behind the beach. He and his wife had had the same dream. And—it turned out on further investigation—the couple's daughters, and their household staff, had all shared it. The whole household was in a gentle mood, so that when the butler appeared to tell the doctor that the young man from yesterday was back and refused to be seen off, Chambers was welcoming. He hurried out to Hame, and the young man explained what had happened to him.

Chambers was amazed but could immediately see advantage for himself in Tziga Hame's gift. The doctor took the young man on an overnight visit to one of his wealthy spinal patients. Chambers later gave an account of this first experiment. He said that, as he sat by his sleeping patient's bed, he'd watched something more effective than sleep smoothing the man's tense face.

Hame spent a week in the rooms of several of Dr. Chambers's chronic patients. Much to the families' puzzlement, the doctor turned up when no crisis was anticipated, but in the morning the patients were better, one even saying she felt she'd been bathed in a whole summer overnight.

When the dream faded, the doctor gave Tziga Hame money so that he could return to Doorhandle and the strange territory that it seemed only he could enter. This was Hame's first commission—his third dream, for which he was paid only expenses and meals. The young man was still proving what he could do, and neither he nor Dr. Chambers had yet thought to put a price on what they regarded as a miracle and a gift.

But, of course, a cure is a salable commodity. Two years after his fall, Tziga Hame had subscribers—sanatoriums, and private and charitable hospitals. He was taking his dreams to any sizable town within two days' travel by sea or rail. He had given up his violin but paid his sister Marta's way through the Conservatory. He had bought himself and his family houses. He was a wealthy man.

✧ ✧ ✧

News spread quickly about the help Tziga Hame was bringing to the suffering. And the fortune he was making. Others were inspired to see if they too could cross over into the dry, silent Place and catch dreams. These early adventurers came alone, to face their failure privately: that moment when they turned on the road to look back at the piled stones of the border marker. Later, some came in groups, egging one another on. A group of clerks from a bank. A group of weavers from a textile factory. A mixed group of philosophy and divinity students. They arrived noisy and stayed noisy if none of them passed through, or were quickly silenced if one of their number was swallowed whole by the innocent air.

All who came to Try and found themselves able to enter the Place assumed that, like Tziga Hame, they would be able to follow the remains of the road a few hours in from the border, lie down, and catch a dream. This was not the case. Most caught a little sleep but nothing else. But some went in often enough to be able to give their friends—or the newspapers—a better description of that territory so few were able to see. They reported that the Place was vast, much larger than the territory it seemed to encompass in the Rifleman Range. They reported that it was never dark in the Place, although no sun could be seen in its luminous, white sky. There, they found, no flame could be kindled. Only humans could cross the border, so no one could take in a horse and cart, and any supplies had to be either carried or pushed in on wheelbarrows. And because no flame could be kindled, machines driven by steam power or internal combustion didn't work.

The explorers boasted, or complained, about their hard rations, the dry, cold food and cold beverages on which they lived. They reported on the uselessness of compasses. Some were so curious about this uncanny Place into which they—special people—had been admitted that they carried in surveying equipment and began to make maps. They formed a club, first meeting in the big parlor of the Inn at Doorhandle. Some, poor and eager to work, offered themselves as porters to those others who, like Tziga Hame, could catch and carry dreams.

The people of Doorhandle were probably the first to notice the changed appearance of those who made repeated trips into the Place. The mapmakers, trailblazers, porters got the look that anyone who kept going in did. They grew thin, rangy, dry-skinned. The dreamhunters took on this look too, but their eyes changed as well. Whereas the "rangers"—as the mapmakers and porters had begun to call themselves—developed crow's-feet from squinting into bright distances, the dreamhunters gradually all came to wear a strange stare, as though the distances into which they looked exhausted them, were full of terrible battles or tormenting mysteries.

The dreamhunters were making their own discoveries. Many had begun to emerge from the Place with dreams for which there was no existing market. They began to advertise these dreams in the classified section of Founderston's daily newspaper. Some pooled their resources and rented one of the small hotels on the Isle of the Temple, a city district of Founderston. These small consortia of dreamhunters would dream to paying sleepover audiences—audiences that were growing quickly as more and more people sampled and were enthralled by these astonishing shared dreams. Dreams as full and physical as lived experiences—but in which people were never themselves, so that the timid could be brave, the infirm could be well, men could be women and women men, and the old could be young again.

Dreamhunters organized themselves for their growing market. They printed posters and flyers. One might describe his dreams as outdoor adventures, another in a careful code: "Dreams for Sporting Gentlemen." One might offer battles and rugby matches; another dreams "soothing to the mind."

An industry had begun.

✤ ✤ ✤

Within eighteen years dreamhunting has become central to the domestic economy and cultural life of Southland. To any historian, the activity has even more the appearance of an apparition than those other appearances that can make the past seem not quite continuous with the present—the invention of the printing press, the discovery of the New World, the invention of the steam engines that drove the Industrial Revolution and—if for a moment I can play prophet instead of historian—those fragile flying machines that are now literally casting their makers' fortunes to the wind. But unlike all these world-expanding inventions or discoveries, dreamhunting is a discovery itself based on *an apparition*, the apparition of the Place, which was in one historic moment not there, then *there*.

In fact, it has often seemed to me that the Place appeared in time to welcome its discoverer, to welcome Tziga Hame and give him his crippling injury. Hame is still indisputably the greatest dreamhunter. He has the widest zone of projection, a four-hundred-yard "penumbra"—to use the language of the profession. He can "mount" any other dreamhunters— if he and others have freshly caught dreams, his will cancel theirs and erase it from their systems. Can it be a coincidence that Hame is both the first and the greatest dreamhunter, and that the Place first appeared to our knowledge when Hame first entered it? It is as if the Place was locked, and Hame was the key that unlocked it. It is as if the Place appeared where and when it did because *that* was where it happened to find Tziga Hame.

12

✧ ✧ ✧

$\mathcal{I}$N A HOUSE NEAR THE TRESTLE RAIL BRIDGE AT MORASS RIVER, A MAN AND HIS WIFE WERE EATING THEIR DINNER. THEY looked up at each other, their spoons poised, when they heard the approach of a powerful engine. The express and milk trains never took the bridge at such speed. They listened to the engine's thunder transmitted all the way along the valley by the resonating timber structure of the bridge. Then the engine was across, safe. The man set down his spoon, the woman sipped from hers. They began to count carriages. One, two—

Silence from the bridge; the roar and rattle receded. The man crossed himself. Two carriages. A special train from Sisters Beach. The great dreamhunter brimful with powerful medicine.

Later the train slid past the little town at the foot of Mount Kahaugh. A boy baiting hooks on a line wound out from a boat in the sea below the mountain saw the train, its windows reflecting the setting sun in long and short flashes as though transmitting a message as it turned and slowed into the spiral. The boy felt the train was signaling to him—a message of farewell. He glanced up now and then to watch for the train's reappearance, to see it come around the curve of the mountain, laboring now, on the inner spiral, two hundred yards above the village. The light it gave back, window by window, was barely gold. Coal Bay had sunk in blue shadow, and only the summit of Kahaugh had fire in its crest of forest.

The train passed through the tunnel that pierced the shoulder of the mountain. It picked up speed, heading east and inland.

It blasted through town stations, hauling the loose leaves of evening newspapers in its slipstream. Stations wired ahead in a relay, and at each the stationmaster came out to see the train hurry through. Stationmasters and porters, and passengers early for later trains, caught glimpses of the figures within the luxury coach—the two men playing cards, the portly man in a bright waistcoat, a white napkin tucked into his open collar. And, alone in the brightest part of the carriage, the slight figure in dust-covered clothes.

The train turned from east to south to west again, the rail line making its miles-wide circle around where the Place was.

Near Founderston it traveled sluggishly through a crossing where signs said SLOW and work was being done on the line. A small girl waiting with her mother at the barrier said, "Ma, a man in that train is singing."

"Yes. He's singing to keep himself awake," the mother said. She listened to the voice, light, hoarse, carrying, and identified the song. She said to her daughter, "It's an Old Town song. 'A Stitch in Time.' "

The train had gone by. The girl asked, "Do you know it, Ma?" And her mother, who had a repertoire of folk ballads and hymns and old prophecy songs, sang "A Stitch in Time" as the crossing guard winched the barrier back out of their way.

> *If I could, I would, my dear,*
> *stitch the next happy hour to our good time here,*
> *sew up the whip, the cell, the noose,*

till that time's a false pocket that lets no true terror loose.
A stitch in Time can save us, love,
now closed between then and then,
a charm to work and spell to prove,
a door to shut and dream to end.

But I am just a tailor,
my art with cloth and thread;
not a dreamer dressed as jailer,
or a savior as the dead.

At Founderston rail yards the train stopped to fill its water tank, and the physician got out and walked along the line, from tie to tie, and up onto the platform. He went into the concourse and bought a carnation for his buttonhole, and a newspaper. He checked his watch by the station clock. It was twelve-thirty a.m.—they were still three hours from their destination. He hurried back to the train and was hauled on board by one of the men from the Regulatory Body who had come out scouting for him.

Tziga Hame looked sleepy. The shot of stimulant Dr. Wilmot had given him eight hours earlier was finally wearing off. The physician went and sat opposite Hame. It was his job to keep the man awake till they reached Westport.

The train left the yards at Central Station. It crossed the iron bridge upstream from the Isle of the Temple. Its occupants looked out on the black river water, the moonlight caught only where its silky surface was flawed by current.

Dr. Wilmot read items from the paper to Hame. "The Grand Patriarch has been sermonizing against you again, I see," said the physician. "Not you personally, Hame, dreamhunters rather. He is troubled by dreamhunter terminology." The physician read: "They speak of a dream's range as its 'penumbra.' This is a word borrowed from astronomy.

A penumbra is the edge of the shadow the moon casts on the earth during a total eclipse. It is the course of a shadow." Wilmot sniffed. "Perhaps he would rather you called it a blast zone. Or, if we're describing circles, perhaps a bubo, like the boils of plague."

Hame's head, which was propped on his hand, slipped. He jerked awake. He'd been asleep for a second, and in the narrow tenements beside the tracks, in people's sleep, shapes had sprung up—people in black, a group of pale-faced mourners—there for an instant, then quenched, sucked down into the graveside earth again.

"Stay awake," Wilmot snapped, and slapped Hame across one cheek.

"Be careful with him," one of the officials cautioned the physician.

Hame got up and began to walk, steadying himself on the long polished table in the center of the carriage. An official opened a humidor and offered Hame a cigar. The dream-hunter shook his head.

The train sped through the small hours toward Westport.

Westport was a big industrial city, a city of mines and mills and shipyards, mostly privately owned. But its richest coal mine belonged to the government. The mine's shaft penetrated a hill to the north of the harbor, a hill wearing skirts of glittering slag. Below the hill and extending out into the harbor was a causeway that, halfway along its length, became a pier. At the end of the pier stood a huge, grim ironwood structure—Westport's Shore Prison. The prison supplied the coal mine with labor. Every day, twice a day, prisoners were conducted in a shuffling column along the causeway and up a cinder-covered road to the mouths of slanting mine shafts. Each shift would return twelve hours later, blackened and bowed down with exhaustion. Every day barges heaped with high-grade coal would set out from the shelter of the causeway to the foundries across the harbor. Or the coal was loaded into trucks at the railhead and taken inland, to Founderston and other settlements, where it was sold for domestic use. Good coal, it burned quite cleanly, its smoke slower to accumulate as stains on city walls and trees.

The special train arrived at the railhead at four in the morning. The officials jumped out onto the platform. There was a flurry. Someone ran a red flag up a flagpole. The physician climbed from the luxury car and put his hands out to assist his patient down onto the platform.

Tziga Hame looked around. He saw a ground mist softening the stones between the rails, and boxcars seeming to float on thin, white vapor. He saw the men waiting for him—prison guards in black brass-buttoned uniforms, and the prison governor in a coat with a fox fur collar. The governor's breath smoked like a dragon's—he'd been drinking hot tea.

Tziga said to the people nearest him that he'd like to stretch his legs, to walk before he slept. He'd make his own way along the pier to the prison.

There was a whispered consultation between officials. The prison governor attempted to shake Tziga's hand, then flinched back when he touched the bandages.

Some of Hame's escort climbed into cars. Others walked with him. The walkers went down from the platform onto the causeway. They left the lights of the rail yards behind them. It was easier to see where the tide lay on the beach, the water striped one way by electric light and the other by the setting moon. The tide was right out, the seabed bare, stinking not of seaweed but of the sulfur in coal. The beach was coated in a silt of coal dust.

Tziga Hame saw that one wing of the prison was lit up. A light burned in every cell. They had kept those prisoners awake all night—after working them all day. As he watched, the lights began to go out. Now the prisoners could sleep. Now that he was coming.

He was asked, "Have you had enough to eat?"

"Yes," Tziga said, "I've had enough to eat."

He'd had enough. Enough of his work, his weakness, his mistakes.

He had scooped a cavity in the chest of his sandman and had hidden his letter to Laura there. He'd put the sand back in and smoothed the place over. The whole time he'd been singing, softly, the song of making. ("It's called 'The Measures,'" Tziga's great-grandfather had told him and Marta when he taught it to them. "It's music and mathematics and prayer too.")

A letter of apology was all Tziga had to offer as a heart for his daughter's servant. He hadn't been able to write "Laura, if I don't come back . . . " and offer a proper explanation. Or any reasonable advice. His mind was filled with murky guilt and misery. He was a fallen man, he knew, and ghostly, as though his sins had sucked the life out of him.

He had practiced "The Measures," and played with sand, and felt the facility of magic fizzing in him—but he hadn't been sure he could make a sand servant. Until the moment when it came to life and stood up before him, his experiments with "The Measures" and hopes for the old Hame magic had seemed only a desperate wish. A wish for someone stronger than himself, someone fit, to whom he could pass his unbearable burdens.

Laura would go to the Place. She would find her servant and Tziga's film of the gutted building—the site of the dreadful dream. She would discover what he and other wicked adults had done. The dream would make it clear to her. She would stop sulking and mooching and living in Rose's shadow. She would catch the dreadful dream, the dream with the great, eclipsing penumbra. She would blot out the sun.

Tziga Hame limped among his watchful retinue to where the causeway became pier and their footsteps sounded hollow. Perhaps he pulled a little ahead of them, despite his limp. They imagined he was eager. How could they imagine *that*— they, who had all taken care to sleep earlier that day, or to chew some Wakeful, who had all done whatever they could to avoid sleeping with him?

Tziga didn't want to sleep. He didn't want what was before him, the strict prison of his dream, nine nights of torture for himself and for the handpicked prisoners who would share his dream—unrepentant murderers, and the men who persistently threatened public order, then when locked up, started prison strikes or riots. Tziga wanted the horror of the dream *out of him now*. He wanted to break himself open and have it leave him at once, and forever.

Hame's escort heard him say, "Enough." Then he veered to one side, limping but swift—a slight man, and fit from twenty years of walking Inland in the Place after dreams. He ran to the edge of the pier and flung himself off it, headfirst, like someone diving into deep water. Except that the tide was right out, and there was no water, only slick black stones at the base of the thirty-foot piles.

THE FAMILY ENTERED THE DREAM
PALACE BY THE DREAMER'S DOOR
ONLY FIFTEEN MINUTES BEFORE IT WAS TIME
for its patrons to retire to their rooms.

Grace stopped in the hallway before the stage door, which led to the oval floor of the palace's amphitheater, and the dreamer's bed, under the huge central chandelier and painted silk canopy. She kissed her family. Her clean, plain face was shining with excitement. "You wait. You just wait," she said to her husband. "I don't know whether you'll run off with the woman in love or with her jealous brother. I like them both. I particularly like the way the brother feels everything in his lips." Grace touched her own mouth.

"Oh dear." Chorley laughed. "But I have your assurance that no one is me."

"Of course not."

He wiped his brow in mock relief. Rose and Laura smiled at each other. They knew Chorley was referring to a time before he and his wife were introduced, when Chorley's friends had alerted him to the fact that his face was appearing on the heroes in the dreamhunter Grace Cooper's romantic dreams. Chorley was disgusted. It was an invasion of his privacy, he thought. Not only had Grace Cooper been eyeing him but now she was using him like a mannequin and dressing him up in her dreams. He confronted the dreamhunter, who at first claimed that his face appeared in her dreams as a result of a poll she'd taken among the society women of Founderston on who they thought was the town's most eligible bachelor. She went on to point out that she'd changed things about him—for example, in her dreams he never spoke. "Your function is simply to be handsome," Grace said. And she said, "The heroes who look like you dress differently too, for instance, they would never wear such *big* cuff links." At this point in the interview Chorley decided the dreamhunter was teasing him and retaliated by asking her out. The way Chorley Tiebold's face turned up on the heroes in Grace Cooper's dreams was Rose's parents' story of how they met.

To Rose and Laura, Grace said, "This really is at the upper limit of what you're allowed, girls." She was warning them not to be shocked, and reminding them how lucky they were. "You'll be the youngest here."

"That's so silly, Mother," Rose said. "Next week we'll be in the Place, and I'm sure *it* makes no fine distinctions about what's suitable for young ladies."

Laura opened the door for her aunt, who stepped out into shouts and applause.

"She's so excited, we'll all be lying awake for hours," Chorley said.

"It'll be worth it," said Rose.

Chorley and the girls climbed the stairs and emerged onto the first-floor balcony through a door in a mirrored panel.

Laura looked up at the massive crystal chandelier. She squinted through its dazzle at the two tiers of balconies, upon which the wealthy visitors of Sisters Beach strolled around or sat on padded benches. People were keeping an eye out for their friends, waving to one another across the space. Most people were in sleepwear—pajamas, nightgowns, and dressing gowns, all in brilliant colors and rich fabrics. The women wore their hair threaded with ribbons, or caught up into silk bags and loosely turbaned around their heads. The only people not in sleepwear were waiters, who wove among the patrons carrying refreshments—or, now, more empty glasses. People craned over the balconies to watch Grace Tiebold speaking to the dream palace's manager. He handed her up the steps to her dais and its huge bed. A bed like an altar. (Laura had overheard one of her teachers say that—in a disparaging way—to one of her classmates.)

Grace climbed into her cloudy bed and sat, looking small and businesslike. She gazed up at the crowded balconies and tucked her hair behind her ears. Chorley kissed his hand to her, and one of his friends called out that they hoped he—Chorley—wasn't on the program tonight. Chorley laughed. He turned away from the pit of the stage and opened the door to the Hame suite. He stood aside for Laura and Rose. "You girls can go in together, so that when Grace joins me for breakfast we won't have to put up with your chatter." He went through the door to the Tiebold suite.

Most of the other rooms were just that—hired rooms—sometimes double, sometimes for families, but all with numbers on their doors and, like the rooms in hotels, used by different people at different times. At the Rainbow Opera in Founderston, the President of the Republic had a private suite, as did the Speaker of the House of Representatives, the Secretary of the Interior, and several very rich men. The Hames and Tiebolds also had suites in the Rainbow Opera and were the only people with suites in the Beholder—a dream palace only half the size of the Opera.

Laura closed the door. She shut out the sound of the crowd. Rose asked whether Laura would mind if they left the room-wide sliding door open between them.

"You can come in my bed if you like," Laura said. "Or we could both curl up in Father's bed."

So it was that the girls lit the branch of candles in the master bedroom and climbed into Tziga's bed (Tziga sometimes had time to enjoy one of someone else's dreams when his own had been discharged). The girls lay diagonally on the bed with their feet touching. Laura felt very close to Rose—Rose sleepy, muted and blinking slowly like a cat. Rose told Laura that one thing she'd miss would be sharing all her mother's dreams. "Because my emptiness won't always coincide with her being full. It'll be like being a child again, and not being allowed to share every dream. Do you remember what that was like?" Rose said. "We'd come here only once in a blue moon, to enjoy one of those nice, vivid, plotless dreams of your father's."

Laura thought of the dreams her father had caught that she had been permitted to share—how *well* they'd made her feel, though she was already whole, healthy, and young. Laura had understood for a long time how valuable her father was. He was valuable, so she saw less of him than she'd like to. How *naïve* she had been to imagine that when it came to something vital—her Try—her needs would come before the needs of the ill, the mad, and the dying he ministered to.

A moth had come in the open window that faced the promenade. It grazed a candle flame and fell to flop around on the polished tabletop. Laura closed her eyes. Some time passed and Rose was quiet. Thoughts were sliding through Laura's head, some bright like sparks in a storm—she wondered where the special train was now—and some obscure—a face she had glimpsed in the audience tonight, a bearded man, someone she didn't know but for some reason was thinking of as a good person, solid and equitable. Laura yawned and let the incongruous thought fly away. The wings of the maimed moth whispered on the carpet. Then Laura was walking down that long staircase in the tower at Summerfort, walking backward in the dark.

Her parents were dead, and she had been left in the care of her older brother. He always kept her close, as though he, and he alone, should be enough for her. But the day had come when she had to go against him—or give in to him for good. She was in agony, she had to make a choice. Her brother had told her that she must either send her suitor away or go away with him. She sent him away. She was too ashamed to look into his face as he stood before her begging her for an explanation, for a word. But they weren't alone. Her brother was by the door, bristling with power, compelling her to be quiet. She didn't look into her suitor's face but at his hands, his slender fingers and clean cuffs.

He fell silent and walked away from her.

That was the moment into which—it seemed—she was born. The moment when her brother left the room to see her suitor to the door. She looked up after them, through the doors to the hallway, at the tall, arched window on the landing. She heard the front door close. She discovered that she had to look at her suitor's face once more. If she did not, it seemed he'd only ever appear to her in memory turning away.

She ran after him, out of the room, and down the stairs.

From the window on the landing, she saw him crossing the lawn to the stables, to where a groom stood ready, holding his horse. She ran into the lower hall. Someone spoke her name. The hall was full of light and the reflections of light. The servants who tried to hamper her flight appeared only as silhouettes. Her brother's stern voice sounded behind her. She didn't pause. She opened the door and sprinted out under the deep portico, down its steep steps, looking back once at the house, its sandstone pillars and pediment.

There was a gale blowing outside, from behind the house, and she was swept up into it. She saw that her suitor's horse was already at the foot of the hill, at the iron gates to the estate.

She didn't take the path but ran across the close-clipped green grass. The wind was frightening and forceful. The tall eucalyptus trees were shedding their dead branches. Bark was flying from the trees in strips like tattered canvas. It was on the ground everywhere, threatening to trip her. She had to run. She must get to him before he was gone. She must have him touch her cheek again. She sped with giant steps down the steep lawn. A tree branch fell in front of her.

She dodged to avoid the fallen limb and lost her footing, dropping onto one knee on the springy grass. As she got up again, she looked to one side and noticed that someone was building a new garden wall. She saw red dust and raw new bricks. She saw laborers in shapeless, gray clothes—their pants legs gathered at the ankles. Then she was on her feet and ready to run again. Her suitor would never hear her call out to him against this wind. She ran.

The heroine ran on, leaving Laura Hame standing on the lawn of the heroine's house. Laura didn't see a woman run away from her. She saw only the wind, one last, fierce gust that flattened her silk robe against the backs of her legs, bent the trees, and cleared a corridor in its own debris. Then the wind stopped blowing, and the garden was silent but for the insects ticking like a cooling engine.

Laura went to look at the wall the laborers were building.

It was a long wall with arches that made frames for the view. It was the sort of wall on which gardeners train climbing roses. The men were making bricks. Laura saw a clay pit and the frames for shaping the slick red clay. She saw a kiln with a blackened chimney. She watched a man stamping the drying, unfired bricks, marking each with the flat of an arrowhead. She saw that, while the clothes the men wore were gray and stained with brick dust, they, too, were marked with arrowheads, in a darker gray. And she saw that it was shackles that gathered their dusty pants legs at their ankles.

Only one of the men seemed to see her. He straightened from his work—mixing mortar—and looked at her. He glanced about him, furtive, perhaps looking for an overseer.

There was no overseer in sight.

The man put his trowel down and came over to Laura. He walked stooped over, seemed at once cowering and eager. He kept looking around him—but none of the other prisoners noticed he'd abandoned his task.

Laura leaned toward him.

He opened his mouth. A trickle of silver river sand spilled from it. His mouth stretched wide. It was packed with sand. He thrust his fingers into the sand in his mouth. The day grew suddenly dark, as though thick clouds had crossed the sun. The garden turned the color of prison clothes—and cold. The world was leaving

Laura. She was dying out of it. She reached out to the man and grabbed his arm. It felt soft, like sand, and yielded, creaking, beneath her fingers.

The man had fished something out of the sand in his mouth. A crumpled paper. He unfolded it for Laura to see, raised it to her eyes.

Before the world grew dark, Laura read the few lines at the foot of the page. She was able to read them because the words assembled themselves around a core of letters she'd already encountered:

> *Yours*
>
> *Cas Doran*
>
> *Secretary of the Interior*

The light faded. The words, paper, prisoner, all the world sank away.

Laura opened her eyes on the Hame suite. The stumps of the candles were bearded with melted wax. Rose breathed peacefully beside her. Rose's eyes moved under her lids, back and forth, scanning some beautiful thing.

Laura lay on her back and looked at the warm pool of candlelight on the ceiling. She knew she couldn't climb back on the dream that had tossed her and taken off without her. She could feel it still, like the beginnings of a fever. She was reluctant to go to sleep again but didn't want to disturb Rose, so she got up and left the room.

The Beholder kept a fire watch, a group of men who patrolled the dream palace's balconies and stairways on their soft-shoed feet. Men with keen noses for smoke, who kept the sand buckets filled and their eyes on a board of switches that, if flipped, would set an alarm bell ringing in each room.

At three a.m. the dream palace was hushed, its guests breathing softly, sleep troubled only by the emotions of the dream. Grace Tiebold lay on her back in the dais bed, her face softly visible in the light of the dimmed chandelier. The dreamer wore her heroine's brother's face and was frowning sternly in her sleep.

The eight men of the fire watch were at their station in a cozy room on the second tier of balconies. The room was like those that opened out onto ballrooms, where chaperones sit to keep an eye on the antics of young people on the dance floor. The fire watch's window opened onto the silent auditorium.

The men spun around, startled, when Laura appeared at the door. "Am I dreaming?" asked one of the younger men—a bit of a joker.

The girl blushed. She asked where the manager was. She said she was looking for someone to take her home.

The men exchanged glances. One cleared his throat, and one scratched his head.

"He's asleep," the girl guessed.

"I'm afraid so, miss. You see—no one ever wakes up." He wasn't apologizing. She was the one at fault, since no one ever woke.

"Dream too rich for your blood?" asked the joker, and arched an eyebrow. He'd just finished doing his rounds, had pressed his ear to several doors and been excited by the sounds of a male curse and a female sigh.

One of his workmates clipped him over the back of the head. "Sorry about him, Miss Hame. He has terrible manners. Would it be acceptable to you if one of us walked you?"

"Yes," said Laura. "But not him." She didn't even glance at the joker as she said this. He found himself blushing.

"I'll see you home myself," said the oldest man. He took off his jacket and draped it over her shoulders. He found a lamp and lit her way down the back stairs to the stage door.

The Strand was empty, its streetlamps pale in the moonlight. The westerly had dropped. The girl walked quietly beside her escort. Now and then she turned to look at the regular flashing light on the end of So Long Spit, miles away across the Bay. Laura thought about the dream. It wasn't the first time she had strayed inside one of her aunt's dreams. She had never mentioned this to Grace. Laura didn't want her aunt to feel that she'd somehow failed to keep Laura's attention. The dream had been exciting, and Laura couldn't see why it hadn't kept her in its grip, why her dreaming self would choose to show more interest in prisoners building a wall and—most of all—why the dream should give her Mamie's father's name. A name formed around the letters on the fragment of paper Uncle Chorley had fished from the mouth of a dead ranger. Did it mean anything? *What* did it mean?

It seemed to Laura that the faraway flashing light was tapping on her eyes, as though asking to be let into her head. But Laura was tired, and her mind remained dark and puzzled.

They reached the gates to Summerfort. The house was above them, hidden by the bulk of the hill, but the man could see the driveway running through flax and tea trees. The drive was paved with broken scallop shells, which shone in the moonlight and slithered noisily against one another when the girl stepped onto them. "I'll be fine from here," she said.

"Good night, Miss Hame," said the man. He stood at the gate holding his lamp high till she disappeared around the bend in the drive.

14

✧ ✧ ✧

GRACE APPEARED WITH THE BREAKFAST TRAY. SHE CARRIED THE MORNING PAPER TUCKED UNDER HER ARM.

Chorley saw that his wife looked pleased with herself, so he didn't hurry to compliment her on her dream. He sat up in bed and stretched out his arms. Grace peered at him speculatively and tossed him the newspaper. He opened it and settled back on the pillows.

The room was quiet; Chorley could hear the sea and the cheerful sound of sugar lumps dropped into hot tea and the crisp crusts on rolls pierced by a buttery knife.

Grace handed Chorley his coffee and climbed into the bed. She put the buttered rolls down between them. The Tiebolds began to fill the bed with crumbs—only Grace giving a momentary thought to the person whose job it was to clean up after them. (She still remembered having to clean tobacco dust and pipe ash off the counter of her tobacconist father's shop.)

They swapped pages of the paper and murmured to each other about the news. For instance, the buzz about who would be the new Speaker of the House of Representatives. They agreed that one man in particular struck them as a good choice. "Solid and equitable," Grace said.

"Yes," Chorley agreed. "Though, for the life of me, I can't

think of anything *else* I know about the man." He shook his head and put the paper down, stretched his legs and said, "Grace, why must I always fall into your villains' heads? I never seem to have a choice. And I can't say that I enjoyed being that jealous brother. He spent the whole dream breathing in clean air and breathing out smoke." He pulled a face, and Grace for a moment saw the luxurious fury of her heroine's controlling brother.

"He's light-headed all the time from holding his breath," Grace said, and kissed her husband on his slightly scratchy morning jaw. "I like that." She sighed and shrugged and nestled down in the bed.

Rose burst into her parents' room. "Laura got up and went home last night," she said. She was waving a note around. "She writes that she couldn't get back to sleep."

"I thought so," Grace said.

Chorley looked down at his wife, worried. Grace's tone was so strange, so knowing. "Laura was very upset yesterday," he said. "No wonder her attention wandered."

"No," said Grace. "*She* wandered. She's done it before. She wanders about in my dreams as if—" Grace screwed up her face. "I was about to say 'as if they're her own,' but when I catch my dreams I follow them faithfully."

Chorley was shaking his head at his wife.

"Listen," she said, "what Laura does—no one does that. Not even Tziga can do that—go exploring, as if it's a world, not a dream."

"Mother?" said Rose. She was disturbed by her mother's tone.

"I thought so," Grace said again, brooding. "I felt her taking a tour backstage."

"Hang on, Grace," said Chorley. "At one time, for months, you imposed my face on the faces of all your heroes—whatever other faces they wore in the dreams you caught."

"It's not at all the same as your face appearing in my dreams." Grace was exasperated.

"But when you did that you were *changing* something, Grace, even if it was unintentional. All Laura does is *change* things a little."

"I don't go rummaging in other people's cupboards," Grace said softly. Then she dropped the subject.

But Rose wasn't about to let it drop. She felt that she could do a better job of defending Laura than her father had. "You mustn't be mad at her, Ma. Laura doesn't mean to be annoying. She's like that at school—always drifting—and teachers think it's insolence. Only sometimes she isn't able to pay attention to what she's supposed to be paying attention to. It's like Da says, her mind wanders. She used to get dreadful grades in Comprehension because she was always supposing that the questions were trick questions and there was some less obvious answer that the teachers really wanted."

Grace shook her head. "I'm not angry at her, Rose."

"Good," said Rose. "At least she's not making your heroes look like anyone else—like, for instance, that handsome lifeguard on the infants' beach, who we think is a smackerel."

"What on earth is a 'smackerel,' Rose?"

"Oh, you know, a smashing mackerel, which is to say a miracle," Rose explained.

Chorley frowned at his daughter. "This isn't George Mason's nephew we're talking about again?"

"No!" Rose was disgusted. "He was brassy and parboiled. The lifeguard is a god!" Then she said that if her parents had finished arguing she would leave them in peace. But only if they had.

They found themselves making promises as if she were the adult and they the children; then they watched her raid half the contents of their breakfast tray and sweep out of the room. For a moment they stared at the closed door. Then

Grace said to Chorley, "Laura isn't just wandering around behind my scenery. Dreams don't have a backstage. It's all real, and it goes on and on, a big world in a small box. Every dream is like the Place itself, vast, and no place to wander alone.

"Look—it's a good day's walk between Doorhandle and Tricksie Bend, but in the Place you can walk for weeks and still find nothing you can recognize from the other side. Tziga and I talked about doing a transverse trip. Our talk inspired a group of rangers, who set out with a lot of food and water and a stash of Wakeful." Grace paused to take her husband's hand. She said, "They were never seen again."

II
The Try

1

✥ ✥ ✥

THE MAIN TRY TOOK PLACE ON THE ROAD WEST OF DOORHANDLE. IT WAS ALWAYS A CIRCUS. THERE WERE DOZENS of officials overseeing the registration of candidates from around five in the morning. Police were present as crowd control. Marquees and refreshment stands were set up for the sightseers, journalists, the candidates themselves, and their families. At the end of each Try day, the grass in the forest clearing was trampled flat. Hundreds Tried at Doorhandle.

At Tricksie Bend, the Try was usually a quiet event, for Coal Bay was a small catchment area, despite the summer vacationers at Sisters Beach. At Tricksie Bend, on the morning of Laura and Rose's Try, the Regulatory Body had to register only forty-five nervous adolescents and two adults.

Laura and Rose arrived with just half an hour to spare. They came with Chorley. Grace was acting as an official and had gone ahead of her family.

As their car had passed through the village, Laura and Rose turned to gaze back through the window at the downhill view of its houses. They exchanged a look.

The time had come. It seemed that within a day they had gone from not being allowed to do something to being pushed into it. For fifteen years they had steered clear of the border, now they were steering straight for it.

Chorley turned the car off the road. It bounced up a hill toward the meadow on the bluff above the river. Other vehicles had already flattened a trail through the dry grass. A small crowd of onlookers was clustered around parked cars and carriages. The candidates were in formation farther up the slope, standing knee-deep in gold late summer grass along a line marked by a shiny blue satin ribbon. The ribbon was strung between two stanchions and extended right across the meadow.

Laura said, "Does that mark where the border is?"

"They line you up along the ribbon," Chorley said. "The border is several paces beyond, I think."

The cars, carriages, horses in nose bags, the small crowd milling under the shade of handheld umbrellas, the short line of candidates, and the finishing-line ribbon were all humble and unceremonious. Rose was disappointed. "It's not what I expected," she said.

Her father told her that Tricksie Bend was favored by parents who supposed their children might suffer from stage fright that would affect their performance. "Of course your mother and I know that's nonsense. But Tricksie Bend is more private. That makes it better for you."

Laura thought that there were quite enough people for her—even the small crowd was intimidating.

Grace came to meet the car. She put her arms on the sill of the driver's window and leaned in. "We were right to delay, Chorley," she said. "There are several reporters up there. They have cameras."

Chorley told the girls to put on their hats and lower their veils.

Laura's and Rose's hats were new—bought to match their first full-length dresses. Before now the girls had worn skirts that stopped at the tops of their boots, halfway between knee and ankle. The hats' wide brims supported veils of bunched organdy. Laura and Rose realized it was with this moment in mind that they'd gotten their new outfits.

Chorley said to his daughter, "You do see now why we wanted you to Try on the quiet side?"

"Yes," said Rose.

"Thank you," said Laura.

"I'm going to stop by the registrar," Chorley said. "As soon as I stop, you two get out and go straight to his table."

Rose and Laura nodded. They turned away from the windows of the car and toward each other. Laura saw Rose's eyes, wide and shining behind the lilac gauze of Rose's veil and through the pale yellow of her own. Over Rose's shoulder she saw a photographer's assistant drop a burning match into a pile of magnesium in a flash pan he held aloft. There was a white flash, and a puff of smoke rolled up from the pan. Laura's vision filled with a shining cloud of green light. (And a day later, there was her face in the paper, her black eyes huge and fearful. The caption took the tone of the article, which disputed the wisdom of letting girls Try at such a tender age. It read "Age of Consent?")

The car reached the registrar and abruptly stopped. "Out," Chorley said.

The girls clambered out and hurried to the table. Grace waited for them, holding two pens—their forms were already filled in and only lacked signatures. Grace pointed at each page, showing Rose and Laura where they must sign. Laura's hand shook, and the pen dropped blots beside her signature. Rangers had crowded around the two girls, jostling the newspapermen away from the table. But they let Chorley through. Chorley signed too—the forms required the signatures of both parents for Rose, and two guardians for Laura.

"Laura!" a newspaperman shouted. "Do you have anything to say about the objection lodged to your candidacy?"

Laura looked around at the reporter, but the registrar was

speaking to her and her cousin. He told them to please make their way up to the line. They were holding up the proceedings. Laura tried to catch her aunt's eye to ask if she'd heard the reporter's question and what it meant. But Grace had her head down over the forms.

Chorley repelled another camera and shouted, "Please! Let these young women collect themselves!"

"That's right, George," said one reporter to another. "Mustn't put the girls off their game." Then, in an insinuating way, "It's an inspiration seeing these girls going on the game."

Chorley Tiebold gasped and lashed out. He knocked the reporter's hat off. The man's comb-over came unstuck and lay in oily tatters against his neck.

Grace grabbed the girls and thrust them before her, around the registrar's table and up the slope to the line. Behind them they heard the registrar shouting, "Only dreamhunters, rangers, and candidates are allowed past this point!"

Space had been reserved for the girls roughly in the center of the line. Grace positioned them more than an arm's length apart, and about three feet from the blue ribbon.

Rose hauled off her hat and dropped it onto the thick grass behind her. She raised her face to the breeze. Laura copied her cousin. Once she had abandoned her hat, she could hear clearly, but she was still breathless, and her heartbeat was shaking her body.

While Grace and the other officiating dreamhunter and rangers conferred, the registrar locked his box and left his table. He made his way up the hill, holding his coattails free of the seeding grass. He was carrying his watch—as if it was a race that the candidates were about to run. He stopped on the slope and straddled one end of the ribbon.

Grace came up to her daughter and niece and touched their shoulders. "Don't anticipate the signal or you'll look silly." Then she said, "See you shortly." She stepped over the ribbon and disappeared into the air. The other dreamhunter and rangers did the same—as though showing the candidates how it was done.

It was the first time Rose and Laura had ever seen the phenomenon that they had known about all their lives and always accepted without giving it any thought. Seeing the people disappear came as a shock. Rose called, "Mother?" tears springing into her eyes.

"Candidates! At my signal," the registrar bellowed.

Downhill the crowd was hushed. Up the slope, toward the blue air over the bluff, Laura saw a pair of skylarks start out of the grass and go up, singing. There was a thistle in the grass directly in front of her. It was a big, healthy thistle, with three bright purple flowers and a woody stem. Grace, oblivious in her sturdy walking boots, had positioned Laura where she'd have to take her few paces through that thistle.

Beside her, Rose said, "Laura!" Urgent.

Laura looked around. The registrar had dropped his hand-kerchief. It fluttered, snagged on the grass. The whole line was a pace ahead of Laura and Rose, already pushing the ribbon with their legs. Rose had waited for her but was leaning far forward, as though she meant to throw herself onto the ground. Laura picked up her skirts and approached the this-tle. She stepped gingerly over it, then jumped forward to catch up with the ribbon.

Where was it? She was too far behind. Laura let her heavy skirts drop—must she spend the rest of her life dragging around in all this cloth? She let out a sob of frustration. The skylarks had stopped singing. She couldn't find the ribbon. The ground was bad. The grass had gone gray.

Laura came to a dead stop. She looked around. There was no ribbon, no candidates, no crowd of carriages, no village, no river, no quiet box beehives, no birds singing, and no

Rose. She heard feet running on hard earth. She saw the rangers converging on her—one girl out of that whole line. They came up to her—but Aunt Grace ran right past her, without a word or glance.

✧ ✧ ✧

Rose walked on, pushing the line. She turned when she sensed Laura failing, saw how sick she looked. Laura was a walking corpse. Then she was a specter. Then she was gone.

Rose stopped, and the shiny blue line of ribbon was carried off by the others ahead of her. One by one the other candidates came to a stop. Some abruptly, some gradually, as if slowed by the drag of the grass. Some doubled back to pass again through the place where the Place should have been for them. Rose did too. She went and stood where Laura had been, where Laura's trail of parted grass came to an end.

Rose felt numb. She didn't know what she should do, so she looked up to see how the other candidates were dealing with what had happened—or failed to happen.

The staggered group, no longer in line, had all stopped walking forward. All but one. One girl carried the ribbon away. It flowed behind her trudging form, a blue V of wake. She began to run, knock-kneed, up the meadow.

"Hey!" Rose shouted. Then she went after the girl, tapping the next nearest candidate, a boy of her own age. "Help me," she said.

The girl was running, blinded by tears, toward the bluff above the river. Rose and the boy pursued her. The boy overtook Rose and tackled the girl. They went down with a crackling thump in the grass, and Rose threw herself down beside them.

"There's a cliff," said the boy to the girl, who clapped her hands over her face and burst into loud sobs, her flesh quivering in her too-tight cotton dress, and her buttons shivering on their rusted wire posts. Everything the girl wore was made over, Rose saw. And she understood the difference between this girl's dashed hopes and her own disappointed expectations.

"I can't!" the girl moaned. "But I have to."

"None of us can," the boy said. "And if we can't, we can't."

The girl paused to listen, then continued to weep.

The boy said, "We're hidden in the grass here, and the grownups can't see us."

Rose leaned up on an elbow and craned over the heads of the grass. She saw the dark trails the candidates had made, and the wind pushing at the rest of the meadow, making ripples of shadow. Rose saw her mother appear and spin to face uphill, searching for Rose. Her mother spotted her almost immediately and started forward—forgetfully—for she rushed straight back out of the world again.

Rose laughed. It struck her as funny.

Her mother came back, wringing her hands, and began to patrol an invisible line.

Rose decided to let her mother wait. Let Grace think about it—that her daughter was sitting somewhere where she, Grace, couldn't ever reach her. The land between Doorhandle and Tricksie Bend, though open to almost everyone, was closed to Grace. As closed as the Place was to Rose.

Rose was angry with her mother, who, it seemed to her, had never encouraged her to consider the possibility that she'd fail her Try. Grace had wanted Rose to become a dreamhunter. Grace was clearly distressed—but was she upset for Rose or for her own disappointed hopes? "I'm not going to cry," Rose thought. "And I'm not going to put up with *her* crying." She lay in the grass watching her mother's misery and feeling a kind of spiteful satisfaction.

Rose's father detached himself from the onlookers, skirted

the barrier of officials, and went to Grace. He didn't offer his wife any comfort but appeared to speak sharply to her. Then he pushed Grace forward, firmly, into the Place again. He dropped his arm once she had disappeared and strode up the hill to Rose.

Rose's father sat down with them. "That was quick thinking," he said to her and the boy. He took the boy's hand and gave it a brief, approving shake.

The weeping girl spread her smeary fingers and glared at Rose's father through them. Chorley reached into his jacket and pulled out a Farry's toffee tin. He opened it and offered it around. Rose and the boy took one each.

Chorley said, "There's plenty to be done by people who don't spend their lives stupefied by one dream after another."

The girl sat up and thrust her blotchy face into his. "That's all very well for you! You're rich. And she's beautiful." She pointed at Rose.

"And you're ambitious," Chorley said calmly. "Stay that way."

"I've always been frightened of dreamhunters anyway," the boy confessed.

"Me too," said Chorley. "But I rather like being frightened." He stood up and helped the tearstained girl to her feet.

She accepted his help but told him that he was an idiot.

"Our people are waiting for us," the boy said. He was frowning downhill. "I bet mine are miffed."

Chorley took Rose's hand. "I'm not disappointed in Rose," he said.

"I hope you're disappointed *for* Rose," said Rose, her voice brittle.

"Yes," Chorley said, and looked at his daughter as though waiting for something more.

"*I won't cry*," Rose told herself again.

The girl was eyeing the ribbon. She said she wondered who got to keep it.

Chorley bent down, bundled it up, and gave it to her.

✤ ✤ ✤

Laura squatted in a circle of rangers. She crumbled the gray-white grass in her hands. She rubbed the turf bald. The grass would never grow back. A fire could have removed all the vegetation, could have inhaled and taken it. But in the Place, it was impossible to strike a spark or kindle a flame.

Laura was wondering, her brain broached by the silence. "Shhhh," she said to the shuffling, murmuring rangers. Her hands were covered in dust. There was an idea in the silence. As she grew still, and the rangers hushed, the bubble of sound that insulated them collapsed and the silence swamped her. It had almost come to her, the thing she must think.

Then Laura thought: "Rose." The name was a blow that bruised her heart. She was alone. Moments ago she'd been a point on an axis, one child in a line of children—one beater on the heath, one soldier in the column—now she was alone.

The shuffling circle of rangers parted to admit Grace, who knelt beside her. "Welcome, Laura," she said.

Above their heads, the rangers murmured it too: "Welcome."

"We have to go out now and get busy," Grace said.

Laura recalled that there were formalities, full registration, the appointment of a guide, and—later—a trip to an outfitter's. Laura got up and followed her aunt out of the dry, colorless brightness.

✤ ✤ ✤

Into color and sense and sound. The meadow was abuzz. Families who had hung back during the Try had reclaimed their children. They stood around in little groups, consoling one another. Laura saw Rose, her face pressed into her father's lapels, her gold hair rippling as she cried. Grace broke away from Laura and hurried to them. Laura stopped. How could she move? She had always followed Rose. Rose stepped out, and Laura went after her. Even today. Rose stepped out, then stopped and put out a hand to Laura.

Now a curtain of nothing more than air—or time perhaps—had brushed Rose from Laura as Laura had gone through it. They were two pips in the core of an apple. But someone had cut the apple. Just now. The voices in the meadow above the river were the sound of a blade hitting a chopping board. Rose and Laura were cut apart. Laura stood, wounded and exposed. Then the rangers came through after her, and they stopped too, stood by her, a retinue for the day's sole successful candidate.

2

✥ ✥ ✥

FOLLOWING THE TRY, LAURA'S DAYS WERE TAKEN UP BY A WHIRL OF AP- POINTMENTS. IT WAS SCARY AND CELEBRA- tory at the same time.

The family went back to Founderston. On the train Rose, quiet and red-eyed, retreated behind a barricade of bags and travel rugs, drew up her feet, and seemed to sleep. The family got home late and went straight to bed.

Every day for the next three days, Laura was up early. She went to the head office of the Dream Regulatory Body to sign forms. She visited shops on the Isle of the Temple— dreamhunter outfitters. Grace bought her walking boots, trousers, silk socks and shirts, and a fawn duster. Laura went to a hairdresser to have her hair cut. She was out early and in late. She scarcely saw Rose. She wanted to talk to her cousin but didn't make an effort to do so. She was afraid she'd start to tell Rose about all the exciting things that were happening to her—and news, like how that boy from the infants' beach was among the ten successful candidates from the Try at Doorhandle. Laura had passed him in the doorway at the of- fices of the Regulatory Body, and she had managed to give him a polite "Good day." But when Laura did see Rose, her cousin's silence silenced her. It was a neutral silence—Rose wasn't punishing her. But it suddenly seemed that the fact they didn't now share everything meant they had to learn how to talk to each other again.

✦ ✦ ✦

Four days after the Try, Laura and the season's other successful candidates were conducted into the Place for their first testing sleepover. They went In at Doorhandle but were first briefed by the Chief Ranger at the Doorhandle headquarters of the Regulatory Body.

The headquarters was in a large, two-story timber building with a veranda that wrapped all the way around its ground floor and was the usual congregation place of rangers who were on their way In or had just emerged from the Place. The ground floor was full of desks, clerks, filing cabinets; in fact, it looked like any ordinary office. The top floor was taken up by a small locked armory and several large meeting rooms.

It was in one of these meeting rooms that the Chief Ranger briefed the eleven potential dreamhunters. He had given this talk many times before, and his tone was one of impersonal efficiency. As he spoke, the eager and restless candidates began to settle, even to sag a little in their chairs. They were tired, and the Chief Ranger's manner was a bit of a comedown after all the fuss of their last few days.

The Chief Ranger began by telling the children that each must carry his or her own food, water, and bedding. He said it wasn't necessary to take a change of clothes—for one thing they'd be In only "overnight"; for another they couldn't expect any rain, or dewfall, or any variation in the weather. They wouldn't be getting wet. The Place was permanently set at what most of its travelers agreed was noon under a layer of thick white mist. A mist that hid the position of the sun but never touched down on the ground, or moistened the air. "The only reason anyone might take a change of clothes was if they were walking many hours In and cared to come out smelling sweet. You won't find any water there," he said. "You have to carry it. Water is the weight you won't ever dispense with. Even if you get rich and hire a ranger to carry things for you, he'll still be burdened with his own supply."

The Chief Ranger had packages of food on the table before him. He showed them the strips of dried meat, cakes of pressed dried fruit, strongbread loaded with nuts and choco-late, and "dreamhunters' bread"—wafers made of rice flour and powdered milk. "You'll learn to live on this," he said. He cast his eyes over the eleven—eight boys and three girls. Sev-eral looked soft, were children who had never had to carry anything much heavier than a rugby ball or book bag. He took note of the two bandy-legged slum runts, and the remaining nine, who were only a little fitter. Behind the candidates were their guides, rangers and dreamhunters leaning on the brief-ing room wall, all thin and hardy from repeated hikes into the Place.

"Well," the Chief said to the candidates. "You'll all build up to something better, I'm sure." His eyes lingered on two who were clearly from wealthy families. They were already os-tentatiously outfitted in walking boots and dusters. One girl had even had her hair cut short, which the Chief Ranger thought was rather tempting fate. After all, what the majority of these children would discover on this first trip was that they wouldn't become dreamhunters. Just being able to penetrate the veil of the Place didn't mean that they could catch dreams or, even if they could, that they could do so with sufficient vigor to make their dreams salable. Most of these children would find employment as rangers—but the Chief Ranger knew very few women who took up that option. That girl had sacrificed her hair to her vain hopes. He hoped she wouldn't regret it too keenly, for he thought she was still rather pretty under her helmet of glossy curls.

He resumed his briefing. "You will each take one of these kits, in which, among other more self-evident items, you will find a signal whistle and a book about its use. I recommend that you study the book and master all the signals before you even consider going In on your own. Which, I might add, you have no hope of doing until you are licensed. And to be licensed you must satisfy the Body that you will not be a hazard to yourself or anyone else either in the Place or out of it with any dream you manage to catch." He went on to talk about the futility of attempting to light a fire in the Place, the importance of consulting maps and reporting any changes in the landscape. As he talked his eyes roved over the whole assembled group. He wanted to make sure they were listening to him. He looked into each of their faces—and was satisfied by their looks of respectful attention. But as his gaze moved, he found himself looking more often and longer at that pretty, attentive girl.

Grace Tiebold arrived at the door of the meeting room. The Chief Ranger waved to acknowledge her and watched every head in his audience—even his own rangers'—swivel to the door.

"Mrs. Tiebold," he said, "I have just finished with the generalities. I'm afraid that, at the moment, these young people are looking on their trip In as an exercise in orientation—which it is not. Perhaps you would like to explain its purpose? I think a dreamhunter will do a better job of explaining than any ranger."

Grace Tiebold said, "Thank you, I'd like that."

The Chief Ranger yielded his place but stayed at the front of the room, watching both the famous dreamhunter and that increasingly—it seemed to him—attractive candidate.

The girl was smiling at Grace Tiebold, who smiled back, a brief, warm look, then moved her gaze to take in all the expectant, admiring young faces.

Grace began by pulling down the Chief Ranger's chart. Several of the candidates gasped.

Grace said, mildly surprised, "Have some of you not seen a map of the Place? You're shocked. Of course, any map of the Place will be shocking to anyone with any understanding of geography. As you can see, this is a map of no *earthly* geography. It is an interpretation of an unearthly geography by the discipline of earthly mapmaking." She looked around at the Chief Ranger and asked if he had a pointer. He found her one, and she returned to the map and tapped it with the pointer. "As you can see, parts of this chart correspond in many ways to normal maps. There are topographical measurements. These hills and valleys have been surveyed." The pointer pattered on the canvas of the map. "Here is a forest," Grace said. "Here is a dry watercourse, here are roads, and ruins. Yes—*ruins*. And then *here* are markings to be found only on maps of the Place. These shadings indicate bands of certain sorts of dreams. And these spots—little dots that on a normal map would show the positions of villages or towns— here mark the sites of certain famous stable dreams, dreams that any dreamhunter can catch, that are always consistent in their content and intensity."

The Chief Ranger's eyes wandered over the large labels of the famous stable dreams. He spotted Convalescent One and Two, Starry Beach, Balloon Wars, Great Players, Beautiful Horse, and Big Member—a title he wished was rather less prominently visible to these children.

Grace rested the tip of her pointer on one spot. "This is Wild River—the dream on which you will be tested."

✤ ✤ ✤

It wasn't the first time that Laura had seen a map of the Place, and she knew it wasn't the bands of color, or the phan-

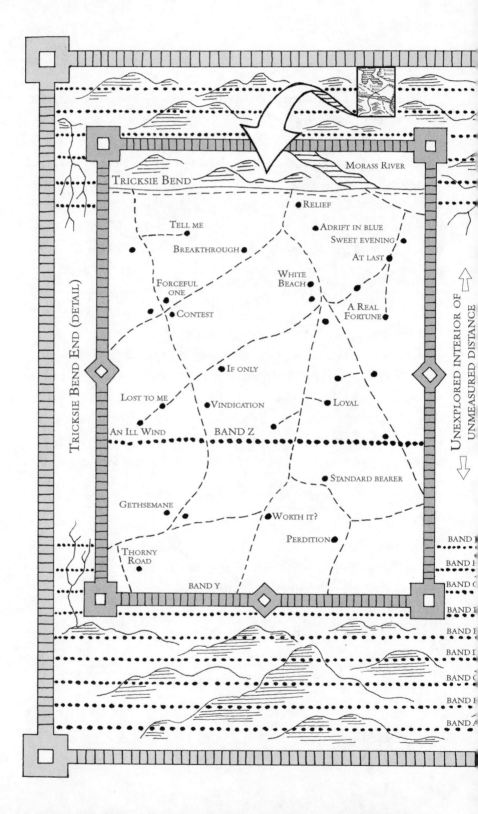

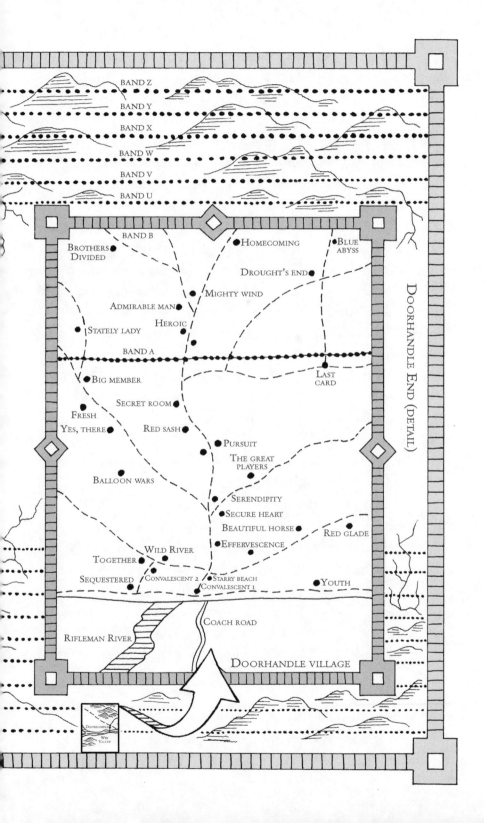

BAND Z

BAND Y

BAND X

BAND W

BAND V

BAND U

BAND B

BROTHERS
DIVIDED

HOMECOMING

BLUE
ABYSS

DROUGHT'S END

MIGHTY WIND

ADMIRABLE MAN

HEROIC

STATELY LADY

BAND A

BIG MEMBER

LAST
CARD

SECRET ROOM

FRESH
YES, THERE

RED SASH

PURSUIT

THE GREAT
PLAYERS

BALLOON WARS

SERENDIPITY

SECURE HEART

BEAUTIFUL HORSE

RED GLADE

EFFERVESCENCE

WILD RIVER

TOGETHER

SEQUESTERED

CONVALESCENT 2

STARRY BEACH
CONVALESCENT 1

YOUTH

COACH ROAD

RIFLEMAN RIVER

DOORHANDLE VILLAGE

DOORHANDLE END (DETAIL)

tom villages, or even Big Member that had caused the candidates to gasp—it was the whole *shape* of the map. The interior of the Place couldn't be measured in relation to known lines of longitude and latitude. Because—Laura knew—the land in the Place represented a much bigger space than the fifteen miles between Doorhandle and Tricksie Bend. Also, the Place had only parallel borders. No attempt to follow the border on the inside had ever resulted in tracing a line from the marker just inside the border at Tricksie Bend around to the one near Doorhandle. The Chief Ranger's map of the Place consisted of two horizontal ribbons of borderland, separated by a feathering of details supplied by those who traveled deepest In from either side. Between the feathering was a broad blank space. No map of the interior of the Place could be set inside one of the surrounding country—as a maritime map of a coastline can be set against a corresponding map of what lies inland from that coast. And that was because the border to the Place was continuous only from the *outside*, not from within.

Laura's aunt Grace was saying, "This is where we are taking you today. It's a dream site at map reference A-8. As you can see, the map is labeled in bands A to I from the Doorhandle side and Z to U at Tricksie Bend, where the Place hasn't been quite so fully explored. I always wonder if we'll eventually have to adopt letters from another alphabet when we find there are actually more bands in the hinterland than there are letters to label them." Grace Tiebold paused and made a thoughtful humming noise. Then she said, "But enough of that. Yes?"

A boy—one of the bandy-legged runts—had put up a hand. He asked, "What's it for?"

"A-8?" said Grace.

The boy blushed and subsided in confusion.

Laura knew that her aunt had purposely misinterpreted the

boy's question. He had probably just asked for the first time that perpetual, teasing question—What was the Place for? Why did it exist?

Grace continued. "A-8 is the dream Wild River. It is highly likely you know it already."

Many of the candidates nodded.

Laura had shared the dream before; it was a perennial favorite, performed at least four times each year in the Rainbow Opera. It was a dream to which older children were permitted to go—a harmlessly exhilarating dream. All who shared Wild River found themselves as either young men or young women—depending on which point of view they fell in with—taking a ride with friends in a sturdy boat down a river. A very beautiful river with a series of increasingly thrilling rapids. The dream always ended with the boat's safe arrival, and stately progress, into a calm lake.

"Wild River is a highly consistent, benign dream. It's ideal for you to cut your teeth on. What we're looking to see is, *first*, whether you can catch and retain it at all. *Second*, how strongly and for how long. *Third*, whether any of you will be fortunate enough to catch the split dream, to carry off both protagonists' points of view."

There was a murmuring among the candidates, who must all have been aware that anyone who caught the split dream would have her or his fortune made. There were only eight dreamhunters who could catch split dreams—of those eight, Grace was by far the most powerful.

"Even given that you're all sleeping in the same place, so boosting one another, this a true test, because you all get the same advantage. The test takes account of that. After the test you'll walk out and catch a train back to the capital. You'll be taken to the Head Office of the Regulatory Body, where you will each individually perform your Wild River for the examiners. Because Wild River is consistent, it's possible to grade the quality of your catch." Grace asked if they had any more questions.

The bandy-legged boy put up his hand again. "Miss," he said—rather betraying his charity school education—"aren't all dreamhunters different? Is the river dream one any dreamhunter can get?"

"Yes. That's why we use it. If you can catch a dream at all, you will catch Wild River. We don't really learn much about what sort of dreamhunter you are unless you catch the split dream. In this test we will measure only your strength—how vivid the dream is—and the dream's longevity, and get some sense of your powers of projection."

Another hand went up, and a boy whispered, "What if you're afraid of water?"

"The dream supplies another *self*—you know that. Though it does happen sometimes that a dreamhunter can change the appearance of a character in a dream so that the character resembles someone in the dreamhunter's life."

Grace went on to tell the boy who was afraid of water about other exceptions to the rule that the dream supplies all its characters. "There are a few talents who are able to make *substitutions*. To supply faces and bodies to order. For instance— the dreamhunter Maze Plasir makes half his income from the sale of 'bespoke dreams' to solitary clients. He can make the characters in his dreams look like people his patrons desire and can't have, or like people they've lost. Plasir makes wishes come true. And he resurrects the dead. His is a very rare— and, I think, rather *dubious*—talent. I'm sure you—all of you— will find that you're one or the other of the same old characters in the usual old boat."

"That's to be hoped," the Chief Ranger added, seeing the disappointment on several of the young faces. Some of the candidates, having joined an exclusive club, now wanted to be singular among the exclusive, to find their own strangely configured niches and sit in them like saints.

"Any further questions?" asked Grace Tiebold.

There were none.

✢ ✢ ✢

The Chief Ranger thanked Mrs. Tiebold, and she spread her hands to herd the candidates from the room—out to the road and the short walk to the border. The rangers fell in behind her. The Chief Ranger was surprised to see Mrs. Tiebold collect a pack from her car, shoulder it, and set off along the road with this latest clutch.

The Chief Ranger had, years before, stopped bothering to check the newspapers to see who had passed at each Try. The successful were always named in the same breathless, gossipy tones in which the social pages reported on who attended Founderston Cup Race Day. It wasn't worth following. He'd notice them only when they either became dreamhunters or came to work for the Body as rangers. However, on this occasion, the man did go back and ask one of his clerks for the day's log to see the names of those who went In. The unlicensed eleven were easy to find. And there were only three girls.

"Laura Hame," he read. That somber, pretty child was the daughter of the dangerous Tziga Hame.

✢ ✢ ✢

Grace and the dreamhunter guides left the eleven guarded by rangers at an encampment at A-8, under a group of trees from which the bark hung in blackened strips. The children spread their bedrolls on ground rubbed bald by successive visitors. Grace and the other hunters walked off out of range. The eleven had something to eat and drink, then lay down.

Laura slipped a black silk eye mask over her face. For the next few hours she listened to the ludicrous sounds of coughs, sniffs, shuffles, and giggles as the stagestruck eleven tried to settle. Someone got up to pee, then everyone did, including Laura. Once they'd done that—a mutual acknowledgment of nerves—the group settled some. Laura noticed the sounds thin out as, one by one, the young people fell asleep.

She felt a lurching drop. It was as if she had been walking and had lost her footing on a tilting stone. She knew the feeling. It was what she always felt when she was in a dream palace and the dreamer fell asleep before she had. There was a moment when she teetered and either fell in after the dreamer or not—and the feeling would pass. Laura very nearly removed her eye mask and sat up to see who the real dreamhunter was, the one who had just fallen so hard into the Wild River. But she didn't sit up, she continued to lie still and breathe deeply. She would go too. She could feel the Wild River beneath her, rushing by under her bedroll. "Ah," Laura thought with relief, falling asleep, dropping through dream water and white bubbles, "here it is."

For a moment it seemed to the fleeing convict that he had fallen asleep on his feet and had dropped through his weakness into a cold, stifling substance, like water. He found himself lying, gasping for breath, on the leaf litter of the forest floor.

The man knew he was finished. He was sick and tired. He couldn't keep up with the others, who could coax but not carry him.

It was black dark in the forest. He and the others from the mass breakout were running, strung out along a ridge.

The man was glad at least to be out. He got up from the ground to struggle on to the clearing he could see ahead, a thinning of the trees on the ridge's spine, where he'd be out of the forest and under the sky.

Another convict took his arm to help hurry him along. It was the young man from the cell next to his. They'd scarcely ever spoken, but had always stood together at the tubs to wash off the mine's black grime. The young man hauled him along. Then the failing convict stumbled and was dragged a little farther, skidding on his knees.

Several of the men nearest him in the ragged line stopped when the sick man fell in the clearing. They waited for him. But he looked up at the star-filled sky and remained on his knees, swaying.

The man who had helped him began to call out to the others—his voice croaking. He was parched. He made no words, only a rattling scream.

Back along the ridge, a line of torches moved through the trees. The pursuers. Their dogs would be bounding ahead of them, nosing through the dusky forest, following the warm trails of the desperate convicts.

There were other fires burning, a long way down on the coast. Stationary fires, the convict thought. Bonfires maybe, bonfires on a beach. He imagined company, singing, fish baking in glowing embers. He turned full circle, looking one last time at all the open horizons before running down to the trees again. He saw why the man beside him had cried out in despair. He saw that both coasts were visible from the ridge and that he and the other prisoners were being driven along a narrowing peninsula. He saw that, as the pursuers came on, their line grew tighter, the lights closer together, and that it would be impossible for any of the escaped convicts to double back and break through that line. He saw that the only real choice was to be swept along by that net and eventually gathered up into it. He saw what was going to happen, and yet he ran.

He felt the raw surfaces of bone grate in his bad knee. He swung his leg out from the hip at each step, as though meaning to fling it away from him.

The continuous line of light was closing on him. He saw his fellows scrambling ahead of him, grubby shapes in the acidic undergrowth of the dry forest.

He was worn out by labor. For years he'd broken stone and hauled stone. His hands were permanently cramped as though clutching a pick. He couldn't run any farther. He lay down to wait. He pressed his face into the leathery leaves on the forest floor.

A dog found him and leapt around, barking and snapping at the air over his head. One of the pursuers arrived and pushed it away. The light of the torches

Dreamhunter

held over him made the long, dry gum leaves on which he lay look like dim flames and their shadows like a bed of coals. He heard one pursuer say to another, "This is the first. But what should I do with him?"

An overseer answered. "I'm tired of even feeding these people. They're all ill-conditioned, and I'm not going to trouble myself driving the worst of them back." He kicked the convict in the ribs. "Do you hear me?" he said. "There's nowhere to take you animals back to. When you set fire to the prison, you burned your own bridges."

The convict realized he was about to be killed. The man was working himself up to it. The convict held out his hands, asking for mercy. In the torchlight he saw his clawed fingers, his broken nails. Was this it then? Was this all? How could it be? "This isn't me," the man thought. "This isn't what I've come to."

He remembered being a boy at the lighthouse on So Long Spit—his quiet, isolated life with his father, tending the light. He remembered how he had liked it when ships had come along the Spit, stopped and off-loaded supplies on the platform his father and the other keepers had built out on the level sand at the low-tide line. The convict remembered being a boy, running on the sand along-side a schooner that was sailing up the ocean shore of the Spit. He ran on the unending, smooth sand and waved at figures lining the ship's rail. He ran into the wind, the same steady wind that bellied out the schooner's sails. The boy waved. A group of four low-flying gannets passed between him and the ship, faster than both, scooping the air back with their black-tipped wings. The gannets flew on toward their colony, far away at the end of the Spit, where—to the boy's eyes—the sand vanished in the sea horizon so that only the colony itself was visible, a thin line of shimmering black and white drawn between the sparkling water and the blank sky.

The gannets overtook him easily, but he made an effort, sprinted, breasting the wind, trying to keep up with the schooner. His shadow ran beside him, and sometimes he was paced by his reflection too, on sand made wet by waves. Reflection, shadow, boy—running, and all keeping up.

3

✦ ✦ ✦

THE HEAD OFFICE OF THE DREAM REGULATORY BODY WAS IN A TOWER BUILT ON A SPUR OF RECLAIMED LAND, FORmerly swamp, at the downstream end of the Isle of the Temple. The tower stood by itself in a walled park whose grounds were planted in water-loving willows and cypresses. From the gallery that circled its upper story there were views of the city, the wide pavements of the west embankment, and, on the east bank, the walls of narrow houses stained by the outfall from jutting privies. Upstream, back along the island, the white marble dome of the Temple itself—St. Lazarus—seemed to hang in the blue air, hazy and weightless, like a daytime moon.

The examiners were waiting in the ring room, some walking around stifling yawns. One complained to another that he was dead on his feet. This season's little clutch of unlicensed dreamhunters had arrived back at the very end of the period he was rostered on. The woman walking with him had just arrived and wasn't at all sleepy. In fact, she felt quite perky. She glanced at one of the clocks. It was an hour yet to sundown.

On their arrival the tired children had been escorted into inner chambers at the base of the tower, where they bathed and were given something to eat. Once they were clean and fed, they would get into nightclothes. Shortly the examiners would take their places, two to each child, in the dream-testing rooms, cabins that lay in the park around the tower like seeds dropped from a tall flower. Indeed, at the moment the sun vanished, the doors in the walls of the antechamber opened and messengers appeared to summon the examiners into the core of the tower. A stair spiraled down to the ground floor and the doors out to the garden and its carefully spaced, isolated cabins. The messengers seemed to want the examiners to hurry. There was urgency in their gestures as they gathered the examiners toward the doors from the room. They kept glancing back at the elevator. Their glances were surreptitious, and they checked as often on one another as on the examiners they were herding. The perky examiner guessed that they had been asked to get themselves out of the way too. She refused to be hurried. Feigning some trouble with the heel of her shoe, she stopped and fussed with it. A messenger came forward and took her arm, helped her to her feet, and hustled her toward the door. She heard the elevator open. She and the messenger hesitated and looked. They saw three men. Two were dark-suited Regulatory Body officials—men from records, or registry. The third was still wearing his top-coat and hat, so he had come from outside the building.

As she was pushed through the inner doors and out of his line of sight, the examiner recognized the man. It was the Secretary of the Interior—Cas Doran.

"Now why"—thought the examiner as the door swung to between her and the Secretary—"should these functionaries be in such a hurry to clear everyone out of Secretary Doran's way?" Doran was responsible for the Regulatory Body. It was in his portfolio. He had every right to be in the Body's offices. "Is he coming now to lie in on one of these candidates' examinations?" thought the examiner. "Even so," she thought, "why should his interest be a matter of any secrecy?"

✢ ✢ ✢

Several hours later the examiner emerged, feeling rather deflated, from a ghostly, muffled experience of Wild River. She
decided to take a walk around the garden to clear her head.

She strode swiftly away from the cabin she'd been in, careful to avoid meeting the eyes of her fellow examiner—though
she was sure he'd agree with her about the poor quality of the
dream. As she walked she thought about how she would word
her unenthusiastic report on the feeble dreamhunter, whom
she would *pass* but whom she should—in all justice—discourage
from taking up the life.

The examiner ducked through a grove of dripping golden
ash trees. She caught sight of some dark-suited figures hurrying ahead of her toward the tower. She was sure that one of
them was Secretary Doran.

She stopped under the trees and waited till the group was
out of sight, then went on cautiously toward a hubbub she
could hear through a hedge of hydrangeas.

A crowd was milling around the open doors of a cabin,
their shoes making dents in the damp lawn. The examiner saw
two of her colleagues sitting on the cabin's veranda with their
heads on their knees. And she saw the dreamhunter Grace
Tiebold leaning on a veranda post, pale, her hand held over
her mouth.

The examiner thought better of her walk. She retraced her
steps through the garden and took her usual route into the
tower.

✢ ✢ ✢

Grace had sent a wire to Chorley from Doorhandle. In it
she had said only that she and Laura were back and she'd be

lying in on Laura's examination. Going by the wire, Chorley thought he could expect them both home the following day.

That day arrived, and Grace and Laura didn't. For that matter, neither did Tziga, who'd been gone for over two weeks now, long enough to have exhausted even his most enduring dream. Chorley had expected Tziga to appear about the time Laura set off on her first overnighter. They had all hoped he'd be back before she left and would be able to take Grace's place as Laura's guide. But when he hadn't arrived in time, Grace had accompanied Laura. Chorley hadn't had word from his brother-in-law.

The next day Chorley got another telegram: LAURA MUST GO BACK IN STOP PROBLEM WITH EXAMINATIONS STOP WILL GO TOO STOP SORRY BUT IT IS ME OR SOME STRANGER STOP WILL TELEGRAPH ON REEMERGENCE GRACE.

✧ ✧ ✧

Chorley was concerned. He took himself to the Head Office of the Regulatory Body to make his own inquiries.

He was shown to the Director's office. Chorley simply asked what the problem was with Laura's examination. "And do you—by any chance—have news of Tziga Hame? We expected him back several days ago, before Laura's examination."

The Director summoned underlings and sent them off to find answers to Chorley's questions. He had his secretary bring in a pot of tea. He poured and chatted and—Chorley thought—acted oddly nonchalant.

Chorley had thought it strange that, when he first appeared in the Director's office, he got the feeling the man had been expecting his visit, had even known what it was about. He was—Chorley thought—now walling himself up behind this

bricks-and-mortar of chatter. The Director had acted helpful, but all his showy activity seemed to Chorley to conceal
something. It was as though the man was stalling.

By the time Chorley's second cup of tea was cool, the underlings had returned with answers—and documents.

The Director read them while Chorley waited. He made a
neat stack of the pages and rested his folded hands upon
them. He looked up at Chorley.

"Apparently your niece caught a nightmare. However, she
didn't describe it as such to the rangers who escorted the season's candidates back from the test site. No one for a moment
imagines Miss Hame was being *dishonest*, just a little shy and
backward. She did manage to let the rangers know that she'd
caught something *different*, and unexpected. Her examiners
were chosen very carefully, and there were more than the
usual number. Your wife insisted on lying in with the girl
too—so, unfortunately, the effect of the nightmare was rather
amplified." The Director paused and smoothed the pages with
his fingertips. He cleared his throat and continued. "It was
decided that it was *imperative* that Laura overwrite her nightmare. There were no dreamhunters in Founderston with any
dream suitable, or sufficiently strong, to do the job. The
child had to be taken back In. Your wife went with her. Mrs.
Tiebold can steer her niece into calmer waters, I'm sure. I'm
certain they will both be back directly."

The Director smiled. "As to Mr. Hame. According to our
records, he went back In seven days ago, after registering his
intentions at the rangers' post at Doorhandle." The Director
paused, then asked, "Did Mr. Hame not go home first?"

"No," Chorley said. "And since he wasn't there for his
daughter's Try, we expected him to turn up as soon as he was
able. Why would he go back In?"

The Director frowned. "I have no idea," he said. It seemed
to Chorley that the man looked *expectant*, as though waiting for

him to begin making excuses for Tziga. As though by hearing what Chorley would say the Director could supply himself with explanations for Tziga Hame's behavior. Not—Chorley suspected—because the Director was disturbed and *needed* Tziga's behavior explained but perhaps because the Director wanted an answer to offer *other* people.

Chorley leaned forward, put his hand out for the papers, and asked, "What were Tziga's recorded intentions?"

The Director sorted one sheet from the pile and passed it to Chorley. He said, "That's a carbon."

Chorley looked at the paper, then sharply up at the Director. The form wasn't in Tziga's handwriting.

The Director seemed already aware of this. "The ranger on duty filled in the form," he said, and waved a hand, as if to wave away any suspicions Chorley might have. "Mr. Hame only signed it. That's not unusual, especially for the great dreamhunters. They are often helpless about anything practical."

The space on the form where the dreamhunter was meant to write his planned destination had only one word in it. The ranger who'd supposedly filled in the form for Tziga had written: "Across."

Chorley saw that the paper in his hand was trembling. He put it back on the Director's desk but kept his hand upon it. Chorley's ears were ringing. He was in shock—a shock that was several parts rage. He wanted to lean across the desk, take the Director by his collar, and shake him. But Chorley knew that showing what he was feeling wasn't wise till he'd gotten away from the office and had a chance to think. He had a suspicion that the document was forged, not filled in for Tziga. He was sure that something was being covered up, hastily and messily, just ahead of his inquiries. He was sure, too, that if he didn't pursue the matter *at once*, the cover-up would tidy itself up and form a solid front.

Chorley Tiebold was a man who'd gotten his own way almost all his life. His whole life experience, and his forceful nature, told him to challenge these lies and whatever lay behind them. His character and knowledge shrieked at him to *attack*—now, decisively. But something else—an instinct deeper than experience—was telling him to let it go, and not let this man know how suspicious he was. For as he sat there in the office of the Director, Chorley was being forced to face a fear he'd had but kept secret from himself. Worries that he'd shaken out of his head whenever they intruded. The fear was this—that Tziga, his sad, secretive friend, had been involved in dangerous things. Things possibly sanctioned by the Regulatory Body but things Tziga was ashamed of and wanted to keep from his family.

Something had gone wrong. The danger had overwhelmed Tziga.

And until he discovered exactly what that danger was, and that it threatened only Tziga and not his family too, Chorley decided he had better keep his new understanding from anyone who had anything to do with the Dream Regulatory Body.

The Director cleared his throat again. "We can't know how Mr. Hame was *in himself*. If he was joking, for instance. Perhaps he wrote what he did only to imply that he didn't like to be asked where he was going. I mean—the great ones in their exploratory phases are often secretive about their sites."

"Yes," Chorley said. He looked at the paper again, at that word, "Across." He didn't imagine for a second that Tziga had intended to make a crossing.

The Director said, "I'm sorry that, at this point, I can't be of more assistance. But if you have further cause to feel concerned—that is, if Mr. Hame doesn't appear within the next few days at Doorhandle, as usual . . ."

Chorley said, "Thank you," put the paper back on the Director's desk, and got up.

"I'll have the Post at Doorhandle send a wire as soon as

Mrs. Tiebold and Miss Hame emerge," the Director said. He stood too. They shook hands, and Chorley left.

✢ ✢ ✢

Laura and Grace were back within three days. A car dropped them at the front steps of the family's house in Founderston. The driver carried their hats and coats and knapsacks into the hall, then Grace closed the front door on him in a definite but not ill-tempered way. Rose ran down the stairs and hugged her mother and cousin, crushing them together in her embrace.

"Sorry for being away so long," Grace said to Rose. "Laura needs a bath." She pushed the girls toward the stairs. "Please see to it, Rose. I'll organize a meal."

Chorley had already organized a meal and baths but didn't like to talk over Grace, who clearly had urgent things to say to him. She was more tired than he'd seen her for years. She was pale and had shiny concavities of dry skin on her lower lip.

"Go on," said Chorley to Rose and Laura.

"Where is Da?" Laura said.

"I told you not to expect him," Grace said testily.

"Why shouldn't I expect him? He should be here," Laura said.

"He's not here, Laura," Chorley said. "We'll discuss it later."

Laura looked from uncle to aunt. "I see," she said. "Once you've got your stories straight."

"Sweetheart, we'll tell you everything we know, once we've had a talk and—between us—yes, sorted out fact from, from other stuff," Chorley said.

Laura glared at them but let her cousin lead her away.

✢ ✢ ✢

Laura lay in her bath, peeling a mandarin. Several other mandarins floated around her, bumping against her body and the sides of the bath.

Rose was sitting on the floor, her back against the full-length mirror, her hair clinging to its misty surface.

Laura had just come to the end of her account of her first dream.

"More convicts," said Rose.

"Yes. That's three dreams we know about. Two of them mine and one that Da once made a point of mentioning."

Rose looked puzzled, then said, "Oh! You're right! The laborers at the end of the original Convalescent One are convicts."

"Convicts mending the rail line, convicts building a wall, one convict with a letter in his mouth—"

"From a real person, the real Secretary of the Interior."

"And convicts on the run after a mass prison break," Laura finished. She dropped peel on the tiled floor and began to feed herself a mandarin, segment by segment. She grimaced. "I have mouth ulcers."

"Ma and Uncle Tziga always get mouth ulcers," said Rose. "And so it begins for you too. The stereotypical silent and secretive dreamhunter just has a sore mouth." Rose gave a barking laugh, then said, "The things I know—I should write my memoirs."

"We should probably keep Cas Doran under our hats," said Laura, as if she thought Rose was serious about her memoirs. "When we were on our way back to Doorhandle, your ma told me that Secretary Doran lay in on my examination."

"Well—you are a Hame."

"I don't like it," Laura said. "It gives me the creeps. That letter—the real letter—was really in a dead ranger's mouth."

Rose wondered aloud whether their classmate Mamie Doran, Cas Doran's daughter, had any opinions on convicts.

"Mamie has an opinion on everything."

"Except hair ribbons and other stuff she's above thinking about," Rose said.

"Poor Mamie's just making the best of being a girl—the best of a bad lot."

Rose said, determined, "I'm not going to be like that. I'm not going to start telling myself I'm *settling* for anything."

Laura batted a mandarin away from her chin and sank down in the bath. "Why do I dream about convicts?" she said.

"The Place is trying to tell you something. Remember how Da said to us that perhaps the dreams are true stories? If they're true, then some of them *matter*."

Laura looked very worried.

Rose sat up straight. Her damp hair detached from the mirror and dropped onto her shoulders. "The real question is this: Who is using dreams to tell stories?"

"Da would say 'God,' " said Laura.

"And *my* da would say 'Nonsense!' "

✤ ✤ ✤

Grace and Chorley were shut in his workshop. She had just finished a detailed account of Laura's first dream and was attempting to eat something. She had trouble with a bit of scone she was trying to swallow and spat it out into her hand. She dropped the chewed mess onto Chorley's workbench and put her face in her hands. "I'm so tired," she said. "I feel as though I'm nowhere."

Chorley ran the tea towel that had wrapped the scones under a tap and handed it to his wife. He said, "The convict in Laura's nightmare remembered being a boy on So Long Spit. Her dream was set in *our world*."

Grace was nodding. Then she knuckled a tear out from under her eye.

Chorley went to his wife. He sat beside her on the workshop's lumpy, developer-stained sofa. He stroked her hair.
"Look," he said. "I'm sorry to have to worry you any more,
but Tziga has disappeared. The Body says he went back In to
hunt another dream. The Director showed me a carbon of his
page from the intentions book."

"I saw it when I was signing myself," Grace said. "I think
the signature is a forgery—I've seen the real thing often
enough over the years. I think the Body is keeping things
from us. We have to decide what to *do*, love. We have to think
about what it means that we're being encouraged to think
Tziga did something as crazy as attempting a crossing. And we
have to think of Laura."

Chorley drew a deep, shuddering breath. Then he said,
"Do you have any idea what Tziga was up to?"

Grace let go of him and drew back. "No," she said. Then,
"Yes. Maybe. Not exactly."

"Which is it?" Chorley's voice was stern. "Yes, no, or
maybe?"

"Dear, I know there are things about dreamhunting that
you disapprove of. You think some of it is a bit distasteful.
Tziga and I never discussed certain things in front of you.
Things we felt you might find offensive."

Chorley wound his hand at her, gesturing for her to go on.
He was too angry to speak. Grace was blaming his attitude for
her secrecy.

"You know that there are different types of dreams—
different classifications. There are healing dreams, and adventure, romance, achievement, enlightenment, indulgence—the
dreams where you find yourself sitting down to eight-course
feasts . . ."

"Yes," said Chorley.

"There's a type of dream the Body classifies as a 'think again' dream. Tziga catches them to take to prisons. 'Think again' dreams are tools in reform programs."

"And how would this get him into trouble?"

Grace's eyes wandered. She looked down as if she was ashamed. Ashamed of what she knew, or suspected—Chorley thought. She said, "I can't see how Tziga might have gotten into trouble with the Body. He's always trusted their judgment. But, Chorley, those dreams were *bad* for him." Grace bit her lip, then went on. "I thought about it a lot this summer, because he seemed more sad and shut into himself than ever. 'Think again' dreams may well do wonders for hardened murderers, but Tziga performs them over and over, so he's the one learning again and again that he's a *sinner*, a bad person."

"So—these dreams are unpleasant?"

Grace looked up into Chorley's eyes. "They're nightmares."

Chorley got up and paced. He made several circuits of the workbench before he spoke again. Then he said, "You should have told me."

"Why me and not him? He's *your* friend. *He* should have told you. I only had suspicions and figured it out—he never actually talked to me about it." Grace raised her voice; she was fighting back. "And you made it quite clear to me that you wanted to know only so much and no more about what we did. About where the money came from, for God's sake! All summer you've chiseled on about how you didn't want the girls to Try. They came of age and suddenly you were full of prejudices about dreamhunting. But Laura and Rose were never going to turn into Tziga."

"Laura is exactly like him!" Chorley yelled at his wife. "And the first time she goes In to catch a dream, she catches something frightening. If that's not like Tziga, then what is?"

Grace began to cry again. "But Laura won't get mixed up in the Body's contracts. We'll tell her not to. She and Rose always had very definite opinions about government contracts, if only because they saw Tziga being whipped off from Sisters Beach several times every summer."

Chorley closed his eyes and tried to calm himself. "If Tziga was so troubled by his nightmares, why did he keep on delivering them?"

"I don't know. If I'm right about it—and how bad it's been for him—I can't imagine what would induce him to keep on. Perhaps he believes he's doing good. He has always tended to think of himself as some kind of savior." Grace patted the sofa beside her. "Sit down, please, Chorley. We have to decide what we're going to do."

Chorley relented. He came and sat beside his wife, and she retrieved his hand and held it hard. After a while she said, "If Tziga is supposed to have disappeared, then I should get together an official search party. I have to do that so the Body thinks I *believe* their story. If they're covering things up, I don't want to give them reason to think they have to cover up any further. We *do* want to find him."

"Something has happened to him," Chorley said.

Grace nodded.

"What about Laura?"

Grace was silent for a long time. Then she said, "Perhaps we should try to persuade the Body to withhold Laura's dreamhunter's license. They're already alarmed by her talent—alarmed and fascinated in equal measures, I think. We might be able to put them off." Grace thought for a little longer; then she told Chorley her plan.

4

✤ ✤ ✤

*L*AURA WAS RELIEVED WHEN HER AUNT AND UNCLE FINALLY ADMITTED TO HER THAT HER FATHER WAS MISSing. She'd known for days that they were hiding grave concerns about him, and waiting to know more before breaking the bad news.

Laura learned that Grace was getting together a search party to look for her father. She pinned her hopes on her aunt's search and tried to put her fears out of her mind. She had remarkably little trouble doing it.

Since first entering the Place, Laura had changed. She seemed to be able to put all her feelings further away from her day-to-day self. It was as if she'd developed an inner hinterland, and, having entered the Place, she'd taken on some of its characteristic distance, silence, and dryness.

Besides, she hadn't really had time to talk to Rose properly. She felt much of what was happening to her was suspended and unreal till she could talk it over with Rose.

The Body kept her busy. She was out for only one sleep in her old bed before being taken In again, to the site of another of those stable, benign dreams. She caught Beautiful Horse and Aerial Picnic. She went to sleep with examiners in the cabins in the garden of the Regulatory Body. She was tested again and again—but no more convicts appeared in her dreams.

On her way out with her fourth dream, a seasonal favorite called Great Players, concerning rugby, Laura met the four of her clutch who had been successful in catching Wild River. They were standing around the potbellied stove in the hall of the Post, consulting charts. They were talking in loud, self-important voices and glowing with excitement. Around their necks, outside their clothes, they were wearing the copper tags that were their licenses.

The little group spotted Laura and began to whisper among themselves. Then, as one, they shuffled over to where she stood waiting for her guides to complete their paperwork.

The tallest boy—the boy from the infants' beach—extended his hand to Laura. "Sandy Mason," he said.

She took his hand and shook it.

The bandy-legged boy asked her, "How's it going?"

"Slowly," said Laura. "They tell me that they need to know whether I'll provide dreams of consistent quality."

The other girl in the clutch who had succeeded in catching Wild River said, "Why won't they just license you and see how your dreams do on the market? I thought the market sorted out the weak from the strong."

"It's not *that* kind of problem with quality."

"You don't think they're making allowances, perhaps, letting you retest because you're his daughter and they just can't believe you're a fizzer?" the bandy-legged boy said, smirking at Laura.

"My aunt Grace often says that dreamhunters are envious and competitive. It seems to be true of you," Laura told the boy. "I caught a nightmare, and the examiners say that's a safety issue."

"Right," said the boy, dubious.

An adult, an expensively equipped dreamhunter with red hair and a taut-skinned, pale face, approached Laura and the clutch. "Children," he said. "I realize it's early yet, but I'd like you to be aware of your options." He pulled a silver card case out of his breast pocket and flicked it open. He passed them all his card. "I often have occasion to hire dreamhunters as amplifiers. It is a very good way for novices to earn while they're learning their trade and building up their own client bases. What people don't tell you—while they're filling your heads with visions of mastery, of ranging hunts and magnificent new dreams—is that you have to learn to outwalk and outwake dozens of other keen hunters. Fit, seasoned dreamhunters. The drug Wakeful is a very bad habit to acquire at your age—and you will be tempted to take it up. There's so much pressure to succeed quickly. I'm sure your families are very eager for you to start earning your fortunes." He looked from face to face, his expression inquiring. "Yes? Are you feeling the pressure already?"

The clutch all looked down at the cards he'd handed them.

"I don't usually solicit children," the man said. "But I happened to be passing A-8 when you were there with your less successful fellows catching your first dream."

"Catching it and skinning it," the bandy-legged boy said, gloating.

"Very good," said the man, and smiled at the boy. "A ranger on picket duty told me what was up and steered me away, but not before I felt one of you fall asleep—crash! Like a hangman's trapdoor. I said to myself, 'I'll look that one up later. There is a dreamhunter among dreamhunters. I'll offer him work.' "

"It was me," said the bandy-legged boy. "I'm the one."

"Good for you," said the man, and gave the boy's arm a squeeze.

"I know who you are, sir," the boy said.

Laura knew too, and she wasn't about to open her mouth in his presence. This was Maze Plasir, about whom her father and aunt always spoke with stiff disapproval.

The boy was saying, "My brother sampled you once."

"And he told you all about it?" Maze Plasir shook his head and laughed.

"Yes, he did." The boy's face had colored, his cheeks and neck suffused with blood, his earlobes purpled, actually throbbed. He glanced around him at the clutch, then seemed to decide to put them all aside. "Never mind this lot," he said. "They're all nice kids from good homes—you know what I mean. My brother, he came home off his ship and he had a dose. He had to stay away from his girl, but he was—you know."

"I know," said Plasir, poker-faced and sympathetic.

"So he went to your place and tried your dream—Fresh."

"Ah," said Plasir, "I have Fresh tonight." He smiled and tapped his head with a forefinger. "It's a favorite with my clients."

The boy's jaw dropped so that all the others could see the glistening strings of spit strung between his tongue and the roof of his mouth.

Plasir said to the boy, "Think about this: after you've caught your very first dream, your brain changes. Your mind becomes an amphitheater in which any other dreamhunter can perform. Empty, you're an amplifier. The greater the talent you have—the more capacity—the greater that amphitheater is. You can make a good dreamer of a poor dreamer, and a great dreamer of a good. I'm a good dreamer, unique, versatile, and—this is the important point—willing to experiment."

The boy was hooked; he was nodding as though he were sitting on a horse at a trot. He folded his chart and put it away.

"Would you like to come with me?" Plasir said. "Would you like to provide an amphitheater for me to perform in? You can earn good money, and learn a thing or two."

"Am I *allowed* to?"

"Don't you know that a licensed dreamhunter is no longer a minor? That's an allowance the law makes to get around the child-labor laws, the law that says you stay in school till you're sixteen. This"—Plasir flicked the copper tags on the boy's chest—"this says you're an adult."

"Great," the boy said. "You're on. I'll go with you."

Plasir put an arm loosely around the boy's shoulders and grinned at the others. "You keep those cards, children. Think about it," he said. He conducted the boy out to his car.

"That man has nearly lost his license many times," Laura said. "My father says Mr. Plasir has reached some accommodation with the Body so they overlook his excesses."

"I'm sorry about your father," the girl said to Laura. "You must be worried."

Laura shook her head, not to deny that she was worried but just because she felt that if she gave any sign of assent she'd be assenting to the fact that he had disappeared.

Sandy Mason said, "Fresh is something nasty about a beautiful young girl. I may come from 'a good home,' but I've heard talk. I never imagined I'd meet anyone who actually *wanted* to be Maze Plasir. But that guy did." Sandy tossed Plasir's business card on top of the stove, where it humped, went brown, then burst into flame and flew up like a tiny black bird. "Everyone else wants to be your aunt," he said to Laura.

"Even me," said Laura.

"That kid's a liar too—and I don't know why it suited Plasir to believe his boasting."

"Maybe Plasir just likes to collect corruptible youth," the girl said.

Sandy pulled a face, then he said to Laura, "Anyway, as I was saying, it wasn't snot-face who went down like the gallows trap. My guide was feeling for me, because my uncle is a dreamhunter who, when he has a dream, falls asleep with such a hard hit he knocks out whoever is in the room with him. Doctors sometimes use him instead of a general anesthetic. That's his special talent. My guide knew to look out for it in me. And I didn't disappoint her, I did go hard—perhaps you felt me? Or maybe you felt snot-face from the slums, who my guide says nearly dumped her like a shaky stepping-stone. But you went after us all, Laura, and it was you who were Plasir's 'gallows trap'—except my guide described it as a landslide. It was a near thing, she said. She's just a ranger, like the others there, and she reckoned half of them nearly fell in after you."

"No one told me that," Laura said.

"No? Anyway—*I* believe you about the 'safety issues' stuff." He put out a hand. "And I want to wish you good luck."

Laura took his hand again and shook it. Then she took the other hands she was offered.

"Dreamhunters aren't all envious and competitive," the girl said to Laura, gentle and reproachful.

"Only competitive maybe," said Sandy, grinning. Then he took Plasir's card from Laura and wrote his own name and address on the back of it. "Keep that," he said.

✦ ✦ ✦

Grace organized her search party, herself and six rangers. They walked eleven days In from Doorhandle, a day beyond the marker left by an earlier—surviving—expedition. They found no sign of Tziga Hame. They turned around and walked back out. Twenty-two days it took them. They emerged thin, dehydrated, and several with suppurating blisters on their feet.

Grace had slept, so she had caught and overwritten thirteen dreams altogether. Several were new to her, and some were unpleasant. She was forced to go off by herself to one of the dreamers' retreats in the forest near Doorhandle to rest up and rid herself of the cacophonous jumble of incidents, characters, and settings. She slept for hours at a time, woke only to feed herself, or draw water at the well, or sit on the veranda in the autumn sunshine watching wood pigeons with their bellies full of fermented berries, bumbling drunkenly from branch to branch and sometimes dropping out of the trees altogether.

She wrapped herself up and slept in the sun, gradually plowing her monstrous mix of dreams back into the air.

✣ ✣ ✣

Grace left it to Chorley to tell Laura that the search party hadn't found her father.

"They didn't find him *dead* either," Laura said. "The intentions book may say 'Across,' but how do you know that 'Across' wasn't his name for a dream?"

"Darling, they didn't find any sign of him, and he hasn't turned up anywhere. It's been over five weeks."

"But couldn't 'Across' be a dream?"

Laura wanted to cling to the last thing her father had done that seemed to her fully *sane*. Sane and reliable. She didn't count his impatience with her on the station platform at Sisters Beach. She went looking in her memories and found herself in summer again, at the sand-sculpting competition. Her father was helping her and Rose make a reclining man from the sand on the beach below the Strand. "Da?" Laura said to her memory, peering back through time at his face in the shadow of his sun hat. "Da? What is it?"

"Laura?" Chorley shook her. She was sitting in a chair in

the parlor of the Founderston house, staring off into the corner. She came to and crumpled. "Where is he?" She was pleading.

Chorley held her. "I don't know," he said, in tears too.

"Where's he gone?" Laura said.

Rose was kneeling on the rug behind her father, who was on his knees before Laura, holding her to him. Rose wrung her hands and pressed them against her mouth. She was afraid to speak, afraid to interfere, afraid to join in their grief.

"I don't know where he's gone," Chorley said again.

"Why didn't he come home?" Laura said, childish and dogged.

Rose scrambled across the floor and embraced Laura too.

"I want him to come home," Laura said, sobbing.

5

✧ ✧ ✧

HE OFFICES OF THE SECRETARY OF THE INTERIOR, PRESSED FOR SPACE, HAD RECLAIMED THE ATTICS OF THE PALACE of Governance, a building that, in former days, had been one of Founderston's grand residences. The attics had been servants' quarters, and narrow back stairs still ran all the way from top to bottom of the four corners of the building. The stair on the east corner was enclosed for all its length, and the doors on every floor were fastened by locks. At its foot this back stair opened on an alley beside one of Founderston's brackish storm drains. At its top the staircase ended in a plain, paneled door. On the far side of that door was the office of the Secretary of the Interior, Cas Doran.

Doran's large, low-roofed room had two old oval windows, whose solid frames bulged above and below the window glass like swollen eyelids. Through the windows his visitors could appreciate keyhole views of the tower of the Dream Regulatory Body—one of Secretary Doran's most tightly controlled departments.

Doran sat with his back to his view. It was his visitors who should be reminded that they were looking out at his domain. Those visitors whose appointments the Secretary scheduled for the early morning also could hardly fail to notice how his windows focused the low sun into his room like a burning glass.

Secretary Doran was an early riser. The people in his outer office were early risers too, because of the pressure of his expectations. They knew that the Secretary always asked certain people to come early. People he wished to catch napping.

It was just after seven when Dr. Wilmot arrived in Doran's outer office. The doctor was still pink from his bath. His hair was so freshly and heavily oiled that its scent was causing his eyes to water, so that he had several times to pop his monocle out of his sweaty eye socket and polish it. Wilmot was on time but had to wait. He polished his monocle so often that it was smeared with cloudy iridescence.

The musical tinkle of a bell by Doran's door signaled that the Secretary was ready for his next—or, Wilmot hoped, his *first*—appointment of the day.

The doctor was shown into Doran's office.

The Secretary of the Interior did not get up from behind his desk—a desk like an altar stone, as heavy as carved masonry but made of some tropical hardwood. Doran had one paper on this slick, dark desktop. Wilmot recognized his own letterhead.

"Good of you to come," said the Secretary, and gestured at a chair.

Wilmot took a seat. The chair was comfortable, but from this angle Doran was now only a silhouette against light striking up from the zinc roof of the assembly rooms one floor below.

"This death certificate . . . " Doran began.

"Esteemed Secretary . . . " said the doctor.

Doran raised a hand. The doctor fell silent.

"A certificate signed by one Dr. Grove—you mention it in your letter."

Dr. Wilmot had not *mentioned* the death certificate in his letter—the death certificate was the *whole subject* of his letter. He said, "Dr. Grove is the consulting physician at Magdalene Charity Hospital in Westport."

"You have written that here," said Doran.

"Secretary. Indeed. It is all there, I believe. I have seen the certificate. I have a copy of it in my private records. I thought that was best. I was sure that was what you would want. The *substance* of Grove's findings are in my letter, Secretary."

Doran read: " 'Tziga Hame expired on the tenth of March, this year, as the result of injuries to his skull sustained in the Westport rail yards on the second of March.' That is the substance?"

"That is what Dr. Grove's certificate says. And from my own examination of Hame directly after his fall, it is the result I expected. Though he did last a little longer than I thought he would."

"He *lasted*—while you returned to your practice."

"There was nothing to be done for the man. My further attendance on him would have been conspicuous."

The doctor could have sworn that he felt the Secretary's eyes shifting from item to item of his clothes, appraising him. Dr. Wilmot was dressed as a successful man should be—a successful man who also prided himself on being something of a *character*, an *identity* at the resort in Sisters Beach. The doctor flushed. He said, "Hame was best left where he was, an anonymous beneficiary of the tender care of the good sisters. I'm sure you agree."

"Yes, I do agree," Doran said.

Wilmot sagged with relief.

"However," said Doran, "your letter, while reassuring in many respects, lacks some vital information."

"Sir. How can I help you?"

"I don't want your bedside manner, Wilmot. I want intelligent compliance with my needs."

Wilmot swallowed and waited.

Doran gave a small sigh. "I have a letter about a certificate. You have the certificate in your private files. But tell me, Doctor, does Hame have a grave?"

The blood left Dr. Wilmot's head so swiftly that his bald spot grew chilly.

"This distresses me," Doran said. "I dislike having to apply for this sort of information myself, but I have done so and can tell you that your discreet Grove and the sisters at Magdalene Charity cannot tell me what was done with the man's remains."

Wilmot opened his mouth but could think of nothing to say. His jaw was trembling with tension. His open mouth made popping noises.

"You silly fish," said Doran. He sounded like a parent at the end of his patience and about to resort to disciplinary measures. He crumpled the letter in his hands. "You can be in Westport in three hours if you take the next train."

Dr. Wilmot got up and left the Secretary's office.

✤ ✤ ✤

In the evening Cas Doran's oval windows opened onto a dark blue late autumn dusk in which only a few lights showed, attic windows in the roofs of the Isle's hotels and dream parlors, and the beacon on top of the tower of the Dream Regulatory Body.

Doran and his friend were sitting in easy chairs at a fireplace on the far side of the room. They were enjoying a glass of wine.

"How is your Mr. Gregg?" Maze Plasir asked.

John Gregg was the new Speaker of the House of Representatives. Various people, including the President of the Republic, would have been alarmed to hear Gregg referred to as
Cas Doran's Mr. Gregg.

"Highly satisfactory." Cas Doran mused for a moment,
then he asked, "How do you do it, Maze?"

"You don't want me to answer that. The less you know the
better, probably."

"I'd like to know."

Plasir looked into the fire. "It's more difficult to do than it
is to explain. So—briefly—the process. Your latest request was
that anyone with any influence should favor Mr. Gregg for the
job of Speaker of the House. You wanted people to imagine
that, for some time, they'd had a good opinion of him?"

Cas leaned forward.

"First I caught Admirable Man. Then I grafted Mr. Gregg's
face and voice and gestures onto the subject of the dream. I
let the dream degrade a little over several nights. Then I
loaded what was left of it—its strongest emotions and impressions—into my apprentice. My apprentice attended performances at dream palaces—the Beholder and the Rainbow
Opera. He was induced to go into his trance once the patrons
of the palace had retired, and he insinuated a few ideas and
impressions into them when they were on the verge of sleep.
He cast his color out on the shock wave of Grace Tiebold's big
penumbra. He caught all the right people. And a week later
Gregg won his appointment."

Doran raised his glass to Plasir. "You make it sound very
matter-of-fact."

Maze shook his head. "It isn't. And I'm afraid I'll be unable
to color any more of the public's opinions for a while. My apprentice has had a breakdown. They do. But I have found a
suitable replacement. The last Try turned up an excellent
child."

"And what is it that makes this child so excellent?"

"He's very impressionable. I am letting him in on mysteries—my most delicious dreams, and certain 'mental disciplines.' He laps it all up."

Doran refilled Plasir's glass. "When will he be ready? I'd like to think that, if I find myself in need of some good propaganda, all options are available to me."

"The coloring of dreams has limited use as propaganda. Did you see the papers this evening?" Plasir asked.

"What in particular?"

"The Temple claims to have ten thousand pledge takers." Plasir sat up straight and put his hand over his heart. He quoted: " 'I swear I will not partake of dreams . . .' Cas, we can't color the opinions of people who won't sleep with a dreamer."

They were quiet for a time. A log in the fire fell apart. The flames covered its coals in a blue and orange membrane, and they tinkled like breaking wires. Then Doran said, quietly, "We'll see about that."

"I'd like to know what your plans are, Cas," said Plasir. "If I know more, I can think about what dreams to catch and how to alter them to suit your purposes."

"My plans, as far as they concern you and your new boy, involve a series of adjustments in the attitude of the general public." Doran mused for a time. Then he said, "It's impossible to have an effective government when it is constantly checked by a very poorly drafted constitution. For instance—my projects would benefit greatly from a longer term in office."

"I see."

"Maze, we are a country that has always found reasons to congratulate itself. Material reasons—our production of wheat and wool, iron and coal. And *moral* reasons—our tradition of democracy. Now, I'm a patriot. Any patriot has sometimes to think like a farmer—a farmer who takes out his gun to kill a wolf and who builds a fence around his water supply."

Plasir said, "I'm not sure who the wolves are, Cas. Though I think I'm getting your drift about the water. I guess you're talking about Shackle Island and its copper mines. I read the editorial your friend wrote, about the islanders' greed and our needs."

"There's no copper on the mainland," Doran said. He leaned forward, excited. "When we were using it only to make things like warming pans and carriage lamps, its cost wasn't a problem." He pointed at the light fixture above his head. "Now we have countless vital uses for that flexible, conductive metal."

Plasir nodded. "And it's easier to present arguments for an invasion to people who have been somehow prepared to hear them."

"I don't like that word—invasion. If the islanders all had a share in the mines' huge profits, things would be very different. But they don't. No—our need is making only a few of them rich. The inequalities on Shackle Island are unjust and offensive to any decent society."

"Cas, you're a visionary."

Doran cast his eyes down. "No, just a practical man who is prepared to think about the future." He turned his hands palm up, seemed to examine them for stains. He said, "I have plenty of work for you, Maze. I have big plans. But things aren't going as smoothly as they should."

"Hmmm?" Plasir made an encouraging noise.

Cas Doran looked up at his friend. "Tziga Hame has no grave. The man was a meteor, and no one can show me where he fell."

6

✦ ✦ ✦

IT WAS LATE AT NIGHT, AND THE HOUSE WAS QUIET. THE ONLY SOUND WAS FROM THE RIVER—A BARGE PASSING UN-der the echoing arches of the nearest bridge.

Grace and Chorley were in bed, clinging together for comfort. They were talking, softly, trying to refine their plans.

Chorley said, "I have to make the Director think that if he lets me have my way I won't be any bother to him in the future."

Grace said, "And he has to imagine that if Laura isn't licensed and goes back to school, she'll never bother the Body again."

"If only Laura *wanted* to go back to school," Chorley said. "She's developed her taste for dreamhunting rather quickly, hasn't she?"

"She knows she's good at it. Talent has its own needs, you know."

"So I've been told. And I've been told that God is in Heaven, and that Jesus died for my sins." Chorley gave a rude, skeptical grunt.

Grace ignored this. She said, "There is one thing we can do to make Laura *want* to go back to school. But it's hard on Rose."

"Rose is resilient."

"Yes, she is. She's probably tougher than all of us put together. My thought is this—we could have Rose board at the Academy, get her out of the house so that Laura hardly ever gets to see her. We can put Rose in as a boarder for a term but tell her it's for 'an indefinite period.' "

"That *is* hard."

"Yes. Hard on me too, Chorley. Rose will think I've lost interest in her since she isn't a dreamhunter."

Chorley nodded. His chin brushed his wife's hair. They were quiet for a time, then Grace said, "I don't want to sleep. I still have bits of my raggedy mess of dreams. I think I'd better get up and read, then go to bed once you and the girls are awake."

"Is Laura expected to go In again soon?"

"No. The Body is making its deliberations. Its decision. And Laura is in mourning, of course."

"*He's not dead*," Chorley said, suddenly. "He *can't* be dead." Grace heard his jaw make a pneumatic creak as he clenched his teeth. Other than that he was motionless—but she could still feel turmoil in his body, his anger, and fear, and suppressed sorrow.

"We could send Laura to her aunt Marta's for a day or two," she said. "She should see Marta. And with Laura gone, we can tackle Rose and have her off to school before Laura gets back."

"All right," Chorley said. "I'll put Laura on the train tomorrow."

"When I'm asleep," Grace said. "Sorry. Chorley, I know how it's been— Tziga and me out at all hours and sleeping when you were awake. Awake and on top of things while we were out of our heads, or full of nonsense. Sorry—I'm saying sorry."

Chorley sighed. "When Tziga was courting Verity, I used to call him 'my sister's creepy suitor.' He was the first dreamhunter I ever met. I never went to dreams. Tziga was this black-eyed, limping, spooky man who managed always to be *there*, watching my friends and me as though we were a pack of happy dogs—which we were. I never knew what he was thinking, but at the time, I thought he saw us all as shallow and simple. But the strange thing was that, as time went by, I got to like being rubbed the wrong way. I liked to feel that he was judging me, because I liked his attention. I'd say to Verity and my friends, 'I suppose that damned Hame will be there as usual,' but I'd wanted him to be there." Chorley made a choking sound, then added, "I want him to be *here*."

"I know," said Grace, and put up her hand to stroke his hair. "I know."

❖ ❖ ❖

When Rose's father told her that she was being sent to board at Founderston Girls' Academy, she didn't react. She was quiet because she was wondering why her da looked as though he was steeling himself for an ordeal. Did he expect her to explode? He certainly looked set to endure shouting, accusations, tears—all kinds of girlish unpleasantness.

Because she didn't immediately react to what he'd said, Rose had a chance to reflect. Why would her mother and father want to send her away? Her father was transparently distressed. Was this only her mother's idea? Was her mother really *that* disappointed in the result of her Try? Would her father let her mother act on disappointment? Rose thought, "They want to protect me from something. Or I'm somehow in the way of their concentrating on Laura. But *I* can look after Laura better than anyone can."

"So," said Chorley, "that is acceptable to you?"

"Are you holding your breath?" Rose said. "Do you think I'm going to start shouting at you?"

"You're being very mature, Rose. It's admirable."

"Why are you doing this?" Rose said.

"It suits us."

"That's the most cold-blooded thing you've ever said to me, Da."

Rose watched the color leaving her father's face. She watched him control himself—not his temper but perhaps his desire to confide in her. She said, "Why don't you just tell me?"

"We don't have to explain ourselves. All you need to know is that, at the moment, it *suits* us to have you board at the Academy. For goodness' sake, Rose, when you were younger you girls used to *ask* to board. You thought it would be fun."

"I remember," said Rose. "And what about Laura? What's Laura going to do when she comes home and finds me gone?"

"That's our concern. You're just going to have to trust our judgment."

Rose shook her head. "Uncle Tziga set out to walk across the Place and you expect me to trust your judgment?"

"Act as though you do, then. Don't give us any trouble." Chorley took a step away from the library fireplace, a step toward her. He put out his hand but didn't touch her. "You're behaving admirably, darling, and I appreciate it."

"A gold star for Rose," said Rose.

✢ ✢ ✢

Chorley called on the Director of the Regulatory Body.

When Chorley arrived, the Director got up from behind his desk, came around it, took his visitor's hand in both of his, and gripped it with great solemnity. "I'm terribly sorry about Mr. Hame," he said.

"Thank you. I did get your letter of condolence."

The Director took a chair opposite Chorley, out from behind the barrier of his desk. He crossed his legs and twitched the crease in his pin-striped trousers till it sat in the center of his knee. "How can I help you, Mr. Tiebold?"

"I'll get straight to the point. I would like the Body to refuse Laura her license. I understand that you do have reservations about her suitability as a dreamhunter."

The Director pursed his lips and inclined his head. "We do feel it would be wrong to let her out on her own too soon. Her ability is so very far ahead of her maturity. We have concerns for her safety, and her mental health. We are also obliged by law to protect the public. *However*, our lengthy deliberation about Miss Hame does not reflect our sense of her worth as a dreamhunter, or our desire to help her take up the life. We'd just like to set her on the right path."

"I'd like to see her go back to school," Chorley said.

The Director covered his mouth. He smoothed his mustache. From behind his hand he said, "There are problems with that. You are aware, I hope, that in giving your consent to your niece's Try you have consented to the examination process? And that, once her license is issued, you and your wife are no longer her guardians? That, in effect, the Body is her guardian till she comes of age? The law was intended to protect young dreamhunters from family ambition. Each dreamhunter represents so much potential earning power, and they come from all walks of life, including families who are not at all accustomed to managing wealth."

"Yes. I understand all that. But my request is very different. The Body doesn't need to protect Laura from my desire to exploit her. I've no ambitions for her. I only want her to be safe." Chorley leaned forward. "Laura is the only child of my only sister. Her father has come to harm. I have always had my reservations about my niece and daughter Trying. *Always*. But it was their wish to Try. And it was Grace's wish. Grace doesn't know I'm here, making this request. This is between you and me." Chorley leaned farther forward and took the Director's hand. "Sometimes sentiment is more important than the law. I cannot bear to give Laura up to the madness that has swallowed her father."

The Director's eyes flashed with appetite and interest. "Do you think that Mr. Hame went mad?"

Chorley lowered his eyes. He tried to seem stricken. He hoped the Director would swallow his act. "Yes," he said, hushed, "I'm terribly afraid for Laura."

"I see. But, Mr. Tiebold, what is your wife's opinion?"

Chorley frowned. "My wife is not Laura's blood relative. If it comes to a confrontation between us about Laura's future, I have the greater right. However, I don't want to openly oppose my wife's wishes. That's why I've come to you. I'm very happy to reimburse the Body for the trouble it has taken with Laura."

"Are you asking me if you can *buy* the Body's refusal?"

"Of course not."

"Miss Hame could return to her studies, but she isn't the same person she was before she caught her first dream. She won't be able to sleep near another, loaded dreamhunter without amplifying his or her dream. She will have to be very careful, all her life."

"Yes. I know."

The men studied each other. One was imagining that his wish would be granted, and the other was thinking, happily, of how many *other* people would believe that Tziga Hame had been insane at the time of his disappearance.

The Director got up. He made a circle of one arm and invited Chorley to stand up into it. He gripped Chorley's shoulders and squeezed gently. "Leave this in my hands," he said.

Chorley thanked him and went home to wait for Grace.

✧ ✧ ✧

"This might work," Grace said. "Laura has never been strong on initiative. If someone decides things for her, she'll simply accept it. With a few tears."

"I'm prepared for tears. And I'm sure she'd really rather be with Rose," Chorley said.

"I'm glad the Director was so receptive. I don't think I could have staged a public quarrel with you, dear. And I'm sure it would be bad for Laura to think we'd quarreled over her."

"I hope we haven't overreacted. I hope we're doing the right thing."

"Me too."

✧ ✧ ✧

Four days later, when Chorley and Grace were sitting quietly, holding hands across the gateleg table in the sunny bow window of their library, Laura burst into the room. Her eyes were puffy from days of crying, but she was smiling. Around her neck, flashing and clanking faintly, hung the fresh copper tags of a dreamhunter's license. "Look," she said, "they let me pass!" Then, "Where's Rose?"

III
The Sandman

ROSE, TEN WEEKS AFTER HER TRY, WAS SITTING IN A CLASSROOM IN THE ACADEMY. THE WINDOW SHE SAT BE-side faced the playing fields and the high brick school walls. Beyond the walls, Founderston showed only its rooftops, attic rooms, and smoking chimneys. A late autumn sun was de-clining in a sky the yellow-white of whey. It was the last class of the day.

Rose was bored. The teacher was pacing up and down be-fore the blackboard, firing questions at her class. Questions about a chapter in their history text—Dr. King, at last. Rose had done her reading, digested the lesson, remembered everything, as usual. She'd allowed herself to answer her cus-tomary four questions and left the rest to the other girls, who were halting and routine in their replies. Rose had soon lost interest in what they had to say. She looked out the window and watched the day die.

She was brought back to the room by the sound of Mamie Doran's cool, smart voice. Mamie was disagreeing with what both the teacher and Dr. King had to say about the balance between individual rights and "the common good." Mamie was eyeing Miss Melon, her head turned sideways like a bird's. Her posture was intensely skeptical, and insolent. "Miss Melon," Mamie said, her voice chiming, "do you not think that people can act in ways that lose them their rights? Convicted criminals, for instance. One citizen takes another's life, and the law deprives him of his liberty. The law won't let him vote. Rights are something we earn by being *good* citizens. Criminals *haven't* earned, they have fallen into debt to society. And you know, Miss Melon, it's impossible to feel much sympathy for people like that. After all, we all know what we have to do to keep on the right side of the law—that is, *obey* the law."

Miss Melon had gone pink, but she tried to sound tolerant. "But Mamie, you can't argue that it is reasonable to make newborn babies subject to rules they haven't invented. We aren't *born* into a contract with society. Our relationship to society is something we negotiate—or rather is negotiated for us by other people, all sorts of people, reformers and lawmakers and artists and so on."

"Yes, just anyone, in fact," Mamie said. "Which is very charming—the charm of democracy. But the point is that we all do inherit the law." Mamie was squinting at her teacher. She clearly thought Miss Melon was dim and illogical.

Miss Melon lost her temper. "Well, Mamie, you should perhaps consider that the law is *all* some people inherit. They don't inherit money or privileges—only duty and duress."

"We all inherit the law *and its protection*," Mamie said, cold and nasty. She said it suggestively, as if to imply that, were she not contained by school rules, and the respect the rules demanded she show her teacher, she *would* show Miss Melon a thing or two.

"Mamie Doran, you are a girl fortunate enough to be born with many personal advantages, and into privilege. I doubt you will ever have reasonable cause to call on the law for protection." The teacher was sharp and final.

Mamie opened her mouth to say something further, and Miss Melon said, "That's enough from you, Miss Doran."

The bell rang. Miss Melon dismissed the girls. Chairs scraped. Rose's classmates all filed out while the teacher busied herself wiping the board with an eraser. After a minute or two she turned around and saw Rose, who was still in her seat. "Rose!" she said, startled.

Rose could see that although Miss Melon was going calmly about her tasks, internally she was licking her wounds. She had thought she was alone. She rallied. "What can I do for you, Rose?"

"Mamie only behaves that way because she's easily bored," Rose said.

"I don't mind when my girls are lively. Or when they debate. And I hope I don't take a disagreement on the meaning of a text as a challenge to my authority. I hope I'm a better teacher than that," said Miss Melon. "It was Mamie's *opinions* I objected to, Rose, not her persistence in voicing them."

"But she does play devil's advocate when she's bored."

"You think so?" said the teacher. "You think she's debating a point, not stating a position?"

"Well—yes," said Rose, "and she *is* the smartest girl in the school."

"And so I should appreciate her?"

Rose shrugged. Then she said, "Mamie annoys me too, but at least she's not timid. If I wanted to, I could talk to her."

Miss Melon came and sat in the seat beside Rose. "And what would you talk about, Rose?"

Rose shrugged again and shook her head.

"How are you enjoying being a boarder?" Miss Melon asked, not bothering to disguise the fact that it was a pointed question.

"Every fortnight I arrive at my own home with a trunk, like a visitor," Rose said. "Boarding isn't bad. The girls I share a room with are nice. But having been sent away is *horrible*."

Miss Melon put her hand on Rose's and squeezed it.

Rose went on. "Laura only answers some of my letters and then just scribbles a few lines. I think she doesn't want to let on how much she's enjoying herself. She thinks I'll be *jealous*, or I'll judge her harshly for being able to enjoy something with her da gone. I wouldn't do that, and I don't want my feelings spared. Sparing my feelings just hurts them, actually. I don't get to *see* Laura. She has a room in a boardinghouse in Doorhandle and keeps going In to get dreams just to build up her stamina—Ma says. I go home and Ma and Da spoil me. We go on outings. I even went up in a balloon. But they won't consider changing my boarding arrangement—as if it matters that they'll lose the fees. They say, 'The arrangements have been made for the half year, and we don't want to trouble our good relationship with the school.' They're inflexible, though they're very sweet to me. But I feel as if Ma's lost interest in me now that she knows I'll never be a dreamhunter."

"I see," said Miss Melon. "And feeling that your mother has lost interest in you puts you in some sympathy with unattractive Mamie Doran?"

"Yes, it does."

"As for Laura—you know she has a lot on her plate. And, Rose, you must be aware that Laura when asked for four pages would often turn in only two. She doesn't like putting pen to paper."

"That's true."

"And do you think that your mother and father and Laura based their opinion of you on your own ideas of your future?"

"Yes," said Rose, quietly. "I was so confident."

"You're the same person that you were before your Try," Miss Melon said. "All that has happened is you have lost a fixed idea of your future."

"And I've lost my uncle Tziga—coincidentally." Rose sounded dry, but she was telling her teacher off.

"Well—yes—and there hasn't been a funeral yet, I gather. That must be difficult for all of you."

Rose drooped. "Yes, I suppose Ma and Da are in limbo about that, and they're not thinking how the weeks are stretching out for me. But they *should*."

"If you can't change their minds, or really know what they're thinking, you just have to be patient. Patient and charitable. 'Faith, Hope, and Charity—and the greatest of these is Charity.' " Miss Melon quoted scripture.

"The new translation says 'Love.' 'The greatest of these is Love.' "

"It does, and I understand that 'Love' is supposed to be more accurate. But it was always better translated as 'Charity' because 'Charity' reminds us of what we owe, not what is owed to us."

Rose lifted her head and smiled at Miss Melon, who said, "I know that you are a wise girl, Rose."

"Thank you," said Rose. "Now about Mamie, I suppose I want to ask you to think about being a little bit more *charitable* toward her."

"If you like, dear, I'll make more of an effort. But is it doing Mamie justice in the long term to let her get up on her high horse?"

"I don't know. Shall we experiment?"

The teacher laughed. "That's better. That's the Rose we all know and treasure." Miss Melon patted the hand she held, then got up. She said, "You should go now, dear, or you'll miss your tea."

✢ ✢ ✢

That evening Rose went to look for Mamie Doran. She found her at a table in the school library, reading a novel behind a barricade of atlases.

Mamie didn't look up from her page. She said, "What do you want, Rose?"

"That stuff you were saying today in history, do you get it from these books?"

Mamie laid her book facedown on the table. "What do you think?"

"I don't know. I'm just interested."

"In our house the dinner-table discussions are often wide-ranging and philosophical," Mamie said.

"You must miss it," Rose said. Mamie had been boarding for over a year, though like Rose's, her home was nearby.

"Miss Melon is no substitute for—for example—father's friend Wilkie," said Mamie. She looked at Rose archly. Then sighed. "Garth Wilkinson, the President," she said, as though she were attempting to educate someone very much her junior.

"What's he like?"

"Gentlemanly. And he likes to do card tricks."

Rose tried to imagine the President of the Republic doing card tricks. "Who else?" Rose asked, curious about Mamie's father's friends and allies.

"Senators and so forth. And"—Mamie's eyes flicked up to Rose's face—"recently we had a particularly interesting man, Mr. Gregg, the new Speaker of the House." Mamie watched Rose with shrewd interest. "Do you know who I mean?"

Rose was surprised to discover that she did know who Gregg was, and even more surprised to find she had an opinion of him. "Yes, I do know Gregg. He's solid and equitable," Rose said. "Someone must have told me that."

Mamie gave a strange, nervy laugh and picked up her book again.

"Well," said Rose, "I just wanted to say that I liked the way you stirred things up in history today."

"You surprise me, Rose."

Rose sat down next to Mamie and leaned toward her, speaking eagerly. "Don't you get tired of everyone being so timid?"

"Timid toward *you*, Rose? Is that what you mean? Of course they're afraid you're going to cry." Mamie studied Rose for signs of tears. "The trouble with you, Rose Tiebold, is that there were a whole lot of things that it never occurred to you to think about."

"For instance?"

"For instance, why did none of your classmates consider Trying?"

Of all the girls at Founderston Girls' Academy who had turned fifteen in the last twelve months, only Rose and Laura had Tried. "I guess their parents didn't give them permission," Rose said.

"That's right," said Mamie. "They come from well-bred, *scared* stock. Their parents probably told them that it is something they can do, if they *must*, when they reach their majority. Like attending the University. Jane wants to attend the University, and her parents say she can, but only once she's twenty-one. You and Laura were expected to *choose* to Try. But my mother says dreamhunters are just fortune hunters—even though your uncle's dreams enriched her father, Grandfather Chambers. It's easy for all our classmates to avoid Trying—all they have to do is avoid the road through the Rifleman Range between Doorhandle and Tricksie Bend. When they go to Coal Bay, they catch the train. Trying is something that other people do—not them. You and Laura did what *other people* do—and then *you* came back to school. They're not going to talk to you about it, Rose. They're embarrassed for you. You'll never be one of them again." Mamie stopped speaking and stared at Rose expectantly. She seemed to want a fight.

"Thank you for telling me that, Mamie," Rose said.

"You're welcome. And now that you have Tried and come back, I can tell you something. I had my fifteenth birthday six months before yours. About a year before that my father bought some land at the back of Awa Inlet in Coal Bay. That's where we have our new summerhouse. It's very isolated. It's also not a place any dreamhunter can go, because it's across the line. When we were building, everyone in the family but me went up and had a look at the progress. I wasn't allowed to. Father didn't want to involve me in one of the official Tries—he said it wasn't necessary for his daughter. So we did it privately. The day after my fifteenth birthday we sailed up Awa Inlet with some officials from the Regulatory Body. We walked from the landing place to our house. We crossed the line. Then we all had a nice lunch and sailed back. It was only a formality, really. No one ever thought that I would go into the Place. And I was very glad that I didn't. I have no particular plan in life—and that's something I rather like. Most things people do seem to me to be rather dull and silly. In my ideal life I'd be left alone to read."

"So—I guess I should leave you alone," Rose said.

"This book is wonderful. But, Rose, I've always enjoyed talking to you. You aren't *dim*, like Jane and Patty and Anne. Also, I'd like to ask you who you thought was right, me or Miss Melon?"

"I'm not sure. But the thing is that you *cared* about your argument. Jane and Patty and Anne are only interested in what Melon says when it earns them lots of checks in their margins."

Mamie nodded. "Ten out of ten—that's Jane. It's like she washes, dries, and presses history instead of studying it."

Rose laughed. Mamie looked startled, then pleased to have

made her laugh. She said, "You can stay put if you like, Rose. But you'll have to find something to read."

"That shouldn't be hard." Rose looked around at all the bookshelves.

"Go and find *The Mill on the Floss*—that might do you some good," Mamie said.

HERE WAS A GATE IN THE HIGH BRICK WALL AT THE FAR SIDE OF THE PLAYING FIELDS OF FOUNDERSTON Girls' Academy. It was always locked. On the other side of it was a narrow night-cart lane. Early one wintry morning a pupil slipped out of her dormitory and hurried across the field to the barred arch in the wall. Another girl waited on the far side of the gate, holding the bars.

Rose collided with the gate so hard it clanged. She thrust her arms through and gathered Laura against the bars. Their smoking breath mingled. They both started to cry and for a time just clung together with the cold iron between them.

"Why didn't you answer most of my letters?" Rose asked.

"I couldn't. It was too difficult. I couldn't think what to write. I can't answer for your mother and father. They say they've sent you away while we regroup. You think that means you're not necessary to the new grouping. But that's not what is going on, Rose. There *is* something going on. Uncle Chorley and Aunt Grace are afraid for me, I think. And no one is behaving properly. For instance—you do know about their fight with Aunt Marta?"

Rose shook her head.

"It's about a memorial service for Da. Aunt Marta talked to the Grand Patriarch apparently. And then he refused Grace and Chorley the use of St. Lazarus. It doesn't make any sense. If someone had asked me what I thought would happen if my father went missing and was declared dead, I'd have sworn that Aunt Marta would be the one to want the ceremony, and Uncle Chorley, at least, would have dragged his feet. First, because he's not religious. Second, because he'd be happy with the excuse of no body so that he wouldn't have to bury Da." Laura began to cry again.

"Shhh," said Rose, stroking her cousin's curls.

"I've had this dream—a real dream of my own I mean. I keep sitting up late in my room at the boardinghouse. I'm trying to be tired to go In and catch something. I'm no good at staying awake. I nod off in my chair, and then Da is standing beside me and he says, 'It's time you went to bed, Laura.' And I look around and he turns to smoke and vanishes." Laura pressed her forehead against the gate and sobbed. "I'm just waiting. I'm going to wait and wait for him to come back. I can't stop. I can't help it."

"I want to look after you," Rose said. "Why won't they let me look after you?" She let go of Laura and jumped back from the gate to look up at the top of the wall. She measured it with her eyes and even flexed her legs like a cat rocking on its haunches before making a jump. She moaned and flung herself back at the gate and clutched Laura again.

"Your da is nearly as bad as I am," Laura said. "Every time I see him he cries."

"Every time *I* see him he puts on a brave face—he's Mr. Sunny," Rose said, disgusted. "I've been trying to eavesdrop on them. I climbed down the shaft of the dumbwaiter, just like we used to when we were little. I listened, but all I could make out was your name, by turns, in things they said. 'Laura' in his voice. 'Laura' in hers." Rose told her cousin that she'd wanted to beat on the walls of the shaft so that they would know she was there. She said she'd felt as though she were attending her own funeral, as if she were listening to her loved ones from inside her coffin.

Laura pressed her face against the gate to kiss Rose's cheek. "I didn't answer your letters partly because I felt they didn't want *me* around either. I was pushing at you, being silent, to see if you meant to leave me too."

"Oh, Laura," said Rose.

"Da did leave me," Laura said. "He did." Then she shook herself. "But I mean to find out exactly what he left me for. What he was doing. He was doing something he shouldn't have. He knew something would happen. He kept trying to remind me of old family things that he'd wanted to teach me when I was little. I just thought he was being weird. And it *is* kind of weird what he thought was worthwhile passing on."

"What?" Rose asked.

"Old Hame songs and stories. I've been thinking about them. It's driving me crazy. It's like I'm being haunted by all this old stuff instead of ordinary everyday life. Just Da being ordinary—sitting on the veranda at Summerfort and chewing his fingernails."

The sun came over the tops of the roofs on the other side of the night-cart lane and threw Laura's shadow and the shadows of the gate's bars onto Rose. The light was bright behind Laura's head, and her face was in shadow. Rose leaned even nearer till she could smell the tea and oats and apricots on Laura's breath.

Laura said that she had been scared to go off on her own and hunt dreams. Twice she had been caught following other dreamhunters, lying down near them, so that she got what they got. "They said I was poaching. But I wasn't. I was trying to avoid getting something odd, like lying down at Wild River and catching fleeing convicts." Since her first sleepover she'd had the feeling that there was a big fuss going on around her, a fuss she knew was about her but couldn't make sense of.

"But I'm tired of it," Laura said. "I'm tired of being miserable and lonely and well behaved. I want to know what really happened to Da. No one in this family believes he suddenly decided to traverse the Place. I have to try to find out what happened. I'm going to catch the train to Sisters Beach today. I'm going to find Uncle Chorley's camera and remove the film from it. I want to see what Da shot on his trip In from Tricksie Bend."

"Uncle Tziga told Ma at the station that he'd left the camera in a dry stream with a blue clay bed about two days In," Rose said.

"I knew you'd remember. That's what I came to ask you."

Rose sighed, then said, "Well, I'm glad something made you come."

"I'm sorry," said Laura. "Look—I thought I should also tell someone where I mean to go. I don't want to go In at Tricksie Bend or fill in my intentions, just in case I find something to follow up. I don't want rangers poking their noses in."

"Already the secretive dreamhunter," Rose said.

Laura didn't respond to this. She said, "I'll go In along the track to Whynew Falls—"

"Hey!" said Rose. She'd made a happy discovery. "I can see the falls now! I always *hated* having to stop. Especially the year Da kept going on up there with Caro Bax." Rose scowled at the memory. She disliked Miss Bax, a Sisters Beach neighbor who had hung on her father's every word through two summers.

Laura smiled at her cousin's excitement. Then she watched Rose get even more fired up. "You know your dream, Laura? The one where you solved the 'ours as D ecre' puzzle? 'Yours, Cas Doran, Secretary of the Interior.' "

"What about it?"

"I'm making friends with Mamie Doran. I'm cultivating her. I've been telling her how neglected I am. How I can't talk to the other girls—which I have to say is true. Anyway, I'm hoping Mamie will invite me to her house."

Laura was surprised and filled with admiration. But this was Rose, her clever, calculating, controlled cousin. Rose was shut out of the Place, of her family home, of Laura's new life—but she'd found something to do, some way to connect.

"I hope to be able to give Secretary Doran a good looking-over and see if I can find out why his name should appear pulled out of the sand-stuffed mouth of a dead ranger, and a convict laborer in a dream." Rose waggled her eyebrows at Laura, pleased with herself. "So," she said, "how long do you think this trip will take you? I should know, if I'm standing in for the Tricksie Bend intentions book."

"About five days. I'll send a wire from Sisters Beach when I'm back."

"You do that." Rose kissed Laura once more, clumsily, through the bars, then relinquished her grip.

"Oh—can I borrow your coat so I look a little less like a dreamhunter on the train?" Laura said. "The new kids only ever work the Doorhandle end, and I don't want to be too conspicuous."

Rose took off her coat and fed it through the bars. Laura put it on. She was shorter than Rose, and it came down to the tops of her midcalf walking boots. Rose said, "Please be careful."

"I will." Laura stepped back from the gate, waved, settled her pack on her shoulders, and walked away.

✧ ✧ ✧

A cold evening at Sisters Beach. Each wave made a hard, definite sound on the sand against the winter silence. The seafront was empty, grilles fastened on the windows of shops, the hotels blind, all their seaward shutters closed.

Laura went up the scallop-shell drive between flax bushes on whose blades dew was beginning to set as white frost. She found the hidden key and let herself in one of the glass doors of Summerfort. She found the house icy and close, all its curtains drawn on the sunny winter weather, the rooms prematurely chilled. The house was dry, but all the empty and unwashed flower vases were dank—the grates swept but not spring-cleaned.

It was horrible. But Laura had the hard work of a long walk ahead of her the next day, so she didn't sit down and cry—for her father, for the family, for their last summer. She swallowed the urge and folded the sorrow back into herself.

3

✣ ✣ ✣

*L*AURA SAW ONLY ONE RANGER NEAR THE BORDER. SHE WAS FOLLOW-ING A FENCE THROUGH FARMLAND WHEN she saw him emerge from the border of whiteywood scrub at the head of the track to Whynew Falls. Before he had turned her way, Laura crouched down in the wet grass and ducked her head. The skirts of her coat spread out around her, making a creased bell. The coat was an old, salt-stiffened oilskin she'd found in the room by Summerfort's main hall, a room that was stuffed with badminton rackets, coats, croquet mallets and hoops, picnic blankets, fishing rods and tackle, and all the other props of the family's idle attempts at living life in the great outdoors. It smelled like old copper coins, but it did the trick, it made the crouching girl look like a large rock. Laura didn't dare turn to watch the ranger, but after a moment she was alarmed to hear a tread and breathing behind her. Breathing, a sound like a bellows working, and thumping footfalls. Laura squeezed her eyes shut and tried to think of what to say, of an excuse, of who else she could be but Laura Hame.

Something stirred her hair. She turned her head, and a cow blew a cloud of grassy steam into her face. There were several cows; they'd come over to see what she was doing. They surrounded her, snuffling and whipping their back legs with their yellowed white tails. They sniffed, then began to lick her coat. They licked, pushing at her, thorough and luxurious. They were black-and-white cows, with mottled pink-and-gray tongues. They were very happy to make the most of this source of salt that had kindly stopped in their field.

Laura held the coat up over her head and reflected that at least it was unlikely the ranger would suppose that the cows were clustered around a trespassing dreamhunter—or indeed that anyone was at the bottom of this scrum of salt-hungry animals.

After some time she pushed the cows away and got to her feet. Her coat, shoes, and bare hands were covered in swipes and strings of gluelike spittle. The ranger was a long way off, already out on the farm road and heading on the gentle downhill toward the coast. Laura took her coat off and shook it, then dragged it along the grass. The cows plunged away from her when she flapped the coat at them. She held it over her head, up in the breeze to dry as she walked.

✧ ✧ ✧

Laura entered Whynew Falls Reserve in the late afternoon, through a half acre of regenerating forest, all indigenous evergreens, whose pale, twisted trunks formed a sunlit filigree before the rest of the forest. She climbed a stile over the last farm fence and went on to the track.

An hour later she was walking between mature mountain beech trees on the track that was just a trough of bare ground surrounded by a confetti of tan beech leaves. The air was filled with their savory perfume. The track had climbed above the streambed, and Laura could see the water downhill between black, velvety beech branches and the dry boulders of the wide streambed. She came to the sign: *CAUTION: YOU ARE NOW ONLY 100 YARDS FROM THE BORDER TO THE PLACE.* She stopped. Despite the height of the stream, and the damp brilliance of the vegetation—despite all the signs that it was winter—for a moment Laura imagined that the rest of the picnickers were about to catch up with her, to come around the corner with their sun hats and baskets and their jackets tied at their waists. Laura could hear the falls, from this distance an endless, deep, sighing sound, only another quarter mile away. It was here, on last summer's walk, that she and her father, Grace and Rose, had sat down on the bank while the rest of the picnic party went on.

Laura stepped past the sign. She walked on, rounding several bends till the sound of the falls grew louder. She came to a tree that had a circle of orange-painted tin nailed to its trunk. She passed the tree. The sound of the falls faded and stopped. Laura stepped into the dry, open country of the Place.

The track went on before her, buff-colored, bared earth running through grass with the white sheen of spun sugar. She stood at a T-junction. There were three paths she could choose. To either side of her the path branched off to follow the border. On her left it led to the main thoroughfare from the rangers' post at Tricksie Bend. On her right it went on for miles, for days, gradually becoming less definite, less traveled. The path before her feet, the tail of the T, led deeper into the Place.

Laura was headed In, but she didn't really want to encounter anyone. So she went straight ahead for a time, then, when she came to a tree twice the height of a tall man, she left the track. She picked her way through the meadow away from the path. When she could see only the very top of the tree, she straightened her course and walked on, parallel to the path but—she hoped—invisible to anyone on it. Every now and then she stopped to consult her map, and to listen. She listened to the silence, then went on. The brittle grass hissed and crackled as she passed through it. It didn't close behind her, and as she went she left a wake of snapped stalks.

Laura had heard her father say that the Place was driest at its perimeter. Like a wound, he had said. Laura wanted to find the streambed that she had heard Grace and her father speak about. It was marked on her map—a two-and-a-half-day walk In from Tricksie Bend, and two days from the Whynew Falls Track. According to marks on the map, the streambed showed the first signs of what rangers called "remaining moisture." "There are places where you can dig down and find damp earth," her father had once told her.

Laura had often wondered, idly, how that could be. If it hadn't rained in the Place for—to the best of anyone's knowledge—twenty years, how could there be any groundwater?

Since her first coming to the Place, Laura's idle wondering about how it worked had become sharp speculation. She had made the investigations she knew other dreamhunters and rangers must have made many times before. She'd tried carrying a burning match across the border, or striking a light once there. She had found that nothing would burn. She'd snapped twigs off the trees and seen the sappy gristle at their hearts. She'd seen that the trees in the Place were not like those struck by earthly droughts. Trees in the Place had leaves, sere, on branches that hadn't had a soaking in living memory. The Place was full of vegetation that wasn't dead but wouldn't revive. It seemed somehow to continue right at the point of death, year after year, as if time had simply stopped.

Laura looked around the dry landscape, a landscape stripped of all animal life—even insects—but without corpses too, without empty chrysalises or the brown skins of cicada nymphs, without transparent, scale-printed cast-off lizard skins. There were no piles of rotted fleeces, the remnants of sheep corpses left after a cold spring in earthly fields. There were no bones, no empty birds' nests, no cold eggs.

Dreamhunter

Because of what it lacked, the Place looked like a mock-up. But it was too vast, and too detailed, for anyone to have made it. If it wasn't a model, or a living landscape, what was the Place? Were dreams its inhabitants? What kind of place had no mortal remains but dreams?

Laura went over all this once more as she walked. And she wondered whether, if someone did perish in the Place, would the Place, after a time, somehow tidy the remains away? Laura thought of her father and abruptly sat down in the dusty grass to cry. She cried hard, but in the dry air her tears hadn't even reached her chin before turning to stiff salt trails on her skin.

She got up again and went on.

✢ ✢ ✢

Laura concealed her trail by struggling through little copses, and by climbing a hill to step along the raised nubs of its stony backbone. Sometimes she came upon signs of traffic—boot-toe-sized steps kicked in a bank, a smooth place where the bark had been worn from a tree branch by the hands of people helping themselves up a steep slope. She hurried through these places, breathing hard. She made her winding but definite way toward the highest rise she could see, a hill whose contours she recognized from her map. From the hill's crest she believed she would be able to see where the land was creased by the stream, somewhere in band Y, in whose dry bed her father had left her uncle's camera.

✢ ✢ ✢

Laura had to call it a day before she reached the summit of the hill. She had been walking for eight hours by her watch, eleven counting the walk from Summerfort to the Whynew

Falls track. She had stopped several times to have a drink and a snack. But now she knew she must sleep.

She pushed her way into a stand of thorns and sat down on a patch of springy heath, unfastened her bedroll, and crawled into the bag of blankets. She lay on her side, munching on a few handfuls of trail mix, washed down with a mouthful of water from the copper spout of her water skin. She coated her lips with wax salve and put on her eye mask, then lay still and listened to the hushed flicker of the tiny leaves of the heath sifting down through the twigs beneath her bedroll. She heard the blood in her ears. She lay still, waiting for sleep to come over her; she lay secret and solitary under a tide of sleep.

The only dream she had was her own. She woke up and could recall only how it ended. In the dream Uncle Chorley had sent her out to see if her father was coming. When she reached the gate of Summerfort, her father had just turned up the track from the beach. She saw him against the evening light, his shoulders rounded and walk tired. She saw the moment he noticed that she was there, waiting for him—the moment he recognized her and picked up his pace, began to hurry to meet her.

Laura woke up knowing she had dreamed something she'd seen, her father hurrying toward her, pleased to see her. She found that she was in tears again, weeping with grief and gratitude. For weeks she had been worried that a deeper sorrow was lying in wait for her—some sort of predatory, crippling sadness made of regret and guilt. She knew that she hadn't fully felt her father's loss—that loss had been absorbed into her global grieving for her old life, her home, Rose, her school routine, a time when all her decisions were made for her and she had only to go along with them. How *kind* of the dream to remind her that, when he saw her waiting for him, her father would hurry forward. Her father—who had gone, who had left her, but who, after all, had loved her.

✧ ✧ ✧

The stream, where Laura first came to it, was in a narrow gorge and bordered by tree ferns with slender trunks and startled tops. The fern fronds were limp and curled, as if they had died just a few days ago. Laura went down between the ferns, her hands skinning the trunks of their furry bark. She walked along the streambed, heading to her right, moving still farther from the main road and its traffic. She wasn't sure that this was the right way but thought it likely, given her father's constant questing after new dreams.

She walked for another hour, stepping from boulder to boulder. The gorge grew gradually shallow and opened out. The boulders became stones and the going easier. The vegetation changed too. There was scrub growing back from the bank and weeping willows at the edge of the streambed, willows with the occasional bare wand, leaves stripped away by the touch of passing human hands. The streambed flattened out, became a trench through fields dotted with thickets of gorse and tea tree. The stream had been the meandering sort and in places had undercut the bank so that blue clay showed beneath fringes of grassy turf, grass roots exposed to the air and the same color as the dry stalks above. Gleaming swaths of very fine river sand appeared between the stones. Laura made her way more quickly on this better surface. Eventually she stopped to drink, standing in the middle of the dry bed, where the vanished water had formed a smooth eel of silver sand.

When she lowered the water skin from her lips, she saw a gleam some distance ahead of her—the brass and oak legs of Chorley's camera, its black concertina lens and shining, lacquered crank handle. Her heart jumped, and her throat grew suddenly tense. Laura's training forced her to stand still at least to screw the cap back on her water skin; then she sprinted to the camera. It was lying just beyond a patch of disturbed sand, an excavation she jumped to reach it. She fell to her knees beside the camera and was for a moment completely still, staring at indentations in the sand under the camera's gathered legs, the imprints of the knuckles of a hand. Laura knew that her father's hand had made the mark when he laid the camera down.

She didn't want to disturb his signs. For a moment she knelt, her hands pressed to her mouth, rocking. Then she took a deep breath and began carefully brushing sand from the box, which she hoped contained an undeveloped film. She knew what to do—she would make sure her hands were clean, then would pull her oilskin over her head to form a tent above the camera while she unwound the wing nuts on its case, opened it, and retrieved the film without exposing it to the light. But first things first. She sat back on her heels, unbuckled the flap on her pack, and found the film canister. She put it down carefully on her knees and thrust her sandy hands under her coat and into her armpits to wipe them clean.

Something moved in the shadow of the overhang on the bank nearest her. Laura started—then instantly recognized the movement, or explained it to herself, as an earth fall, the bank giving way.

Then, suddenly, she was up and running.

The earth hadn't fallen, it had collected itself and stood up out of the shadow.

Laura rushed across the stream. She jumped at the far bank, and caught hold of two handfuls of grass. They came away in her hands, roots and all. She fell backward but onto her feet. She dodged the gray, blurred bar of an arm—an arm!—that snatched at her as she scrambled away again. The sand, a welcome softness after her long tramp on hard earth, was now treacherous; it yielded behind her boots, offered no resistance from which she could spring away from the thing that was chasing her.

She looked back, saw a huge, heavy, glittering mass looming after her, moving forward with great fluid strides. Laura screamed and veered for the bank again. She ran at a ramp of fallen sand and tufts of turf. She waded up it, then lunged at the lip of the bank. Her feet came down on the edge. She saw a crack appear before her. A seam of grass roots ripped open, the lip broke off, and she was dumped back in the streambed.

There was no air between her and the monster, no open space. Laura scrabbled along the raw earth of the undercut bank, then was cut off by more earth—earth in motion and in the shape of an arm. The monster set its arms on either side of her body with a thud that shook the bank and sprinkled her face with gobs of turf. The creature's chest loomed above her like a stone lid. She saw the grains of sand on its torso seething like smoke, rearranging themselves into the shapes of muscles under skin. She screamed again and turned her head. "No!" she howled, and "Please!" She closed her eyes.

She was sitting in a warm puddle. Her bladder had let go, and the urine had pooled on the inside of her oilskin. Laura moaned and whimpered, now only able to make inarticulate sounds. Then she broke out again, as a rodent cornered by a cat will, alternately bolting or frozen in fear. She battered at the arms and chest and felt her hands sink into the yielding, sandy stuff, then—horrible—the sand come to life and consolidate to force her fists out of it. She screamed and thrashed until she was covered in sand. It seemed she was buried in the creature itself. She fought to a standstill and was still miserably conscious, gasping for breath, gagging on sand, spitting it out of her mouth.

Once she was quiet, the monster released her, only hovered again, hemming her in. Laura lay motionless. She gave herself up—but then nothing further happened. The monster was there, still and silent. Waiting.

After a time Laura stirred. She looked up at the monster's arms, to see if there was a chink it might let her slip through. Then she shortened her focus to look at the tombstone lid of its chest again. It didn't move. It let her make these slight movements.

Finally, Laura looked up into its face.

It was a lopsided, lumpish face—and very solemn. The sand and clay from which it had been formed was crusty and uneven, and stained red, as though mixed with blood.

Laura saw that the monster was watching her and waiting for something. She saw letters scored into its sandy forehead. Three letters: "N-O-W."

Now she was finished, Laura thought. *Now* she had gone too far, asked too much. She had struck out on her own at last, and *now* she was going to get it.

Laura cowered from the creature. "Don't hurt me," she begged. "Please. Please let me go."

The monster simply watched her and waited.

Then a thought came to Laura, as cool as rainfall—a memory, a song.

> *The final measure is his Name.*
> *Four letters, and four laws.*
> *The first gives life, the last speech,*
> *though they are the same.*
> *Two letters remain within,*
> *death and freedom.*
> *Make his name his Own and he is.*
> *If your Will departs he will.*

Laura remembered her father, the last time she had seen him, at Sisters Beach Station. He had said, "Those are capitals. Name, Own, Will, Name."

She remembered the song, and her father's words. She stared at the letters on the monster's forehead, and her right hand drifted up toward them. It was as though her hand had a mind of its own. She stretched out her forefinger, and for a moment, in the spell of her terror, she nearly used it to erase the "W" in "NOW." But as soon as her fingertip touched the letter Laura understood that erasing the "W" wouldn't make the monster disappear. She somehow knew that it would remain invulnerable till she had completed the spell that made it. Understanding seemed to rush down her finger, hand, arm, and fill her body. She simply knew that there was a "NON," an *end* to the spell, but first she must supply a second "N." A final letter, which—the song said—would give speech.

Laura wrote with a trembling hand on the creature's forehead. She knew as she did so that she was opening her father's Will. For, as she altered her father's handiwork and added to his spell, she experienced a deeper form of recognition. Some kind of music—more than the remembered song—flowed from her into the sandman. A soundless music made of calculations. The single letter formed by her fingertip was—she knew—a compressed phrase of information, instructions, laws.

Laura lowered her hand. The word, the name on the sandman's forehead, now read "NOWN."

The sandman moved. It sat back on its heels and then knelt before her. In a low, harsh, arid voice the sandman said, "Laura Hame, I am your servant."

4

✥ ✥ ✥

*L*AURA HAD NO SPARE TROUSERS, AND NO WATER IN WHICH TO WASH. SHE SHRUGGED OFF HER COAT, abandoned it, and sat in a patch of dry sand some distance from the creature.

She watched it. It didn't move but turned its head to watch her in return. She saw that while the front of its body and its face were, in their texture, like the crudely clawed together sand around the excavation, from the *back* the creature was shapely and statuesque. Laura wondered whether the sandman had been formed like the sculpture she and Rose had made for the Sisters Beach sand-sculpting competition. If so, then only its face and the front of its body would have been formed by its maker's hands. And, she thought, perhaps the creature's back bore the stamp of the spell alone, not its maker's hurried efforts.

Its maker—her father. When Laura had opened her eyes and read the monster's name, she had recognized it from a song her father had taught her. And when she had finished her father's spell, it was as though she had heard his voice, singing a music made of calculations.

Laura pulled her pack to her and put it on. She crouched over the camera and picked at the wing nuts with weak fingers. Her body was still trying, though only by reflex, to complete her task and carry her out of there, away from the creature. She was crying. Her corded velvet trousers clung, clammy, at the backs of her thighs. She fiddled ineffectually with the camera, then stood up.

For long moments Laura simply looked at the sandman. Then she said, "Come here," and as it got up and moved toward her—with heavy, thumping steps and a dry hiss of sand on sand—she backed away. She pointed at the camera. "Pick that up," she said.

The sandman stooped, like something being poured. It seized the camera, and the tripod's splayed legs closed together with a "clop." The sandman swung the camera over its shoulder.

"I want you to walk ahead of me," Laura said. "Walk along the streambed." She pointed the way.

It moved ahead of her, and she followed. She wanted to keep it in sight.

❖ ❖ ❖

Laura didn't pause until she had reached the crest of the highest hill. She walked for hours, and her thighs were chafed and stinging.

"Go in among that brush," she told the creature—pointing at a stand of low trees. The creature pushed its way into them.

"Stop," said Laura. "Put the camera down."

It put the camera down, carefully.

"Sit," she said.

It sat, so she was able to sit too. Her head was swimming. She unfastened her bedroll from her pack and spread it out on ground that was gritty and covered in sinewy tree roots. "Nown," she said, naming the creature. "You can call me Laura."

"My dear Laura," said Nown.

Laura flinched. She told Nown not to say that. Then she told it to sit still.

It was sitting still. She didn't like to look at it. When it had spoken she had seen the back of its mouth, a shallow cave, without tongue or teeth or any physical equipment with which it could produce its voice—its harsh, low-pitched whisper. She knew she was looking not at a body but at a conglomeration of earth and magic.

Laura had to sleep. She was afraid to close her eyes, but her eyes were closing. She had slumped onto the bedroll. Her thighs were burning—probably breaking out in a blistered rash.

"We're hiding," she explained to the creature. "You must be very quiet. People may come."

"There are no people," the creature said. "Or I would see them. People are very easy to see here. Only people burn. Everything else is dead. The trees give off no soft fire. People shine through the dead forests and grasslands. If there were people, I could see them. Someone has stopped here before. They have dropped the salt of their fire. They have dropped waste."

Laura listened to this. Her eyes had closed. She felt herself slipping, felt herself melt her way through the surface of sleep, felt the world turn from solid to liquid grease around her. She was afraid of Nown, so before she lost consciousness she said to it, "Don't hurt me."

✧ ✧ ✧

Laura slept for a long time. When she woke she found that, at least, her trousers had dried. Nown was sitting in exactly the same place and position, with the clenched legs of the camera inclined against him and its boxy head drooping behind his own. Laura bundled her bedding and scrambled up.

The sandman didn't get to his feet until she told him to. She told him to follow her and set out.

On any journey in the real world, as often as not there would be something to welcome, the sun coming up over the eastern horizon perhaps, or the heat going off the day. In the Place there was only a sense of covering a distance to reach a goal, either In or out. Laura and her servant moved across the landscape, leaving a trail of broken grass in their wake.

Laura was in shock. All she was able to do was head back to the border. She held to her original plan: to find out what was on the film her father had made and then decide where to go. There would be clues on the film to instruct her—Laura hoped. But instead of—or as well as—clues, her father had left her this. This creature coming after her with his steady, hissing gait.

It occurred to Laura that, having gone looking for knowledge, she should recognize it when she found it walking softly behind her. She understood that she should ask the sandman some questions. She paused to let him catch up with her. But as soon as she stopped, he stopped too.

They were on the lower slopes of a hill, winding their way through parched thornbushes. There was room for Nown to walk beside her, so she told him to. She didn't like him standing so near her but understood that she could, without embarrassment, tell him to keep up with her but maintain a certain distance between them.

When Laura had the sandman where she wanted him, she began to interrogate him. She said, "Were you waiting for me?"

"In the streambed?"

"Yes. In the streambed. Were you waiting there?"

"Yes."

"Is that what my father told you to do?"

This time Nown answered at once, readily, "Your father

told me to chase a spying ranger, and find out who had sent him."

"So you chased him—the poor man?"

"He ran fast, and he wouldn't tire."

Laura said, "Do you know you killed him?" As soon as she said it she realized that in fact, they were talking about the ranger who had been killed when he appeared on the road right in front of the Sisters Beach coach.

Nown didn't answer her.

Laura wanted to know what sort of creature he was. How dangerous he was. What he was capable of. So she probed some more. She asked him, "Do you not *mind* that you killed him?"

Nown was still silent. After a while Laura looked at him—an impassive object. She said, "I asked you a question. Why don't you answer me?"

"I was considering your question," he said.

"And your answer is?" she demanded, feeling a little thrill of power.

"I wasn't told to kill the ranger."

"Then it's lucky for you that you *didn't*," Laura said. Then she explained to the sandman how the ranger had been killed when he had stumbled out in front of the coach.

They walked on for a time in silence. Laura weighed the sandman's silence, his hesitation before speaking. She looked on his silence as a guilty one, then she looked on it as puzzlement. Then she tried to see it as profound consideration.

Laura tried to come up with another question. She needed to think about the way Nown expressed himself as much as the answers he gave. She asked, "Are you *glad* that you didn't kill him?"

Nown was silent.

"Are you considering my question again?" she asked.

"Yes," he said.

She wondered whether he was stupid. Slow, obdurate, and earthy. Then she thought about what he'd said earlier, when he was trying to explain to her how he knew there were no other people about. She said to him, "How do you know the difference between the forests here, in the Place, and the way that forests are *supposed* to look if you've only ever been here? You *have* only ever been here, haven't you?"

Nown said, "I am the eighth of myself."

"Do you mean that you are the eighth Nown?"

He didn't reply.

"Were none of the others called that? Nown?"

"No one has ever called me Nown."

"But that's what it says." Laura pointed at his face, the four capital letters scratched into the sand above his brow bone. Then she realized that she had been saying "noun"—like "noun, verb, adjective," not like "known" without its silent "K." She asked Nown whether he remembered what the other sandmen had done. He told her he did.

Laura thought about this. She asked, "What did people call those others?"

"Servant."

"Who were they, the people?"

"Hames. The Hames who could sing true."

When she had touched the sandman Laura had felt an ancient, complex music in him. She was sure that she'd heard it before. Her father had been singing it the morning he left Summerfort. He was, Laura remembered, playing with the cold, glutinous oatmeal in his plate; he'd made an oatmeal face and was singing over it. He'd called the song "The Measures." He'd been practicing—practicing a spell, singing "true." And he'd made a point of mentioning all the songs his great-grandfather had wanted to pass on, and how foolish he'd been when he was young not to value them—his Hame inheritance.

Laura asked Nown, "Where's my father?"

"I don't know."

"He's dead, isn't he?"

"No," said Nown. "If he were dead, I would be undone."

Her father was alive. Laura said it to herself, over and over, "He's alive, he's alive." She was so happy that for a while she hurried, and Nown stumped along behind her, and the camera he carried rattled as he walked.

Laura wiped her eyes and looked at her servant. She wondered whether he could only answer the questions put to him, couldn't voluntarily expand on an answer. Then she recalled again that he had expanded his answer about the dead forests of the Place and the "soft fire" that plants and people gave off. He'd spoken as though he was explaining something surprising to *himself* as well as to her. Laura racked her brain for another question, one that might yield another telling answer. Then she had it. "Did you catch the ranger?" she asked.

"Yes."

"I thought so. He had sand in his mouth."

"He bit off my fingers."

"What were your fingers doing in his mouth?"

"He was eating a paper."

"A letter from Cas Doran?"

Nown said, "I don't know." And then he unfolded one of his hands from the camera's legs and touched his own chest. He began to work his hand slowly into his chest. This looked horrible, shocking, as though he had begun to scratch in a very private place. Laura told him to *stop it at once*. He withdrew his hand, returned it to the camera's legs. Laura watched this with relief, then remembered the camera. She asked Nown whether he had been with her father when he was making his film.

"No."

They walked along for a while without speaking. Laura kept

licking her lips in order to keep them moist and flexible enough *to* speak. She couldn't leave her servant alone. She had to worry at him. Again a sense of her own power came over her, like a wave of heat, like faintness. It was a new sensation to her, a physical sensation of force and weakness mixed together. Laura asked her sandman whether he had to do anything she requested.

"Yes."

"Anything?"

"Anything I am able to."

"And what would *stop* you?" she asked. "Scruples?"

"Oceans, high walls, strong locks, swift rivers."

Laura stared at him. She asked him what he would do if he didn't *have* to obey her.

"That I can't know," he said. He was quiet again, apart from the sound he made as he moved—almost the same sound Rose made when she was wearing her best silk pajamas and walking briskly—a silky susurration. Laura supposed he had finished his reply and was about to ask him another question, when he said, "I am not the one who need not obey you."

Laura went over this in her mind. *I am not the one who need not obey you.* "Who is the one?" she said, baffled. Was he talking about some other person? Or some other monster *she* might be able to make? Then Nown further surprised and puzzled her by making a remark, rather than merely replying to her question. "Perhaps you will introduce me to him," he said. "The one who need not obey you."

Laura found herself squinting at Nown. "Did you just make a joke?"

"I hope I made a prediction," Nown said.

Laura said that since Nown was supposed to *obey* her, she should at least be able to understand what he was saying. She was beginning to enjoy questioning him, as though it were a game they were playing. She was tired, but Nown was distracting her from her tiredness, and from the stinging rash under her trousers. She wished she had some Wakeful—but at least the conversation was keeping her going.

Then, dizzy with vanity, Laura asked him—this creature compelled by his nature to be wholly honest to her, and who, in the absence of her father, owed his existence to her—"What do you make of me?"

He didn't answer.

"Are you considering my question?"

"I am making sure that I am, truly, unable to answer you," Nown said.

Laura, peering at him, could see he was thinking. She could see thought in the busy swarming of the grains of sand in the sockets of his eyes. "I am thinking till I am sure that I *cannot* think of an answer," he added.

"So—you don't make anything of me?"

"I might," he said. "I can't say. It's not my business to make. I have been made. It seems to me a great step from being made to making."

"It's just a figure of speech, Nown," she said in exasperation. Then she thought that *that* was what he was, a figure of speech and sand. She tried again, this time saying, "I mean— what do you *think* of me?"

"I think you are tired," he said. "I think you are keeping yourself alert with this game of questions."

Laura felt that he was an adult and she was a child. She hated the feeling. Yet though she hated it, she had to admit that it was probably true. For Nown was a being who had been made eight times and could remember his earlier selves. He had appeared in time, in history, on eight occasions. He had lived with her distant ancestors. He must have experienced things, unimaginable things.

"Like *himself*," Laura thought. "*He's* an unimaginable thing." It was possible that the sandman might have been made only in emergencies and not *kept*. But still, he must have seen a great deal—and so he could make her feel like a child.

Laura's thoughts went on for a while gnawing at this least of their differences. She yawned and scrubbed her face with both hands. She sneezed—her feet and Nown's were raising dust as they walked, a dust made of dry earth and of the grass that disintegrated when they stepped on it. Then Laura thought of another question. She was tired, and it was vague, lazy, general. It was the sort of question that infants ask their mothers when they want to be talked to but have nothing to say in return. "What else do you think?" she said, then added, "About me?"

"I *see*," he said. "My mistress is walking beside me. I look at her, and she burns before me in a world in which everything else has lost its working heat. I see Laura Hame, the daughter of my maker, Tziga Hame. I see another Hame whom I must obey. I see another Hame, not so different from all of them."

"But a little different?"

"Younger. The first girl, who asks more questions. Who gives fewer orders. Who has not yet thought what I am good for."

Laura glowered, then yawned so hard that her jaw clicked. "So—what are you good for?" she demanded.

"I could carry you as well as the camera."

Laura actually flinched from him. Her heart began to hammer. "No," she said. "No, that won't be necessary."

5

✧ ✧ ✧

DESPITE THE FRESH DAY AND HARD FROST, THE GYMNASIUM AT FOUNDERSTON GIRLS' ACADEMY SMELLED as usual of sweat and sour dust. The gym was a big, echoing room with knotted ropes hanging from its high roof beams and all its walls lined with climbing frames. The windows were at the very tops of the walls, transoms operated by dangling chains, several of which were fouled in their pulleys. The day's earliest classes had stood in steaming huddles in their skimpy gym clothes till spurred into activity by their instructors and group captains. No one had minded the jammed windows, but by midmorning the gym was airless. The sun was cutting right through the upper third of the huge room, and a ceiling of warm air had begun to drop down at least to head height.

The girls were doing folk dancing, for exercise rather than for a performance. The hockey field was deemed too dangerous for play—till its frost-stiffened grass and frozen puddles were fully thawed.

Rose was in charge of one circle of dancers and was trying to persuade one of her classmates to be nice. Patty and Anne had had a falling out. Patty had a ball of candle wax and had molded it into a sheath around her right index finger—the only part of her body she would allow Anne to touch. Rose normally had no trouble sorting out this kind of thing, but she was having trouble today. The easiest option would be to find Patty another partner—but no one must be permitted to reject even pinched, prim Anne. Founderston Girls' Academy had a motto—*Fidelity, Equality, Justice*—and Anne was going to bloody get all that from Rose.

Rose coaxed Patty into handing over her wax thimble. Surely it was unhygienic for both of them, Rose argued. She took the wax to the wastebasket and came back to find that Anne was being danced around but that Patty had pulled down her sleeve to cover her hand. Rose held her breath and began to count.

She was saved from temptation to violence by the gym teacher, who called her name.

Rose went over to the woman, who was leaning on the piano, where Mamie—the most musical girl in the academy now that Laura had gone—was playing a country air. The gym teacher said, "Rose, could you climb up there and see if you can open a few more of those windows?"

"Sure," said Rose.

"Sprightly, sprightly!" Mamie said to Rose, obviously imitating the gym teacher's remarks about her own piano playing.

Rose smiled at Mamie, then edged her way through the spinning cogs of the two groups of dancers, reached the wall, and began to climb. She went up the center of a frame, where the varnish had been worn away from its timber rungs. She climbed into warm air, and then into the sunlight.

The windows were rheumy, coated with dust and crusted with cobwebs. But Rose didn't need to be able to see out of them. As soon as her face was in the sun, she was instantly happier. She perched on a windowsill covered in the corpses of flies and moths, and played with the window catch. She took her time and did some thinking.

Rose's teachers relied on her to take the lead and show other girls what they ought to do. No problem was beneath her notice. She was patient and firm, she would always find time and ways to talk the other girls out of silliness, or to help them articulate real problems to those who could solve them. She had been an advocate, had stood up beside others, steadied them when they had to explain themselves to house mistresses or to the headmistress. "Rose will go with you," others would say. It had been a great privilege—especially for a day pupil, a girl who hadn't shared everything with those who offered her their trust. But Rose's patience had run out. Why should she go on doing what everyone expected of her? Be nice to Patty, Anne, Jane, and so forth, and be obliging to teachers? Why should she? It seemed that the less *trouble* Rose was to the school, and her parents, and her so-called friends, the more they seemed to feel that it was perfectly acceptable to leave her *alone*.

Far below, the gym teacher called out, "Rose?"

"This chain is badly caught," Rose called back, "but I am making some progress with it." She bent her head, turned away into the light. She rattled the catch. Then, to her surprise, the window came open with an awful squawk, and its top whacked her on her forehead.

The teacher called up to her, "Oh, good, you finally managed it! You can come down now. You've only ten minutes to change."

Rose wondered what they'd all do if she refused to come down. But now wasn't the time to make experiments in rebellion. She wanted to find a mirror and look at her forehead to see if the window had left a mark.

She clambered down the frame and sprinted across the now empty gym into the noisy fug of the changing rooms. She pushed through the pink and pale bodies. Then she came to a baffled stop before her spot. There was a younger girl sitting on the bench under her clothes on their hook. The girl was holding Rose's laundry bag on her lap.

"Are you waiting for me?" Rose asked.

"For ages," said the child. "Miss wouldn't let me into the class. She wasn't *listening* to me. I'm late. Your father is waiting for you in the head's office." The child was peering at Rose with an expression of keen curiosity. "He's wearing driving goggles on top of his head and kind of stomping his feet," she added.

Rose stood still and frowned at this messenger. The school encouraged parents to make appointments. Of course, in an emergency any parent could appear and ask for his or her daughter to be pulled out of class. But normally Rose's father and mother would observe the school's protocols. Was there a family emergency?

Rose dismissed the messenger, stamped her bare feet into her shoes, stuffed the rest of her clothes into the laundry bag, and pulled her blazer on over her wool shirt and shorts. Then she sprinted out of the gym and through the school to the administrative building.

Rose's father wasn't in the head's office. He was standing in the open arch under the gatehouse. The porter was holding the gate open, and her father's car was parked by it. The sun had just looked over the roofs but had not gotten past the eaves of the building opposite. Her father was in shade still, and his head was haloed with a cloud of his breath. Rose reached him and touched his arm. She was worried to see how tense he looked.

He didn't acknowledge her touch but only walked through the gate, tipping the porter. He held his car door open for Rose. She got in, and he walked around and climbed in beside her.

"What is it?" she said.

"Where is Laura?"

Rose considered telling her father that she didn't know. She did stall. She said, "Why?"

"Rose!" He was angry, and very anxious. "We've had her landlady at Doorhandle let us know when she comes and goes. A week ago Laura was with us. But when she left Founderston, she *didn't* go back to Doorhandle. *A week*, Rose!"

Rose swallowed. Her father took this as further reluctance to report what she knew and leaned toward her, gripped her shoulder, and gave her a quick, hard shake.

"Ow!" said Rose. "Let go! Laura has gone to Sisters Beach, to go In at Whynew Falls and recover the film in your camera."

Chorley removed his hand from her shoulder and sat back in his seat, staring through the windshield with the expression of a man confronted by a frightening obstacle.

"Is Laura in danger?" Rose asked.

He didn't answer. He just reached across her and opened her door so that she could get out again.

"She's probably out by now, Da—resting at Summerfort. She told me she'd send me a wire. She made sure someone knew where she was. Me. I hope you don't think I should have told her not to go."

Chorley gave Rose a cold, bleak look.

"Look," Rose said. "Someone had to get the film out of the camera."

"Your mother was going to do that."

"When? It might hold clues, you know."

"Yes, we know."

"Well, why take so long about going In to get it?"

Rose's father didn't reply. He shut his eyes and shook his head.

"I wish you would tell me why you're so worried about Laura," Rose said.

"Tziga disappeared."

"It doesn't follow that you should be worried about Laura."

Chorley muttered something about Laura's "state of mind." It sounded pretty feeble, Rose thought.

She closed her door again. "Come on," she said. "I'm going with you. I'm sure I can be of *some* use."

Chorley opened his eyes again. He nodded to the porter, who was waiting to crank the car. The man stooped in front of the hood, cranked the motor, and the car rocked—he cranked again and the engine caught and ran. The porter stretched his back and gave them the thumbs-up.

As Chorley pulled away from the school gate he said to his daughter, "What did you do to your head?"

He had noticed. Rose felt a little less neglected. "There was a stuck window. I got whacked by the frame."

"Doesn't the Academy employ a caretaker?"

"Certainly. And since I'm not going to be a dreamhunter, I've apprenticed myself to him." Rose waited for her father to glance at her and then gave him a "you deserved that" look.

AFTER MIDNIGHT SUMMERFORT WAS
DARK AND STILL, GLITTERING UN-
DER A SEAL OF FROST. LAURA LET HERSELF
and her servant into the house. She lit a lamp and led Nown
to the kitchen. As he followed her down the hallway, Laura
looked back to see if he had trailed sand indoors, as Grace was
always telling her and Rose not to. She saw that his feet left
no mark on the floor, that the prints of her feet, damp from
the icy grass, were the only ones visible. It seemed that Nown's
sandy soles were thirsty and had mopped up any moisture. He
left nothing of himself behind.

In the kitchen Laura showed Nown the wood box. She
opened the iron door on the range, made balls of paper with
the yellowing pages of an old *Summertime Weekly*. She struck a
match and put it to the paper, then sprinkled wood shavings
on the first thin flames. Laura told Nown to keep the fire going. The wood range was a wet-back stove, and she hoped
that, in an hour or two, the fire would have heated enough
water for a bath.

Nown squatted by the hearth. Laura stood behind him, swaying with tiredness. "What am I going to do with you?" she said.

"You could send me to fight your enemies," he said.
Prompting her, she thought.

"I don't have any." Her head was swimming. She imagined

enemies, in silhouette, like shadow puppets. She imagined her sandman tossing them left and right. She had a little glimpse of what her life might be like if she asked Nown to throw his weight around.

"I think, for now, I should keep you secret," she said. She was too tired to think. And that was what her father, aunt, uncle, and teachers had always instructed her to do—"Use your head," "Be responsible."

Laura left the kitchen, found a blanket, wrapped it around herself, and went back to doze by the stove. She wasn't disturbed by Nown's movements as he went back and forth between the wood box and the range. After an hour, the moon cleared the steep hill at the eastern end of Sisters Beach and shone through the room's latticed windows.

Laura was hungry but unwilling to stir. She wondered whether she might be able to ask Nown to find something for her to eat. She imagined him buttering slices of bread and presenting her with a sandy sandwich. She laughed and opened her eyes.

Nown had the range door open and was using his hand as fire tongs, rearranging embers in order to put in more wood. The flame strained up through his fingers, didn't wrap them—it was as though the fire knew that there was nothing in him to satisfy its appetite. Nown stayed squatting by the open range, peering in at the flames.

Laura asked him what he saw. Was that fire at all like the "soft fire" of trees and people?

"It is brighter than creature fire," Nown said.

Laura asked Nown what else he saw; for instance, how did he make his way around obstacles that had no heat that he could see?

"I see spaces and shapes. Objects like myself manufactured by people, and objects nature has made." He touched one of the roughly hewn blocks of the hearth. "This stone is made of many things lying quietly together. But inside each thing, everything is in motion. Nothing is wholly solid."

Nown could see things that Laura could not. He could see *inside* the stone. She questioned him further and discovered that he couldn't see colors, that he had no idea what colors were. She tried testing him by pulling faces and asking him what he could see. She tried a smile, and what she hoped was a skeptical expression; she tried a frown, and a look of fear. He was able to guess most of her expressions. But Laura was determined to sort out, if not their *differences*, at least the things that she felt made her *superior* to him. She said to him, "A frown means what? A smile means what?"

Nown's impassive face changed—there was a perceptible upward flow in the smoky grains of sand. "A frown means you're frowning. A smile means you're smiling," he said.

Again Laura had the strong suspicion she was being teased. She frowned at him.

"But I will watch your face for frowns, Laura, if that is what you want," he said.

"You would do *well* to," Laura said tartly. "For now you can fetch me the cookie tin." She pointed at the pantry.

She watched Nown cross the room and thought that, even exhausted and numb as she was—even *surprised* by him—somehow *having* him seemed natural to her.

Nown came back and put the cookie tin into her hands. She took it from him but was staring past him at the cut-glass pantry doorknob. Was it her imagination, or had the glass clouded, marred by his abrasive touch? She got up to take a closer look, then lost her nerve—was she really ready to know that her servant could unconsciously destroy things at a touch? *No*—that was more than she needed to know right now. She decided that she must not confuse her servant, overburden him with trivial questions and instructions. It was important that he respect her, *and* her judgment.

She left the room, trailing her blanket but trying to look queenly. She called out to Nown to follow her. She led him upstairs. She showed Nown her room and told him to make a fire there—then remembered to add "In the hearth, please." She took the cookie tin into the bathroom, put the plug in the tub, and turned on the taps. She sat on the edge of the tub and crunched her way through five dry vanilla wafers.

The bathroom filled with steam. Laura closed, then locked its door.

The steam formed skeins, seemed to bale itself up near the ceiling. Condensation appeared on the insides of the bathroom windows, and droplets ran, zigzagging, down their bobbled glass.

Laura shed her filthy clothes. She kicked them into a corner. She stepped into the hot water, sat, then slid down. She left the taps running for a while, and the water chimed in a rising tone as the bath filled to its rim. Laura floated down the bath and turned the taps off with her toes. She submerged her head, then came up for a breath and rested her head on the tub's rim while water drained, sizzling, out of her short hair.

She managed to eat another wafer, this time dipping it in her bathwater, then draping it—a wafer-shaped paste—onto her tongue. She thought of the open door of the kitchen range—she hadn't told Nown to close it. She thought of the camera on the kitchen table—she hadn't thought to ask Nown to carry it upstairs. Her thoughts were fragmentary and helpless, her limbs heavy in the hot water.

✧ ✧ ✧

When Laura woke up, the bath was still warm, but only just. She woke abruptly, slipped down in the water, then lifted her head to listen for a noise she was sure had woken her. She tried to sort the sound out—whatever it was—from the wash and slap of the little waves her sudden movement had made in the bathwater. She was looking up at the ceiling and saw the swinging squares of pebbled light appear there as the headlights of a car swept across the glass of the bathroom windows.

Summerfort was nowhere near the road—the car must have come up its driveway.

Laura held her breath. She sat up in the lukewarm water and listened to the still house, the wintry grounds. She heard car doors slam, and then the latch on the front door making its familiar musical rattle.

Laura flung herself out of the bath, slipped and slithered across the bathroom floor to the wicker cabinet where towels were kept. She grabbed a towel and draped it over her shoulders. She fumbled with the lock on the door. The bolt was slippery with condensation. It gave way suddenly, and she skinned a knuckle. She opened the door and looked around it. She saw lamplight, and the crown of her cousin's glossy golden head appear—Rose was coming up the stairs.

Laura dashed down the hallway to the door of her bedroom. Rose had reached the top of the stairs. She saw Laura and called out to her. Their eyes met. Rose looked relieved. She was holding a lamp but raised her other hand to gesture— she seemed to be saying something about Laura's towel. Then she turned and spoke to someone over her shoulder. It was Uncle Chorley, of course.

Laura wrenched opened her bedroom door, went into her room, and leaned against the door to close it. She stayed there, a puddle of water forming around her feet.

Nown was standing by the fire. When she came into the room, he turned and looked at her. In the firelight his eyes were hidden under the deep shadow of his gnarled forehead.

There was *no lock* to Laura's bedroom door. She gripped the doorknob in her slippery hand and held it closed. Rose was now on the other side. "Laura?" she said.

"In a minute," said Laura.

"Rose? What is it?" Uncle Chorley was there too. That was his hand slapping high on Laura's door.

"Go away," said Laura.

She panicked. She abruptly released the doorknob and crossed the room in several bounds, leaving her towel behind her. Then she was next to Nown, beside the fire, its flames warming the water on her chilly skin. For a moment she was closer to her servant than she had been since he'd cornered her. He was looking down at her with calm expectation. All the fine, crystalline river sand in his form was alive in the firelight—*alive!* Laura was quick. She put up her hand and caressed her servant's forehead. She did what she had known how to do since she'd first touched him. She didn't think of what she wanted, or "Will it work?" but simply acted on the information she'd gleaned from that touch. She erased the "W" in his name.

Nown collapsed with a gentle, mineral sigh.

The door burst open behind Laura.

✧ ✧ ✧

When Rose came into the room, she saw Laura's towel at her feet. She picked it up and carried it over to her cousin, held open, ready to drape her. Before dropping the towel onto her cousin's shoulders, Rose turned back briefly to her father in the doorway. She frowned at him and made a little movement with her fingers, sweeping him away.

Rose's father had frozen, his mouth open. Rose was angry with him, and embarrassed on Laura's behalf. She wished he would just take the hint and step out of the room. Her father hadn't quite caught up with the fact that she and Laura were young ladies now.

Rose turned her attention back to her cousin. She settled the towel around Laura, meaning to mask her breasts and backside, and then to dry and warm her. It was only then that Rose saw that her cousin's face, shoulders, breasts, stomach, and thighs were coated in sand, as though a blast of wind had blown it at her. She saw that Laura was standing up to her ankles in a mound of sand. She saw that Laura's hand was raised at the level of her head, and that Laura's fist was clenched, as though she had been knocking on an invisible door.

Rose took a step back. She stared at the mound. The sand was mostly smooth but was in places mealy with lumps of clotted clay. She saw, peeking out of the pile, what looked like fingers of a clenched clay hand.

Chorley came up beside his daughter, then he touched his niece's arm. Rose stepped forward again, so that she and Chorley flanked Laura. They began to try to talk to her. They spoke over each other.

"Laura?" said Rose.

Chorley said, "Take a hold of your towel, dear."

"Are you all right, Laura?" Rose said.

"What is all this?" said Chorley, pointing at the floor.

Rose didn't understand what her cousin was up to; she simply helped Laura hold her towel.

Laura's eyes slid sideways. She looked at her uncle. She looked wild and furtive, then she dropped onto her knees and began to scrabble through the mound. Perhaps she had seen something. Something buried in the sliding mass of silver. She was moving the sand around with all the messy diligence of a digging puppy. It was Chorley who first saw what Laura was looking for. He saw the corner of an envelope sticking out of the sand. He bent and picked it up. Laura jumped to her feet, dropped her towel, and made a snatch at it. Her sandy skin rasped against her uncle's clothes. Chorley reeled back, holding the envelope up over his head.

"Give that to me!" Laura said.

Chorley held off his niece with one arm, brought the envelope down to his eyes, and shook the sand from it. The letter was addressed in Tziga's hand—"Laura," it said. The letters of her name were faint, the ink scratched away, the surface of the envelope itself distressed and furry—as though it had been rolling around in sand. But since the letter was addressed to Laura, Chorley surrendered it to her.

As Laura waded out of the mound, clutching her letter, one of her feet hooked free another paper. Laura didn't notice it, but Rose picked it up. Laura went over to her bed and wound herself up, sand and all, in her eiderdown. She tore her letter open. Chorley watched his niece's eyes go back and forth, climbing down the page, reading. He became aware of Rose beside him, making crackling noises as she unfolded the other piece of paper. He looked over her shoulder at a large fragment of a letter. He and Rose read,

> . . . It is reasonable to suppose that he will attempt to enter the Place on a quiet section of the border, and without registering his intentions at a rangers' station. Follow him and find out where he goes.
>
> And—this cannot be stressed enough—do not sleep when, or where, Hame sleeps.

Chorley was surprised to hear his daughter saying, under her breath, "Yours, Cas Doran, Secretary of the Interior." Then Chorley thought of the fragment of paper he'd found in the mouth of the man run over by the Sisters Beach stagecoach. The fragment had read: "ours as D ecre." The paper Rose was holding was another piece of the letter whose partial signature he had pulled from the sand-stuffed mouth of that dead ranger, nearly four months ago, on the day that he last saw Tziga.

Rose understood more than *he* did, Chorley realized. He and Grace had been protecting their daughter from knowledge she already had. She'd been keeping secrets—not her own, perhaps, but Laura's.

Chorley tried to catch his niece's eye. He said, "What does your father have to say?"

Laura looked up from the page only to say, "*Get up.*" She appeared to be speaking to the mound of sand. She said, "Pull yourself together." Then she laughed, a ragged, unhappy sound.

✦ ✦ ✦

"My dear Laura," the letter began. Laura, reading it, heard Nown speaking, not her father. "My dear Laura," Nown had said. Later she had seen him working his hand into his chest— to fetch out this letter, she now knew. The letter had lain against his heart, or had lain inside his chest alone, instead of a heart. Laura had asked Nown about her father—she had requested information, and Nown had reached for the letter. *If only*, she thought.

My dear Laura,
Please excuse this clumsy scrawl. I haven't much time, and my hands are hurting me. I'm writing only to tell you what I must.

I've made a mess of things. I'm afraid I intend to leave my mess for you to tidy up—a shameful thing for any father to do.

Laura, you must listen to what the Place tells you, what it will tell you if it speaks to you as clearly as it has to me since the beginning. I wasn't ever prepared to listen to it. I should have let it make something of me— what it needed me to be. Instead, I took what I wanted from it. I really always knew that the Place wanted me to do something for it. What I wasn't able to understand was that it was warning me, warning me what I must not *do.*

Laura, I've made terrible mistakes. I don't want to tell you what I've done because I know that, if I try, I will betray myself even further by defending my actions when, in fact, they are indefensible. Indefensible and unspeakable. Can you blame me if I can't speak about it? But see—I am defending myself. Maze Plasir, who is as guilty as I am, would not try to make excuses for his part in our crime. Plasir, it turns out, is a more decent man than I am.

This is my excuse, Laura—for the little it's worth—I loved your mother for too long before she consented to be my wife. I loved her too much, till it wasn't love, till it was only excessive sentiment and miserable longing, as lonely a habit as habitual drunkenness.

I must stop this. I must remember everything I have to tell you.

*Your aunt Marta knows "The Measures." It may be that you will find need of them, though I have given you someone—*this *someone. He will be able to help you, to carry you places where you wouldn't be able to walk on your own. His patience, his stamina, and his loyalty are infinite. I hope that you will make good use of him, and that his usefulness to you will make up for my failings.*

Laura, I have left you with a terrible task. But you need only do it once, if you do it properly. When you're ready, catch the dreadful dream. Overdream someone with the right-sized audience—your aunt in the Rainbow Opera. Pick the right occasion, then break and enter, break and enter their minds. Make them see that the dreams are ghosts. That the Place is a tomb—the tomb of the future.

Laura, love, I am so sorry for involving you in my ludicrous life.

Laura twisted the page in her hands and tucked them out of sight under the bedclothes. At that moment her confusion was the only reason she had for not answering her uncle's question, or simply handing over the letter.

Her father's last line was like the darkness following a lightning flash. The letter had dazzled her, but after she'd read it, only its final line stayed with her. She couldn't understand it. Laura was her father's child—had he involved her in his life? *Ludicrous.* What a word—it was too deflating, too bleak, too adult for her to understand. There had been a moment—a moment between Nown's collapse and this, when she thought she would get an explanation, receive instructions, be released from the lonely prison of her puzzlement. But Laura found her father's letter unfathomable. And she was *ashamed* of it.

"Well?" said Chorley. His voice sounded like a grating hinge.

Under the covers Laura had begun to tear the letter into pieces. Her uncle saw what she was doing and dived at the bed. Suddenly he had one corner of the paper, and Laura was rolling around over the other fragments, kicking, and slapping him with her free hand. She shouted at him. "It's *my* letter!"

Rose came to Laura's aid. She took her father by the arm and hauled him away. She yelled, "Let Laura keep it!"

Chorley shook his daughter off. He said to her, "She *isn't* keeping it, she's tearing it up! Why won't she let me *help* her?" Then, to Laura, "Why won't you trust me?"

Rose, seeing Laura in tears, began to cry too. Laura was still shredding the paper, tearing it into smaller and smaller pieces. "Da wouldn't want you to see it," she said to her uncle.

"Let *me* be the judge of that," Chorley said. "You're still only a child, Laura."

"You don't need to know." Laura shook flakes of paper off her ink-blackened fingers. She and her uncle stared at each other, each looking through tears on the other's anger, pity, and compassion. They didn't look away till Rose said, "Where did all this sand come from?"

IV
Open Secrets

1

✣ ✣ ✣

CHORLEY HAD TO LEAVE HIS CAR AT A GARAGE IN SISTERS BEACH. LAURA COULDN'T BE TAKEN BACK THROUGH RIFLE-man Pass, where, for her, the border was. So they caught the train. They went in their usual style and had a compartment to themselves.

Laura refused to answer their questions. After a time she found it easy to disregard them. She felt chilly and light-headed. Her hair hadn't dried properly after her bath, or her scalp was damp. She inclined her head into the padded corner of her seat and let her uncle and cousin talk. At one point she found herself telling her uncle a *story*. She said that her father had left her a sand castle—that he had built a sand castle in her bedroom at Summerfort. She'd only just found it. "It fell apart when you hammered on the door," she said.

Her uncle's face was like the reflection of the moon on water, pale and unstable. Laura couldn't seem to look at it properly. Chorley was reminding her that her father had been *dead* before they had left the house at Sisters Beach, two days after her Try. He said, "You're just being insolent, Laura."

Rose said, "Laura, when I asked where all the sand came from, why did you lie down on your bed and pull the covers over your head?"

Laura slid farther down the seat. She heard Rose say, "She has beads of sweat on her top lip. I think she's unwell, Da."

The seat beside Laura depressed as Chorley sat down. He prized her out of her corner and felt her forehead. Laura said to him she was going to have her dream about the mice—she always dreamed about mice when she had a fever, dear little mice running all over the place so that she couldn't lie down anywhere. Beneath her uncle's hand, her head felt like a teapot stowed under a cozy—something was brewing there. Rose seemed to be counting the stops between Sisters Beach and Founderston—but weren't they on the express? They were discussing where they might have the train stop. She heard Rose say, "Do you think she is very sick?"

"She's very hot. But I want to get her home. I'd rather not hand her over into anyone else's care."

"No," said Laura. She was agreeing with her uncle, she wanted to be taken home. She tried to explain that she was only tired because she'd walked so far. Her water was in her pack, wouldn't someone *please* give her water?

There was a little flurry around her, as if the mice had arrived. Then someone put a cup to her lips, and she took a few sips of cool water. Her teeth hurt. She heard Chorley say to Rose, "Do you have any idea what she's been up to?"

"I told you—she went to get the film from your camera."

The camera. Laura asked them had they remembered to collect it from the kitchen. "After all my trouble," she said. She saw Rose frown and slap her forehead. They had forgotten it.

Laura said she wanted to lie down. "Let me," she begged. Then she said, fearful, "*You stay over there. Stay where you're put.*" Then she called his name, "Nown!" and began to cry, and put her right hand—her writing hand—up into the curling column of the music that had appeared around her and was smoking away from her body, the music she had felt singing between Nown and her when she gave him his voice.

✣ ✣ ✣

A week later Laura's fever had gone, but it had left her as worn out as her ordeal of walking.

The doctor had been in that morning. Before he'd left her, she'd asked him to tell her aunt and uncle not to tax her with questions. He'd said he would do that for her, but in a few days she'd be as right as rain. He was the family's doctor and specialized, he'd said, in exhausted dreamhunters, but he was distressed to see one exhausting herself so *early* in her career. He had gotten up to leave and patted her foot under the covers. He'd said, "You'll be back on your feet in no time. If you're anything like your father, you're as tough as a bug."

Her illness and its dispensations couldn't last forever.

Rose appeared in Laura's room after lunch. She was flushed, as if she'd been running, and was wearing her school coat and hat. When she saw Laura looking at the coat, Rose took it by the lapels and gave it a little shake. "When Da went back for his car and the camera, I remembered to tell him to look for my coat." Rose came and sat on the end of Laura's bed. "They're sending me back to school. Da is developing that film—they mean to have a look at it tonight, I think. I'm being kept out of everything, as usual. I know you're not going to say much to them, but, Laura, you *are* going to talk to *me*, aren't you? They keep bushwhacking me—they told me the cab would come at two, but it's here already. I have to go. But—look—I figure that, if they're in such a hurry to send me away, then there's still something they're frightened of."

Laura grabbed Rose's hand. Then she had a fit of coughing.

"We only have a minute," Rose said. She looked over her shoulder at the door. Then she helped Laura sit up and gave her a sip of water. "Tell you what," Rose said. "You let me know what's on the film. Put it on a postcard. Then meet me a week from Wednesday, in the sculpture room at the Museum. That's ten days from now. That's when I have a day off." Rose leaned over Laura's pillow and kissed her.

"Bye," Laura rasped. "Wednesday week, the sculpture room."

✧ ✧ ✧

There was just over two minutes of film, showing, in ghostly black and white, the remnants of a burned building. A ruin sketched as if in black ink against—

"Is that water?" Chorley said to Grace.

"No, it's sand," Laura said.

"A dry seabed, I think," Grace said.

The first shot came to an end, then a second began, the same view, but the camera was unsteady.

"He's picked it up," Chorley said.

The camera turned, slowly rocking, through one hundred and eighty degrees, till it showed a range of gray hills.

"That's the view back the way he came," Grace said. "That's a kind of map."

The film came to an end, the projector flicking through what was left on the reel—Chorley's cataloging marks—and lighting their faces in flashes.

2

✢ ✢ ✢

*S*IX DAYS LATER LAURA WAS BACK IN
DOORHANDLE. SHE DROPPED HER
BAG AT HER BOARDINGHOUSE AND ASKED
her landlady to lay a fire in her room. Then she went out
again.

She ran along Doorhandle's plank pavement toward the
rangers' station. It was raining heavily. She ducked through
fountains that streamed from jutting downpipes. The duck-
boards were slippery, the spills of summer oozing out of their
timber—dog piss, liquor, horseshit, ice cream. The boards
seemed coated with saliva, not rain, a surface on which even
Laura's rubber-soled walking boots sometimes slithered. It
was dark; the guttering on all the verandas drooped and drib-
bled fringes of rainwater. There were no people or animals in
Doorhandle's streets, but still those streets were noisy with
drumming, splashing, splattering, never-ending rain.

By the time Laura reached the rangers' station, the rain
was through the shoulder seams of her coat. The station was
warm; its rooms were steamy and smelled of wet wool. It was
crowded, and everyone there seemed set to head In. There
were lines before the counter in the supply depot, and all the
customers were cradling ration packets and the bottled lime
juice they used to keep their water sweet. The shelves were
thinly stocked. The station had been like this for days, as

everyone who had the option of escaping the awful weather packed up and walked off into the only reliable dry place.

Laura didn't plan to go In that day. She would spend a night at the boardinghouse, climb into her bed, and listen to the rain on the iron roof of her gable room.

But first, she had to buy a special kind of map.

Laura already had a book of charts, what she was after now was a book of profiles. These books contained views of the landscape of the Place from the points of entry at Doorhandle and Tricksie Bend. The pages in books of profiles were made of semitransparent paper, so that the next view of hills appeared faintly through the view on the page before it, as it would to anyone shifting focus from the hills in the foreground to a range farther away. The profile books were essential to anyone who planned to penetrate deep into the Place. Because the pages were transparent, the reader had only to flip the book over and go back through it in order to plot a course out again. Each newly issued book of profiles represented the landscape of the Place for as far as anyone had journeyed In from either end. The latest issue—the one Laura wanted—was titled simply *Profiles: Seven Days In from Tricksie Bend*. She wanted to see whether she could plot a course to the dry seabed of her father's film using a combination of his shot of the hills back the way he had come and the landforms in a book of profiles.

The books were expensive items, and Laura had to join the line in order to ask for one at the counter. As she waited her turn, she looked around at the gathered rangers and dreamhunters. Even after all her trips In and her examinations, Laura wasn't quite used to the sight of this collection of thin, fit, brown, crop-haired people. They were the *other* family to which her father and Aunt Grace belonged. As Laura mused over this family likeness, she noticed a boy trying to catch her eye. He was a few bodies behind her in the line beside hers. He had been staring at her till she felt it and looked back at him.

He was the boy from the infants' beach, the one who had written out his name and address on the back of her copy of Maze Plasir's business card. Laura had lost Plasir's card and couldn't remember the boy's first name. She gave him a small smile of acknowledgment and looked away.

His line was shuffling forward faster than hers; he would soon be beside her. She racked her brain. His name was Mason. What Mason?

"*Sandy!*" Laura thought, and giggled with relief at the very moment that Sandy Mason fell into step with her.

"What's so funny?" he said, and grinned.

Laura told him she had only just remembered his name. "It's Sandy Mason, isn't it?"

"Alexander," the boy said.

"But you wrote 'Sandy' on Plasir's card."

The boy blushed. "Sandy isn't a good professional name," he said.

They reached the counter at the same moment. He deposited his armload of rations and watched carefully while the clerk added up the total. Laura paid for her book and an oilskin satchel in which to keep it. They came away from the counter, Sandy with his purchases in a flour sack, Laura with a sealed and wrapped package clutched to her chest.

Sandy licked his lips. He said, "Have you earned anything yet?" He was looking at the book longingly.

"No," said Laura. "But I am writing an article for the *Ladies' Journal*—'My Winter Dreamhunting.' "

"Really?"

"No," said Laura.

Sandy's blush spread up into his ears. "I suppose it *was* rather a rude question," he said.

"Yes," said Laura.

"Do you always put people on the back foot?" Sandy was clearly preparing to defend himself.

"Well—if it helps them get their other foot out of their mouth," said Laura.

For a moment they continued to stand dumbly in the middle of the store, clutching their purchases and getting in people's way. Then Sandy showed what he was made of by trying to continue the conversation. He said, "How are you, then?"

"Not bad," said Laura. "And how are you?"

"I don't know. Still Trying, it seems. I've been working at Pike Street Hospital, amplifying my uncle—I told you about him, the one who works with the surgeons, supporting the anesthetic."

Laura nodded.

"But apparently I am not 'opened' enough yet to be much of an amplifier. My uncle says I should spend a few months catching different things and 'opening' myself. He's sponsoring me, which makes it easier."

"Good," said Laura. "Plasir didn't seem to mind taking that boy unopened." A moment after she had said it, Laura realized that it could be taken two ways. Sandy looked shocked. She clapped her hand over her mouth, then apologized. "I was only trying to use your term—'opened.' I mean—I didn't mean anything else."

Some rangers went past them, one saying, "Excuse me," pointedly.

"We're in the way," Sandy said. He gestured with his chin at the door, beyond which was a wide veranda littered with umbrellas and covered in muddy footprints. Laura followed him out.

It was cold outside, and the street was uninviting beyond the veranda's beaded curtain of dribbling rain.

"I really didn't mean—you know," she said again.

"Good. For a moment I thought you were one of those girls who'll say anything for a laugh."

Laura, irritated again, said, "What *can* such girls be thinking?"

Sandy lost his temper with her. "You're impossible to talk to—you're so scratchy!"

"Well—if I agreed with absolutely everything you said, that would be scratchy too, believe me," she told him. "I had a friend like that. He was very accommodating—and very abrasive."

"You *had* a friend?"

"Amazing, isn't it?" she said, then, "He's gone now. But not because I was impossible to talk to."

"Do you mean your father?"

"Fathers aren't friends," Laura said, impatient.

"No, they're not. My father is more of an opponent. He made me wait two years past the legal age to Try. He set impossible conditions—which I met, actually."

"I thought you were nearer my age," Laura said, though she knew he was not. She didn't want him talking down to her.

"Do I *look* your age?" Sandy said. It seemed his disgust in her was complete. "No, I do not. I look as though I should be doing *better* already. I should be a brown-skinned veteran with specialty dreams and dedicated clients." He was shifting from foot to foot, a picture of frustration and impatience. He said he had a thirty-five-yard penumbra already, unopened, and his uncle should be working for *him* by now.

Laura was surprised. "Who measured your range?"

"The examiners. They do that. Didn't they give you your figures?"

"No, they didn't."

"They're supposed to. Why wouldn't they? You know, that was what was behind the trouble we had with that boy who went with Plasir. *Range*. After our examination he was nagging everyone else for their results, *their figures*. It was like the bloody changing sheds—" Sandy remembered he was talking to a girl and blushed again.

"That boy seemed to think he knew what Plasir wanted," Laura said. She was wondering about Plasir, whom she knew she'd have to talk to. Her father had mentioned Plasir in his letter. He'd implied that the dreamhunter knew things. Laura hadn't even begun to think how to approach the man.

The boy was saying, "Plasir's penumbra—his *range*—may be tiny, but he can overdream almost anyone."

Laura suddenly realized that there was a great deal she didn't know about differences in talent. Her father and aunt had almost always talked as if it was all a matter of *degree*—great and small. She tried to explain her thought to Sandy and then said, "You'll have to give me a full rundown, I think."

"Sure. But you know, it really isn't surprising that your father and aunt didn't go into a lot of detail. For them it was a case of *them* and everyone else. Your aunt's a split dreamhunter, as catchy as flu, and has a three-hundred-yard penumbra. And your father once overdreamed eight dreamhunters who all had his own Starry Beach, *and* on their first night with it. His penumbra was estimated at somewhere between three fifty and four hundred. He was a god, basically—if you don't mind me saying. Even if he only ever caught single-point-of-view dreams."

"I'm going In tomorrow to catch Starry Beach. I want to have a look at it," Laura said. She watched Sandy swallow and try to collect himself. He began to apologize. He said he realized that it might be hard for Laura to hear people talk about her father. She saw that he thought she had changed the subject because her feelings were hurt.

"My uncle is organizing a memorial service," she said. Then she put out her free hand and touched Sandy's upper arm. She had a moment of surprise at how little her fingers were able to encompass—how big his arms were compared with her own. Then she remembered she had meant to say something, had only touched him to get his attention. "Don't be sorry," she said. She removed her hand, and they stared out at the rain. After a time he told her that he'd taken a room at Mrs. Lilley's.

Laura's room was at Lilley's too—no surprise, really. Mrs. Lilley was the kind of landlady who kept an eye on her lodgers, so her house was often recommended to the parents of young dreamhunters. "Shall we go, then?" Laura said. She didn't wait for him but held her package over her head and darted down the station's steps and onto the plank pavement.

They arrived at the boardinghouse wet and breathless to find that another lodger was entertaining his parents in the parlor and Mrs. Lilley's daughters were setting the table in the dining room. They had nowhere to go but to their respective rooms. Laura noticed that Sandy seemed to feel he had to make something up to her. He climbed backward up the stairs in front of her, beginning several sentences, clutching his side—he had a stitch from their run—and getting nowhere.

Laura interrupted him. "Do you have a fire?"

"No," he said.

"I can give you some coals in my warming pan," she said. She unlocked her room, left the door ajar and him outside—mindful of the house rules, which said that there were to be *NO visitors in lodgers' rooms at ANY hour.*

Laura took the warming pan from its hook and used the poker to roll some coals out of her fire. She called Sandy in to pick the pan up. Then, as he hesitated in the doorway, she said, "My feet are wet. I want to change before tea."

"Dinner," said Sandy, taking the warming pan.

"Dinner at teatime," Laura said.

"And there's the difference between us," he said. "You're used to having *tea* while I am having my *dinner*."

Laura told him to go away. She closed the door on him and sat on her bed to remove her wet boots and socks. She put her boots on the hearth and hung her socks from the mantel by placing her parcel on their tops. She was feeling irritated but happier. She'd been preoccupied with her big problems—her father's letter, what he had meant, whom she might confide in once she *understood* what he meant—so was grateful to be presented with a minor puzzle, Sandy Mason's behavior.

Sandy was as displeased and contrary as Rose could be when things weren't going well for her. Most of what Laura said seemed to offend him, yet he also seemed troubled if she let him know he'd offended her. He seemed to want to prove to her that his *manners* were better than hers. Or if not his manners exactly, then his morals. Sandy thought he was somehow *better* than she was, more mature, more realistic. All his carrying on seemed to imply that, since she wasn't trying to make money, she was only playing at being a dreamhunter, perhaps in an effort to make herself appear more substantial to herself. Perhaps he thought that she was some kind of dabbler—and that it was significant that she came from a household where dinner was served at eight. But, Laura decided, she would let Sandy think what he liked. He could imagine she was a posh girl with a hobby if he wanted to. Laura didn't like being alone—when she was alone she felt all bent out of shape by her burdens. Squabbling with Sandy Mason made her feel human, nearly as human and alive as she had felt while asking her sandman questions.

IN THE MORNING THE RANGERS AT THE BORDER POST BEYOND DOORHANDLE WERE HAVING TROUBLE WITH SOME youths throwing stones. They were locals who had decided to alleviate their cabin fever by harassing rangers. They had hidden themselves in some bushes by the roadside a little way beyond the stone cairn. In fact they had removed some stones from the cairn as ammunition and were now throwing them at anyone who came near the landmark.

The rangers couldn't catch them, couldn't get past the border without crossing over Into the Place. Stones were sailing through the air at them from a spot only twenty yards away—a spot along the everyday road—where they couldn't ever walk. The rangers had sent someone to the sheriff's office for help and were loitering around just out of range, with a gathering of dreamhunters intent on going In that morning. The dreamhunters were feeling the cold. It was still raining, and they had umbrellas, but they had left their heavy winter coats back in their rooms since they wouldn't need them once they were across the border.

Time passed, and the gathering of dreamhunters clustered under their umbrellas like mourners at a rainy graveside. There was no sign of the sheriff. Doorhandle was having a delightful moment—letting the employees of the Dream Regulatory Body, who had virtually taken over the village ten years before, feel *its* power for a change. The news of the stone throwers made its way back to the shelter, so the dreamhunters who had been filling in their intentions stopped there, where there was a fire in the stove. They waited to hear that the problem had been sorted out, the culprits chased off or collared.

The rangers near the cairn were therefore quite surprised to see a couple of dreamhunters come scampering up the road after word had been sent to the shelter and the flow of people stemmed. They were more surprised when the two rushed past the tortoise back of joined umbrellas and ran on, headlong, toward the cairn. The two had their packs held up over their heads. When stones began to fall around them, making pockmark splashes in the mud, the big one, the boy, pushed the girl behind him. They continued on that way, like an engine and its carriage, into the shelter of the cairn. They crammed together there, laughing. The boy picked up a stone from the cairn and tossed it into the bushes. It was answered by a furious volley. Stones clapped and thumped on the far side of the cairn. The two put their heads together and had a consultation. They filled their hands with stones. The girl ducked out into the road, threw her handful, then dived through the space beyond the cairn and vanished. Stones splattered into the puddles where she had been. The boy poked up his head, feinted, provoked another volley of stones, which he ducked. Then he jumped to his feet, threw his handful, and plunged through after the girl.

There was a burst of clapping from the watching dreamhunters. Others were inspired to make a dash for it, and after a few more minutes the wet road was pimpled by flung stones and littered with mangled umbrellas.

✛ ✛ ✛

When the last of their followers had overtaken Sandy and
Laura, greeted them, and hurried on in squelchy shoes, they
found themselves alone. Their jackets steamed, and their
dripping pants legs left trails of clotted dust behind them on
the road.

Sandy had asked Laura that morning whether she minded
if he went along with her. He'd felt surprised—and surprisingly happy—when she said she'd welcome his company.

They walked to where the road forked, into road and
track—the track beaten and scoured of dead grass. There was a
sign on a tree; it told them they were only an hour from
Starry Beach.

"I set my alarm and got up really early," Laura said. She
stretched and yawned. "I'm ready for a nap."

Sandy had kept himself up late. He'd read old issues of the
Founderston Monthly Illustrated that Mrs. Lilley kept in piles in the
hall. He had searched the magazine's pages for any mention—
or better, any pictures—of Hames and Tiebolds. The whole
time he had been skimming and swooping, Sandy had felt he
was studying for an exam. In what subject he didn't know.

He had already done the Hames in history. He knew—for
instance—that they were one of five families who had come to
the country from the island of Elprus after a volcanic eruption. The Elpra who crossed the seas all settled in Founderston—then a jerry-built settlement around a fort and river
port. They were welcomed for their highly cultivated skills in
silk making—and for the relics, the bones of St. Lazarus. The
relics were housed in the Temple. The islanders stayed together as a people in the streets they built in what, over one
hundred and fifty years, came to be known as Founderston's
Old Town. In fact, up until eighty years before Sandy was
born, the Old Town was predominantly peopled by the dark-
skinned, curly-haired people—people named Hame, Tuce,
Vail, Zarene, or Bartholem. It would be still, were it not for a

cholera epidemic and the two contaminated wells in the Old Town, which caused more than half the epidemic's deaths.

The Tiebolds were another story. Sandy had encountered plenty of Tiebolds in his history courses at school. They were impossible to miss; the histories were full of them, sometimes scoundrels but usually worthy citizens. The family appeared as politicians and soldiers, scientists and churchmen—the current Grand Patriarch, Erasmus Tiebold, was a cousin of Chorley Tiebold's father.

Of course, the most *famous* Tiebold was, in fact, a Tiebold by marriage. Grace Cooper was only eighteen when she first entered the Place and discovered she could catch dreams. Her father owned a tobacco shop, and her family hadn't the resources to rent rooms, and so Grace was at a loss how to sell what she caught. But she had always been an avid reader of the social pages, and it was her knowledge of who was who in society, of the habits, hobbies, and tastes of the rich—as reported in *Founderston Monthly Illustrated*—that helped her form an idea.

The story Sandy had heard was this: Grace Cooper had turned up one day at a famous dressmaker's when a certain racy lady of fashion was there for a fitting. The dreamhunter told this perfumed person, "This is what I can do for you." She was invited to turn up at a house party at the woman's country place. The woman said to Grace, "You shall be my rabbit in the hat."

On her first night in the country house, full of a dream she had caught only two days before, and ready to sleep deeply— because she had deprived herself of sleep in order to keep the dream fresh—Grace lay down and filled forty rooms with her dream. The guests found themselves fleeing cross-country, night and day, as two lovers pursued by enemies who wanted to keep them apart. Grace set the sleepers afloat in boats down dark streams fringed by bulrushes. She laid them down in an embrace in the sweet damp summer grass. Some of the male guests found themselves in the head and body of the woman as she watched her lover defy their pursuers, filled with fear and admiration for him. Some female guests found themselves in the mind and body of the man as he lay over his lover touching her tenderly and gazing into her face. Some sleepers moved from one to the other. And all woke moved, refreshed, excited by their thoughts and their bodies. They could talk of nothing else all the next day. It was beyond anything that any of them had experienced, or even heard reported.

At breakfast their hostess pulled her rabbit out of the hat—she introduced her guests to her young dreamhunter. Grace Cooper was an overnight sensation. From then on she was very much in demand in certain circles, at some houses, though it must be said that there were mothers who would keep their daughters away from any house at which Grace Cooper was to be a guest. Grace was the toast of—as the newspapers said—"the fast set." Grace Cooper and her dreams were disturbing to polite society in a way that Maze Plasir was not. Plasir conducted his business with privacy and discretion, and could only project his dreams into rooms right next to his own. Grace Cooper, despite the frivolous content of her dreams, had powers of projection rivaled only by those of Tziga Hame. When she dreamed, her dream was shared by as many people as could be packed in comfort into some two hundred square yards of space. Many people tasted her dreams, and her influence was great. For instance, it was for Grace Cooper that the first dream palace, the Rainbow Opera, was built. Shortly before the Opera was completed, Grace Cooper had married the dashing, but debt-laden, Chorley Tiebold.

Yet as Sandy walked along beside Laura, this Tiebold-Hame, he wasn't feeling too starstruck. In fact he felt he could be of some use to Laura, who had been a sheltered schoolgirl up until only a few months ago. There was so much that Laura didn't know and should, Sandy thought. She had become a dreamhunter naturally, but haphazardly. Her father and aunt hadn't bothered to explain the life, had possibly only ever talked about it in a vague, self-glamorizing way. Her father may even have hoped she wouldn't become a dreamhunter—the fact that she had attended Founderston Girls' Academy suggested quite different ambitions. Laura Hame was dabbling, wasting time and money, buying the texts like a good schoolgirl, wearing the correct uniform, but—to Sandy Mason's mind—she was adrift. After all, what had she said about catching Starry Beach—that she wanted to "have a look at it"? As though the Place was a big store and she was a lady of fashion out shopping with a fat purse.

"So," Sandy said, breaking into the perfect, uncanny silence of the Place, "you want to catch Starry Beach to 'have a look at it' but not to sell it?"

"There's something I want to learn."

"About Starry Beach?"

Laura said, "Have you ever shared it?"

"No. I told you, I come from south of the Corridor. I only shared dreams once I came north to stay with my uncle."

Laura nodded. Then she seemed to decide to confide. "In Starry Beach the friends around the bonfires wonder about a line of lights moving through the forest on the hills above them. I caught a dream where I was *among* the lights on the hill. My dream was a reverse view of Starry Beach. Starry Beach is a healing dream, and my dream was a nightmare. I guess I'm just checking all the angles."

Sandy was perplexed. "You mean," he said, "you want to know what the two dreams *mean* in relation to each other?"

"Yes."

"That's a very strange approach to dreamhunting."

Laura shrugged.

"And that's your plan?" he said. He thought she was very odd—one of those people with an impractical amount of intellectual curiosity.

"Ah," she said. "My *plan*. I also want to learn how to walk for days and days. And I want to learn how to make something."

"Make what? Are you talking about the material world? You know dreamhunters don't really deal with the material, except money, water, and shoe leather."

Laura Hame wore an airy, secretive look. She said that all the girls at her former school were making beaded snoods for St. Lazarus's Day gifts.

"What the hell is a snood?" said Sandy.

"A woven bag to wrap around loosely bundled long hair," Laura said, deadpan.

They walked along in silence for a time. Sandy, who felt he was being teased with stories about snood-making, tried again. He said, "You know, I think it's pretty slack of the Body not to have given you your figures."

Laura said, "They might have, I may not have been paying attention. I don't pay attention sometimes."

"You drift," Sandy said, pleased to have one of his own views confirmed.

She didn't answer. She had the look of someone who was listening, trying to identify some distant sound. Then she stopped, squatted, and touched the ground. She seemed to pet the surface of the road.

"What are you doing?"

"I don't know," she said. "Whenever I come In, for the first hour or two I get a funny feeling." She stood up again and resumed walking. "It's as if it's telling me something."

"You hear the Place talking to you?" Sandy tried not to sound too skeptical.

"I don't hear it. I begin by knowing I'm being talked to, then I get a very strong feeling. I feel I want to *console* the Place, as if it's crying. Or—or I have to *save it* somehow."

Sandy told Laura that all that meant—probably—was that she had an affinity for healing dreams. "They are all around here. If you feel you want to *stop the suffering*, it's because those dreams are here. Perhaps you're a Healer, like your father."

"Maybe."

This was enough of an invitation for Sandy. He went on to educate Laura about affinities. She listened with interest. He was right, she had only a sketchy knowledge of what was what— the pedigrees of dreamhunters.

There were Soporifs, Sandy told her, like his uncle, who could send people off to sleep. Sandy told Laura he thought she might be a Soporif, if the way she'd nearly knocked out the rangers at Wild River was anything to go by. There were Novelists, Sandy went on, very rare dreamhunters who could catch split dreams. Laura's aunt Grace was the most cele-brated example. "Wild River is a split dream, but none of us caught its split version," he said.

"I didn't even catch Wild River," Laura said. "I told you that."

Sandy ignored this. He knew she'd caught a nightmare. But he figured that, since the Body had licensed her, it must have been an isolated episode. He told her about Healers, with their affinity for healing dreams, and Hames—any dream-hunters with big penumbras. "A whole class of dreamhunters is named after your father!" he said. "Imagine."

There were Mounters, who might not have big projection zones but could easily overdream others. "Your father was a Mounter, too. So is Plasir—he is also what is politely called a Gifter and impolitely a Grafter. Depending on your point of view, he either grafts real people's faces and bodies onto characters in dreams or gives people what they can't have, or what they've lost."

Last, Sandy said, there were Colorists. "Coloring is illegal. I have heard a Colorist can infiltrate dreams and suggest things. They're secret persuaders."

Laura was staring at him, apparently horrified. "What do they persuade people to do?"

"Alter their opinions, invest their money, sell their houses, vote a certain way, leave town, get married, change their wills, like or dislike someone, form suspicions—all that."

"But how? How can they catch dreams to do all those things?"

"I don't know. Because it's illegal, no one talks about Coloring."

Laura was quiet. Sandy let her think—he'd given her enough for now.

After a little they reached Starry Beach. The dream site was in a clearing among trees with polished white limbs. The patch of ground was dusty and interrupted by hollows where people had been bedding down for the last twenty years.

Laura and Sandy were stopped short of the clearing by a couple of rangers. The men were sitting together and swigging from a bottle. They were surrounded by dirt-caked picks and shovels. They had been digging a new latrine, they said. They were having a break before closing and covering the old one. "There are a couple of dreamhunters at the site already. They're asleep. Men from St. Thomas's Lung Hospital. You'll have to wait till they wake."

The rangers finished their meal and went back to their digging, off behind a screen of trees. Sandy and Laura waited quietly. Sandy hadn't run out of conversation, or *lessons*, for Laura, but while he was making his lesson plan he became distracted by something the girl was doing.

She was playing with the dirt. She was sitting cross-legged, scraping the dusty earth together until she had a small mound before her. Sandy was reminded of his neighbor's daughter making mud pies on the back steps of her house. Laura pressed the mound together and patted it smooth. Then she began to shape it. Sandy saw her form deep eye sockets and a rough, flattened nose. While she worked the dirt, her face was blank and dreamy.

On the far side of the clearing, there came the sounds of stirring bodies, coughs, and murmurs. The dreamhunters were awake. They sat up, one scratching his head. They looked around them with slitted, blissful eyes, then yawned, stretched, got up, and shook the dust from their bedrolls. One spotted Sandy and Laura and said, "It's all yours, kids."

Laura's head jerked up; she stared at the man, startled. As she got to her feet, she knocked her dust sculpture to nothingness with her knee.

The dreamhunters stuffed their bedrolls into their packs. Sandy and Laura came into the clearing and stood waiting for them.

"Is it still raining?" asked one man.

"When we left it was," Laura said.

The dreamhunters shouldered their packs, waved, and left. Laura and Sandy spread out their bedrolls at the base of one of the skeletal trees.

✢ ✢ ✢

They didn't catch Starry Beach. When she had lain down to catch her first dream, Laura had run off on her own with the fleeing convict while her successful test mates plunged together into Wild River. By himself, unsupported by other dreamers who were catching the predictable dream, Sandy

Mason had to go where Laura Hame went. It really was as though the Place was determined to communicate something to Laura through her dreams.

Later, once he had caught it a couple more times and learned to wake up before it turned from an "achievement dream" into a nightmare, Sandy came to name the dream and make it part of his repertoire. He registered the dream as his own, and the following year, in the new issue of the charts, the name of the dream appeared in small print under the still stable Starry Beach. The map reference read: "The Water Diviner—Alexander Mason." The dream's name was coupled with Sandy's name because it was his claim and he first performed it. It didn't fall under the description of "dreams for the public good" so wasn't commandeered by the government. Sandy had an exclusive on the Water Diviner for a year, and he made good money out of it—but only once had he learned to wake himself in time.

The boy went out in the afternoon and cut a forked branch from the hazel tree by the stables. He stripped off all its leaves and twigs and took it out to the lip of the crack—the relic of an earthquake half a century before—a scar on the home paddock, filled with blackberry brambles. The boy did what he had seen the water diviner at the agricultural produce show do. He balanced the branch between his spread palms, a fork in each hand, fixing it in place with his thumbs. With the hazel rod held that way, the boy paced along the edge of the crack. He only walked with the rod, didn't point it. The water diviner had shown him how to go slowly and hold the rod loosely.

The boy circled the crack, and the rod failed to move, so he went on up the hill behind the house and stables, among the rocks, and there, after an hour walking back and forth, the hazel rod suddenly flipped down in his hands and pointed at a patch of rocks and ferns. The boy put the rod down and moved the stones with his hands. He pulled out ferns by their roots, dislodging more rocks.

Water bubbled out, at first in little, pushy knuckles, then in a steady trickle. Clear water, though it came out through a crack lined with coal.

*The boy's father had been worried about water, his plans for the farm con-
strained by a shortage of it.*

*The boy poked the rod into the coal crack to mark the spot, then ran off to
find his father. His father would be so pleased with him. "At last!" he thought.
"At last I'll be praised. At last I'll be noticed for the right reason."*

*But the boy couldn't find his father, who wasn't at the house or in the stables.
A stockman said he had gone into town.*

*The boy set off down the road that passed through fields where the stubble
had been burned off after the harvest. The slope beside the boy, undisturbed by
rain or wind, was charred still, black against the white sky and as glossy as an
ember. The boy was running, and he startled several crows who were picking
over the burned field. He didn't see them until they separated themselves from
the silky black slope. It was as though the fragments of the hill had broken off
and fluttered away into the sky.*

*The road turned down toward the town. The sun was low, setting into a band
of smoke from the burn offs. In its light the sandstone of the town shone clear
gold. The new bridge spanning the slow, green river looked like something built
by spirit. The boy could see the builders though, still at work, the mason presid-
ing over his laborers, who were busy on the bridge rail mortaring the mason's
strange, unlearned carvings into place.*

*The boy searched for his father at the post office, the butcher's, and the gen-
eral store. He told people his news, bubbling out of his usual silence like a spring
released from a seam of coal.*

*He crossed the bridge between the convict laborers and their guards, who
lounged against the finished coping, their rifles pointed skyward. The guards
were keeping a close eye on the men, whose chains had been removed so that they
could clamber over the outside of the structure without the risk of falling into the
river, and being dragged down and drowned by their leg irons.*

*The setting sun made the smoke pall lovely, lit it up in layers of crimson, ver-
milion, and tangerine. The light went pure orange, the orange of orange oil.*

*The boy came to the church, whose sandstone glowed. The building was
locked, so he wandered around the churchyard. He was no longer really looking
for his father but only turning around staring at everything, in awe of the light.
The tombstones changed from rose to flame, as though each one were staring a*

bonfire full in its face. The air was close and reeked of woodsmoke. All the birds had stopped singing.

The boy reached a place where there was a tree stump among the tombstones. It was the stump of a giant eucalyptus, recently felled, and then its remnant chipped at and reduced. It was still huge, and still gave off the fiery perfume of its resin. The stump was like another tomb in that light, scarcely more red than the stones, though its bleeding timber would be red in any light.

The boy climbed up onto it. He got sap on his hands and feet. He stood on the stump and looked around. The sunset was so violent that it should have been making a noise. The light cast the shadows of the far hills up across the sky, bristling rays of opaque blue in a huge, bright, slicing pane of orange light.

There was a noise in the churchyard. It was not the noise of a bird inspired by the sunset. It was a moan. It might have been a human sound, only there was no human consciousness or intelligence or character in it. It seemed to come from a very dark place. It was a sound of absolute despair.

The boy climbed down from the felled tree. He followed the moan, creeping softly among the tombstones.

The sun went down. The billows in the sky seem to roll and swell as they filled with purple shadows. The light went blue.

The boy stopped. He listened. He heard the sound again, a muffled rustling, then a terrible, raw-throated moaning.

A little way off, between two tall headstones, the boy could see a pile of color—color still, even in the blue twilight. It was a heap of white, red, yellow, and purple flowers. The boy crept closer. He saw a fresh grave, piled high with late summer flowers and wreaths, laurels painted black and gilt. Nothing stirred, but the ground moaned again, then shrieked, thumped, scraped, and rustled.

The boy stood staring, his hands spread as though he held his hazel rod, wavering in his loose grip and turning—turning down to what he had divined.

4

✦ ✦ ✦

ON THE DAY ROSE HAD ARRANGED TO
MEET LAURA, SHE HAD SOME DIFFI-
CULTIES. IT WAS STILL RAINING, AND SHE
had Mamie Doran in tow. Rose had been rather startled by
her success in cultivating Mamie's friendship. The girl was
usually cool and offhand. She never showed any sign of
needing to be liked; all her actions said: "You can take me or
leave me." Rose had wooed Mamie, had recommended her
for choice parts in play readings. She'd asked for Mamie's
help sorting rags for one of the school's church-related charity drives—had kept her good company and plied her with
paprika chocolate cookies from one of Farry's jumbo
cookie barrels. When Mamie got chilblains, Rose bought her
lavender-scented hand cream. When Mamie had a cold, Rose
sat on the end of her bed and read to her. This was an unexpected pleasure. Rose didn't really approve of Mamie's manner, her sour talk about people, but Mamie was better read
than Rose and had more adventurous taste in books. Before
the second term was halfway over, other girls were speaking of
Rose and Mamie as they had once spoken of Rose and Laura.
So it was that Mamie naturally assumed they would spend
their free day together.

Rose had tried to discourage Mamie by making her plans
sound as dull as possible. Her attempt to do this was compli-

cated by another girl from the dormitory, a girl Rose rather liked, who tried to invite herself along too. "We could take a tram to Kirks," the girl said. (Kirks was a big department store with a cavernous, overheated tearoom.)

"We could go to a matinee," Mamie suggested, speaking only to Rose.

Rose didn't know whether Mamie meant a play or a dream. She was so distracted by wondering she nearly asked which— then remembered she didn't want anyone to go anywhere with her.

"I'd like to do that too," said the other girl.

Mamie had her back to the girl and didn't look at her when she spoke.

Rose was uncomfortable. She nearly said, "Of course you can come!" But then she'd be committed to company. Instead she said only that she was *determined* to go to the Museum. She tapped her sketchbook with her gloved hand. Let them think she was a grind and trying to get ahead of everyone else in their art class.

"We can do your thing, Rose, and then do mine," Mamie said. She was still giving the other girl the cold shoulder.

The other girl gave up and drifted off to sit in the bay window of the common room.

"Only if you're sure you won't be bored," Rose said to Mamie.

"Of course I won't. So we agree—the Museum, then a matinee? And we could have lunch at Kirks—to honor certain people in their absence." Mamie glanced at the girl she'd driven off and gave one of her sly smiles.

✛ ✛ ✛

When Rose and Mamie came out of a street onto the west embankment's wide pavement, they saw that the Sva River was the color of overbrewed coffee and only a few feet from the bottoms of the arches of the nearest bridge. It was an alarming sight, and they were relieved to turn away from the river to climb the zigzag steps that led to the Plaza before the National Museum.

They left their coats and umbrellas in the cloakroom, showed their school passes, and went in.

Rose checked her watch. It was half an hour till her rendezvous with Laura. She should just take Mamie to the sculpture hall and start sketching something.

The sculpture hall was in a covered courtyard in the center of the building. It had been roofed only recently, by the same architect who designed the glass dome at the Rainbow Opera. It was a lovely, light-filled room that mainly displayed copies of classical statues. When Mamie and Rose arrived, they found that the roof was leaking and that several curators were marking the spots of the leaks—one standing, her head thrown back to regard the failed lead seal far above her while her toe tapped, keeping time with the drips that fell into the puddle by her foot.

Two guards appeared with buckets. Rose and Mamie hesitated in the entrance and were told, "Just mind the puddles. It's quite dry everywhere else."

Mamie said to Rose, "Are we quite sure this is a *nice* thing to do?"

Rose only pointed with her pencil. She set a course between the statues in search of something she could sketch. The "splish splish" behind them changed into a "tock tock" of drops hitting the bottoms of zinc buckets.

"I wonder if the Opera is leaking," Rose said, then, "What kind of matinee did you mean, Mamie? A play or a dream?"

"Rose, you forget that some of us aren't allowed to go to dreams yet. My mother says all but a very few dreams are *too strong* for girls."

"Oh," said Rose. "Do you believe her, Mamie?"

"It isn't a question of whether I believe her. I'm obedient to my parents' wishes. Aren't you?"

"Um," said Rose. Then she stopped dead.

Laura was standing at the other end of the hall with her back to them. She had her hands on the naked back of a male statue and was caressing its contours thoughtfully, from the shoulders to the buttocks.

Mamie sniggered.

Rose hurried toward her cousin—before the guards could notice what she was doing. As Rose approached, Laura removed her hands. She turned and smiled, then lost her smile when she spotted Mamie.

Mamie was smirking, looking from Laura to the statue. "I suppose you had a previous arrangement to meet your cousin here, Rose," Mamie said, "but why didn't you just say?"

"I wasn't sure she'd show up," Rose said. She widened her eyes at Laura, trying to convey the *necessity* of lying to Mamie. Then she asked her cousin, "What were you doing?"

"Waiting," Laura said. "I came in out of the rain when the Museum opened."

"Not that!" Rose snapped. She gestured at the statue. She was furious with Laura for embarrassing her in front of Mamie Doran—for being so peculiar, doing something so *dirty*, then being vague about it.

Laura seemed baffled, so Rose pointed at the statue.

"Oh," said Laura. "Um."

"Oh? Um?" Rose fumed.

"I was thinking of making a sculpture."

"You could have taken an interest in the little bronze ballet dancer over there," Rose said.

"I studied her too, before you arrived," Laura said. Now she sounded smooth. She had assumed a polite, public face again.

Mamie was showing some tact too. She had moved a little way off and was studying another nude—a saint clothed in her long hair.

Rose took Laura's arm and walked her a little ways away. "Are you well?" she asked. "We haven't much time. I promised to spend the day with Mamie."

"Why on earth?"

"Shhh."

Laura sighed. She said she was fine. She'd spent a few days In, where it was warm, catching dreams to "open" herself. "Me and Sandy Mason—the boy from the infants' beach. I went to catch Starry Beach but managed to get something else with convicts. The last one was a bad dream that ended well. This was a rather lovely dream that ended horribly—though not for the convicts. Honestly, Rose, I'm sick of those bloody convicts. Anyway, I erased it myself, overwrote it with Convalescent Two. I have a few nights' work boosting one of the resident dreamers on the medical ward at Pike Street. I got the job through Sandy's uncle."

Mamie joined them. "Perhaps we should all just go to Kirks? The air is clammy in here."

Rose looked around the room at the light from the overcast skies shining coldly on the frozen figures, on dark bronze and pale marble. "All right. Lead on, Mamie," she said. She tried to sound friendly.

Mamie took Rose's arm and looked across her at Laura, whom Rose already had hold of. "Isn't this nice, Rose?" Mamie said. "Your old friend on one arm, and your new on the other."

✢ ✢ ✢

Rose got lucky at Kirks, where Mamie ran into her mother and some other society ladies. Rose had to endure a few uncomfortable minutes when Mamie not only introduced her to Mrs. Doran but delivered a speech in praise of Rose's achievements.

"Well," said Mrs. Doran, when her daughter finally finished, "cream rises to the top." She looked around her circle. "Don't I always say that? Cream rises to the top." To Rose she said, "I'm hoping that one day Mamie will be made prefect too."

"I'm sure she will," said Rose.

"And this is Laura, Rose's cousin," Mamie added.

The ladies smiled nervously at Laura.

"We won't join you," Mamie said to her mother.

"But you *must*! Rose dear, take your cousin and Mamie up to look at the selection. Choose whatever you like. It'll be my treat."

Mamie went red. She glared at her mother. Rose saw her chance to have a moment alone with Laura. She took her cousin by the arm and led her away to the cake counter, where the glistening creams and glazed fruits shone up through the glass.

"You've sure hooked and landed Mamie," Laura said.

"I know. Now I only have to scale her, bone her, cook her, and eat her."

Laura pulled a face. Then she said, "I can't wait for your next free day to talk to you properly. Have Aunt and Uncle relaxed at all?"

"Not to the extent of having me live at home again. But my board is only paid for this term. I doubt they'll send me back after St. Lazarus's Day. I don't feel they're scheming anymore. Perhaps they gave that up once you got your license. They're indecisive and depressed and soggy now. Ma is working much harder than she needs to. Escaping into dreams, really. Da is still tussling with your aunt Marta about the memorial service."

Laura said, "People in Doorhandle—rangers and villagers—keep being friendly and helpful, and it turns out that they are all doing Aunt Grace favors."

"Yes—they're keeping tabs on us. The headmistress stopped me in the corridor yesterday and said, 'I've just had such a nice chat with your father.' I waited to hear about the chat, but that was all she had to say. Da had called in and been *terribly charming* to her, and she just couldn't resist sharing her good luck."

"They're avoiding us because they're so bad at being secretive," Laura said. "If they saw more of us, they might just blurt out their fears." Then she told Rose what they had found on the film in Chorley's camera.

Rose said, "Why did your da film the view back the way he had come? Was he leaving directions?"

Laura shrugged.

Rose stared at her suspiciously. "Directions for you?" she said.

"I don't have the stamina yet for a journey like that."

"Good," Rose said. Then she asked if Laura could stomach Mrs. Doran and her friends. "Can you sit and be a friendly nonentity?"

"Yes."

"Can you, Laura? Can you remember I'm cultivating Mamie, and just eat cake and keep your mouth shut?"

"No. I can't eat cake if I have to keep my mouth shut."

"Ha ha."

"What I can't do, Rose, is wait for your next free day. There's someone I have to go and see. Someone creepy. I'd rather you went with me."

"I'll cut class. I'll climb the wall if I have to. Who is it you have to see?"

"Never mind that now, just meet me on the steps of the Temple. Two o'clock, Friday."

Rose reached for Laura's hand and held it. Her heart turned over. If she could only get Laura alone for a few hours, she knew she could fully unthaw her cousin. "I'll be there," she said. "So, are you ready to brave the ladies?"

Laura nodded.

"You be bland and I'll be duplicitous. Lovely word that— duplicitous. Sounds like a prehistoric animal. *The lame duplicitous was pursued by the ravening erroneous.*"

Laura folded into her funny, panting giggle. And Rose felt tears come into her eyes because she had made her cousin laugh. Happiness had never been like this before. Now it came like sun showers, the sun and the rain together. Happiness was happier than it had been—sharp, piercing, and snatched, like a breath while swimming in surf.

5

✤ ✤ ✤

THE ISLE OF THE TEMPLE WAS A
LOVELY MIRAGE OF STONE DOMES
AND SPIRES STANDING IN THE STREAM OF
the Sva River. The Isle's Temple, St. Lazarus, was a site of pil-
grimage. All the hotels, guesthouses, and convents on the Isle
had, for over a century, accommodated pilgrims. But by the
time Laura's father fell from the Sisters Beach coach, business
wasn't what it had been. *Faith* wasn't what it had been, and
there were fewer pilgrims than in former times. The hotels
had needed customers and welcomed dreamhunters as guests.
It was an ideal arrangement. Over the years the streets and al-
leys and winding staircases of the Isle had filled with dream
parlors. Of course there were rumbles of disapproval from
the Temple and the throne of the Grand Patriarch. The
church preached against the "houses of unholy worship" and
"strangers sleeping together." But it had made sense, for
safety reasons, for dream parlors to be set up with the broad,
swift waters of the Sva between the dreamers and overcrowded
buildings of the Old Town on the east bank, and the prome-
nades before the white houses along the west.

By the time Tziga Hame's daughter had become a
dreamhunter, the Isle was as full of the commerce of
dreamhunting as it was of the business of the Orthodox
Church. The offices of the Dream Regulatory Body stood at

one end of the Isle, and the Temple stood at the other. Between them, as well as several charity homes and hospitals and church libraries, there were countless shops that outfitted dreamhunters in work clothes and their opulent nightclothes. There were sleepwear emporiums for dream palace patrons. There were saunas with steam rooms (dreamhunters and rangers all suffered from sinus complaints as well as mouth ulcers because of the arid air of the Place). There were small, specialist dream parlors and larger salons, with shuttered windows and high, boasting perimeter fences. (The dreamers who performed in salons didn't have dangerous projection zones, but they put up fences to *imply* that they did—it was a form of advertising.) And, finally, there was the Rainbow Opera, looming above its high fence, its perimeter patrolled by guards who regularly cleared away loitering, hopeful dream-pilferers.

Maze Plasir's dream parlor wasn't easy to find. Rose and Laura wandered around looking for forty minutes before Rose thought to buy a newspaper and find his listing. The girls put their heads together and searched the three columns devoted to advertisements for salons and parlors on the Isle. They found it—"Maze Plasir: Adventure, Satisfaction, Solace. Dreaming Feast After Fasting tonight, 9 p.m." Below the description was a street address.

The cousins set out again. They hurried and clung to the walls. They were the only young women abroad in those streets and felt conspicuous. They were so nervous and rushed that they missed the head of Plasir's street on their first pass. They turned back and went more carefully, then found it, a narrow, dog-legged alley. It was dry and clean, though, and not too forbidding. This passage led to a narrow path beside the river, with only an iron rail between them and the high, brown flood. The path passed around the water-stained basements of several houses, then plunged between

two, down a tight, short passage to a private door. A black
timber door studded with bright copper nail heads.

Rose pulled the chain that hung above the door, and they
heard a bell ringing somewhere in the house.

The door was answered by the bandy-legged boy who had
tested with Laura. His appearance had improved—he'd filled
out, his skin was clear, his hair slicked back with pomade, his
clothes new and neat. He looked at Laura with lowering suspicion, and his top lip lifted. "What are *you* doing here?"

Laura said, "Mr. Plasir gave me his card too."

"And what about her?" The boy looked Rose up and down.

"We're keeping each other company on our errands," Rose
said. "I'm Rose Tiebold. And who are you?"

"Gavin Pinkney."

"May we come in, Gavin?" Laura said.

The boy stood aside. He said that Plasir wasn't in, he was
taking his exercise, but he would be back shortly.

Gavin showed them into a sitting room lit only by the coal
fire and the slivers of light that came through its fixed shutters. There were several wingback leather chairs and a massive
leather sofa. There were brass ashtrays on stems beside every
seat. There was a gateleg table and, in its center, a silver plat-
ter holding sparkling balloon glasses and a cut-crystal de-
canter filled with brandy. The walls were decorated with a
frieze of dancing Eastern maidens, prancing horses, pheas-
ants, peacocks, and gilded palms. There was a clock on the
mantelpiece, all its workings visible, fidgeting and glittering
under a glass dome. The room smelled of tobacco and furniture polish. The house was hushed.

"Are you here alone?" Laura asked the boy.

"Not this minute. The cook's come in to make me and Mr.
Plasir our lunch."

"And how are you?" Laura asked.

Gavin began to boast. He had been apprenticed to Mr.

Plasir. They went together into the Place, where Gavin said he was able to catch some dreams that Mr. Plasir said were special only to him. The boy said he didn't just have casual work boosting Plasir—no—he had an *affinity* with Mr. Plasir's sites. And Plasir was teaching him some special mental disciplines, things that most dreamhunters knew nothing about.

Laura said, "From what I hear, Mr. Plasir wouldn't require boosting."

"Then why are you here if you haven't come to take up his offer?" said the boy.

"My business is with Mr. Plasir, not you."

Gavin shrugged. His eyes went back to Rose, and again he scanned her from top to toe. He swallowed nervously, licked his lips, then said he had to go back to his reading. "I'm studying the dream almanac." He left Rose and Laura alone.

They sat down, hip to hip, on the sofa. Rose said, "I don't like people who breathe through their mouths."

"Yes, revolting," Laura said.

Half an hour later the girls heard the street door, and the clatter of Gavin's footsteps as he rushed from somewhere else in the house to speak to Plasir. Their voices murmured a moment, then the door opened and Plasir came in with a look of cool curiosity on his pale, taut face.

Laura and Rose stood up together. Plasir said, "Please," gestured to the sofa, and took a seat himself opposite them. The girls sat down again. Rose put her arm around Laura's waist. Plasir had not offered to shake their hands.

"To what do I owe the honor of this visit?" he said. "Are you considering my offer?" He smiled at Laura.

"I am dreaming Convalescent Two in concert with the resident dreamers at Pike Street Hospital," she said. "I have work enough."

She was at a loss. She had hoped that once she got here she would think of some way of picking Plasir's mind while giving nothing away herself. She was afraid just to ask. But asking was all she *could* do. She said, "I want to ask you some questions about my father."

Maze Plasir looked surprised. Then he looked at Rose.

Rose said, "Laura didn't think she should come here on her own, so I agreed to come with her. I'm only here to keep her company—so you shouldn't look to *me* for clues. I haven't any idea what she's going to say."

"Anything I can tell Laura concerning her father concerns you too—since you're Chorley Tiebold's daughter."

Laura could feel Rose looking at her; she could even feel her cousin's breath on her cheek. Laura knew that Rose wanted to consult with her, to say with a look, *Wasn't there something funny about Plasir's remark, something suggestive?* Laura thought there was too, but she would reflect on it later; she wasn't about to be swerved from her purpose.

"Come then," Plasir said.

Laura said, "My father left me a letter."

"You mean—a suicide note?" asked Plasir.

"Not quite," said Laura. "In the letter he mentioned your name in a way that made me think you might know something about what he was *doing*. The things he was doing that he never talked about."

Plasir's expression said, "Is *that* all?" He leaned forward. "You *know* what he was doing, because he did it publicly."

"You're only saying that to make me feel stupid," Laura said. "If you don't intend to tell me anything, just say so. Otherwise, won't you please just *tell* me?" She was begging him.

Plasir made dampening signals with his hands.

"My father disappeared. He got on a special train at the end of summer, and we didn't see him again."

"Yes, I read the papers. But the papers said he attempted a

crossing. To attempt a crossing—alone—is insane, or suicidal."

Laura didn't answer.

Rose said, "When we were staying in Summerfort, Mother and Uncle Tziga would go In from Tricksie Bend. That end of the Place was less explored. They wouldn't have to walk so far to find new dreams. Mother would catch a dream, and sometimes she'd get the express to Founderston to play at the Rainbow Opera, but mostly her audience followed her to Sisters Beach and the Beholder. But at least three times each summer, a special train came for Uncle Tziga."

Laura said, "My father always said that dreams travel better in summer—because there are longer hours of daylight."

Rose said, "We would be on holiday, and they'd be working hard."

Laura said, "But Da was never *happier* in summer. He *should* have been, but he wasn't. *We* were all happier, we were on holiday. Aunt Grace was happier, catching new things—"

Plasir interrupted her. "You want to know where he went? Where the special trains took him?" He looked at them with raised eyebrows.

Laura nodded.

"Most of what I'm about to tell you is public knowledge, or part of the public record," he said. "You could put it all together from newspaper reports if you wanted. It's not often discussed, though, or discussed in any detail."

Plasir waited, gauging their attention, their *need*. He said, "For years dreams have been part of a program of prison reform. Your father was one of a handful of dreamers who were able to catch dreams that could inspire and *improve* people. Dreams like that are rare and precious. They are never for the open market. They are classified under the Intangible Resources Act as 'Dreams for the Public Good.' The Department of Corrections took your father and his dreams to prisons." Plasir looked from Rose to Laura, making sure they understood him. "The prisons supply labor for public works," he said. "You must have seen convicts building roads?"

Laura shook her head.

"Or perhaps you don't travel anywhere off the beaten track?" Plasir said.

"*I've* seen convict laborers," said Rose. "Laura sleepwalks. She never notices anything."

"When the government first came up with the scheme, its merits were debated in the newspapers. This was six or seven years ago. You wouldn't have been reading the papers then."

"Is that all?" Rose said. She seemed to be hoping he had finished.

"I too have a contract to perform dreams in prisons," Plasir said. "Dreams as rewards. While Tziga Hame worked in rehabilitation, I offered rewards and incentives—and education."

Laura was shaking her head, trying to hear the sense in the thick of his words. There was something implied in this talk of incentives and rewards.

"And, of course, as a Gifter I am able to alter dreams. For instance, I can catch a dream about a killing, then change the face of the victim to fit a certain crime, a particular criminal. Many a murderer has been brought to a better understanding of what he has done by my dreams. Imagine a criminal being able to experience what his victim suffered. You can see how *effective* it might be. How educational."

"I see," Laura said. "You worked on rewards and education, and my father was working in rehabilitation. He gave prisoners inspiring dreams."

"Yes," said Plasir. The way he said it, the word sounded open, like "Yes, *and* . . ."

"Then why did he never talk about it? And why, in his letter, did he say he'd done terrible things?"

Plasir said, "I am unwilling to be the person who casts a shadow on your memories of your father."

If Laura hadn't been given a task to complete by her father she would have listened to Plasir's warning. She would have stood up, called Rose to follow her, and gone away. She hadn't *promised* her father, after all, she had only opened his letter. But the letter was part of a bigger legacy, a legacy she wanted. She suddenly understood this as she sat facing Maze Plasir in his darkened parlor. She knew now, for sure, that she wanted to put her hands into sand and shape it, she wanted to sing to the sand, to make it get up and speak to her. Speak to her again. Laura felt that, to take what she wanted, she must accept her father's whole legacy. Besides, she really did need some clues about why convicts kept appearing in her dreams. She said to Plasir, "I need to know."

He seemed to settle deeper in his chair. He said, "The Department of Corrections subscribes to dreamhunters in order to reward prisoners for their cooperative labor. But if prisoners don't cooperate, the Department uses dreamhunters to *punish* them." Plasir stopped and waited for his listeners to react. When they didn't, he went on. "It has been noted by prison reformers in other countries that in our prison system convicts are well-clothed and housed and fed. They're not whipped or starved. Foreign prison reformers hold up our system as a kind and humane idea. But there are always agitators in any prison population. And there are always prisoners who are prepared to protect agitators." Plasir had spread his hands, palms up. He said, "Well—imagine." Then he waited.

"My father took nightmares to the prisons," Laura said.

"Yes."

Laura was aware that Rose, beside her, had put a hand over

her mouth. Laura said, agonized, "But why would he do that? He always earned enough. He was famous, and celebrated. Why would he agree to do that? He couldn't possibly have believed it was right."

Plasir said, "Was there something he didn't have that he badly wanted?" The way he asked it seemed almost gentle. Again he waited, but Laura said nothing.

"When it was first suggested that uncooperative convicts might respond well to the threat of nightmares, Tziga and I were already under contract to Department of Corrections. He was already selling his inspirations to the prisons, and I was selling my rewards. We both had an affinity with nightmares—but for some reason he could find many more than I. More and worse. But, as I say, we were both under contract, so it was suggested that I offer Tziga an inducement—a very strong inducement—to help him get over his misgivings about the scheme."

Rose jumped to her feet. She yelled at Plasir, "Don't tell her!"

He glanced at Rose and shook his head. "You're a clever girl," he said, then, to Laura, "Do you know that your father and I were once friends? I knew him before he became socially ambitious. Before his eyes lit on those beautiful Tiebolds. In fact, I was with him when he first saw Verity Tiebold. I watched her too, and spoke to her. She made a strong impression on me—too." As he watched Laura, he looked sad. "Do you see?" He said. "I had *several* dreams that worked. The one he liked best was Stately Lady."

"That's enough," Rose said. She put out a hand to her cousin, then withdrew it again, apparently afraid.

Laura felt surprisingly alert, but not agitated. Had Plasir's words injured her? She wasn't sure. If there was pain, it was coming slowly, raining on her, changing her temperature. She said to Plasir, "You gave him back my mother. And for that, he agreed to sell nightmares. The Department of Corrections paid you both for this work. That's it. That's all of it."

"What were you expecting, Laura? A criminal conspiracy?" Plasir said. "I think you will find that the public supports the penal system *as it is*. The public knows what goes on. They may not want to be bothered with the details, but they know. The general public isn't fond of details. They know that this is a civilized nation, where no one is tortured or lives in squalor. That's all they want to know. There's no scandal here, Laura. No crime. If you made a fuss, your father's reputation might suffer, that's all. As it is, people regard him as a kind of saint—a scary saint, one who came out of the invisible realm carrying beautiful visions."

Laura found herself trying to work out, in quite a cool-headed way, whether Maze Plasir hated her father. She said, "There's nothing to be done then?" She said that, but she thought: *"When you're ready, catch the dreadful dream"* and *"Your aunt Marta knows 'The Measures.' "* She thought of her father's instructions, and his story about the song St. Lazarus heard in the tomb. Then she asked Plasir if he had ever seen the convicts *in dreams*.

He looked surprised. "No," he said. "Have you? What are they doing, these convicts?"

"They're waiting to be seen. They're waiting to be heard," Laura said. She got to her feet. "Thank you for talking to me," she said. She put her arm around Rose's waist.

"Yes, yes," said Rose, "let's go."

But Laura had one more question. She asked Plasir whether he still took his rewards to the prisons.

"I'm still under contract. My business alone won't support me. My parlor is very exclusive; at most I perform for five clients a night. They pay very well. But even five wealthy customers a night will not keep me in style."

He was making excuses, Laura thought. He was saying "it's necessary." But *he* knew what he was doing was wrong—whether the public cared or not.

"Please, Laura. I want to leave," Rose said.

"We'll let ourselves out," Laura said, as if this were an ordinary visit, as if Plasir had politely stood up to see them out, as good hosts do when their guests get to their feet. Laura led Rose from the room and from the house.

V

The Measures

1

✤ ✤ ✤

MARTA HAME, THE RETIRED DI-
RECTOR OF THE CHOIR OF ST.
LAZARUS AND SISTER OF THE DREAMHUNTER
Tziga Hame, lived in a large timber house a half-hour walk
from a train stop twenty miles south of Founderston. The
house was surrounded by orchards that belonged to it but
were worked by a neighboring farmer. The retired choir mistress was still several months short of her fortieth birthday but
dressed like an elderly widow, in black from neck to ankle,
her only adornment a small gold crucifix. Marta Hame was a
very religious woman, and despite her retreat to the country,
she was still on the boards of several church charities and was
known to be a close confidante of the Grand Patriarch himself. The local postman could testify to this—for letters were
exchanged, often daily, between the Palace at the Temple and
the house in the apple orchard.

The postman was waiting for the train that came through at
eight in the morning. The train came and stopped, didn't just
snatch the mailbag from the hook-topped pole beside the
track.

Four passengers got off. A farmer jumped from the steps of
a third-class carriage, and his wife handed down their baskets, then herself. Another man stepped from the second-
class carriage onto a box the conductor placed for him—he

was a traveling salesman with a sample bag. The passenger
who climbed down from first class onto the platform wore a
beautiful camel hair coat. He was tall and had gold hair, and
for a moment the excited postman imagined he was witness-
ing one of the Grand Patriarch's rare visits to his friend. But
the Grand Patriarch generally arrived by car, and with some
followers, and this man wasn't even carrying luggage. Besides,
as the man approached, the postman saw he was too young to
be the Grand Patriarch. Too young and clean-shaven, and
unaccompanied—but very like His High Reverence, Erasmus
Amon Tiebold. "Of course!" the curious postman thought to
himself. Then, as an experiment, he said to the man, "*Good
morning*, Mr. Tiebold."

✧ ✧ ✧

Chorley said good morning to the postman, slightly annoyed that he'd been recognized. This was silly of him, really.
How many other men of fashion got off at this country station? Chorley had never learned to be inconspicuous, to
dress modestly, to travel cheaply. He hadn't managed to do
those things even when—as a young man—he couldn't afford
to do otherwise.

Chorley left the train stop and tramped on up the road.
The postman rode past and peered at him. The bike's front
wheel wobbled, then the bike tipped in a rut, dumping the
postman onto the road beside Chorley.

Chorley helped the man to his feet. He picked the bicycle
up. Its chain was broken.

"Thank you," said the postman.

Chorley retrieved the mailbag. It was dripping mud. He
held it out to the postman, who said again, "Thank you, Mr.
Tiebold."

"Do you have any mail today for Marta Hame?" Chorley asked.

The postman explained that he hadn't sorted the letters yet. He usually sorted the mail at the station but—

"But today he was in a hurry to see where I was going," thought Chorley.

"—and sometimes I sort the mail *at* Miss Hame's. I have a cup of tea with her. She's a friend."

"I see," said Chorley. "I only meant to offer to carry Miss Hame's letters—if you have any for her. To spare you the trip, since you've torn your trousers."

The rip was in the worst possible place. The postman found it, blushed, and went knock-kneed in an effort to conceal it. He explained that a third of the mail was usually *for* Miss Hame anyway.

Chorley gestured at the torn trousers. "That—and the broken chain on your bike—needs immediate attention." He looked around at the rail line and the farmland, then back at the postman. "What *will* you do?"

The postman answered with dignity. "I will make my way slowly up to Miss Hame's and seek assistance there."

Chorley put out his hand for the mailbag.

The postman clutched it to him. "*With* the mailbag," he said. "It's my responsibility."

Chorley shrugged, tipped the man a salute, and strode on up the hill.

✢ ✢ ✢

He recognized the house from Tziga's description—a description given offhand but so detailed and interesting that Chorley had felt the question he had asked was being answered. "Why do you spend so much time there when Laura's here?" (Chorley *had* meant "When we are *all* here" but didn't want to make any demands on his own behalf.) "It's very peaceful," Tziga had explained. "And there's no other place near it." Tziga had described Marta's house—and his description was an explanation. He'd explained everything—without burdening Chorley with the truth. For as Chorley stood where Marta Hame's driveway turned off the road up to the house, he knew he was looking at the place his brother-in-law had hidden with the tired fragments of the final days of each of his terrible nightmares.

Marta Hame's house was handsome, but it looked haunted.

As he crossed its yard, Chorley heard singing, a light, low voice singing not a melody but a complex, modulated chant. The singing was accompanied by the sound of a stick thumping on a wooden floor. Marta was giving a lesson.

It's only a lesson, Chorley thought, though the chant seemed to pull him around inside. It made him feel queasy.

When he knocked at the door, the singing stopped and a dog began to bark. Chorley heard the bark coming closer as the dog raced to the door. He heard its nails skittering in the hall, and then Marta hushing it.

Marta opened the door. She was clutching her woolly coated boyar by his collar. She hauled him back out of Chorley's way. She looked stern—at the dog—and amazed to see Chorley. "I'll put him out," she said. She shuffled around him, pushing the dog out with her legs. She closed the door on her dog, who barked briefly, then whined a little, then yawned while still whining, then fell silent and trotted off into the yard.

"Can I take your coat?" Marta said. She was a short, broad woman, with her gray and black hair wound into a tight knot at the nape of her neck. She had Tziga's deep-set, dark-circled black eyes.

Chorley gave her his coat and followed her into the nearest room, a sunny front room with a piano, and a cello leaning on a chair, and with *Laura*—Laura was there.

Chorley asked his niece just *when* she had planned to tell him and Grace where she was. "You told us you would be sleeping at Pike Street, dreaming with the resident dreamhunters, but we had hoped you might come *home* during the day."

Laura got a stubborn, defensive look. "I spent two of those days with Rose. Didn't she mention it?"

"No," Chorley said.

"Perhaps you haven't *seen* Rose," said Laura with transparent false nonchalance. "But that's all right, I guess, since you always know where she is—where you've *left* her."

"Please do not speak to your uncle like that," Marta said. She was standing in the bay window, facing the yard. She said, "Laura, would you go out and rescue the postman from Downright?"

There was barking outside. Laura went out to deal with the dog, and Chorley joined Marta at the window. He saw Laura running toward the postman, who had put his broken bike between himself and Downright's doggy enthusiasm. Chorley caught Marta's eye. "I knew I didn't have long before the postman descended on us with his broken chain and torn trousers."

"What on *earth* did you do to him?" Marta said.

Chorley lost his temper. Laura's criticism had stung him, and he wasn't going to take a telling-off from Tziga's sister. "Why would you imagine I've done something to the man?" he said. "What do you think I am?"

"A Tiebold," Marta said. She turned away. Her profile looked like a portrait on a medal, cold and minted. "Your sister tormented my brother," she said.

"What are you talking about? Verity loved Tziga!"

"She tormented him for years before she would marry him," Marta finished her sentence.

"She was *afraid* of him!" Chorley shouted.

Marta flinched. She stared at Chorley, her eyes wide, while he glared back at her.

Then, all at once, Chorley saw how hopeless it was, his having come here to *beg* Marta to cooperate with him and Grace in organizing the memorial service for her brother. There was too much between them—too much made of too little. Years of neglect on his side. He had taken her brother—one of only two surviving relatives, counting Laura—and made him part of *his* tribe, the Tiebolds. He hadn't discouraged Laura from regarding Marta as her "dull auntie." He hadn't invited Marta to family celebrations—and neither had Tziga, but then Tziga would *never* remember to host family celebrations anyway. If Chorley ever remembered Marta and felt uncomfortable, he would remind himself that she had her church and choir. Marta was respectable (that was another thing Laura had always called her, mockingly, "My *respectable* aunt"). Grace and Tziga hunted dreams and wore themselves thin, while Chorley stayed at home with the girls and was *loved*. He was the one who got the love. He had been neglectful and disrespectful, and he didn't deserve Marta's help. And he *did* deserve to have Laura answer back when he started his ineffectual nagging.

Chorley folded, slumped down on the window seat, bent over with his face in his hands. He said, "Please, please, for God's sake, let us hold this service. Help us do it."

Marta put her hand on his shoulder. She said, "Chorley Tiebold, you don't believe in God."

"But *you* do," said Chorley, muffled. Then he jumped up from under her hand and went across the room to lean on the fireplace. He gripped the mantelpiece with both hands but couldn't prevent his shoulders from shaking. "The only reason you won't help us bury Tziga is that you think he's still alive," he said. His words were strangled but audible.

He listened to Marta's silence and supposed she hadn't heard him. But then she asked, "Why would that thought upset you?"

Chorley heard her footfalls; she came close to him. He tried to get a grip on himself. "If Tziga was alive, why wouldn't he let his daughter know?" he said.

"Or *you*," Marta added.

He hadn't said it. He'd kept his mouth tightly shut.

"You—his best friend," Marta said, rubbing it in.

Chorley dropped his head till it pressed into the jutting shelf of the mantelpiece.

"Do you think Tziga's dead?" Marta asked.

"I don't know what I think. What I think changes every hour. But I know it's wrong to let Laura go on hopelessly hoping."

Chorley heard her move even closer, then her voice at his shoulder. "*Think*," she said. "Think why you're so determined to hold a memorial service."

"I want it settled somehow for Laura," Chorley said. "For all of us. And Tziga was a great man. A public figure—"

Marta interrupted him. "*No.* I mean—why do you want to be *seen* holding a service?"

Grace and he had agreed, over a month ago, that it was vital to have some public show of their belief in the official story of Tziga's fatal disappearance. Grace had said, "If *they*—whoever they are—imagine that we think they've *lied* to us, then they'll never relax enough for us to learn anything. A memorial service will, perhaps, make them drop their guard. Besides, I'm scared that, if we don't somehow discourage her, Laura is going to go looking for him days In from Doorhandle. She isn't strong or experienced enough to do that."

Chorley wiped his eyes on his sleeve and faced Marta. "So—you won't go along with our plans for a memorial service, even for the sake of appearances?"

"I'm a religious woman. I never pray for the sake of appearances," Marta said. "And—who knows—*I* might be holding out a foolish hope." She shrugged.

Chorley stared at her for a long moment, then said, *"Where is he?"*

The question hung between them in the quiet, plain, sunlit room. Marta put out a hand, a shy hand but one without the slightest tremor, and laid it on Chorley's. "Listen," she said. Her hand was warm. "I'd like you to go out and help the poor postman restore the chain to his bicycle. Now, don't protest, I know you're a mechanically minded man, Chorley Tiebold. While you do that, I'll write a letter for you to carry to my friend. He will tell you what to do."

☙ ☙ ☙

Chorley sat on the steps and restored the chain to the bike. He got some grease on his trousers. The postman sat in a cane chair at a wicker table, sorting the mail. Every so often he would look expectantly along the veranda. He clearly hoped tea would appear. Downright sat at his feet, sighing.

Laura came and sat near Chorley. He asked her whether Aunt Marta was giving her singing lessons. Despite her impressive piano playing, Laura had never shown much interest in learning to sing.

"I wanted to learn some more of the old songs," she said. And then she sang one of the Tailor's, a short song:

> The past is a purse;
> the future a note of promise.

Past blights are poison in the ground,
rotted crops or living corpses.
Against the time the debt falls due
is time itself, and only time.
The dry seconds are sand in a glass,
and a servant made of sand.

"That wasn't what you were singing when I arrived," Chorley said. "It was something older. Something foreign."

"It's in Koine, demotic Greek, with some additional Cabalist-type words. It's a song they say St. Lazarus heard in the tomb."

"Sing it," Chorley said.

Laura got up and backed off from the steps till she stood in the center of the yard. She clasped her hands, as if it was important that each hand hold the other still. She began to sing. She was still practicing—that much Chorley could hear, because her voice faltered sometimes. The chant was made of complex shifting tonal patterns, of strings of words that didn't sound like sentences, because each word sounded like a *new* word, as if no word was used twice, as if the language of the song had no use for "and" and "to" and "it." Laura scowled in concentration. Chorley even saw sweat start on her face, beads big enough to tremble as a breeze came up. For as she sang, a wind did come up and sweep around the yard, around and around till it had raised a little dust devil, which danced for a moment, circling Laura. At the same moment Laura lost her place in the chant and broke off with a coughing sob, the dust devil collapsed and vanished. "Damn it," she said, panting.

"That was pretty impressive," Chorley said, then added, "sweetheart."

Marta appeared. She held out her letter. Chorley wiped his

greasy hands on his trousers and took it. The letter was in a sealed envelope. The envelope was addressed to "His High Reverence Erasmus Amon Tiebold"—the Grand Patriarch.

✢ ✢ ✢

Laura and Chorley stayed one night at Marta's. The adults enjoyed a diluted version of the young dreamhunter's Convalescent Two—in its ninth night no longer salable but strong enough to be felt. Uncle and niece caught a train back to Founderston together in what each thought was a friendly silence.

Laura didn't wonder about the oil-spotted, unopened envelope her uncle carried, or notice how his hand went to his jacket pocket now and then to check that the letter was still there.

Chorley didn't notice how Laura sat, her face turned to the view of paddocks and poplars and ditches filled with blackberry, or how her lips moved and fingers flickered as she mouthed the chant and counted its measures.

They failed to notice what they should have noticed, that Chorley was nursing his hopes and Laura her secret resolve.

For Laura was planning to make herself a sandman.

2

✢ ✢ ✢

LAURA SPENT SEVERAL DAYS AT THE
HOUSE IN FOUNDERSTON. SHE LET
HER AUNT AND UNCLE FUSS OVER HER. GRACE
was at home during the day but sleeping at the Rainbow
Opera, where she was dreaming Balloon Wars. During those
days Grace made plans for what they would all do in the summer, "as a family." Chorley and Laura nodded and made attentive noises. Chorley wrote a letter asking for an audience with
the Grand Patriarch. And Laura practiced "The Measures" in
the bath, in her bed at night, whenever she was left alone.

When she was ready, Laura took her pack, maps, food,
money, bedroll—and one other thing. She left a note for her
aunt and uncle and caught a train to Sisters Beach.

She went on up the track to Whynew Falls and trudged for
two days In through the silent country to the dry riverbed.

The sand disturbed by her father's digging, and by her
flight and struggle, hadn't settled. With no wind or rain to
erase them, the signs stayed. Laura looked at the imprint of
Chorley's camera, and the marks where her fingers had clawed
at the bank, and last, at the excavation, which looked like a
shallow grave. She tried to imagine what her father had seen
when he sang a body up out of that grave.

For the first time Laura let herself really think about what
she planned. It seemed to her that she had been drawn back to

this place by a series of unconnected impulses. She had asked her aunt Marta to teach her certain old songs that Marta and Tziga were taught as children by their great-grandfather. She had memorized and mastered one song—the long, complex chant Marta called "The Measures." Before she left Founders-ton, Laura had removed something from her jewelry box—the rust-stained rock she had picked up from the railbed five months before. She had kept her hand closed around the rock in her pocket as she rode on the train to Sisters Beach. She had mouthed "The Measures" at the carriage window, and her hand felt her heart beating in it, as though the rock in her hand was a heart.

She had been planning this for weeks, the plan like a pulse in the back of her mind. She'd fondled the statue in the Museum, touched it in order to feel how to *shape* it. Laura had formed a strange notion. She felt that she wanted to learn who Nown really was—if he was somebody in his own right, not just an occasional powerful wish wished by a succession of powerful Hames. Laura was planning a kind of experiment that, she thought, would let her look on the *real* face of her sandman. She had realized that she didn't want to look on a face like the one she and Rose had formed in the sand of Sisters Beach during the sand-sculpting competition, a face with the marks of their tools in it, clumsily made. No—Laura wanted to look into her sandman's *true* face.

Standing in the dry riverbed at map reference Y-17, Laura was about to attempt something that no Hame had attempted before. She *knew it* too, knew it in her body and brain, and in her mouth, where the words of "The Measures" seemed to sit on her tongue and fizz like sherbet dissolving.

Laura took her coat off. She put down her pack and the heavy water bottles she had carried and scarcely touched to drink—for she might need water for her work. She found an undisturbed patch of river sand and began to dig. She dug with one of Grace's narrow gardening trowels, which she had taken from its hook on the porch of Summerfort. It wasn't a very effective digging tool—Grace only ever used it on Summerfort's potted plants—but it did spare her hands.

When she had cleared a long, wide trench and had dug down to damp sand, Laura rested and had something to eat. Then she excavated some sticky clay from the bank of the stream. She wet her hands and worked the clay till it was firm but plastic. She spent an hour carefully fashioning two hands, hands nearly three times the size of her own, with long, thin fingers, big knuckles, and backs marked by branching sinews. She did her best. Art was one of two school subjects at which Laura had done well. (The other was music.) The girls at the Academy had often crowded around her table in art class to admire her work.

When she had finished making the hands, Laura looked up to check the light. It was a reflex—of course the light hadn't changed, no sunset would come to hurry her along.

Laura washed the clay from her hands. She stepped down into the excavation and began to scrape the damp sand together. She bulldozed with her palms. After a time she had scraped together a long mound. She stood up and walked around it, measuring it with her eyes. Then she knelt once more and began to work.

She disappeared into her work. She became invisible to herself.

Laura shaped a pair of long, sturdy legs. She shaped square heels, round anklebones, and a thick Achilles tendon. She modeled squared calf muscles, strong thighs, and a narrow pelvis. She made a form remembering the statues she had looked at, and the one she had been moved to touch, much to Rose's embarrassment. "How could Rose have known?" Laura thought as she finished with the buttocks and began to shape the small of the back.

Then, while the back was still only roughly shaped, Laura paused and thrust her hand into her coat pocket.

Nown had had her father's letter hidden in his chest. It had served him as a heart. Laura had a different plan for her sandman. She fished the rust-stained rock from her coat pocket and pushed it through the sandy back. She shoved it deep into the body she imagined lay before her, with its knees, feet, hipbones, chest, and face—*its own true face*—all hidden in the sand. She withdrew her empty hand and closed the hole, smoothed the place over. She then shaped the symmetrical trapezoid muscles and shoulder blades. She fashioned wide shoulders and strong arms. She made sure the elbows were level with the waist, and wrists with the tops of the thighs. She got his proportions right. She laid the clay hands at the ends of the arms, backs down and curled fingers up. She blended the join between sand and clay, and sprinkled a coating of dry silver sand onto the still damp blue clay so that—when he was dry—his hands would be the same color as the rest of him. She made a powerful neck and as shapely a skull as she could fashion.

Laura sat back and began to laugh. She'd forgotten to make ears. She looked at the clay on the bank, and the place both she and her father had dug, and felt too tired to move. So she wrapped her coat around her and lay beside the facedown, earless figure and went to sleep.

There was no dream at that place in the riverbed. Nothing marked on the map, and nothing even for Laura.

✦ ✦ ✦

When Laura woke up, she opened a can of condensed milk and poured it on top of several dry rounds of strongbread. She looked at the facedown figure. It was beginning to dry in the air, its surface turning a soft, granular silver. Laura was careful as she moved around it. She didn't want the vibrations of her footsteps to shake any sand from the figure, making cracks in his skin.

She went to the bank and scooped out two balls of clay. She fashioned each into an ear, a left and a right, like the hands. She had to dampen and remold the sand of the figure's head in order to attach the ears, though each had a cupped back, like a shell, that held it firm.

Laura lay down once more to gather her strength. She had been in that place for sixteen hours by her watch, through a sleep and two meals. She began to sing, lying there, looking into the sandman's ear. She didn't feel any need to get up and lift her hands to the mist-covered skies. She sang in a quiet, clear, intimate voice. An unfaltering voice. And, as on other occasions when she'd managed to get through "The Measures" without making a mistake, Laura began to feel the spell build around her, a force like a wind funneling up around her body. Nothing moved, though; her clothes and hair stayed still, and no dust devil got up to dance for her as it had when she sang in Aunt Marta's yard. The force sucked at her, like air pressure so low it was almost a vacuum. Laura grew cold. She finished her song shivering. She shut her mouth. The air began to shimmer around her.

Laura lifted her own cheek and ear from the riverbed. She leaned up on one elbow and bent over the back of the figure's neck. There, on the bumps she'd made to suggest vertebrae, Laura scratched the letters with the tip of her finger. She wrote his whole name:

NOWN.

The cold, shimmering, sucking force around her leapt into her body and out again through her finger. She heard the spell again, a whole song that seemed to shout only this: *"Soul of the spell! Come out of the earth! Wake! Speak! Obey my will, and know your name!"*

Laura flopped back, exhausted.

Nown's arms moved up from his sides, turned palm down, and pressed. Laura was only feet from him. His hand brushed by her as it moved. She saw the back of the head she had shaped stir, a crack appear in the sand where what she had shaped came to an end and the earth itself began. Laura watched Nown lift his face from the riverbed. He came up shaking off clots of sand. Only not *all* the sand fell. Instead it sorted itself out, some grains rising like steam against Nown's face, settling there and shaping it.

He turned toward Laura, his skin of sand still rearranging itself. She saw his skin move to make sharp ridges of eyelids. She saw his nostrils become dark and deep, then flare, as though he drew breath. She saw his lips split in two, and teeth rise up before the hollow of his mouth, and sand run from the hollow, leaving only enough for a tongue. She saw thin gaps appear in the fence of his teeth, but nothing in his eyes, no lines to represent irises, no holes for pupils. His eyes stayed smooth—widely spaced in a face as handsome as that of a classical statue. Except that, having no human model, the face was too symmetrical.

Nown got up, separated his sandy self from the sand of the riverbed. He stood above Laura, looking down at her. He opened his mouth again—and this time didn't dribble sand. He said, "Laura Hame, I am your servant."

3

✤ ✤ ✤

*L*AURA HAD DONE WHAT SHE WANTED TO DO. SHE HAD MADE HER OWN NOWN. THAT DONE, SHE WAS LEFT with only her duty. She had to follow her father's instructions. She felt that, if she followed them faithfully, she might somehow find him again. Sometimes this was what she felt, and sometimes she thought it was crazy to have feelings like that, and that her father was lost to her forever.

Laura knew where she had to go next because of the film her father had made. She believed that she would find her father's "dreadful dream" near the burned building. The film had shown its black beams flickering like the shadows of twigs stirred by a breeze against a bay of naked sand. The film had stopped, then started again with the building, shot from her father's shoulder. He had held the camera and turned himself around, to show the view back the way he had come, and hills like a page in a book of profiles.

Laura was looking at those hills now from the other side. She could see them rising in the distance, above the scrubby country across the dry streambed. She knew that, beyond the hills, she would find the ruin and the dream she had to catch and carry.

It was as if, for months, Laura had gone about her business turned side-on to her own intentions. From the moment she had read her father's letter, she had meant to do what he told her. She had felt that if she followed his instructions she could conjure *him* too, make him reappear. But she had not thought clearly about what following her father's instructions would actually entail. She hadn't thought about catching the "dreadful dream" and overdreaming her aunt Grace.

Laura tried to make plans as she lay on the ground looking up at her sandman. But any thoughts about what she should do next were driven out of her head by the sight of him—the *fact* of him.

She—Laura Hame—had raised a thinking, speaking being from nothingness, or time, or family tradition. It was very confusing. She had made *a person* out of river sand in the Place, and the rock she'd kept. She had made her sandman out of longing and disappointment and indecision. She had made him as though she were making her own father, rather than a replacement for her father's servant.

Laura had made someone to look after her. And here he was, big and strong, and *wise*—she was sure of it—and looking at her to see what she would ask him to do. Waiting for her to make decisions.

Laura was too exhausted to move and couldn't decide what to say to him.

Hello again. I missed you. I needed you.

Looking up at Nown, Laura felt she had finished everything she *wanted* to do. She felt safe, not just because he'd arrived again to protect her but because she'd put something of herself into him—where it was safe for now—something she felt she was too young to use wisely.

Laura realized that she needed to rest. So great was her need that, when she closed her eyes, she immediately fell asleep.

✧ ✧ ✧

Laura woke when she turned over and snuffled up a little sand. She sneezed and sat up. She was thirsty and needed to pee. Time had passed. Nown stood as he had before. He was looking out over the low bank of the riverbed and through the curtain of grasses at the hills Inland.

Laura asked him what he was doing.

"Listening," he said.

She crawled over to her pack and found her water bottle. She took a long drink, not bothering to ration the liquid. Her work was done, and Nown could carry her out again.

This thought came to her calmly. He had suggested it once, and she had shied away from him. Now she couldn't see anything wrong with the idea. Perhaps *this* Nown was less uncanny—more hers. She looked at him again and began to laugh.

Nown had no nipples, or navel, or whatever lay under the fig leaves on the copies of classical statues at the Museum. Before making this Nown, Laura had studied the most beautiful statue she could find, but it had had a fig leaf. She had made her Nown facedown, hoping to discover his true face—but she also wanted to find out what was underneath the fig leaves on statues. Of course she had a vague idea—she'd seen plenty of small children of both sorts, girls and boys, running around naked on the beach. But she was quite sure men were different from little boys.

Laura finished laughing and wiped her eyes. She imagined sharing the joke with Rose—then sobered up when she remembered just how much she'd have to explain first.

Nown had watched her laugh. But when she was quiet he lifted his head again and listened.

"Is someone coming?" Laura said. She clapped her hand over her mouth, regretting having laughed so loudly.

"No," Nown said.

"Then what are you listening to?"

"I am listening to it. It is listening to you."

Laura shivered. "The Place?" she said. "Is the Place listening to me?"

"Yes. I can hear now. I am nearer to myself than before."

Laura stared at Nown for so long that her neck began to hurt. She climbed to her feet and stood rubbing it. Did Nown mean that each new Nown was *better* than the one before? That he was made to make progress toward some *perfect* sandman? He couldn't mean that, could he?

"What do you mean?" she said.

"I can hear now. I am here with myself," Nown said.

"How?" she asked, then realized it wasn't the right question.

Nown answered her anyway. "I don't know."

"Are you more yourself? More your *true* self?" Laura asked, then blushed—feeling she had asked for a compliment or a show of gratitude.

Nown was looking at her intently. She knew it by the way the gleaming black grains of iron sand sorted themselves out from the mix in his face and flooded his wide open eyes till his eyes, brows, and the bridge of his nose were banded with glittering black. He answered her. "Yes, I am."

Laura was pleased to have helped Nown. Pleased with her own speculation. She didn't for a minute consider that her servant might have spoken obscurely.

Nown stood, his face striped black with the force of his attention, and waited for his mistress to help him understand what he sensed. Then she was talking again, and his desire to understand disappeared into the flow of time, for her will was the flow of time for him.

She said, "My father wrote in his letter that I must listen to the Place. He meant the *dreams*. He meant me to do something about the convicts in the dreams."

"Yes," Nown said. "I think that is what he wanted." He

touched his chest, wherein he had once carried Laura's father's letter—or where, at least, the *eighth* him had.

Laura saw that he remembered the letter and was curious to know if he knew what she'd put into him. When she asked, he said, "It's a rock you wanted to throw at your father. To throw at the train that took him away. It is anger and unhappy love in a rock."

Laura began to cry then. She covered her face with her hands—raw under their nails from scraping sand—and sobbed. Her sandman made no move to comfort her, and after a time she simply finished crying.

Nown was listening again, it seemed. And Laura imagined that it might be embarrassment that made him look away through the grass to the hills Inland.

She told him to pick up her pack. He did. Then she told him to pick her up.

His arms were faintly warm, like sand under a winter sun. They softened to accommodate her. She rested her head on his chest, heard a faint creak of sand moving on sand—but no heartbeat. "Back to Summerfort first," she said, "for provisions."

Nown began to walk back the way Laura had come.

VI
The Rainbow Opera

CHORLEY'S APPOINTMENT WITH THE
GRAND PATRIARCH WAS ON A SUNDAY
AFTERNOON BETWEEN THE MASSES AT NOON
and three. On Sundays the Isle of the Temple was quiet. All
dream parlors and palaces were closed until sundown. By one
the cafés were open and serving whatever it was possible to
prepare in an hour.

Chorley crossed from the west bank on the enclosed iron
footbridge slung under the rail bridge. He was early. He
stopped at a café for coffee, and crepes with honey and nuts—
a Sunday favorite. The café was across the square from the
Temple. Chorley ate and watched pigeons fossick for crumbs
among the iron table and chair legs. Then he paid, stored a
coffee-soaked sugar lump in one cheek, and crossed the
square. He went around the Temple to the gates of the Grand
Patriarch's Palace. He presented his appointment card. The
guards, men in long embroidered capes—beneath which they
cradled repeater rifles—let Chorley in. An usher led him upstairs and along galleries under high vaulted ceilings covered
by frescoes. Their footsteps echoed.

Chorley had expected to be taken to an office or an audience chamber, but instead the usher showed him to the
Grand Patriarch's private rooms.

The Grand Patriarch was just finishing his lunch. He was sitting at one end of a long, polished table and tilting his bowl to spoon up the last of his soup. There were a few slices of black bread and a pot of tea in front of him. When Chorley appeared, the Grand Patriarch called over the solitary servant in the room and had him pull out a chair for Chorley where a second cup and saucer sat waiting for him.

Chorley sat down. He turned this way and that to check how many people were in the large, gloomy room, and whether they were near enough to hear him if he spoke. There were two guards, one by either door, the servant, and a young priest, who stood closer.

The Grand Patriarch set the bowl back on its base, laid his spoon down, and removed the napkin he'd tied around his long beard to keep it clean. He wiped his mouth. His beard, dented where it had been tied, began to spring back into shape. For the next few minutes while they talked, Chorley watched the beard expand and restore itself to its square, golden magnificence.

The Grand Patriarch held his hand out to Chorley, palm down. He offered his ring for Chorley to kiss—but Chorley only took the hand and shook it. The Grand Patriarch smiled faintly.

"Cousin," Chorley began. "I will call you Cousin because I am not a parishioner, and I intend to presume upon our relationship."

Erasmus Tiebold took up the teapot and poured Chorley a cup.

"Er—thank you," said Chorley.

"How was my friend when you saw her?"

"That was more than a week ago," Chorley said—he couldn't resist telling his kinsman off for not responding more quickly to his request to see him. "Marta was well—a week ago," Chorley added, then took the sealed letter from his jacket and gave it to his kinsman.

The Grand Patriarch broke the seal and read the letter. It wasn't long. Erasmus Tiebold finished and looked at Chorley over the top of the page. Then he gestured to the young priest, who came over. The Grand Patriarch handed the young man the page, then said, "No, don't read it." Then he gestured at the branch of candles in the middle of the table. The young priest held the corner of the page to a candle flame. The paper flared up. The Grand Patriarch pointed to his empty soup bowl, and the young priest laid the paper there to burn and backed away from the table.

Chorley watched this and realized that, if his family really had found itself on the wrong side of something, a secretive, sinister something that had to do with the Regulatory Body, then this secret, sinister something had *opponents*. This man, the head of the Orthodox Church and his father's cousin, was an opponent. This man—and other men and women. Marta, for instance. Chorley realized that he wasn't here just to look for Tziga, he had come to show that he was willing to sign on to some sort of *resistance*. If they would have him.

Chorley actually had no idea what Cas Doran and the Body were up to—but they had taken Tziga from him, he was sure of it. He blamed them. They were his enemies. And his enemies' opponents were his friends.

Chorley leaned toward his kinsman, his eyes fierce. "Tell me what to do," he said.

The Grand Patriarch laid his hand on Chorley's. "Only this, for now," he said. "You must take passage to Sisters Beach by sea. Catch the packet boat from Westport. The schooner *Morningstar*, which sails every week. You must leave the *Morningstar* at the first place she stops."

The Grand Patriarch lifted his hand and leaned back. He

took up his teacup and sipped, raising his brows to urge
Chorley to taste his tea. "Don't bring anything back with you,"
he added. "And I hope to see you on your return."

✣ ✣ ✣

Grace sat on the bed and watched her husband pack.

"I won't be back till after St. Lazarus's Day," he said. "I have
a table booked for you at Bacchus. The booking is for six-
thirty. And Rose wanted to go skating in the afternoon."

"Goody," said Grace, who didn't like skating.

"She won't expect you to take her," Chorley said.

"Still, I had better. She won't mind if I'm groggy." Rose
would know that her mother would be tired. Grace performed
a dream called Homecoming on the evening of St. Lazarus's
Day every year. The site of Homecoming was three days In
from Doorhandle, and Grace was setting out herself the following day.

Grace didn't like watching her husband set off somewhere
before her, or in this case without her. Nor did she like how
small his suitcase was. Chorley wouldn't usually travel anywhere
overnight without a selection of clothes and a case of toi-
letries. He liked to look his best.

"What are you hoping to find?" she asked.

"I'll tell you what I do find," he answered, "that's all I can
say." He changed the subject. "Does Laura know you expect to
see her on St. Lazarus's Eve?"

"Yes. Rose has spoken to her. And she sent us a postcard
from Tricksie Bend."

"She's at Summerfort again?"

"Yes. Chorley—she's looking for clues. She got the camera,
but she's still looking."

Chorley put on his coat and picked up his suitcase. "Well—
maybe soon she won't need to look anymore."

Grace watched her husband's slow, growing smile. He looked like a man with a confident hope in his future happiness. Grace couldn't share his hope. As she watched him standing there with his suitcase, she felt that he was leaving her. Leaving her alone with her fear.

2

A WEEK BEFORE ST. LAZARUS'S EVE, NOWN CARRIED LAURA, ALONG WITH HER PACK AND PROVISIONS, UP THE Whynew Falls track and into the Place.

The sandman loped along, his stride and speed almost unvarying. Sometimes Laura asked him to put her down so she could walk for a bit. "To get my blood moving," she told him. She walked and raised a sweat, and the dust of chaff stuck to her face and prickled in her nose. Nown could run with her without raising a sweat or tiring—of course. She had him hurry when she was sleeping. She hoped he would run her right through dreams.

They had passed the stream at Y-17 before she was quite ready to sleep—Nown had carried her there in ten and a half hours. Nearly thirty hours after that, Laura fell asleep in his arms on the upward slope of a crumbling, fissured hillside. And Nown *did* run her through dreams.

Laura dreamed she was a young man who had found a place above a waterfall where he could look down and see the picnickers who came and bathed. She dreamed that he was waiting at the end of the summer, on a day when the track was quiet and a certain girl came to the pool in the company of his sister. Laura left the young man waiting. She then dreamed she was a hunter, walking through brush at evening beside a ravine from which a terrible smell was coming.

She woke up, moaning. They were at the foot of the far side of the hill. "Nown! Stop," she complained. "You hold the heat so. You're like a hot stone. Put me down."

Nown put Laura down, and she staggered around till he steadied her. She asked for water and sat on the ground to drink. "I had the beginning of a dream about a man in too tight trousers," she told Nown, then laughed. "*Funny* feeling. And I had a nightmare." She shivered.

Nown said nothing. He didn't even tell her she should eat. Not that she needed telling.

Laura got out her strongbread, some nuts, and an apple. She looked around as she ate. They were in a narrow valley between hills that were more like dust heaps in a midden. Laura almost expected to see human rubbish—old bike wheels or bits of broken bedsteads smeared with ash. It was a horrible place, and if there had been any wind, she was sure she would have been breathing dust.

It had been windy when she and Nown had crossed the paddock before Whynew Falls Reserve. Nown had been impervious to the wind, which had left him as untouched as a rock—when she had expected him to smoke in the gale like the crest of a dry dune.

Laura couldn't tell, from where she sat at their base, whether the hills were the same shapes as those in her father's film. She hoped they were. She hoped these were the last of the hills. She and Nown couldn't go around these because they were so crumbled away that the ravines between each hill were choked with boulders and heaped shingle, all harder going than the climb.

Laura pitched her apple core at the next hill. "What am I doing?" she said.

"Eating," said Nown.

"I keep forgetting just how literal-minded you are," she said. "I keep imagining you're marvelous."

Nown was silent.

Laura looked up at him. "Would you like to be able to eat?" she asked. She wondered whether he was envious of things he might know she could do, like taste food.

"I have watched eating often. Vitas Hame asked the fifth to hold up the arch by his fireplace for many years. The fifth could see the dining table. Vitas Hame often had guests. Feasts."

Nown was telling her that some ancestor of hers had had him play statue and support the roof.

She asked Nown to show her how he'd stood.

He put his feet together and stretched his arms up over his head, the heels of his hands horizontal as though pressing a great weight upward.

"How unkind," Laura said.

"It was the service asked."

"I won't ever ask anything like that," she promised. Then she had Nown pick her, the pack, and the water bottles up again. She told him not to let her fall asleep till they got to where they were going. "I want to be ready to sleep when we get there."

They went on, up the next hill, Nown climbing on his legs and with one hand. The arm that cradled Laura had lost its elbow joint and become a flattened sling. Her pack and the water bottles rested in a hollow Nown had made in his back.

At the summit they found lesser hills below them, a rumpled cover of vegetation, dead pasture on hills any wind would have made bald, grass like a haze, and more hills piled in the hazy distance.

Laura walked for a time. Nown broke a path for her, parting the grass.

✤ ✤ ✤

Sixty-five hours In, by Laura's watch, they came to where more sky was visible than at any other place in the Place. The sky was still white but like steam gathered under an immense high dome. They looked down from a low hill onto what appeared to be a wide harbor, a seabed of sand and rocks that shelved down to several deep, branching channels. On a spur of land with an apparently man-made, straight-edged shoreline were the remains of a huge timber-frame building.

"There," Laura said. Nown let her down, and she went ahead. She held his hand as if she were leading him, though he was the one anchored on the slope.

They climbed all the way down and walked to the head of the causeway—for Laura could see now that that was what the squared headland was, a wide bank of hewn stones mortared together and paved on top. The ruin stood on a hammerhead of embankment at the end of the causeway. Its main beams were of tree length and girth, the surfaces of their wood scabbed and glossy black.

Laura took her pack from Nown, untied her bedroll, and spread it on the ground. She was thinking—whatever the nightmare was, it should relate to the fire, to this particular place. She imagined being penned in by smoke and herded by flame.

She squatted by her bedroll and drank and ate a little. She said to Nown, "I'm afraid."

He made no sound, no comforting noises, not even a grunt of acknowledgment. He didn't offer encouragement, or remind her that having come so far she *must* want to find out.

"My father wanted me to do this," Laura said.

Nown remained silent.

"Is he still alive?" Laura asked. She needed to know now. If she couldn't ever expect to see her father again, then she didn't need to do this, she didn't need to sleep here.

"I don't know if he's alive," Nown answered. "The eighth knew that. I am the ninth. I know only whether *you* are alive."

"Know, or believe?" Laura imagined her father standing in the shadow of a passion fruit vine that grew over the arch of a gate. The gate to a garden in the afterlife.

"I can't believe. I can only know," said Nown.

Laura thought about that. She said, "There's a nightmare here that my father caught to take to the men in prisons. Something to frighten them into obedience. Something worse than the worst sermons about Hell. My father wanted me to catch it too—and show it to other people, so that they'll know how bad it's been for the prisoners. It's like the little children working in mines and factories fifty or so years ago—everyone knew about that, but they didn't feel how heartless it was till people wrote describing the conditions. Then public opinion changed the law. If people experience what the prisoners are forced to, they'll be shocked, indignant, and—I hope—compassionate." Laura was wiping her hands, which were covered in oil from the peanuts she had eaten. She said, "Anyway, that's what Da said I should do. He always thought that, with any encouragement at all, most people will behave kindly." She mused for a moment, then said, "I should probably tell the newspapers too. Write them letters explaining what I know."

Nown said, "Your father had injured his hands. Shall I hold your arms?"

It was a practical suggestion. And given what she knew about his nature, Laura was surprised that Nown had offered any suggestions. But this one was *coldly* practical, and she felt like a condemned criminal sitting on deathwatch with a polite warden. She lay down. She looked up at Nown and said, "All right. But gently."

She couldn't stop shivering. She was afraid to close her eyes. "Is it cold?" she said.

"I don't know."

Laura yawned and her jaw shuddered. She was tired after all. She listened, but there was nothing to hear. She was adrift in her body, in the quietest place in the universe.

Weak from a long sickness, heavily encumbered with what he did not know—perhaps the bedclothes—the man moved. He came to and moved. With no result. His eyes were open, but it was dark. Pitch black, as though death had pressed its thumbs into his eye sockets. He turned his head. A thin cloth pulled tight against his face as he turned. He opened his mouth and sucked in air to call out, and the cloth came into his mouth, a bubble of lily-scented satin and air that smelled of damp earth.

His hands stirred. He meant to lift them. He meant to pull the cloth from his face. His hands moved up only inches and were pinned by pillows of satin, an upholstery over hard walls. His hands scraped and slithered. He heard the noise his nails made.

He heard the box.

He began to scream. The reverberations of his screams gave him the whole shape of the box, narrow-walled, low-roofed, unyielding. Its lid was screwed down hard and would not give. Earth was piled above the lid, airless earth, pressing down hard.

He screamed and moaned, he fought the box in a frenzy of terror. He struggled and scuffled, strained his head up so that it beat against the coffin's lid. He chewed his shroud, took it into his mouth to tear it to get a little more air. Any more. He bit at his lips, and through his lips, and through the shroud. He managed to make a hole in the shroud, yet still stifled on the condensed vapor of his own breath. He bent his hands back and pressed upward, clawed till the satin tore and he was through to the wood. He beat on the lid of the coffin. He strained till his wrists cracked.

Then he stopped. He made himself lie still and listen. He forced his panic back. He thought he heard birdsong. He thought he heard the world above him, daylight and the open air. He listened. He listened. He listened. He hoped to

*hear someone coming, someone who could help him. He hoped. He listened.
Then he burst out of his hope as he couldn't burst out of the coffin. He went mad
with activity, he convulsed. His bowels let go, and the trapped air turned foul.
He scraped at the lid till his nails ripped away from his fingertips, then till his
fingers were broken. He didn't feel it—he felt only the grip of the box.*

*He forced his hands up as far as his face, to find flesh that did yield, his own
mouth the only space he could thrust his fingers through. His lips were in tatters,
and his broken hands were full of his own torn hair.*

He kicked and thrashed.

It was dark.

It would not break.

It was dark.

He was shut in, shut in, scuffling on in the stifling dark.

Laura woke and reared up. Her head collided with something above her, on top of her. She screamed.

Nown released her hands, and they flew out, making rents in his arms and shoulders, bashing sprays of sand from his body. The sand flew wide, stopped in the air, then rushed back into Nown's body.

Laura scrambled up and away from Nown. She stood, shaking her arms and howling. She had bitten her lips, and blood was dripping from her chin. She cried like a child, in terror and despair. She had caught the dreadful dream. She would find herself buried alive if she slept, when she slept, night after night. It wasn't over.

The dream went on. Laura knew that it did. The buried man suffered. He waited to die in a mess of blood and filth. He didn't have any hope. He was a penned thing.

Laura walked back and forth, shaking her hands and crying. Her arms were aching. She could see bruises and sandy welts on her skin. She pulled up her sleeves and showed Nown the marks he had made. She roared at him and shook her arms under his nose.

Nown got to his feet.

Laura rushed at him, put her arms around him, and pressed her head into his creaking chest. "Be human!" she begged.

Nown said, "How?"

Laura continued to cry. Nown was unrewarding to cling to. Stony, then yielding. If she pressed his sand, it cracked and shifted.

Suddenly he picked her up, his hands under her armpits. He lifted her, then lowered her. Lifted her again, then lowered her. He swung her gently from side to side.

Laura was shocked; she hung from his hands, stiff and stunned. Then she realized that he'd seen people do this to coax their small children out of crying. She was being dandled, like a baby. She stopped crying. "Nown?"

He lifted her to his eyes.

"I'm not a baby," she said.

He put her carefully down.

✣ ✣ ✣

Laura packed up her bedroll. She drank some water, then set Nown walking in front of her, toward the hills.

As they went she thought about her father on the platform of Sisters Beach Station—his gnawed lips and bandaged hands. She wondered how he had managed not to think of her as a child. As *his* child, whom he should protect at all costs. But between the nightmare and the station, her father had shaped and sung his Nown into existence. Laura thought that she must judge her father now like God, not like a girl of fifteen.

Laura had a heart, but she still had to do what her father had asked. She would take the dream to those who profited from their willingness to terrify other people with it and dreams like it. They would all be there—on St. Lazarus's Eve. The President would be in his suite with his family. The Secretary of the Interior in his, with his family. Government secretaries and deputy secretaries, captains of industry—they would all be there. Laura had no doubt that she could overdream her aunt. She was the same size as the dream now. It was packed into her, tamped down, compacted under tremendous pressure, like a huge, horrible charge.

*O*N A SUNNY SATURDAY TWO DAYS BE-
FORE THE FIRST OFFICIAL DAY OF
SPRING—ST. LAZARUS'S EVE—A COUNTERMAN
at Farry's looked up to see Laura Hame. He smiled. "You are
the first of your family I've seen this season," he said. "Welcome back."

"I'm here alone," she said.

The counterman was puzzled. He watched the girl touch
her hair—the ends of her curls that showed under the red velvet hat she wore. Her hair was damp, freshly washed—and
short.

Of course—one of the inseparable two had passed and the
other had failed. He had read that in the newspaper. She was
thin, he saw, and had lost none of her summer tan. She was
beginning to look like a dreamhunter. She even had the dry,
scabbed lips of those who hunted far Inland. "What would
you like, Miss Hame?"

"I'd like some raspberry lollipops, and a hazelnut log. And
some toffee shells and musk cream. The cream in a jar,
please. I'll make the musk creams up myself."

"For Miss Rose," the counterman said. He knew each girl's
favorite candy.

"Yes, a Saint's Day present. Could you put the shells and
the hazelnut log in pretty boxes?"

Her tongue was mauve, the counterman saw. She was already chewing that drug they used.

As he assembled the boxes and jar of musk cream, the counterman thought about everything he had read in the papers. He'd forgotten it all when he'd first seen her. He'd seen her and smiled, as he would at the first cherry blossoms or daffodils. She'd made him think about summer. He'd always liked those girls.

As he put the boxes in a bag, he said, "I was sorry to hear about your father."

"Thank you," she said, and took her package from him.

✥ ✥ ✥

At that time of year, off-season, the Sisters Beach train had only two coaches and a mail car. It was never an express. The conductor had an easy job. He kept his eye on the third-class carriage, since there were people on and off it at every station. But he had only two people in the private compartment of first class—and those two had tickets all the way to Founderston. In fact, he looked in on them only once, to ask if they would like their beds turned down. The compartment was a sleeper.

The girl was nearest to the door. She told the conductor no thank you. "My father will do it," she said, and gestured at the man in the seat beside her. The man was huge, bundled in a coat and travel blanket and wearing a broad-brimmed hat.

"Shall I turn up the heat in here?" the conductor asked.

"Would you?" she said. "Father feels the cold."

The man didn't acknowledge the conductor. He didn't turn from the window. It was dark outside; there was nothing to see.

"Can I do anything else for you?" the conductor asked. He raised his voice to reach the man.

"No. That will be all, thank you," the girl said.

The conductor moved away from the door before sliding it shut. As he did so, he let more light into the compartment, whose lights were turned down low. The light from the carriage passage made a reflection appear in the carriage window. A reflection of the man's hidden face. It gave the conductor a fright for a moment—though it must only have been a trick of the light. The conductor closed the door. He walked off shaking his head, telling himself he hadn't seen—couldn't have seen—the face of a statue, stone but with eyes full of a seething *aliveness* that wasn't quite like life.

✦ ✦ ✦

Laura wanted to sleep in order to escape her memory of the dreadful dream. But she knew that once she slept, she would be back in that stifling box. She dared not close her eyes, but there was nothing to look at. It was night, and the carriage window was black.

She slid along the seat and huddled against her sandman's bundled form. She said, "There's nowhere else—nowhere to go."

Her servant turned to her. She peered up into his face. It was statuesque and superficial and offered her no comfort. "I hate this dream," she said.

"And you are going to give it to other people," Nown said.

Laura stirred uncomfortably. "I'm doing what my father asked me to do," she said. "We need to make people see what it is like for the prisoners. To make them feel pity."

"Do people who are frightened feel pity?"

Laura considered, then said, "The dream frightens me.

But it does make me feel sorry for the prisoners, and responsible." She gripped the sleeve of the coat Nown was wearing. "You must stop acting as if I'm a child and you're an adult. You're not an adult. You're not really a person."

"Do you think you should be talking to an adult about what you plan to do?" Nown said.

"You're doing it again!" Laura pushed herself away from him. She retired to the opposite corner of the compartment and glowered at him.

"Laura," Nown said. "Why do you think that the Hame servant cannot be undone until after its final 'N' has been inscribed?"

Laura remembered how she'd undone the eighth Nown—wiped him out of existence. She recalled with horror the dry sigh of his undoing. "I'm sorry," she said. "I'm sorry I did that to you. Or the eighth you."

"That isn't something I have feelings about," Nown said.

"Do you have feelings?"

"I find I feel afraid for you, Laura. No Hame can undo a servant without first giving it a voice so that it can talk to its maker, give its maker an account of what it has done, what it has been asked to do."

"I have to do this, Nown," Laura said, desperate. "This is what my father wanted me to do! The only thing he asked me to do!"

"Your father said to me, 'Laura isn't very good at thinking for herself.' "

Laura cried at her servant, "Stop! You're *hurting* me!"

Nown fell silent.

Laura turned away from him. She put her eye to a gap in the compartment's curtain and watched two men standing in the train's hallway and smoking pipes. They looked peacefully involved and very human.

Laura wiped her eyes on her sleeve, then put a wad of

Wakeful into her mouth—her fifth in three days. Her tongue went numb, then a moment later the drug roared into her head like oxygen and electricity and fury.

The train slowed into the first turn of the spiral at Mount Kahaugh.

4

✣ ✣ ✣

AT HIGH TIDE, LATE IN THE AF-
TERNOON OF ST. LAZARUS'S EVE,
THE SCHOONER MORNINGSTAR TACKED TO-
ward the ocean shore of So Long Spit, where it put in to its
first stop, an ironwood platform built at the low-tide line,
beside the lighthouse.

The head keeper and his son waited on the platform. They
had tied up their boat and were ready to catch the line thrown
to them from the deck of the schooner. Between them, the
seamen, the head keeper, and his boy brought the schooner
alongside the platform. They were all practiced at this
monthly maneuver, and it was easy on a day like this—a day
with a calm sea and only a light breeze.

The seamen delivered the lighthouse supplies, boxes of
canned food, barrels of flour and rice, and whale oil. All were
winched over the side in a rope net. The head keeper and his
son guided the net gently down onto the platform.

The captain of the *Morningstar* was supervising the unloading
and passing the time with the keeper, handing on the news,
wishing the man and his family a happy St. Lazarus's Day.
When the captain had done that, he glanced over his shoulder
and leaned closer to confide. He spoke in a loud whisper—for
the deck and platform were separated by eight feet. "We have a
visitor for you," he said.

"Someone from the Keepers' Service?" the head keeper asked, worried.

"I don't know his business. He just asked to be put off—though his passage is paid all the way to Sisters Beach." The captain looked over his shoulder again. "Here he comes," he warned. "I told him to stay out of the way till we had finished unloading. I wanted to let you know."

The seamen unrolled a ladder. The passenger appeared beside them, a tall, well-dressed man sporting a hat with earflaps. One seaman passed the man's bag over the rail. The head keeper stood under the ladder as the passenger straddled the rail and lowered himself onto it. The keeper helped the man onto the platform, then ignored him for the next several minutes while the *Morningstar* cast off. Then the keeper's son jumped down into their boat, and his father began to pass the barrels and boxes to him.

The visitor didn't offer to help—which was fine by the keeper, who thought inexpert help slowed down any job. They were finished in only a few minutes; then, "Sir," said the keeper's son, and practically snatched the visitor's bag from him.

"Careful, boy." The keeper understood that his son was in a hurry. His boy liked to race the *Morningstar* along the shore for a little way. It was a game he had played for some time now.

The keeper handed the visitor down to the boat. He was feeling a little awkward, since he had tried a number of times to catch the man's eye and had been avoided. Nor had the man made any attempt to introduce himself.

The keeper and his boy took an oar each and pulled to shore—not quite straight since the boy was too eager and was putting a little more into each stroke. They bumped onto the sand, and the boy jumped over the side and waded in to hold the bow as the visitor made a well-timed leap onto the beach beyond where the waves were breaking. The keeper and his son ran the boat a few feet up the beach and began to unload.

This time the visitor offered to help.

"Oh, no, it takes only a few minutes," the boy said. His eye was on the schooner, whose sails were set and filling as she came around to head along the Spit and a little out to sea.

The keeper and his boy went back and forth with boxes and barrels across the short stretch of sand between water and the first clumps of spinifex, marram, and pink-flowering ice plants. As the keeper worked, he spoke to the visitor. "We have inspectors from the Lighthouse Keepers' Service who visit. We have surveyors, and bird-watchers, and the parish priest, Father Paul . . ."

None of this inspired the visitor to volunteer his name or mission. He watched the keeper. His face was tense—and tender around the mouth, as though he were near to tears. "Come on up then," the keeper finally said.

He led the man to the sandy track up onto the crabgrass, and under the wind-tortured pines that had been coaxed to grow in soil hauled in by carts from the farm at the base of the Spit. The keeper pointed out the three houses and said, "There are nine of us here permanently. Myself and my wife, my boy and my two girls; the second keeper and his wife—they have a baby on the way—the third keeper, and the reserve man." The keeper shot a glance at the visitor, trying to read him.

The priest, Father Paul, had asked the head keeper to stay quiet about "the reserve man"—the man who had come five months before and was now fit for a few duties, like cleaning whale oil smoke from the lamp. Whale oil burned bright but not clean, and it took eight hours every day, seven days a week, to keep the crystals clean.

The head keeper had taken the reserve man in as a favor to Father Paul—and it wasn't the first of that sort of favor.

The reserve man was called Mr. Thomas—but he wasn't the keeper's first "Mr. Thomas."

Of this latest Mr. Thomas the keeper knew only this: that he had been injured in an accident in the rail yards of Westport and had been given up for dead by a dandy of a doctor. For weeks he had occupied the bed nearest the door in the crowded men's ward of Magdalene Charity Hospital. He had lain with the curtains drawn around his bed, and the sisters waiting every moment to sew him into his bottom sheet. For weeks he lay still, balanced on the border of life and death—and then lived. No one came to claim him. And when he was waking—but not yet awake—the sisters claimed that he somehow disturbed the sleep of their other patients. It may have been their unwillingness to keep him on the ward that brought him to Father Paul's notice. The priest took an interest in him, and when he had improved enough to travel, Father Paul brought him to the lighthouse to convalesce. Mr. Thomas. And all Father Paul's *former* Mr. Thomases had been in hiding from the law.

✦ ✦ ✦

Chorley could see that the new lighthouse was built only a little way from the base of the old one—a timber structure whose wood had rotted. The new one stood on four steel legs and was of plate steel, like the hull of a ship. The lighthouse had a widow's walk at its top, around the windows that let out the light.

As they came up the track, Chorley caught sight of a man standing on the widow's walk, wiping his hands on a smudged rag. Chorley shaded his eyes to get a better look but couldn't see for the scintillating dazzle behind the man—the setting sun reflected in the crystals of the lamp.

Chorley hadn't known what to say—or whom to trust. The

keeper had mentioned a "Father Paul" among their visitors. Father Paul might connect this place to the Temple.

Chorley had followed the Grand Patriarch's instructions. He had gotten off the schooner at its first stop.

There were several huts in the lighthouse's windbreak, Chorley saw, but only one that had a porch. The sun colored the salt-silvered weatherboards of the huts. The ground under the pine trees was as russet as oxidized iron. The setting sun was warm on Chorley's back.

"Wait," said the keeper, and touched Chorley's arm. "Look."

Chorley looked where the man pointed and was in time to see the last sliver of the sun disappear below the horizon. Then he noticed the keeper's boy, who was some distance along the shore, sprinting, apparently racing the schooner.

"That's a regular game of his," the keeper said. "And look—" He called Chorley's attention away from the boy.

Chorley turned, stunned into obedience.

The shadow was climbing the lighthouse. It was the shadow of the sea horizon, the shadow of the world. And when the sun vanished from the very tip of the tower, a sliding glitter showed in the tower top, then a bright flash as the light came around to probe the open sea.

"Now my boy will turn back," the keeper said. Sure enough, the boy was looping back. The *Morningstar* had changed her heading to sail away from the Spit.

"He always does that, you say?" Chorley asked.

"Yes. We lead very quiet lives here, and he's learned to find a lot of pleasure in little things."

Chorley hadn't shared Laura's first dream, had only had it described to him by Grace. But he knew that the man in Laura's dream, a convict broken by hardship, had remembered being a boy racing the schooner along the shore of So Long Spit. The convict in Laura's dream had remembered being *this* boy. And so Laura's dream had taken place in a time *further on from now*. Laura's dream was about something that would happen *in the future*.

The keeper said, "My lad is bound to pepper you with questions, sir, the moment he reaches us."

"Sorry," Chorley said. "I haven't introduced myself."

"I did think you might be another Mr. Thomas," the keeper said.

"Mr. Thomas?"

"We have had several Mr. Thomases here. Named after the apostle Thomas. Doubting Thomas."

"You mentioned a Father Paul."

"Yes. But I shouldn't have mentioned anyone without knowing who you are."

"I think I *am* another Thomas who has his doubts," Chorley said.

The keeper smiled. He said, "None of us here knows anything much. We're only hospitable. *We have all been the world's guests, and we must pay for the world's hospitality.*" This last thing he said as though quoting someone. He took Chorley's bag from him, and they turned back to the light. The boy came up behind them, his bare feet thumping on the crabgrass. He eyed Chorley, panting.

Another person appeared ahead of them on the path. A person in shirtsleeves with a grubby rag slung across one shoulder.

Chorley cried out and ran up the short slope. He pulled Tziga to him and held him. Then, horribly, Tziga jerked back in Chorley's arms and began to flop around. Chorley lost his grip, and Tziga dropped at his feet. Tziga's jaw was clenched, his breath hissing through his nose, his legs and arms trembling spasmodically.

The keeper and his boy hurried to help. The keeper pulled a rubber stopper out of his pocket. He forced Tziga's mouth open and wedged the stopper between his teeth. The keeper said to his son, "Run and tell your mother that Mr. Thomas is having another of his turns."

Chorley fell to his knees beside his brother-in-law. He was afraid to touch him.

"He has these fits," the keeper said. "It's because of his injury."

Chorley had had no trouble recognizing Tziga. He had appeared above them on the track, his face indistinct in the dusk but his stance instantly recognizable. Chorley now saw the changes in Tziga's appearance. Tziga had one mutilated ear, dents and lumps of shiny scar tissue on his forehead, one eyebrow smeared nearly out of existence by scarring, and one cheekbone caved in. All the injuries were on the right side of his head. Chorley found the courage to touch Tziga again. He helped the keeper, who was gently restraining Tziga's quaking arms.

The tremors gradually quieted. "He will come to shortly," the keeper said. "He's always very tired and disoriented after these fits."

Chorley asked how often Mr. Thomas had fits.

"Every few days. It's very hard on him."

A woman arrived with the boy, a lamp, and a blanket. She spread the blanket over Tziga and put the lamp down on the turf beside them.

"It's best not to move him till he is awake," the keeper said. "I have to go and fetch the boxes up from the beach before it's completely dark."

He and the boy went back down to the water, leaving Chorley alone with his wife and Tziga.

After a time the woman got up too. She said, "The men will be back and forth. Let them know if he wakes up before I return. I've left my girls minding the cakes, and I don't quite trust them." She turned back toward the house with the porch.

Chorley could smell the cakes, their cinnamon and sugar. He could smell pines, eelgrass on the ponds among the dunes, and the sap from the green claws of the ice plants he had stepped on. He imagined he could hear the waves on both shores of the Spit—the ocean and Coal Bay.

Tziga was lying curled like a sleeping dog, his arms stretched out in front of him. Chorley put his head down to listen for his brother-in-law's breathing. It wasn't yet quiet; it still sounded as though Tziga was recovering from a steep climb. Chorley felt Tziga's slick face and ran his fingers over the scar tissue. Then he touched Tziga's throat and tested his weight by pushing up his frayed shirt cuffs to clasp his bony wrists. Chorley lifted a hand and kissed it. The hand smelled of charred benzene spirit—whale oil.

Tziga's eyelids fluttered.

"Wake up," Chorley whispered.

Above them the beam of light probed the dusk. A warning, and comfort to all within its thirty-mile range, it too seemed to say, silently, urgently: *"Wake up. Wake up."*

5

✦ ✦ ✦

HORTLY BEFORE THE EVENING PER-
FORMANCE BEGAN, WHEN MOST OF
THE PATRONS WERE ALREADY INSIDE AND
in their sleepwear, the guards at the Rainbow Opera set out to
patrol the Opera's perimeter. It was generally a dull, everyday
job. It had been years since anyone had succeeded in parking
himself near enough to the Opera to pilfer a dream. These
days guards were mostly for show. The Opera's prices were
such that it wasn't a likely haunt for drunks and troublemak-
ers. On St. Lazarus's Eve, things were only a little different.
Busier. Security a little tighter.

There were more cars and carriages, chauffeurs and
grooms than usual parked in the space around the perimeter.
The President of the Republic was at the Opera, so his guard
of honor—a dozen military men with sabers and pistols—were
standing to attention by the President's vehicles, while other
rich patrons' chauffeurs and grooms lounged around smoking.

The Opera's guards always patrolled in pairs. Each pair was
responsible for one section of the building's blind outer wall.
The two men who were in the best position to raise the alarm
that night had been assigned the quietest section, a forty-yard
stretch that faced the river at the far side of the perimeter
from the main gate. This stretch of wall was interrupted only

by the dreamer's door—a stage door by which the dreamer entered the Opera—and, right beside the door, a drinking fountain in an alcove.

The men set out, making their way around their stretch, one swinging the padded club he carried, the other thumping the wall with his gloved hand as he walked. When they came to the alcove, they stopped and stared. Where there had been a drinking fountain, there was now a statue.

The statue of a man, a little bigger than life-sized, was crammed into the alcove, a beautiful, bald-headed figure, who should have been posed like a sentinel. Instead, the statue was stooped and had his head over at an angle to fit into the arch.

The guards were curious. One tapped at the statue with his club while the other ran his hand down the figure's muscled side. The statue was finished but not polished, he noticed—its surface was still gritty. One man called the attention of the other to a cloth that had been crammed behind the statue. He crouched down to try to pull it free. It was a worn piece of gabardine—perhaps a workman's drop cloth. He couldn't free it, but as he was working he noticed that the drinking fountain was still there behind the figure; the statue seemed to have been posed as though sitting on the bowl of the fountain. The guard pointed this out to his companion. They spent a few minutes puzzling over this whimsical addition to the Rainbow Opera's decorations. Then they walked on, one pausing to check the lock on the dreamer's door as he went by.

✣ ✣ ✣

The four oval balconies were full of the Opera's patrons. Many were wearing the latest spring fashions in sleepwear. The men wore quilted crimson or gray robes, and the women were mostly in white and darker gray, floating silks trimmed with swansdown. The people milled around in the balconies and up and down the red-carpeted staircases, visiting with friends. Waiters wove among them, carrying trays of sweet wine or chocolate liqueur mixed with fresh cream.

The people paused in their talk to applaud as Grace Tiebold appeared under the dome and began to climb the spiral stair to the dreamer's bed. At the Rainbow Opera, the dreamer's bed was on a raised platform in the center of the auditorium, at the same height as the second balcony. The long train of Grace's embroidered robe trailed after her around the turns in the stairs. Despite her elaborate costume, the dreamhunter looked girlish, small and thin, her light brown hair bobbed, her wrists, neck, and ears bare of jewelry. At the top of the stairs she turned to make a curtsy to the President of the Republic. He was on his private balcony, isolated from the rest of the second floor by locked doors. Grace bent her knee and inclined her head, then raised her arms to the rest of the public, who clapped and cheered. Then, as she always did, Grace turned and blew kisses toward the balcony before the second-floor private suites belonging to her family. The crowd looked where she threw her kisses to see that, this evening, only the dreamhunter's daughter and niece were in attendance. The girls were, as usual, the youngest two people at the performance. The patrons noticed that Rose Tiebold was fulfilling every expectation people had of her by growing more beautiful with each passing month. "But she won't be out this summer," one society matron said to another consolingly—they had girls coming out that season, and the competition for good husbands was always hard enough without the added complication of half the eligible men falling for the same girl.

✢ ✢ ✢

Cas Doran wished the President of the Republic a good night and retired to his private balcony. His son, Ru, had ordered some more chocolate. Ru was posted at the rail, looking out over the auditorium and waving to his friends. Doran said, "Ru, I'll be back out shortly, save me some of that chocolate." He went into his suite and shut its padded door. The sound of the Opera's crowd retreated completely.

Maze Plasir was waiting for him. Plasir had his new boy with him. The boy stared at Doran with wide eyes, then looked to his master for a cue as to how he should behave. Plasir nodded faintly, and only then did the boy extend his hand. Cas took the limp, sweaty hand and shook it.

"Gavin knows that he must regard this as a very great privilege," said Plasir. He looked at the boy. "Don't you, Gavin?"

"Yes, Mr. Plasir."

"I've been telling Mr. Doran what a talent you are," Plasir said.

"And I had heard already from the examiners," said Doran.

Maze Plasir seemed to be taking a great deal of pleasure in their little act of patronage. He said to the boy, "Now, Gavin, you're Mr. Doran's guest, but you mustn't bother his *other* guests."

"Yes, Gavin. You must keep to your room." Doran waited for the boy to agree.

Gavin swallowed, then nodded.

"You'll be very comfortable. The room will be my daughter's when she is old enough to attend these things." Cas Doran put his hand on the boy's shoulder and walked him to the bedroom. "Sleep well, dream well," he said. He closed the door on the boy.

"They'll be ringing the bells in fifteen minutes," Plasir said. He began winding his scarf around his neck and buttoning his coat. "I came up the stairs from the dreamer's door. I could still smell Grace Tiebold's perfume in the stairwell." He smiled to himself.

"And you persuaded your boy to think that he's here only for the benefit of the experience?" Doran asked.

"He's the best I've ever had," said Maze. "But simple—or single-minded. He believes every bit of flattery he hears. He's hungry for it, and totally credulous. That's the profile of an ideal Colorist. I can guarantee that he'll go into his trance when he hears the bell. He'll catch everyone when they're dropping off. I hope he will still be performing his little repetitions by the time Grace Tiebold falls asleep, so that, in the first minute of her dream, he might be able to get his ideas out to her whole audience. Even if he isn't able to do that, he will color the dreams of everyone in the suites on either side of this one, and yours, of course."

"I don't mind that. I look on it as quality control. Your Colorists are very convincing, Maze. I still find myself congratulating myself on my judgment regarding Mr. Gregg and what a fine Speaker he's made." Cas Doran laughed. "I find myself thinking 'What a solid, equitable man.' And I hope I'll wake up tomorrow thinking how wonderful Garth Wilkinson is. How he should be enshrined. How desirable it would be that he remains in office."

"Knowing what I know," Plasir said, "I'd discount *any* idea I had while dozing off in a dream palace."

"You and I are the only ones who know how good you are, how *priceless*," Cas Doran said—he was a cool man but passionate in admiration.

Maze Plasir smiled. He finished buttoning his coat. He said he'd leave when the balconies had cleared. They went to the door together, Doran saying, wistfully, that he hoped his son had left him some hot chocolate.

"Sleep well," said Plasir. "Dream well."

Ru Doran was still leaning over the balcony rail. When his

father joined him, he turned, eyes bright, and said, "Is that Mamie's friend? That beautiful girl?"

✢ ✢ ✢

Rose stood straight and held her head high. For a moment she could feel all eyes on her. The attention was like a hot spell of sunlight on a dull day, and, heated, Rose put up a hand to lift her hair off the back of her neck. The stares had made her self-conscious, but her gesture was unself-conscious, it was innocent and arresting—and, of course, it only encouraged various people to stare harder at her. Out of the corner of her eye, Rose saw some hulking boy on the balcony of the Secretary of the Interior's suite imitate her mother and blow a kiss her way.

"Who *is* that cocky so-and-so?" Rose muttered to Laura.

Laura seemed even more dazed than she had been all afternoon. She was still sucking on one of Farry's raspberry lollipops. She had arrived at lunch with one in her mouth already and her duster's pockets stuffed with a dozen more. Her lips were stained red, and looked raw now—though when she'd appeared in the restaurant she had only looked childish.

"Laura!" Rose said, and turned her cousin's head so that she would look across the space at the balcony opposite them. Rose felt Laura's jaw clench under her fingers. Laura said, "That boy?" exuding raspberry-scented breath. "Well, he's with Cas Doran, so perhaps he is Mamie's older brother."

Rose decided that she would *now* have to share some news she'd been withholding if her cousin was going to be able to appreciate why it might be uncomfortable to have Mamie's brother kissing his hand at her. "You know I am spending the first two weeks of the summer with the Dorans," Rose said. "On Mamie's invitation."

Laura shrugged.

Rose had expected her cousin to laugh—to see right away that she could hope to hear some *good stories* as well as Rose's views on Cas Doran's character, opinions, and interests. The whole point of Rose's campaign of making friends with Mamie had been to get near enough to Mamie's father to make an assessment of him and his associates. Yet when Rose was at the Dorans' over the coming summer, making her assessment of Mamie's father, there might be *other* intrigues for her to share with Laura—like, for instance, how Rose would manage to cope with Doran Junior's flattering attention.

But Laura didn't laugh. She only stared at the Doran men and the President, her eyes shiny and dull at once, as though another skin had grown over their surfaces. Laura hadn't even waved to her aunt Grace. She was slumped on one of the ottomans by the balcony rail, her side to the amphitheater and hunched down, as though she wasn't happy to be seen.

Laura had been vague and absent at lunch—but friendly enough. She had remembered to bring Grace and Rose St. Lazarus's Eve gifts. Rose was rather surprised at this, since it was normally the sort of nicety that slipped Laura's mind. Laura had turned up with two beautiful packages of Farry's finest confections—a hazelnut log for Grace, and Rose's favorite sweet, musk creams.

Rose had her package open on her lap and had already eaten three. Her lips were greasy and her mouth perfumed. She would save the rest till they were in bed and could share them—though Laura seemed content to stain her mouth with those cheap boiled lollies.

Rose flipped her hair again and stood up, stretched, and took a deep breath. The tall gas flames around the coping of the Opera's dome sent unsteady light down through the stained glass. The houselights began to dim, a little at first to hurry the patrons to finish their conversations, wine, chocolate, cups of roasted rice tea, and at least *think* of retiring to their rooms. As the houselights dimmed, the fluttering, multicolored radiance that came through the dome grew stronger, till the whole auditorium began to look as though it were underwater.

Rose spotted another young man—this one on the third floor. He was leaning over the balustrade opposite and waving at her. She waved back. She said to Laura, delighted, "I'm beginning to see what my life is going to be like!"

Laura merely asked her whether she was sleepy.

Rose wasn't. She'd gotten up early that morning but wasn't tired at all. In fact she felt jittery—either picking up her mother's performance nerves or wound up by all the attention she was getting. She didn't answer Laura because she caught sight of the latest male admirer making his way down the staircase to their level.

The lights dimmed another notch. The crowds on the balconies began to thin. People called out to one another, "Good night. Enjoy." Some of the padded doors were already fastened. The waiters were gathering empty cups and glasses.

Rose grabbed Laura's arm. She pointed, wanting to show her cousin the man hurrying up to them.

Laura said, apparently to herself, "I like things the way they are." She sounded very definite—and as though she was arguing with someone—but no one there with them on the balcony. But then she *did* speak to Rose: "I love the way the torchlight shines through the roof. Your mother looks like an enchanted sleeping queen."

Grace wasn't asleep. She was propped up on her elbows and eating an apple.

Laura looked up at Rose then and said, plaintive, "I always liked the Rainbow Opera." She was talking, Rose thought, as if she had just discovered a plot someone had made to burn the building down.

"What is it, honey?" Rose said, concerned. But before

Laura could answer, the young man appeared beside them. "Hello," Rose said, and held out her hand. "I am Rose Tiebold."

"Pleased to meet you." The young man was briskly polite. "*Again.* Alexander Mason," he said, and shook her hand.

"Oh, you," said Rose. It was the boy from the infants' beach. He had done some growing. He seemed friendly too, but looked at Rose for only a moment before turning to Laura. He offered her a bright, eager smile.

"Oh—Sandy!" Laura said. "Sandy—*what are you doing here*?" It sounded like a lament.

Alexander Mason frowned. "You're not happy to see me?"

Rose thought he was risking an even worse rebuff. She was impressed.

Laura showed more life than she had all day. She jumped up and grabbed Mason's hands. She gripped them hard and drew him to her till they stood chest to chest with their locked hands between them—rather like, Rose thought, singers about to perform a love duet. Rose took a closer look at Mason's heavy, freckled face and thought that he wasn't really her idea of handsome. But Laura looked inspired. Then she looked confused. She released Mason's hands. Rose heard him draw a sharp, shocked breath.

Rose said, "The Hames can be very dramatic." She patted Mason's arm. "Don't let it worry you."

He glanced at her, frowned again, then said to Laura, "Have you been chewing Wakeful?" He sounded managing—stern, paternal. If Laura hadn't been behaving so badly toward him herself, Rose would have been tempted to kick him.

The lights went down another notch. The bells began to chime, the balconies to empty.

"No, I've been sucking a lollipop," Laura said. She didn't seem at all offended.

"That would be one way of disguising Wakeful," said Mason.

"Why would I? I am going to sleep tonight, to dream," Laura said. Her voice was dull.

"I am here with Uncle George," Mason said. He addressed Rose this time—and changed the subject, she was pleased to see. She wasn't used to being ignored. "Your mother asked my uncle to come and help her. She's been having trouble falling asleep." Mason looked over the rail. "There he goes," he said, and pointed to the balding, burly man climbing the spiral stairs to the platform. "Since your father's away," Mason said to Rose, "he can't object. Besides, Uncle's a portly old gent."

"She's so *sly*," Rose said of her mother. "She loves being boosted. Da would have a fit. Your uncle isn't palsied and doesn't carry a cane—so Da would *still* object."

Rose imagined that she could hear people murmuring, even above the bells. She looked around and saw—yes—they were pointing Mason's uncle out to one another, then looking her way. She resisted an urge to thumb her nose at them.

"Everyone will fall asleep at once," Laura said. "Since your uncle is a Soporif. They'll go down and stay down." She looked around, turned her body and her head as though searching for an avenue of escape. Then she froze, staring.

Rose followed Laura's gaze and saw that her cousin had caught sight of a pregnant woman. But why should her cousin look frozen with fright at the sight of a pregnant woman? Rose reached for Laura's hand, and her hand collided with Mason's—he had reached for Laura too.

Laura turned away from them. "I'm going in," she muttered. She walked into the Hame suite and—much to Rose's surprise—closed the door.

"I am always upsetting her," Mason said.

"Oh, poor you," Rose gushed. Then she said, sharp, "And

you only sometimes *mean* to." She had decided to blame him for Laura's peculiar mood.

His face went dark. "You girls," he fumed. "You think you own the world."

"I shall," Rose said, with as much hauteur as she could muster—which was a lot. "You had better get back to your nice little room, Alexander," she said. She turned on her heel and went into the Tiebold suite.

Rose knocked on the connecting door. Laura opened it.

Laura said, "I am going to go to bed by myself. My sleeping is all over the place these days. I don't want to spoil it for you."

"All right. If you like."

"Have you got your musk creams?"

"Yes." Rose produced the box and opened it. Half the creams had gone already. "Take one," she offered. "They're very good, though the taste is a little different from the last box I had."

Laura took one. She said she would eat it in bed. She leaned toward Rose and kissed her cheek. Then she closed the door. And Rose thought she heard the lock turning.

Rose got into bed with her box of creams. She turned the lamp down low. She took one sweet and slowly excavated the musk cream from its cup of toffee. She was cozy but not at all sleepy. She had too much on her mind. For instance, she'd connected three things in her thoughts—Laura's sudden, inexplicable fondness for raspberry lollipops, her agitation on seeing Alexander Mason, and her horrified look at the pregnant woman. "*No*, no, *no*," Rose said to herself, shaking her head. She had been reading too many "educational books." (Founderston Girls' Academy had a secret club—the Educational Books Club—which circulated novels that girls their age were not usually allowed to read. Novels in translation with stories in which married women had affairs, then killed themselves.)

Rose was more excited than worried by the thought that her cousin had "gotten herself into trouble." After all, if something like that happened, they would all look after Laura. Nothing like that could make the family falter in their love. However, Rose's father might *murder* Alexander Mason . . .

Rose's thoughts circled, excited and—it seemed to her— loud. Time passed. She finished her musk creams. She tossed and turned. Finally she got up, found a book, and turned up the lamp to read. It was one of her father's books, bought to research a trip the family had planned and hadn't taken. It was about castles in France.

For a time Rose was lost, floating down a famous river with a guide who delighted in stories of witch trials and walled-up wives.

She heard the clock on Temple Square strike midnight. And sometime after midnight, she heard the screaming start.

✦ ✦ ✦

Shortly after the clock struck twelve, the two guards were ambling past the alcove and the dreamer's door as they had countless times that night. They had just met another pair of guards and exchanged reports. All was well.

The moon was up, its light pulsing through gaps in fast-flying cloud. The wind was higher in the upper atmosphere than on the ground, though the river's surface was ruffled, its ripples not black but speckled with the same gray light as the cloud. The torches on the Opera's roof had become fluttering banners of fire. They gulped and snapped above the men. The ground was wet and reflected the moon and the torch-light.

The light was unsteady but came from everywhere, so it shone into the empty alcove, shone on the water fountain where the men *had* seen a statue.

The guards stopped. They gaped at the empty arch and the fountain. There was nothing there; even the bundled drop cloth had gone.

One guard clutched the other's arm. He pointed. The dreamer's door hung off its hinges, and the carpeted stair within was sprinkled with broken glass from the first of the electric candles.

As the men stood staring they heard another smash, and the faint light shining down the stair diminished. They heard something heavy vaulting up the stairs. Beyond that, from the building's interior, came the sound of screaming—of a multitude of people calling out in an agony of terror.

The guards shouted for help, then ran inside. They sprinted up the short staircase to the first floor, their boots crunching on broken glass. The light ahead of them receded as lamp after lamp shattered. They plunged on.

✧ ✧ ✧

Rose heard her cousin call out in horror and despair. She heard Laura's voice above the horrible cacophony of the others. Rose jumped out of bed and ran to the connecting door. It was locked. She hammered on the door and called to Laura. Then she rushed out of the Tiebold suite to try the outer door to the Hame suite.

That door too was locked. Rose gave up twisting its handle. She looked around her and listened.

The first thing Rose saw was her mother—thrashing about in the wavering light that came through the dome. Grace flung herself up in bed, her movement convulsive. She threw her arms wide and yelled. For a moment Rose heard her

mother's cry soar above all the others—because it was different, because it was a cry of rage. There was blood running on
Grace's face and throat—the ends of her fingers were black in
the light, black with her own blood.

Rose shouted to her mother. She saw Grace's head snap
around and her mother's eyes find her. Rose saw her mother's mouth shape her name. Then Grace leapt out of the
dreamer's bed. She upended a carafe of water onto Alexander
Mason's uncle, who had been lying top to tail with her and was
now struggling, tangled in the covers, with both hands pushing into his own mouth.

Rose didn't see him wake up, because her attention had
been seized by something else.

On the first floor, in the stretch between the dreamer's
door and the public staircase, someone was in a fast, thun-
dering run. As he ran, he struck out at each light. Rose saw
the hot fuses quenched beneath a fist. She saw the spraying
glass and heard each bright smash.

For a mad moment Rose thought she was looking at her father. And then she realized that she *was* looking at her father's
hat and coat—a black fedora and gray gabardine coat from two
years before. But the hat was too high up from the floor and
the coat so strained that its back was splitting. Who was that in
her father's clothes?

Grace was still on the platform. She was shrieking at the
fire watch. Above the din Rose heard, "Sound the alarms!"
Grace pointed furiously at the control room behind the
milling men. "The master switch!" she roared. "Wake them
up! Wake them all up!"

Rose saw the man in her father's coat and hat plunge up the
stairs from the first to the second floor. He was coming toward her floor and the private suites. The fire watch was on
the second floor too, and it was for their control room that
the man in Rose's father's clothes was headed.

He flung himself among them, traveling in the light now, a shadow in a pale greatcoat. The men reeled back, some as he scattered them left and right, others without having been touched. They fell back from him and raised their hands as if to fend off—what?—*the sight of him*?

Rose saw her father's fedora float to the floor. She saw the man—the shadow—leap sideways into the control room. As he bounded through the men, his body curved and elongated. For an instant he left his feet on the floor and cast himself out like a net, a net that Rose saw fall onto the man whose hand was clutching the master switch.

Rose could make no sense of what she was seeing.

Above the screams, Rose heard the sound of dry earth falling. Her father's coat had jumped with the man, but then it twitched and deflated. The coat lay on the control room floor, and a solid, man-shaped shadow sat astride the man who had reached for the switch. Rose saw the shadow turn back to disentangle its feet from her father's empty coat.

Grace was running down the spiral stairs from the platform, the bright trail of her robe flowing behind her.

Rose leaned over the balustrade and yelled at her mother—she didn't want Grace to come up to the second floor. She didn't want her mother to come anywhere near that *thing*. But Grace didn't hear Rose, for at that moment the howling voices of the maddened dreamers reached a crescendo, a sound of such misery that it slapped tears from Rose's eyes. Rose felt the dream leave the building, like a devil taking flight and carrying souls away with it.

In the control room the men of the fire watch cowered as the shadow got up to rip the electrical cable away from the board of switches that would have sounded an alarm in every room. The figure stood for a moment in a fountain of sparks, then dropped the cable. He waded through the cowering men and ran out of the room.

Rose turned around to see her mother appear at the head of the staircase. Grace paid no attention to the fire watch but ran straight to her.

Rose staggered back from her mother. Grace's face was streaked with blood. Her cheeks were gouged by nail marks, her lips bitten and bloody, her hair savaged, her scalp bleeding. This bloody apparition grabbed Rose and stared at her, checking her all over. A look of relief filled Grace's mutilated face, and despite all her injuries, she began to look sane.

The door to the Hame suite opened. Rose and Grace turned to see Laura walking out onto the balcony, slowly and unsteadily. She looked tiny with her thin limbs and short, sweat-soaked hair clinging to her skull, and childish in her white pajamas with forget-me-nots embroidered on their collar. Laura was clumsily unwinding bandages from one hand with the opposite hand, which was itself still half-bandaged. Spirals of gauze hung from both her hands. There was blood on her lips. And there were bruises on her arms. Dark bands of bruise, as though she had been tied but not rope-burned. Rose remembered that, all day, Laura had kept her arms covered, sometimes holding the ends of her sleeves.

"Laura," Grace said.

Laura looked up at her aunt and cousin. She looked, but didn't react to what she saw. Her face was blank, closed. She shook the bandages from her fingers' ends and looked around. Then she began to shout.

Rose couldn't make any sense of what her cousin was yelling, though she could hear Laura clearly, since the screams behind all the Opera's padded doors had, for the most part, subsided to sobs. What Laura yelled was maddeningly ridiculous, and, briefly, Rose felt like joining in—or adding, "Verb! Adjective! Adverb!" Because Laura was shouting, "Noun!"

The shadow appeared. He burst through one of the doors

from another private suite. He had run around the balconies through all the partitions. He had broken down all the doors.

Rose saw a massive, glittering, silvery statue. A statue that moved and looked around with eyes banded black, as though encrusted with tiny flakes of jet. The calm, noble face turned her way, then swung toward Laura as she stretched out her arms to him.

Rose tried to tear herself away from her mother, who was clutching her, grappling with Rose as she tried to struggle free and go to Laura. To *save* Laura.

Laura stretched her arms out to the statue, and it swooped her up and rushed away into the nearest stairway—the one that led down to the dreamer's door.

Rose ran after them, then stopped when she saw the sparkle of broken glass on the carpeted stairs. Her feet were bare.

✤ ✤ ✤

Nown held Laura close, his body almost curled around hers. He took the stairs at a tumbling run, but he kept his feet, for, whether they fell on the tread or the edge of each step, the sand from which they were formed spread, and shifted, and held him balanced.

They erupted into the moonlight, Nown landing with a thump on the pavement. He straightened, and then very deliberately turned and seized the broken dreamer's door by its handle. He lifted the door back into its frame and pulled it shut. It was just a gesture, for closing the door did nothing to dampen the noise of crashes, sobs, and frenzied shouting coming from inside the Opera.

Over her sandman's shoulder Laura saw light bloom in the streets around the Opera as curtains were pulled back and people looked toward the festively lit building, the source of the hellish howling that had woken them. The houses nearest the plaza were normally safely beyond any dreamhunter's maximum range, but Laura saw that the people leaning out the windows of these houses were brushing at their faces, over and over, as though to remove an obstruction only they could see.

The scene blurred and tilted as Nown began to run. He ran for the gate in the Opera's perimeter fence. It was open. There were men clustered around it. Two stricken chauffeurs had stumbled through it and were on all fours on the road, retching. Opera guards still seemed to be trying to control who came and went, while two of President Wilkinson's uniformed bodyguards stood over them shouting. One bodyguard was waving a revolver back and forth as though it was a hose and he was watering a lawn. He was trying to clear the way for the President's car. Laura recognized the car not only by the armed men standing on its running boards but because she caught a glimpse between them of Garth Wilkinson himself, his face stark white and his chin and starched dress collar smeared with bloody foam. The car slid through the gate, sounded its horn, and sped away.

Nown followed it. He plunged through the gap in the crowd, then lurched left, toward the river. Over his shoulder Laura saw bristling beams of pressure lamps at the head of the main street into the plaza. She heard pounding footfalls and police whistles. Then she caught sight of the man with the gun, arm extended, sighting along his barrel. "Nown!" Laura yelled. She drew her legs up and ducked her head down between her shoulders. Nown jerked sideways and stumbled. A spray of sand stung Laura's ear. Nown flung himself onto the ledge between the perimeter fence and the river, ran for a few steps along its narrow course, then lost his balance. Laura felt him falling and flung out her hand to grasp the fence. Her fingers closed on a bar, then, in a desperate snatch, his did too, only inches above hers. But for a moment Laura had held them both—a moment in which she'd learned he was too heavy for her to hold. They swung above the river, and Laura saw a thin stream of sand fall from Nown's shoulder and disappear hissing into the smooth water, followed by a smoking stone, the bullet.

Nown flexed his elbow and drew both of them back against the bars. He let go his grip to prize her locked fingers free. He was speaking to her. She could feel the low muffled reverberations of his voice in his chest, but her ears were deafened by the sound of the shot, or the screams, or even the horrible hiss of his dry vitality dropping away into the river. She'd heard *that*, so why couldn't she hear him speaking?

Laura released her grip and Nown bundled her close to him again and sped away along the ledge, fearless, his balance and momentum unimpaired. He skirted the Opera and sprinted through the Isle's alleyways. There were people behind them blowing whistles, and others closing in from the right—people everywhere, the whole Isle apparently awake and blundering around the streets.

The harrying calls came nearer, and beams of light that ran along the eaves of the buildings they passed between as their pursuers entered the street they were on. Nown hesitated and cast about, then he stooped and rolled Laura into a dark alcove by the door to a coal cellar. He pushed her up against the padlocked door and pressed himself into the space after her. Laura saw with horror the moonlight and fleeting torchlight closed off. The sand of her servant's body creaked, and then it was seeping around her. She was sealed in.

Laura stuffed the heel of her hand into her mouth and bit down. She hadn't any bandages to protect her. She thought of the clamor in the Opera, the cries of distress. She thought of the polished paint and glass of the President's car marred by bloody handprints. She thought of the long, raw claw marks on her aunt's face and neck.

It had happened. She had done it. She hadn't been able to spare Aunt Grace—the dreamer she'd had to mount. Or Sandy Mason—whom she hadn't imagined would be there—or any of the other innocents. She hadn't spared the pregnant woman, the sight of whom had appalled and very nearly stopped her. She'd gone through with it. She'd followed her father's letter, kept faith with him, done what he said must be done. She'd stuck to her resolve.

But early that morning, before her train had come to Founderston and after she'd seen Nown off it—pushing him onto the track near the muddy riverbank—Laura had sat down to mix Wakeful into the jar of Farry's musk cream before spooning it into the toffee shells. She'd done it so that Rose, *Rose at least*, would be spared waking up in her coffin.

It was over. And *now*, for now, she'd do this—bite on her hand till blood ran down into her sleeve. She could hear the pursuers right beside her hiding place. Their lanterns would be passing over Nown, balled into the alcove like a big stone stopping the mouth of a tomb.

The men passed on, and Laura was safe. Buried, but safe.

✤ ✤ ✤

6

ECRETARY DORAN WASN'T CARRIED
OFF BY HIS BODYGUARDS. FOR ONE
THING, HE HAD ONLY TWO OF THEM, MEN
in opulent silk dressing gowns worn over evening dress, who
might be mistaken for his guests. For another thing, unlike
President Wilkinson, Cas Doran wasn't incapacitated by the
nightmare. He'd sampled nightmares before.

Once he had managed to drag his consciousness and his
intelligence free of it, Doran first checked on all his people—
his bodyguards, who had been awake throughout and who had
stationed themselves at the door to the suite, where, they reported to their employer, they had heard someone smashing
through all the doors that sealed off the row of private balconies. Doran checked on his son, Ru, who was vomiting into
a basin in the bathroom. He checked on Maze Plasir's apprentice, and found the young Colorist uninjured, but rigid
with fright—he had wet his bed. The boy was too shocked and
ashamed even to attempt an apology. He stood by the bed,
shivering so hard that the silk of the drooping crotch of his
pants made a wet flapping noise. Doran stripped the quilt
from the bed and wrapped it around the boy. He took him
into the suite's sitting room and sat him beside Ru, who had
stopped being sick and had some of his color back. One of
Doran's bodyguards told him that his lips were bleeding and

passed him a towel. Doran pressed it against his mouth and went to the door to the suite, where he stood listening to shouts and breakage and pounding feet. Then, distant at first but coming closer, police whistles.

Doran and his bodyguards exchanged glances, then Doran unbolted the door.

The balcony was empty, but the doors at either end were wrenched out of their frames, timber splintered around latch and hinge.

A phalanx of blue uniforms was thrusting its way up the spiral staircase of the dreamer's dais. The staircase was packed with struggling bodies in torn silk nightwear. Doran spotted several members of the Opera's fire watch among them. George Mason was on his stomach on the dreamer's bed. Two men had hold of his kicking legs and were trying to drag him toward the thrashing maw of the crowd packed at the top of the stair. Mason clung with both hands to the bed head.

Another cluster of police emerged from the main staircase into the auditorium and fought their way through the crowd, striking all around them with their black truncheons. In their midst Cas Doran glimpsed the slight form of Grace Tiebold. The dreamhunter was hustled out of the building.

The police on the dais had secured Mason. They threw a quilt over his head and gathered themselves around him and defended the bed till reinforcements arrived—another fifty or so constables who erupted into the auditorium through every entrance. Several were carrying rifles.

The melee blew apart everywhere the armed police appeared, people scattering from the sight of the guns and truncheons, those who were staggering suddenly fleet. The crowd began to press out of the Opera into the surrounding streets.

Doran turned to his bodyguards, his son, and the shivering Colorist. "I think we might venture out now," he said.

Dreamhunter

Rose had emerged from behind the door of the President's suite, where she'd been hiding with her mother for a terribly long time—though it was perhaps only ten minutes. The police had appeared and carried Grace off. The mob had poured away after them. Rose had taken a seat on an ottoman on the balcony. She was quietly beside herself, her mind in good working order, her thoughts progressive in direction—but her feelings seemed to have gone to sleep. She'd been shocked before in her life, when she'd failed her Try and found she couldn't enter the Place and wouldn't become a dreamhunter. But this—she supposed—was what it was like to be *in shock*.

Rose had discovered that her cousin was on friendly terms with a monster.

Laura had called on the monster's help and had fled the Opera wrapped in its glistening, inhuman arms. This discovery was such a dislocation in Rose's sense of what she knew about Laura—never mind *the world*—that Rose had the impression that if the world wasn't quite itself, then *she* wasn't herself either. Any moment now she'd do something strange, like poke out her own eyes or jump off the balcony. She would do so solely out of a crazed urge to check that what she had always thought was true—Rose and Laura, Laura and Rose, together in a world without monsters—was *still* true.

Rose wound a lock of her long hair around her fingers and dragged on it. The steady pressure made her tilt her head, then stoop. She concentrated on the fiery patch of pain. Then someone near her said, "It's Rose, isn't it?"

Cas Doran and his party made their way from the balcony of his suite, through the smashed, skewed doors of the suite belonging to the Speaker of the House, and onto the President's balcony. There they found a girl sitting slumped and knock-kneed on an ottoman and tugging severely on a lock of her long golden hair. Doran removed the towel from his bleeding mouth and said, "It's Rose, isn't it?"

Rose let go of her hair and her head bobbed up. She straightened and looked at him, Ru, the bodyguards, Plasir's apprentice. "The police took my mother away with them," she said.

"For her own protection," said Doran. "But—did they just leave you here alone?"

Rose glanced over her shoulder at the door to the President's suite. Its surface was dented and gouged. "The crowd followed the police. They were throwing things at Ma. Mostly only their slippers, thank God. I was behind the door when it opened. Suddenly everyone was gone." She rubbed at her scalp. "Ouch," she said. "I think I've pulled my thoughts into line."

"I'm glad to hear it," said Doran. The girl was a little hysterical, he thought. It was to be expected. He caught her under her elbow and helped her up. She flopped against him, then said, "Oh—Mamie's father." She sounded as though she was making a note of it, her tone musing and cautious.

"We'll get you out of here," Doran said. "Come along."

The building was emptying. There were ambulances in the plaza. People were being seen to, bandaged, offered blankets and sweet tea.

Doran took a blanket and draped it around Rose. He got the attention of a captain of the police and called him over. "I'm rich in witnesses," the captain said, "but of course they all want to go home. I have my men taking names and addresses."

"Good," said Doran. "Were there any serious injuries? Or arrests?"

"There were people who couldn't be calmed down. We took some into custody. Others were taken in ambulances to Pike Street Hospital. I imagine the Regulatory Body will want to interview witnesses?"

"Yes."

"The dreamhunters have gone to the city barracks. They'll be safe there. I have to say, Secretary Doran, some of what I'm hearing sounds like plain nonsense. Half these people were running around while still asleep, I think."

A disheveled youth, his blanket floating behind him like bat wings, barged past the police captain shouting, "Rose! Rose!"

"Sandy!" Rose said.

The police captain seized the boy by the collar of his pajamas.

"Where's Laura?" the young man asked. His eyes stayed on Rose's face while his fingers grappled with the policeman's hand, slipping, for they were covered in bleeding bite marks.

Doran spotted the copper tags that swung flashing through the gap in front of the boy's pajama jacket. He said to the police captain, "This is another dreamhunter. You should make sure you catch any who were here. It's almost certain that the nightmare has printed itself on them. They'll be reproducing it in a diminished form for the next few nights."

The young man looked at Cas Doran then, his eyes wide. He moaned.

"Sandy, your uncle is with my mother at the city barracks," Rose said.

Cas Doran thought, "This is George Mason's nephew, asking after Laura Hame, desperate with worry."

"Where is she?" Sandy Mason said again.

Rose's eyes flicked sideways—met Doran's gaze—then returned to Sandy's face. "She ran off. She was scared. I had bare feet, there was glass on the stairs." Rose was explaining how she and her cousin had become separated.

Cas Doran knew—because it had been described to him—that the nightmare he had just experienced was Tziga Hame's Buried Alive. Hame had had Buried Alive the night he jumped from a pier while walking under escort between the Regulatory Body's special train and Westport's Pier Prison. Hame's family seemed to accept the fiction that he had disappeared while attempting a solo crossing of the Place. The story—the cover-up—wasn't Doran's idea. He knew nothing about it until it was done, a sloppy deception, a forged signature in the Intentions book at the ranger station in Doorhandle. Hame's sister-in-law, Grace Tiebold, had organized a search party and had taken it In looking for a body.

There was no body. No body mummifying in the Place, or, in fact, where it *should* be, in a pauper's grave belonging to Magdalene Charity Hospital in Westport. But Hame's family seemed prepared to accept his passing without a body to bury. They were even planning a memorial service. Cas Doran knew all this, and he also knew that Tziga Hame's sister, Marta, opposed the planned service. She was a very religious woman and—Doran figured—the only reason she could have for not wanting the proper ceremony was if she thought her brother was, in fact, still alive.

Cas Doran looked back at the Opera, its walls blackened by heaving, magnified shadows. He looked at all the tattered fingers and clawed faces and thought, *"Hame is alive."* Hame's nightmare had not been felt in the world since he disappeared. And yet tonight, when the Opera's patrons were expecting a seasonal performance of Homecoming, here it was, bursting out of an unknown grave—*Hame's grave*—like a blood-soaked revenant.

Doran set his hands on Sandy Mason's bullish neck

and held him hard. "Who was Laura Hame with?" he demanded.

Sandy looked baffled. "She was with Miss Tiebold. That's why I'm asking Miss Tiebold where she is."

"Laura was in bed with me," Rose said.

Cas Doran studied Rose's face and saw that she was much more composed than she'd been only moments before.

"We didn't sleep. We were talking. When the screaming started, Laura got scared and bolted down the stairs to the dreamer's door," Rose said, looking from Doran to Sandy.

Sandy was stricken. He writhed out of Doran's grip. "We have to find her!"

"Oh—yes," said Rose. She laid a hand on Cas Doran's arm. "Mr. Doran, could you please have someone take me home? Laura will have run there."

"No. I won't feel clear in my conscience unless I take you home with *me*, Rose. Mamie's mother wouldn't forgive me for failing to do so. I'll send some people around to your house to find your cousin. I'm sure you're right and she's there." Doran regarded Sandy. "As for you, Mr. Mason—the police and Body officials are gathering exposed dreamhunters so they can be quarantined. It's a matter of public safety. I'm sure you understand. And you will need some easing through it." Doran patted Sandy Mason's shoulder. "We'll let you know how your friend is as soon as we locate her."

Sandy slumped, but nodded.

Doran signaled to a bowler-hatted Regulatory Body official. The man came to him.

"I have a dreamhunter here," Doran said, one hand resting on Sandy in a proprietary way. "And Maze Plasir's apprentice is standing over there with my son. Also, Miss Tiebold tells me that her cousin—the dreamhunter Laura Hame—will have run home."

"She didn't sleep," Rose said again. "We were talking." Then her eyelids fluttered as if she were about to faint and she began to laugh, semi-hysterical again.

The official took hold of Sandy and escorted him away.

"Your cousin's beau?" Doran inquired.

Rose stopped laughing and said, "I'm sure *I* wouldn't know." Every inch a Founderston Girls' Academy senior asserting her sense of what was proper. She was squinting against the headlights of his car, which his chauffeur had driven slowly and inexorably through the thronging people. The chauffeur put his hand on the top of the windshield, stood up, and called to Doran. "Sir!"

"Good work!" Doran called back. He took Rose's arm. "Come," he said tenderly. "There's no need for you to try to think it all through now. I'm sure we'll find your cousin and she'll be all right. Your mother will be perfectly safe at the police barracks, and cared for—I'll see to that myself. We'll send for your father—wherever he is. You must be worn out. If, as you say, you didn't sleep, it is safe for you to sleep now."

"All right," Rose conceded.

"And I'm sure Mamie will be delighted to find you in the morning," Doran added, and smiled at his daughter's friend.

As he climbed into his leather-scented car, Doran looked back at the Rainbow Opera and thought, "Someone planned this. I don't just have opponents, I have *enemies*."

He would have to step up the timing of his plans. He'd have to hurry along the rangers who were laying a rail line for handcars across the silent plains beyond the gorges at Z minus sixteen. He'd have to take less time and less care than he liked to purchase more properties around Founderston—untenanted houses whose bedroom windows were being fitted with bars and bedroom doors with deadlocks.

Dreamhunter

For Secretary Doran had a dream—up his sleeve, that is. A dream called Contentment. Contentment was not a nightmare; it was a gift. A gift to anyone whose vision of a better world included himself surrounded by happy and peace-loving people.

7

✧ ✧ ✧

WHEN IT WAS QUIETER LAURA AND
NOWN LEFT THE ISLE OF THE TEM-
PLE. THEY WENT BY THE RAILWAY BRIDGE
to the east. He carried her, walking from board to board
along the top of the bridge, over the running water that was
deadly to him.

He cradled her, his arms so long in comparison to her
body that he could warm her bare feet in one hand—a cold
hand, but it kept her toes from the night air. He held her as
he could hold heat, and her breath blowing against his fake
collarbone warmed him all the way to the back of his neck.

Nown strode on, stepping on every third tie on the track,
passing beneath the windows of the houses that backed onto
the railway line in the Old Town. There was no one looking
out of those windows. Not a soul to see them go by.

It had been raining and the ties were wet, the rainwater sitting on spills of engine oil. But Nown's sandy soles never
slipped, and their progress was smooth.

They passed through the Old Town and into the suburbs,
over crossings whose striped warning barriers were up, salut-
ing the sky. Nown stepped aside for one train. They went on
past backyards where damp work clothes and aprons and dia-
pers hung from clotheslines. They passed properties where

dogs erupted from their kennels only to balk, whining, then scuttle back into shelter again.

Nown carried Laura beside ditches choked with brambles, and banks covered in newly planted trees—budding birches and willows.

The rail line east would eventually bring them to the stop near Marta Hame's house. That was where Laura had asked Nown to take her. At her aunt's house she'd be safe. She could read the papers; see what they had to say about the nightmare, and about the letters she'd sent to explain it. She could be quiet and learn how to separate Laura from what Laura had had to do. She could discover what else there was for her. Because there must be something, mustn't there? Not something *further*, but something *else*.

Laura lay quiet. She didn't stir till they reached the country. Then her head moved from where it rested against Nown's shoulder to look around at the slender birches that clacked and ticked in the night breeze.

She said, "You make me feel like God on the Sabbath— sleepy, that is. But I know that when I sleep I'll have the dream again." She was so tired that even her terror was dull. "I only want to stay awake," she said.

Nown was silent.

Laura needed to occupy her mind—to stand upright and alert in its darkness. She tried to think back beyond recent events, all that had happened and felt inevitable. Then she remembered something. "Nown," she said, "in the train last night, did I tell you to stop talking to me?"

"No."

"I think I did."

"You said, 'You're hurting me.' You had told the eighth, 'Don't hurt me.' "

Nown had let himself be guided by an order she'd given his earlier self. He'd tried to help her, and she'd silenced him.

It was wrong that he was so easily silenced.

Laura hitched herself up in his arms. She felt the smooth bandage of sand that wrapped her feet separate, and round out into fingers once more. She climbed her sandman, flexed her legs so that she could get her arms up over one of his shoulders. Laura looked behind him—not back along the track but at the back of his neck. She looked at the letters of his name. N-O-W-N. She thought of the words of the song her father taught her: "*Two letters remain within, Death and freedom. Make his name his Own and he is.*"

She reached around and used one finger to erase the first "N" in his name. It now read: "OWN." She knew that, if she properly understood the spell, she had just set her servant free.

Nown hesitated. He faltered, but he didn't stop walking.

Laura sank back into the cradle of his arms, and he once again picked up his pace, kept on steadily striding along between the rails.

Shortly before dawn it began to rain. Laura watched the big drops absorbed by Nown's sandy skin. She saw the rain spots join together to become dark patches. Nown stooped his shoulders, and bent his head over Laura to shelter her from the rain. His face was near to hers.

She said to him, "You might melt."

And he said, "If I melt, you can make me again."

Acknowledgments

I would like to thank Natasha Fairweather and Julia Wells in London, Frances Foster in New York, Lisa Berryman in Melbourne, and Shona Martyn in Sydney. And, as ever, my first editor, my husband, Fergus.